BLOOD BROTHERS

DALLAS BARNES

ROUGH
EDGES
PRESS

Blood Brothers
Paperback Edition
Copyright © 2024 (As Revised) Dallas Barnes

Rough Edges Press
An Imprint of Wolfpack Publishing
1707 E. Diana Street
Tampa, FL 33610

roughedgespress.com

Paperback ISBN 978-1-68549-629-6
eBook ISBN 978-1-68549-628-9

BLOOD BROTHERS

FOREWORD

Dallas Barnes, a former **LAPD Homicide Detective,** is the best-selling author of eight novels. **Blood Brothers** is his first novel based on experiences gained while working in critical positions for five Native American Indian Tribes. Each of the tribes were involved in casino operations and contemporary gaming.

- **Morongo Resort & Casino** – Cabazon, CA – Director of Security
- **Blue Water Resort &Casino**—Colorado River Indian Tribes – Parker, AZ—Gaming Supervisor
- **Fantasy Springs Resort & Casino**—Cabazon Tribe – Indio, CA—Director of Surveillance
- **Agua Caliente Casino & Casino**—Palm Springs, CA—Tribal Gaming Commission
- **Augustine Casino**—Coachella, CA— Director of Surveillance

Additionally, Dallas Barnes served as:

- Director of Security—**The Hyatt Regency Resort & Casino**—Lake Las Vegas, Las Vegas, NV
- Director of Security—**The Signature- MGM Grand**—Las Vegas, NV

Combined, Dallas Barnes has a total of forty-three years of Police & Gaming experience. It is safe to say he knows of what he writes.

1 THE GREAT WHITE FATHER

"The idea of full dress in preparation for a battle comes not from a belief that it will add to the fighting ability. The preparation is for death, in case death should be the result of the conflict. Every Indian wants to look his best when he goes to meet the great Spirit."

Wooden Leg—Cheyenne

The three Indians sat in silence, cross-legged and bare chested, on the carpet of their eighteenth-floor room at the Marriott on Pennsylvania Avenue in Washington, D. C. They were big men. Mojave's. All over six feet tall. Two leather-faced elders and a young buck with a ponytail. Spread on the floor around them lay an assortment of colorful cosmetics. Max Factor, L'Oreal and Cover Girl had replaced powdered charcoal, red clay and cactus blossoms. The finger-traced swaths of color

1

on red skin looked ominous. There hadn't been an Indian attack in the United States since the early 1900s of years. In fifty-three minutes, history would be changed.

They had driven to Washington, D.C. from Parker, Arizona in a six-year-old Chevy pick-up truck. The twenty-seven-hundred-mile trip took four days and two tires. After another three days of waiting in sterile polished corridors at the Department of the Interior and the Bureau of Indian Affairs, they were disillusioned, frustrated and nearly broke. Washington had not received them as the elected government officials of a sovereign nation that they were. Instead of the meeting at the Department of the Interior they expected they got two parking citations and a coupon for a ten-dollar discount at Gold Finger Massage. The Secretary of Interior sent a fax to the Marriott. Floods in Ohio had forced revisions in his busy schedule. The three Tribal Council members were invited to re-schedule their meeting in a month. They had sixty-two dollars and a Visa card to get them home.

It was seventy-two-year-old, hawk-nosed, Russell Stoner, the Tribal Chief, who made the decision. Laboring down the weathered steps of the Department of Interior on knees stiff with arthritis, after another fruitless three hours wait, he warned, "We will not return home like women with nothing, but broken promises."

"You're right," twenty-eight-year-old David Rollins quipped sarcastically. "Let's show them. Let's take the towels from our room."

The old Indian's dark eyes found the younger man's face. "Only a boy giggles when another man pisses on his fire."

"Pisses on our fire," Rollins mocked with hands in the air. "Oh, that's great, but you're right, Grandfather; forget the towels. Let's have our picture taken in front of the Marine Memorial. Wasn't one of those guys a Navajo?"

"I told you we should have left him at home," Paul Manygoats said, taking the Chief by the arm to help him down the steps. Manygoats was a big rotund man with no neck. He wore a suit bought when he was thirty pounds lighter. "All he's done is watch MTV."

"Except when you were watching Playboy," the younger Rollins shot back.

"We will go see the President," Chief Stoner said as they reached the bottom of the steps. His tone was matter of fact. Manygoats sensed the old man was serious.

"Okay if we stop by the hotel first?" Rollins questioned with a look at the two older men. "I'd like to put on a better jacket."

"Get the truck," Manygoats ordered soberly.

They stopped at a drug store two blocks from the hotel. The old man picked out the cosmetics, carefully checking each color. Rollins, the raven-haired young buck with the ponytail was now as sober as his older companions. "Are you real Indians?" a shallow cheeked blonde asked as she rang up the purchase at a checkout stand. She was staring at the plaid Pendleton shirts, the turquoise jewelry, the bolo ties.

"No," Rollins said flashing white even teeth, "We're Puerto Ricans."

The young brave had worn war paint before, but only for Tribal ceremonies and pow wows. As the old man's boney finger traced a green saw-toothed line along his cheek, Rollins felt a stirring deep in his soul. It was as if his spirit were swelling inside his body. His throat tightened and his pulse quickened. The old man felt it through his finger. "Be still, listen to the silence," the chief whispered.

It was dark and raining when they left the hotel. The war paint on their faces drew little attention as they crossed the busy lobby. Washington was much too sophisticated to react to three Mojave Indians in face paint. Their naked upper torsos were covered with jackets. The old chief held a crumpled time worn parchment clasped in his right hand.

They drove the five blocks to the White House in silence. Young Rollins was behind the wheel. The windshield was streaked with rain. The wiper blades, cooked brittle in Arizona's heat, squeaked as they swept back and forth across the sand-pitted glass. "It is a good rain," Manygoats said from the passenger's side of the pick-up. Chief Stoner nodded agreement as his eyes surveyed the night lighting and reflections. "It will bring many bugs."

The President was in his bedroom on the second floor of the White House. The First Lady and their teenage daughter were in an adjoining study watching television. The door was closed, but the President could hear occasional sounds of a sit com laugh track mixed with their laughter It was comforting to him. Little else in the day had been. The results from the latest polls lay in an open file in front of him. His popularity had slipped another six points and was at the lowest point of his presidency. It was the economy. Someone had to be the focal point of the collective fear gripping working America and he was it. The economy had brought him into office, and he knew somehow, he had to turn water to wine or his fate as a one term President would be sealed. Unlike many of his predecessors, he hadn't come to the White House a wealthy man. Like many Americans his success was the result of hard work and sweat. Somehow, somewhere he'd lost that identity. He had become what he vowed he wasn't, a politician. As the incumbent, he had to defend four years of political reality, while his opponent, who seemed to be gaining momentum every day, talked about his plan to rebuild the foundation of America. Fear was creeping in. He was becoming more and more defensive. Perhaps it was his age, the President considered. Only forty-six when he took the oath of office, he was now approaching his 50th year. How in the hell did Trump do it? The warmth from the fireplace crept through his slippers, relaxing him. He remembered rainy winter nights in the south when he sat with his mother crowded near a pot-bellied stove. He closed his eyes and listened to the rain splatter on the balcony outside. Maybe one term was enough. Maybe it was time to go home.

The pick-up truck pulled to the curb and stopped. The three Indians stared out the side window. It was clouding with condensation. Manygoats wiped it with the meaty palm of his hand. Beyond an open eight-foot-high spiked wrought iron fence the expanse of the south lawn stretched to the White House which stood bathed in chalky night lighting. "Do you suppose he is home?" Manygoats asked quietly as if someone were listening.

David Rollins wondered if his grandfather and Manygoats were as frightened as he. He supposed not. His mouth was dry and bitter. He wished he had taken time to relieve himself. He gripped the plastic steering wheel to keep from trembling. Looking at the distant White House through the wet glass, the young Indian remembered a line from a summer Bible school class. "Through a glass darkly."

Chief Stoner laid a hand on the knee of both men. "It is time to go."

Manygoats opened the door and stepped out into the rain. Chief Stoner followed him. David Rollins pulled the ignition key out, then thought about it and tossed it onto the dash. He patted the steering wheel affectionately and slid across the seat.

A group of Japanese in bright yellow raincoats and plastic hats, standing a short distance away spotted the three Indians as they stripped off their coats exposing painted chests. Fingers were pointed and the air bristled with excited bursts of Japanese. A cellphone camera swung toward the three men. They ignored it all and tossed their jackets into the open bed of the pick-up. A rapid transit bus labored by, its heavy tires hissing on the black wet street. If the evening commuters lining the windows saw the Indians, none reacted.

The rain, the fear, the chill of the night, David Rollins wasn't sure which it was, but it excited him. Defying it he raised his painted face to the downpour and gave a soul deep yelp that cut through the night. The knot of Japanese shuddered and pushed together.

As if they had done it many times, the three Indians stepped to the wrought iron fence. David and Manygoats joined hands, interlocking their fingers for strength. Rain matted their hair and ran down their faces. Chief Stoner, ignoring his pain and age, stepped onto the bridge of their palms and they propelled him up and over with a collective war hoop.

Manygoats was next. David Rollins leaned into the fence and grabbed two wrought iron bars. They were cold and slick from the rain. The heavier Manygoats grabbed David's bare shoulders and walked himself up the back of the younger man's legs. David grimaced and grunted under the strain of the man's three hundred pounds. Grabbing a fence bar above David to steady himself, Manygoats stepped up onto David's bare shoulders. First the left, then the right. Boot heels pressed deep into flesh. David's muscles trembled.

The wrought iron shafts of the fence were tall with their spikes. The White House, fearing some martyr may impale himself intentionally, had opted for the protection of height. Even standing on David's shoulders in a stooped, precarious position, George Manygoats found himself staring at another two feet of cold hard steel. The shudder of the flesh and bone beneath him reached up through his boots to warn him the boy would soon collapse.

Rain dripping off his chin, flesh cold with fear and exposure, George Manygoats' mind took him back to a dark muddy rain slick hill side in South Viet Nam. They had won the battle but lost the war. He and four others from a platoon of thirty-three young marines were the only survivors. "Die fighting or die pissin' in your boots!" the gunny admonished just before he vanished in a flash of fire, mud and hot steel. George gritted his teeth, grunted and jerked himself up. He was thirty-two years older and one hundred and fifty pounds heavier than he was as a combat marine, but the old Indian's upper torso cleared the top of the fence. His legs did not. The top of a wrought iron shaft caught the material on the inside of his left leg. The denim material ripped and swung him back into the fence. He landed with a loud thud, but he was inside. "Semper fi," he mouthed, gathering himself up.

The Japanese stared in awe.

The fence proved far less a challenge to young Rollins. He jumped, grabbed high on the top, pulled a knee up to a horizontal brace, raised himself and jumped. He landed on his feet near Chief Stoner and

Manygoats. Wiping rain from his face he stared in awe at the distant White House. It looked big and distant. David's heart pounded in his chest like a war drum.

In the White House security office on sub-level one a red light winked on a control panel and a pre-recorded electronic female voice announced. "Intruder, south lawn. Intruder, south lawn."

Lieutenant Lawrence Hanes, the duty Watch Commander, a veteran of eighteen years with the White House Uniform Division of the Secret Service, reacted by laying aside a copy of the Washington Post. "Bet it's that goddamned poodle again."

"Let's see," a trim black officer at the control console said reaching for the joystick of a pan-tilt-zoom camera.

The two men concentrated on a series of closed-circuit television monitors in front of them as the camera panned blurring images "You want me to broad-cast an alert?'

"Intruder, south lawn," the recorded voice warned again in a flat business-like tone.

"Not yet," the Lieutenant answered staring at the screens.

"What the fuck!" Lieutenant Hanes blurted as the automatic lens brought the colored image into focus.

"Indians!" the young black officer punched a button labeled, "Alert One."

On the wind-swept roof of the White House, Secret Service sniper Greg Sellers, dressed in a black jumpsuit and rain gear, stepped into a heated two room sentry booth where his partner sat watching Netflix. "Gotta take a leak," Sellers said, moving to the rest room door.

Sellers unzipped and pulled an annoying earpiece from his ear just as an electronic alarm on the wall went off. "Goddamn." He grabbed the night scope equipped rifle leaning against the wall and ran. His partner was already scrambling out the door.

In the Security Control Room, the air was electric with tension as the Lieutenant and the Duty Officer watched the images on the screen. The three rain-soaked Indians, glistening with war paint, were hunched and moving abreast toward the White House. The Lieutenant grabbed a microphone. "Three intruders confirmed, south lawn! This is not a drill. Release the K-9's. Hold fire. Three unidentified males on camera, sector two."

Agent Sellers was pushing his earpiece in place and kneeling at the roof's parapet when he heard only a portion of the tense broadcast. "...fire. Three unidentified males on camera, sector two."

Sellers swung his infrared scope. The blue-white figures came into view. "Got a picture!" he announced as his partner knelt beside him and took aim.

"I'll take the one on the right," the older officer said. Both were oblivious to the rain.

Sellers would later testify to a Board of Inquiry headed by the Attorney General that he misunderstood the word "take" as a command to fire. Sellers held his breath, took aim at the man on the left and pulled gently on the trigger. The gun popped sending a burst of fire into the rain.

David Rollins knee exploded in a shower of splinters and blood as the high velocity, armor-piercing, projectile ripped through his leg. He fell, not feeling the pain. "Grandfather," he cried.

Chief Stoner was turning to the youth when Sellers fired a second shot. The bullet hit the old man just to the left of his navel on a downward track of about forty degrees, puncturing his spleen, large intestines and exiting his lower back. He fell and reached for the boy.

Finding a wet leg in the grass he grasped it. "Ahhh!" Rollins cried in pain.

The older Secret Service sniper, not wearing an earphone because he'd been on break, assumed Sellers had received an order to fire. After the two shots were fired by his younger partner, he took careful aim on the remaining man and fired.

Paul Manygoats, the autopsy would later reveal, died instantly. The bullet entered his left eye, penetrated the roof of his mouth and exited the back of his neck severing his spine and destroying two vertebrae.

The video seized later from the Japanese tourists by the FBI clearly showed Manygoats stagger when he was hit, then walk in a half circle, before falling to flail about in the grass like a dying chicken. Hard Copy would air the video tape three nights later as an exclusive.

The shots woke the President. Sitting in the high-backed chair facing the warmth of the fireplace he awoke uncertain what he heard. His wife and daughter entered from the adjoining room. "Bob, did you hear that?"

Suddenly the room's lights went out and the doors burst open. "Get on the floor!"

The President's daughter and wife screamed.

"What the ...?" The President questioned, but a Secret Service agent cut him short, grabbed him and pushed him to the carpeted floor.

"Down! Everybody down!" another voice shouted, grabbing the two frightened women. Outside they could hear dogs barking. Soon the sound of a helicopter mixed with it. "Stay calm," the President urged his wife and daughter.

A dark silhouette appeared in the doorway to the hall. "Is the Eagle secure?" a voice demanded.

"Eagle secure," the agent at the President's side answered. There was a gun in his hand.

"Listen closely," the silhouette said calmly, "on my command we move to the elevator and down to the safe room."

"Ready," two voices answered simultaneously. Now there were sirens outside.

"Move!" the voice barked.

The train of ambulances, Secret Service vehicles and police cars lit the night with flashing lights and piercing electronic sirens as they raced over the wet streets to Georgetown University Hospital. CNN was the first to break the story. "Terrorists strike at the White House." All over the District, an army of reporters and news crews scrambled into the wet night. The White House, on high security alert, remained silent as an unseen coalition of Secret Service, Marines, FBI and other React Team members moved into position to protect the President.

Deep in the bowels of the White House, more than sixty feet underground the shaken, but calm, President paced. His wife and daughter were with him when the Chief of Staff and a Senior Secret Service agent came in. They were rain soaked. "May we talk in private, Mr. President?"

The First Lady and the President's daughter were escorted out. When the door closed the Chief-of-Staff spoke. "There were three of them, Sir. One is dead. Two wounded. They appear to be Indians."

"Indians! What the hell have we done to India?"

"No, Sir. American Indians. Native Americans."

"What?" The President said in disbelief. "Are you sure?"

"The youngest was carrying an Arizona Driver's License, Sir." the Secret Service Agent answered.

"What did they want?"

"We don't know, Sir," the Chief-of-Staff offered.

"How did they get here? What kind of weapons did they have? I heard shots."

"Appears they were driving a pick-up truck, Mr. President," the agent answered. "We found it at the curb near the fence."

"And the weapons?"

The Chief of Staff and the agent exchanged a look. The Chief of staff wasn't about to answer. The agent took a breath then, "We haven't found any weapons, Sir."

"They were unarmed?"

"I didn't say that, Sir." The agent hedged. "We're still searching.

"Where are these men now?!"

"Georgetown U, Sir."

"Get the car, Leon. We're going over there."

"Mr. President, I would advise against that. The press...."

"Get the goddamned car, Leon!"

"Yes, Sir."

CNN as well as the networks carried what they thought was the arrival of the President's motorcade at the hospital. Surrounded by a small army of Secret Service agents the President was glimpsed being rushed inside. In reality the President had arrived ten minutes earlier in a nondescript ambulance.

The President met with the Emergency Room staff in a third-floor doctor's lounge. He listened to the detailed medical evaluations. One man was DOA. Another, the oldest of the three, was in critical condition and the youngest was stable, but facing extensive surgery to save his leg.

"Has either said anything?" The President questioned.

"The old man keeps repeating a name," the surgeon answered.

"What name?" The President pressed.

"John Fox. Agent John Fox," the doctor answered.

"We ran the name, Sir," a Secret Service agent offered. "The FBI has an agent by the name of John Fox. He was born in Arizona. His mother was a Native American."

"Where is he?"

"He's assigned to the office in Palm Springs, Sir."

"Get him here," the President ordered.

"Yes, Sir," the agent moved for the door.

"The old man was carrying this in his hand, Mr. President." The surgeon unfolded a tattered parchment. "Had a death grip on it He wouldn't give it up until we put him under." The doctor offered it to the President. "Careful, Sir, it has blood on it."

The President took the document and unfolded it. It was dog-eared and blood splattered. He read aloud. "Greetings to all concerned from the President of the United states, Ulysses S. Grant. Be it known to all men that on this day, May fourth, and in this, the year of our Lord, eighteen sixty-nine, a treaty is formed, between the United States of America and the now duly recognized sovereign nation of Mojave Indians.....that no man shall violate the mutual peace or raise arms against one another."

The President stopped, lowered the wrinkled treaty. The silence in the room was heavy.

"Mr. President," the Chief-of-Staff said, "we had no

way of knowing what their intent was, or that they were unarmed."

The President looked to his Chief-of-Staff. "I'll bet they've heard that before."

2   SINS OF THE FATHER

> "A warrior will follow the path of his father
> He will look in the quiet waters and find his
> father's face
> and in his chest beats his father's heart."
> **Lone Wolf—Apache Warrior**

Two thousand five hundred and sixty-six miles west of Washington, D.C., in nighttime Palm Springs, California, an electronic chirp of a cellphone on a bedside night-stand woke thirty-four-year-old FBI Agent John Fox. He reached for the phone in the darkness and quickly silenced it. His wife stirred at his side and then settled. Cellphone in hand, Fox eased out of bed and walked from the room. He was nude, but the dark house was comfortable. He walked to the den and looked at the LED display on the phone. The number "9" winked at him. It was a code to call Tom Roberts, the Special Agent in charge of the FBI office in Palm Springs. Fox, the agent in charge of operation CAT, Catch A Thief, guessed one of his bank men had been picked up the police somewhere and now he'd have to drive to some goddamned little department somewhere in the deserts heat and drink shit coffee while interviewing a foul smelling, unwashed suspect. Crooks had much better working hours than cops, Fox decided, punching an auto dial he walked toward the kitchen, nearly stepping on a sleeping cat in the hallway. "Move your ass, Smokey," he warned. "I don't sleep, you don't sleep."

Opening the refrigerator, Fox selected orange juice. Telephone to his ear, he took several heavy swallows. On the third ring a male voice answered. "Three-four-six."

Fox recognized the voice. It was Tom Roberts. "Tom, it's John. What's up?" He instinctively looked at the time displayed on the kitchen's microwave oven. It was one-sixteen. He was already working on the shit report he'd have to write after this shit call-out. Banks were a real pin in the ass assignment.

"Get dressed. I'm going to pick you up in twenty minutes," Roberts warned in his ear.

Fox was surprised. The Special Agent in Charge rarely rolled on callouts. Something was wrong. Fox tensed. "Someone down?" he questioned.

"No. You're going to Washington, and it's a ten-thirty-five." The number code told Fox it was confidential information.

"Washington?" Fox was puzzled. "Come on, Tom. Pam just got home from four days out. Can't someone else go?" He was betting it was some mundane advance work for a visiting Head of State or yet another Federal task force the Bureau was volunteering bodies for.

"The call was specifically for you and it came from the White House."

"What?" Fox's surprise was now shock.

"I'll be there in twenty minutes. Be ready." Roberts hung up.

"Damn," Fox muttered. He was certain it was all a mistake.

"Do you have to go?" His wife's voice asked from the shadows behind him.

Fox turned to her. The room was dark, but the ambient lighting filtering in from outside silhouetted her nudity. Pamela Fox was a shapely brunette with long hair and long legs. She stood with her arms folded beneath her breasts. Fox crossed and drew her into his arms. "I have to go to Washington," he complained into her hair. She was perfumed and warm from the bed and although they had made love before falling asleep, he was still hungry for her. Pam was a stewardess, a veteran of eight years with United Airlines, working long haul turnarounds between the Far East and L.A. Matching schedules was difficult for them at its best. She had been home less than twelve hours. Now they were facing separation again. "The president's daughter getting bullied at school again?" Pam whispered, kissing his neck.

"I don't know," he answered.

"John, I don't want you to go." He could feel her warm breath on his neck. "I don't want to be alone. Please."

"When I get back," Fox said resigning himself to duty, "We're going to do something about our schedules."

"I hate being alone." Pam raised her face to him. They had talked before. Pam confessed she had gone to a counselor, started a drug regimen. "Pam, I'm sorry."

She pushed away from him gently and walked into the shadows. "Sorry doesn't fill our bed, John. How soon are you leaving.?"

"I'm being picked up. Maybe half an hour."

The silhouette paused and turned to him, "How long will you be gone?"

"I don't know."

"I love you, John, but this hurts. It really hurts." She whispered.

Fox was ready when the two cars arrived. The sight quickened his pulse. One was a California Highway Patrol car. The other he recognized as Tom Roberts' unmarked government sedan. They slid quietly to the curb in front of the condo on South Palm Court and stopped. No one got out.

Fox picked up his tote bag. He was dressed in a dark suit. His nine-millimeter Browning was on his side. "Time to go," he said kneeling bedside to kiss Pam on the cheek. He tasted the tears on her shadowed face. She reached and drew him tight to her. "Goodbye, John." Her tone was mournful. He could feel her form beneath the robe she wore.

"Pam, I'm...," She silenced him with a finger to his lips.

"Go," She whispered.

"We're going to March Air Force Base," Tom Roberts said following the escorting highway patrol car. Its red lights were flashing, and the yelp of its electronic siren filled the night. They were driving seventy miles an hour over the quiet city streets. "The C.G.'s Lear is taking you to Andrews in Washington. Someone from the Washington office will meet you there." He was talking loud over the roar of the engine and the yelp of the siren.

"What the hell's going on, Tom?" Fox was worried.

"Officially I don't know shit." Roberts answered as they sped across the dark desert floor leaving the lights of Palm Springs behind. They were at a hundred miles an hour and gaining speed. "But just before I got the call concerning you, a flash Teletype came in. Someone tried to hit the White House tonight. There were casualties."

"Jesus," Fox muttered. His anxieties swelled. He had no idea how his talents or experience could help in a matter that clearly would be handled by the Secret Service, but if someone had tried to kill the President, and they wanted his help, he would do what he could. "Any idea who? Islamic? How many?" There were a thousand questions. Fox knew transporting agents from the West meant it was damn serious. He also knew he wasn't the only one being called.

"I don't know."

"Is the President safe?"

"Yeah, I learned that from CNN" Roberts complained.

Fox's anxieties were giving way to excitement. This was more of what he had joined the Bureau for. He was fast approaching the mid-point in his career with eleven years of service. Miami, Atlanta and Los Angeles had preceded the assignment to Palm Springs. Fox, with a combination of hard work, perseverance and savvy had become one of the Bureau's best bank men. Miami, with its notoriety for brutal bank robberies had served as his boot camp. There Fox had met them all, the intellects with scams and notes, the take-over artists with their rapid-fire machine guns and the bombers. He had talked with hostage takers, safe-crackers and wheel men. He knew what they wanted and why they wanted it and seldom did money have anything to do with it.

Fox reasoned his success was rooted in athletics. Football. Pop Warner through Arizona State. Age seven through twenty-two. Fifteen years. The training and regimen of the game not only toughened him to physical abuse, contact and a hunger for contest, it also forced him to make quick, hard decisions and if it was the wrong decision, to immediately make another one and never watch the clock and never ever give up. Time was an ally, not an adversary. Those who stuck with the game plan, won. Football was far more than twenty-two men in a physical contest. It was in the abstract, geometry and mathematics, linked to intellect. The best prepared, the best plan always won. It was that fucking simple.

Forcing him into sports was one of the few things his father had given him. Although Fox felt the benefit, he had gained was incidental. James Fox was really feeding on the vicarious rush he got from a son standing in the limelight. Wasn't it really because he was his father's son?"

What Fox remembered most about his nineteen years as his father's son was a relentless avalanche of verbal abuse and a cloudy memory of a mother who abandoned him at age six, followed by three step-mothers whose chronological age seemed closer to his own than his father's. Even his career choice seemed to push him further into his father's shadow. James Fox had been the legendary leader of the FBI task force that broke the backbone of the mob's grip on Las Vegas. Now, crime families had been replaced by corporations. Ironically the tough, broad-shouldered James Fox, who for twenty-eight years, faced many of America's most hardened criminals, fell victim to one of the universe's most basic principles. Gravity. James Fox and two other agents were flying into Denver in an icy storm in pursuit of a serial killer, when their small two engine plane fell from the sky. John, a senior at Arizona State at the time, hadn't seen his father in eight months.

John Fox expected the death of his father to change his life, and it had, but so subtly he had hardly noticed. Like a salmon coming of age and returning to the river of its birth, in a natural born migration Fox found himself turning to thoughts of the FBI. After graduation from college he abandoned plans for law school and applied. He was soon enthusiastic about his choice. He was back in the game. A game even more exciting than football. A game dependent on physical and mental assets. A game whose outcome sometimes meant life or death. Fox seldom allowed the thought although it often teased at his consciousness. He was still in the game to please his father.

The ride to March Air Force Base went quickly. The sleek executive silver jet belonging to the Commanding General of the Base sat idling, turbines whining, strobe lights flashing, on a runway apron, when the cars arrived. The Highway Patrol car and the unmarked FBI sedan were now led by a blue Air Force Police jeep. Roberts and Fox climbed out of the car and walked to the open door of the craft. The ground crew stared, wondering what the night passage was about. "Well," Roberts said, extending a hand to Fox. He was a tanned, mustached man looking more like a golf pro than an agent. "Hope you have a good flight."

Fox wasn't sure what to say. He didn't know what he would be doing, or when he'd be back. He took Roberts' hand, shook it and climbed aboard. Christ, it seemed he was saying goodbye to everyone.

The cabin was small and compact, but comfortable. It smelled of leather. There were six cushioned high back seats. Fox chose one near a small illuminated conference table. A Lieutenant in a blue jumpsuit closed the cabin door and sealed it. The turbine grew louder, and the craft moved. Fox was strapping himself in when the Lieutenant reached him. "Evening, Sir." He was a young man with intense blue eyes and a service cap resting on his eyebrows. "I'm Lieutenant Bowen. That's Captain

Collins up front. We've got a good jet stream working this evening. We'll pick it up at about thirty-seven thousand. Have you at Andrews before daybreak."

Fox nodded appreciation. The Lieutenant moved for the open cockpit. It was bristling with soft instrument lighting and terse radio traffic. Outside runway lights were winking by. It was ironic, Fox thought, Pam had flown home less than eight hours earlier, now he was flying away. He loved it, but yet hated the separation. The craft turned, braked to a halt. The pitch of the turbines grew into a roar and they lunged forward. The acceleration surprised Fox as he was pushed into his cushioned seat. The runway thumped by in a blur and the cabin tilted up as the G force compressed him down. The craft cantered sharply to the left and the G's shifted again. Fox gripped the arms of his seat.

The flight crew stayed in the cockpit. Maybe they had been told not to talk to him, or maybe it was just the discipline of the need-to-know world they worked in, Fox reasoned. It was likely piloting the C.G.'s executive aircraft had taught them not to make idle conversation.

The cabin was warm, and Fox didn't remember falling asleep, but when he awoke there was a boxed flight lunch setting on the conference table in front of him. He ignored the sandwich and ate two carrots and drank a carton of orange juice.

Life as an athlete and an agent had taught Fox not to ignore opportunities to sleep. So, he did. When he awoke it was to the sensation they had slowed. The wing strobe lights were slicing through wisps of clouds. They were in descent. Fox straightened in his seat and willed himself alert, shaking off the sleep and jet lag he knew would haunt him. He wanted to be ready for the briefing he was certain would come. He wondered who else had been called from the West. Maybe some of the crew from the

L.A. branch. They were good men. He missed working with them. Working bank robberies in Palm Springs gave him ample opportunity to go to L.A. The crooks loved to drive to the Springs to rob banks. Somehow, they expected it lessened their chances of apprehension. Fox, being transferred to the Springs twenty-four months earlier, had changed those odds.

The cloud cover thickened, and the view Fox hoped for of Washington at sunrise never came. He was surprised when the tires yelped and suddenly, they were on the ground. He was awake now and eager to be out of the airplane. He could feel, and almost taste, the heavy humidity in the air. It was a sharp contrast to the dry desert air in Palm Springs. Rain began to bead and snake horizontally across the cabin's windows. As soon as the craft braked to a halt, Fox unsnapped his seat belt. The door was opened and a rush of cool moisture laden air rushed in. It was tinged with jet fumes. An Airman in a raincoat stepped aside as Fox climbed out to meet two men. They were younger than he, tall and ramrod straight, in matching raincoats. Unmistakably FBI. The Palace guard, Fox concluded. The Palace guard was a cadre of select agents assigned to Special Ops at the Hoover Building. "Agent Fox?" the man on the right questioned.

"Yeah," Fox extended a hand. The man took it. "I'm Agent Eckles. This is Agent Palmer." They shook hands. "If you will come with us please."

They marched across the wet tarmac to a waiting, unmarked sedan. Eckles opened a rear door. Fox climbed in. Palmer entered from the opposite side. The doors swung shut and they were rolling.

Fox knew not to ask. If they had any instructions, he would already be listening to them. It was awkward. They shared careers, responsibilities, even identities and he knew these two men would defend his life with their own. As he would theirs, but yet they had nothing to talk about. Fox opted for the universal icebreaker. "Been raining long?"

"Couple hours," Eckles answered, and then added his own question. "Palm Springs?"

"Clear," Fox answered.

The remainder of the ride was in silence. Fox knew the District. They skirted the downtown area. He wasn't surprised. The briefing wouldn't be held at the Hoover Building. Although there was ample conference space, it was less than a discrete location. Especially if the Press was onto something, and with an attack on the White House, they were. News crews would be stationed all over the District by now. The FBI Building always provided a good background for field reports.

Traffic on the beltway was light. The unmarked sedan slowed and exited at Washington Circle. Georgetown looked sullen and gray under the mantle of morning rain. It was a world away from Palm Springs. Fox silently cursed himself for forgetting his raincoat. He felt awkward and displaced. The conclusions he made earlier regarding the trip were now failing him. He couldn't prepare for what he didn't know, and he hated being unprepared. Preparation was a requisite to success. No preparation, no success. What the hell was going on? Why wouldn't someone tell him? Then, the hospital came into view. A tangle of mobile news vans with microwave dishes and colorful station logos crowding the street in front of the main entrance made it easy to spot. A police car with flashing lights warned the street was jammed. A knot of cameramen and reporters filled the sidewalk, waiting with umbrellas, steaming coffees and the hope of a shot of something for primetime. Cameras and lights took aim at the sedan as it swept by and swung into a subterranean entrance where a security officer in a yellow slicker waved them through.

Two agents waited on the parking level. One of them opened Fox's door as soon as the car stopped. "John Fox?" the man questioned.

Fox stepped out. "Yeah." He noticed the lapel pin, the coil running to an earphone. Secret Service.

"Follow us, please?" Fox walked between the two men, toward an elevator. The FBI agents made no effort to follow.

The agent on Fox's left raised an arm and spoke to his lapel. "Shadow-six to twenty. The package is coming up."

"Are you armed?" The other agent questioned, as the elevator doors parted after he punched the call button.

"Yes," Fox answered.

"Do not reach inside your jacket for any reason in the presence of the President," the agent warned, leading the way onto the elevator.

"The President?" Fox questioned. He was shocked. His pulse raced.

"Do you understand?" The agent pressed, as the doors closed, and the elevator climbed.

"Yeah, I understand." An instrumental version of Yellow Submarine was playing on some hidden speaker above them in the elevator car. Fox found it appropriate.

The President was on the telephone when Fox was escorted into the doctor's lounge. His fist impression was that the President was much taller than he expected, and he wasn't wearing a tie. Everyone else in the room was. Among those crowding the room Fox recognized the President's Press Secretary, the Director of the FBI, the Director of the Secret Service and the President's Chief-of-Staff. There were others. Several were involved in muted conversations on cell phones. Others were conferencing. Fox's arrival didn't seem to impress anyone. One of his escorts spoke with the Chief-of-Staff who promptly tapped the Director of the FBI on the shoulder. "He's here."

"John, how are you?" the Director said, reaching Fox. He took his hand and shook it firmly. They had met at Bureau conferences and retreats. The greeting offered some comfort. Fox still had his gun and the Director had acknowledged him. "This is the President's Chief-of-Staff."

The Chief-of-Staff wasted little time on formalities. He knew he was dealing with a subordinate. "The President will be asking some questions. Your answers should be brief and concise."

"Yes, Sir," Fox answered, returning the shorter man's hard look. He noticed the President hang up the telephone and turn toward them. Fox straightened his stance.

"Is this Agent Fox?" the President had his hand out, as he reached them.

Fox took the hand, opened his mouth to speak, but the Director filled his hesitation. "Yes, Sir, it is."

"John, I appreciate you coming," the President said, shaking his hand. "Do you have an uncle by the name of Russell Stoner, he's from Arizona? Mojave Tribe, I believe."

Fox felt the blood draining from his face. His mouth went dry. The years fell away as the shame and embarrassment of seven-year-old John Fox standing in front of the school principal, accused of provoking a classroom fight, returned. His ears burned as the memory of a finger pointed in his face returned, "You may fight at home," the principal warned, "but this isn't a reservation. Here you are going to learn to act civil, not like some damned wild Indian!"

His FBI father had committed a Bureau sin. He had married an Indian instead of a white Mormon. The marriage was to last just one child. Choosing career over marriage James Fox requested a transfer to Atlanta. John, a mere six-year-old wept for his mother. His father did not. "She loves her goddamned reservation more than you and me, Boy."

In Arizona, John Fox was a half-breed. The west was still cowboys and Indians. The credo dictated, "You could fuck an Indian, but you sure as fuck never marry one." It seemed James Fox finally realized he had an albatross hanging around his neck and cut himself free. The boy who grew into a man remembered Clair, the gentle woman with a soft voice, but he also remembered the stinging bias and prejudice. Indians were the low life that lived in squalor on the fringe of civilization. They were dim-witted people who drank too much and always had a handout. They were a defeated nation. A people with no spirit or ambition. He had distant dream-like memories of reservation shacks with uneven bare floors that smelled of urine, dusty gritty glasses full of watery goat's milk, and rusty hulks of automobiles full of spiders and weeds. He didn't need a mother who allowed him to be carried away without protest. Hell, wasn't that the Indian way? No fight in them, unless they were drunk. In Atlanta, Fox wasn't a half-breed. He was an athlete. He was to learn ten years later; his mother had died. Diabetes. He heard his father telling his third stepmother. "Most of them die of it," James Fox added in anger. "Cause they're so goddamned fat."

If the FBI demanded anything, it was truth. Thus, eleven years earlier when John Fox filled out his application, fearing anything else might be less than truthful he checked American Indian under "Race." It had never drawn comment, until now. Fox's heart was in his throat.

He was facing not only the President of the United States, but the agony of his past as well. "What was the name, Sir?" Fox coughed out the question.

"Chief Russell Stoner," the President repeated. "He asked for you by name. He has refused to talk to anyone but."

"I...I can't explain that, Sir," Fox stammered. "My mother was Indian, but I...I grew up in Atlanta."

"Would you be willing to talk to him? See what he wants?" the President questioned. His concern was sincere.

"Yes, Sir."

Fox was escorted to the Intensive Care Unit by the same two Secret Service agents that met him in the basement. A nurse, two doctors and an orderly gave him curious looks as the trio marched by in the wide corridor.

Chief Stoner, wearing a clear oxygen line under his hawk nose, still bore traces of green war paint on his lined face. L'Oréal's Forest Green eye shadow had stood the test. Ashen-faced and silent the old man looked dead. An IV line traced to a swath of adhesive tape on his wrist. A blue hospital band encircling the other wrist made it look frail and boney. Above the bed several monitors beeped with the erratic pulse of his struggling life. A nurse stood bedside adding notes to a tablet. She paused as the two agents and Fox entered. "Has he said anymore?" the senior agent questioned.

"No," the nurse answered.

The agent looked to Fox, then to the old man. "Mister Stoner, Special Agent John Fox is here." He spoke loud as if to a deaf man.

The old man's eyes opened. Blinked. They were bloodshot and teary. Fox wondered if the man could see. When the old man's eyes found his he knew the answer.

They were tired and reflected the pain the old man was feeling, but the dark eyes were riveting and alert. It unnerved Fox. He felt as if the old man were looking into his soul.

"Did you hear what I said, Mister Stoner? This is John Fox."

The old man raised his right hand. His knuckles were knurled with age and arthritis. He gestured them away.

"You want us to leave?" the agent questioned.

"John Fox is to stay," the old man gasped from a throat dry with oxygen.

The agent made no effort to mask his displeasure. He looked to his partner and they turned away.

Fox moved closer to the bed rail. The old man held his look. The nurse watched the vital signs.

"I don't know you," Fox said to the old man.

The eyes blinked. "I know you, John Fox. I held you as a child."

Fox's heart raced. His mind struggled with a tangle of emotions he couldn't fathom.

"I am your mother's great uncle," the old man said with effort. "She was a good woman. She made a fine son."

Fox wet his lips. "What is it you want from me?'

"You are a Federal man," the old man explained. "The President will listen to you. Tell him we came in peace. We came with the Great White Father's promise of peace, but they would not listen."

"Who would not listen?" the Fox asked. He was being drawn into the old man's words like a rabbit in a snare.

"The men at the Department..." The old man paused to cough. It was a soul deep, gurgling cough and he struggled with it. When he finally stopped, he was weaker. He gasped a breath, reached to take Fox's hand that was on the bedrail. Grasping Fox's hand in his own which was gnarled with age and arthritis, he went on. "The Department of Interior. They took our river, our crops died. We want to build a casino."

"And they won't allow you?"

"Many other tribes have casinos. They call them White Buffaloes. The White Buffalo has returned with food for all, but they would not talk to us."

"Why?" Why won't they talk to you?" Fox wanted an answer. He wanted it to be over. He wanted away from the old man and his pain. He wanted away from his own pain.

"Because we would build our White Buffalo on the river," a boney finger pointed as if the old man could see the vision, "and the river runs to Las Vegas, Many travel the road to Las Vegas."

"But they would stop at your casino," Fox probed for understanding. "And you think Las Vegas is blocking your casino? Is that what this is about?"

"It is about much more," a boney finger warned and then the hand fell to the bed. The old man was gasping for breath. "It is about a man's word."

"Do you understand what you've done? Do you know the consequence?" Fox didn't understand the anger growing inside him, but he felt it.

"Life is not easy," the old man breathed heavily, "but it is life."

The nurse looked to Fox. "I'm sorry, I think we should stop."

"Will you tell the President, John Fox?" The old man questioned with effort.

Fox nodded agreement.

"Your mother was a good woman," the old man whispered. Fox pulled his hand away carefully. He nodded and turned away.

The Chief-of-Staff ordered the room cleared when

Fox returned to the doctor's lounge. Fox faced the President and the Chief-of-Staff. He told them of the conversation, nearly word for word. The President listened intently. He waited until Fox finished before he asked questions. The Chief-of-Staff seemed annoyed with it all, but he deferred to the President. "So, they meant no harm?" the President speculated. "Coming to the White House was simply to demonstrate no one would listen to them?"

"That's my understanding, Sir," Fox agreed.

"And he asked for you, knowing of your Indian heritage, knowing you would be a conduit he could trust?" The President seemed impressed with the scheme.

"It was a reckless unlawful act that got one man killed and two others wounded," the Chief-of-Staff defended.

"He said life is not always easy," Fox quoted, "but it's still life."

"Did you know of any of this, Leon?" the President said with a look at his Chief-of-Staff.

"I'm aware many tribes are seeking to exploit gambling for quick revenues, but I think caution has to be ..."

The President cut him short with another question. "Do the Mojave's have the lawful right to build a casino?"

"They are a Federally recognized Indian Nation."

"I know, I saw the treaty," the President interjected.

"Yes, they have the right, but these matters have an approval process. In this case..."

Again, the President interrupted. "So, what we've got here is not an attack on the White House, but a protest against a Federal Bureaucracy by three unarmed men with a hundred-year-old treaty in their hands."

"Mr. President," the Chief-of-Staff argued, "an intrusion at the White House is a matter of the gravest concern."

The President grabbed the bloody treaty from a countertop. "So's a treaty, Leon. It's so important that three men were willing to die for it. Goddamnit, let 'im build their casino."

"Mr. President, this shouldn't be an emotional decision."

The President was angry. He stuck the wrinkled treaty in the Chief of Staff's face. Fox stood transfixed, stiff with amazement. "This is a Constitutionally binding agreement signed by the eighteenth President of the United States, Ulysses S. Grant. We are bound by law to honor it."

"You yield to this," the Chief-of-Staff argued, "and every time some nut wants something, he'll be crawling over the fence at the White House to get it."

"Maybe that's the problem, Leon. Maybe we've got too many fences between us and the people. Get it done!" The President turned and marched from the room.

The Chief-of-Staff gave Fox a look of disgust and followed after the President.

The silence in the lounge was heavy after the door swung shut behind the Chief-of-Staff. Fox felt very alone. He felt his life had just changed. The old Indian was right, life wasn't easy.

3 FLY AWAY HOME

"The white man thinks fences will protect his riches.
Our riches have no fences."
Three Paw—Lakota Chief

Donald DePalma sat on the second-floor balcony of his twelve-room mansion in the Lakes District of Las Vegas having his morning coffee while watching Good Morning America. It was his morning ritual. Four miles up the hill and fifteen hundred feet higher than the fabled "Strip," DePalma was among the chosen few with a commanding panoramic view of the sprawling gambling Mecca. The Luxor's massive pyramid, the blue-green Rio, the towers of New York, New York and the sprawling glass face of the MGM Grand stood like distant silent monuments in the morning sun.

At thirty-eight, "The Don," as DePalma was known, was a billionaire plus. Earlier in the year, Fortune Magazine had featured him on a cover at the groundbreaking of his ninth casino, the four-thousand room Casa Grande. "Bus boy to Billionaire," the story was titled. The publicity had brought in the Asian investors he needed. "Momentum," The Don remembered quoting to the reporter from Fortune. "As long as you have momentum you have growth." Looking at the veil of smog hanging over the city below him The Don knew momentum in Las Vegas was becoming critical. "Only so many K-Marts in one town, Kid," his father had warned.

Realizing Las Vegas was reaching its saturation point, The Don had secretly turned his sights south, along the Colorado River to where the Southwest corner of Nevada met Arizona in Laughlin. There was still money to be made in Vegas, but there was big money in Laughlin. Seeing a growing rift between the rich and the poor, and the sinking of the American middle class into a blue-collar swamp, The Don formulated a plan to exploit those who could no longer afford the ever-increasing cost of Las Vegas. There were millions of seniors in the American southwest and the Don was about to get his share of their retirement funds.

Vegas was for the rich, the business conventioneer, while Laughlin was fast becoming the west coast capitol of the working man. Seeing this, DePalma bought up two hundred and forty acres of river front property in Laughlin. He was now well into development on "River Gold Resort." River Gold was a no-holds barred casino with an ambitious gaming menu anchored in thousands of slots and almost as many busty women providing more than you could drink. The hard-core gaming center would be cloaked in a facade of family themes and attractions, water parks, thrill rides, headline show rooms, day care, pet hotels and RV parks. "No room over a hundred bucks," was The Don's order for the marketing plan. "We'll draw them in and then nickel-dime them to death."

In six weeks, The Don would go public with River Gold. It was his first venture outside the security of Las Vegas, and he knew it had to go right to succeed. The construction of the Casa Grande was still strapping his assets and the acquisition of the raw land in Laughlin had eroded his cash reserves, but The Don was betting, and it was the betting that was the rush, the announcement of River Gold would bring in the needed investors. A news bulletin put it all in doubt. The smiling trio on his TV disappeared as a sober news anchor appeared. "We are interrupting our regularly scheduled programs for an anticipated statement from the President in the aftermath of last night's shooting at the White House."

DePalma sipped his coffee and watched as the scene switched to the President at the White House. The President stepped to a podium bristling with microphones. DePalma silently wondered what it would be like to be President. Hell, his business enterprises were as big, or bigger, than many governments. And unlike the U.S. Government, his made money. He decided he'd make a good President. Probably, better than the man he watched.

"Good morning," the President said. "As most of you know, last night three men climbed over the fence here at the White House. It was raining and it was dark. The forces dedicated to protecting me and my family did not know the men were unarmed, or that they were Native Americans. Nor did we know that they carried a copy of a treaty signed by President Ulysses S. Grant."

The White House press core sat in stoic silence as the President studied them. "There has been much talk recently about a contract with America. These three men carried one with them. A contract Washington has ignored, a contract we have failed to honor, and a contract now stained with their blood.

"The fence these men climbed is made of more than cold steel. It's made of indifference and shame. President Grant made peace with the great grandfathers of these men. They were Indians, Native Americans. He gave his word that we, the United States of America, would honor it. We have not."

"We have built too many fences in this country," the Presidents' hands gripped the podium. "We have separated the people from the government. We have forgotten we are a government of the people. Unfortunately, a man had to die. His death must not be in vain. I have ordered the Secretary of Interior, the Director of the Bureau of Indian Affairs and the Chairman of the National Indian Gaming Commission to tear down the fences. If the Mojave people want to build a casino near the Colorado River, on their reservation, we have no right to build fences in their path."

"What!" DePalma gasped, bolting to his feet. He knocked over a small patio table sending a china coffee pot and cups crashing to the tile floor. Splinters of white china slid across the patio. The Don knew the CRIT reservation, made up of the Colorado River Indian Tribes, that snaked along the banks of the Colorado River ninety miles south of Laughlin near Parker, Arizona. More important than a rag-tag band of dusty Indian wannabes was the sprawling ribbon of asphalt, known as U.S. Interstate 95. It ran for nearly five hundred miles from the Mexican border near Yuma, Arizona straight to Laughlin, Nevada. U.S. 95 carried millions of tourists, and dollars, from Arizona and all over the Southwest. It was the major artery, the life blood of the river gambling town. An Indian casino built anywhere along the path leading to Laughlin would bleed millions from the Don's plans. It was a disaster and DePalma knew it. He watched in stunned shock, hardly able to breathe. He had spent hundreds of thousands of dollars on buying the Arizona Congressman representing the highway leading to Laughlin as well as providing whores and the best rooms on the Strip for the Goddamned Director of Indian affairs. He clenched his fists and gritted his capped teeth as the President continued. "When President Grant and the CRIT tribes made peace well over a hundred years ago, amnesty was granted on both sides...now, we here today, once again find laws and promises broken on both sides. Therefore, knowing these men came without malice, I grant them amnesty...and ask them, as they have asked us, to forgive, and join in tearing down the fences. Thank you." The President turned and marched away.

It was a reporter from the Washington Post that was first to stand. The veterans in the White House press corps knew the man wasn't a fan, or a supporter of the incumbent, but he was on his feet applauding. Soon the NBC White House correspondent joined him, and then a CNN reporter. The momentum of the ovation grew as more and more reporters pushed to their feet to join in the spontaneous applause. Soon they were all standing. The chorus of hands joined in celebrating a rare moment in the Presidency that rose above politics.

In Las Vegas on the patio of the home on Lake Shore Circle there was an exception. The slippered foot of Don DePalma kicked the television set off its stand to send it crashing to the floor. "You bunch of fuckin' Indian loving' assholes!" the Don screamed in anger.

John Fox watched the President's speech in a waiting lounge at Dulles International airport. He had flown to Washington in an Air Force staff jet. He was flying back to Palm Springs, via Denver, United coach. Mentioning his wife's position, as a stewardess, he hoped to get bumped up to business class upon boarding. He felt smug listening to the President's speech. He had heard the private debate between two of the most powerful men in the world. His fifteen minutes of fame, Fox mused. He was eager to get home and tell Pam. He had called her earlier, but she hadn't answered. It was early in Palm Springs he reasoned, maybe she was still sleeping. He was almost relived. He wouldn't be able to share much more on the phone than what time his flight was. Details. The bureau had taught him telephone conversations were far from private. Pam would be among the few he could tell, but only in person. If word ever got back to the Director, or the White House Chief-Of-Staff, that he had discussed what he heard or saw his career would be over. Discretion and "need-to-know" had become a way of life. In this instance Fox welcomed it. He was glad the moment linking him to his haunting Indian heritage had been private. In another four years the President, even if re-elected, would be leaving office, his Chief-of-Staff would be joining some corporate board and the Director of the FBI may have his sought-after seat on the Supreme Court. John Fox, he hoped, was already old news. A private behind the scenes moment, that may have been a turning point for the CRIT Indians, was proving to be little more than an embarrassment for him. Fox had breathed a sigh of relief with the President's announcement of amnesty. A blood link to a felon, especially some nut who had climbed over the fence at the White House, could have bought him a permanent assignment in Alaska. His career would be over. Now, there was a good chance he could turn this whole mess into benefit. Tom Roberts would want to know what happened, what it was all about, but since the request came from the Executive Office, he wouldn't push too hard. Fox was already planning to be vague and ambiguous. The mystery of it was much more exciting than the reality. He would be remembered only as the one the White House called. And no one would ask why.

Fox was comfortable with what he considered his pay back. If the Indians had ever given him anything, it was now repaid. Being part Indian, Fox decided, was much like once being a quarterback. It was something he once was, but now it was behind him. He was no longer an Indian or a quarterback. He was an FBI agent assigned to Palm Springs. He wished old man Stoner well, even hoped he would recover. Hell, he would be going back to the reservation a hero. The Indians could use a hero, Fox decided. It had been a while since they had one. Although winning a battle didn't mean winning the war. Fox wondered if the CRIT's really knew what they were getting into. Palm Springs was dotted with a patchwork of Indian casinos. Although they generated millions of dollars, it seemed to Fox more than "White Buffaloes," as Chief Stoner had suggested, they were the White Mans "cash cow." Indian reservations were Federal lands held in trust by the government. Crimes occurring in "Indian Country", as the Reservations were called, were investi-gated by the FBI. Assigned to banks, Fox evaded Indian crime in Palm Springs, but he routinely saw the intelli-gence coming from the casinos. Extortion, bribery, fraud, racketeering, embezzlement and murder. Money, more than solving the Indians' problems, seemed to add to them. The Mob may have been pushed out of Las Vegas, but it seemed to Fox as if they landed firmly on their feet in Indian Country. The thought was painfully poignant. His father may have screwed much more than one Indian.

"United Airlines, flight six-oh-three, non-stop service to Denver, is now ready for boarding at gate three," an amplified female voice announced from a public address system. Fox gathered his tote bag and pushed to his feet. He was looking forward to Palm Springs with its dry air and purifying heat. There, he could get back into his role. There he wouldn't have to face old Indians with gnarled hands who spoke of a past he only wanted to forget. A flush of guilt swept over Fox. He winced as it settled deep in his conscience. His thoughts had followed the path to the realization he was the epitome of what the old Indian had spoken of. His life had been born in the womb of an Indian. Now, he was seeking to deny it, to distance himself from it, declaring he was pure and innocent. The United States had done much the same. Born on Indian land, the young country grew and prospered gaining strength until it turned on its benefactors and slaughtered them. Greed and blind ambition were cloaked in the romantic history of the Indian wars. Fox, considering himself an honorable man, knew he would have to reconcile it. He damned himself for even allowing the thought, but it clung to his inner being like a blood stain on white cotton. "Ticket please," a stewardess asked.

Fox fumbled in a jacket pocket. He was at the mouth of the jetway. The stewardess glanced at his ticket then tore away a portion of the boarding pass. Fox moved down the damp cool air of the jetway. Damn, he had forgotten to ask about the upgrade. No matter, he just wanted on board, wanted strapped into his seat to sleep. Flying always brought him deep dreamless sleep and he was eager to retreat into it.

The flight to Denver became a numb void. Instead of

leaving the haunting spectacle behind him, it robbed him of rest. Fox hung of the edge of sleep, annoyed with the heavy perfume of the woman beside him and a passenger behind him who kept bumping the seat back. The one time he raised the window screen, the country far below was hidden beneath ominous, dark clouds. Hiding its face, Fox thought. He was relieved when the descent into Denver was announced.

"For your convenience our calls are being answered automatically," Pam's voice said on the answering machine. "If you'll leave a message at the tone, we'll return your call as soon as possible."

"Damn," Fox muttered into his cell. An electronic tone sounded on the line. "Pam, it's John. I'm in Denver. I'll be in Palm Springs in two hours. Flight two-ten. See you in two hours. Love ya." He dialed her cell phone. Why wasn't she home? On its third ring he knew it wasn't going to be answered. He pushed the cellphone back into a pocket. Maybe she was in the shower. The thought of her wet naked beauty made him smile. He knew she be waiting at airport.

Facing a forty-minute wait before the Palm Springs flight boarded, Fox browsed a gift shop. Anything was better than the idle thoughts he was certain would take him back to the old Indian with make-up on his face in a room smelling of antiseptics and alcohol, but the gift shop betrayed him. It was challenge enough to try and find a token gift for a stewardess in an airport shop, but the sight of the newspaper's headlines ended the search. "President declares, 'Tear down the fences... Amnesty for the Indians... President sends personal physician... Secret Service defends shooting."

Turning away from the books and newspapers offered little in the way of options. The shop was crowded with an assortment of Indian lore. Arrowheads, moccasins, feathered tee shirts, painted dishes and an array of toy drums, bows and arrows and feathered headdresses. Leaving the shop, Fox sarcastically wondered if the Indians got a royalty.

The low-pressure system that sucked the mantle of moist clouds over the Midwest yielded to high, broken strata and sunshine as the 727 descended toward Palm Springs. Fox leaned to a window as the craft banked into its final approach. "Please return your seat backs and tray tables to an upright position in preparation for landing," a practiced voice ordered. Below the textured complexion of the desert floor yielded to a deep green. A patchwork of intricate, cultivated fields were interlaced with swath after swath of golf courses. Endless rows of tile roofs snaked like intermingled worms along networks of asphalt. Blue pools reached up into the sky like blue/green emeralds. Surrounding it all was the harsh, seemingly barren, hostile desert. From his perch in row twenty-three A, Fox decided it looked much like an island. An island in the desert. An island he called home. An island he was glad to see.

Fox expected to find Pam waiting outside the security gates after landing. She wasn't there. His eyes continued the search as he walked through the terminal toward the baggage area and the street beyond. He paused at the sliding glass doors and reached for his cell phone. He knew he'd had a massage waiting from her. His bewilderment grew. No messages. He punched the button for her cell and listened. "Hi, you've reached Pam Fox. Leave me a message and I'll return your call as soon as possible."

"Pam, it's John. Just landed. Where are you? Call me."

He punched the call button for their home. As it rang his eyes searched the faces moving by to the busy street and those gathering around a luggage carousel expecting to find his wife. On the fourth ring in his ear her voice spoke again. "For your convenience our calls are being answered automatically," Pam's voice said smoothly, "If you'll leave a message at the tone, we'll return your call as soon as possible."

"Hey, girl, this is the FBI, better known as your husband. I'm at airport. Did you get my message? Where are you?" He hoped his voice would be interrupted by hers. It wasn't. Cell phone in hand he walked toward the glass doors leading to the street. A rush of warm desert hair sweep over him reminding him he was in Palm Springs. The warm air was comforting. He was on the edge of a chill after Pam's not answering again. "What the hell could it be?" He pushed aside a growing gut feeling that something was wrong and waved to a waiting cab for a pickup.

4 ALL THE KING'S HORSES

"Wounds of the flesh bring blood.
Wounds of the heart bring revenge."
Two Birds—Oneida

Fox's condo on South Palm Canyon drive was little more than fifteen-minute ride from the airport although with his growing anxiety John Fox felt it was much longer. He silently cursed the traffic signals and slower cars from the back seat of the cab as the graying senior driver wormed the car across the face of the city. "Home for you, or just visiting?" The driver questioned with a glass in the rearview mirror as he slowed for yet another signal.

"It's home," Fox granted the man as he watched the red light, willing it to change.

"Me too," Driver answered. "They say a hundred and

three today," I'm from up in Utah. Been here ten years. Love it."

"Lights green," Fox urged.

Fox pushed money at the man when he finally pulled to the curb on South Palm Court. Maybe Pam was on her way to the airport. Maybe called out on a flight. It had happened before. Managing their schedules was a constant challenge. Digging in a pocket for a key, Fox remembered Pam's annoyance when he got the call out. They had been apart for five days. Maybe if he could get some time off and coordinated with her, they could do a couple days in Vegas. Hit a couple shows, a little fine dining, Craps. She liked rolling the dice. They'd been married in Vegas. He promised himself he would make it happen.

A walkway shaded by towering palms lead to their front door. Fox pushed the key in the lock swung the door open. "Pam," He called with a shout. The living room was dim with closed curtains and blinds. Fox tossed his carry-on bag onto a chair and moved for the kitchen. There was no answer to his call. "Pam," It was louder this time. Again, no answer. A quick look into the kitchen showed nothing. Smokey the cat found him and started snaking around his legs. He turned, moving for the master bedroom and bath. The master bedroom, like the living room was in shadows. Light spilled from beneath a closed bathroom door. Relieved, Fox moved to the door, "Honey, I'm home," he mimicked with a smile. "Ready or not." He swung the door open. Time stopped. Shocked gripped him like a hot bolt of lightning.

The glass door to the shower was open and Pam's lifeless body, dressed only in bra and panties hung from a chromed shower nozzle with a nylon bra, twisted rope like, strung tight around her neck. Her head was bowed with her long hair masking her face. Her arms hung slack at her side and her polished toes nails hung just inches from the shower floor. A puddle of urine lay pooling on the shower floor.

John Fox's scream was loud and animal like as he grabbed for his wife. Fox lifted the lifeless form and pulled at the knotted nylon around Pam's neck. Her flesh was cool to his touch. He lifted and jerked at the knots on the shower nozzle. "Pam," he screamed in desperation again as the shower door banged as a lifeless leg bumped it. Fox struggled with lifting and pulling at the tight knots. "Hold on, Baby, hold on," he cried again and again, pulling, tugging but the unyielding knots held.

It was a concerned neighbor in a connecting condo who heard the chilling screams and the thumping on the wall who called nine-one-one. "No, I don't know what's going on, but it's serious. A man is just screaming and screaming. He won't stop. No, I don't know him. We just come down here on weekends. I'm retired. I'm not going over there."

It was six minutes after the call that the first of three patrol cars arrived on the scene. The first two officers heard the man's screams and found the front door ajar. On entry they found Fox in the bathroom. He was sitting on the floor now, cradling the lifeless form of his wife in his arms, trying to give her breath, mouth to mouth. Broken shower glass covered the floor. The door to the shower had been broken and twisted from it hinges. Water dripped from what was once the shower nozzle. Swaths of blood arched over the shower tile. Fox's torn fingers and hands were covered with blood. "Come on, Baby, breath. Please, breath." The two officers struggled to pull him away from the body.

Fox couldn't remember the arrival of the EMTs and the ambulance, but he rode with them enroute to the hospital. He knew it was shock, but the pain numbered him and stole his voice and even his thoughts. Fox sat in the hallway outside the doors to the emergency room. He was and oblivious to the blood stains on his shirt and hands. It was caking and turning a dark rust color. His mind was numb with soul-deep, agonizing, pain. The horror of it was too painful to allow. He remembered the officers pulling him away from Pam when the paramedics arrived. He remembered fluids gurgling from her nose and mouth when he tried heart massage. He remembered the bittersweet taste of her lipstick when he tried to breathe into her. He remembered her hair, he remembered her touch and, he remembered her love. He raised his hands to his face as deep sobs gripped him. He wept. The deep, painful sobs shook his shoulders and back. Fox's FBI partner in Palm Springs, a black man by the name of Terrance Bell, had arrived and sat at Fox's side. He slipped an arm around Fox's shoulders and held him as he wiped his own tears away. Roberts, the OIC of the Palm Springs Bureau paced nearby with a cellphone to his ear. The suicide death of an agent's wife was going to create a helluva wave. No matter what, as the OIC, he was going to have tough questions coming from the Director in Washington.

God refused to send a doctor out of the emergency room to say a miracle had occurred even though Fox prayed silently for it. It was as if he waited, there was still a chance. Finally shock and the rejection of the unimaginable yielded to painful reality. Pam was dead. Fox felt he was too. Suicide. How could such a dark horror have crept into a love he shared with his wife, his love. How could she do this. Why would she do this. There were no secrets between them. But there must have been. Cold, dark, haunting secrets, unshared. Secrets he could not fathom. Who could? Had he killed her? What did he do, what did he say? What had he not seen, not heard?

Answers ran and hid. Seemingly there were none. No one was coming. There was no help on the way. Hope and reason, like Pam were not only gone, they were dead. Without comment Fox finally stood up and simply walked away. Bell, hesitated a moment, exchanged a look with Senior Agent Roberts, who nodded agreement. Bell pushed up to follow after Fox.

Bell drove while Fox sat silent on the passenger's side. Palm Springs was basking in the late afternoon heat. The streets teemed with tourists and shoppers. People were smiling and laughing. How could they? How could it go on? How could it be normal? Fox silently cursed them.

After pulling to the curb in front of the house Bell turned the car off. Fox looked to him. "Thanks, but I need to be alone," he said in a tone Bell chose not to challenge.

"You sure?" Bell questioned and then felt stupid for asking.

"Yeah, " Fox climbed out of the car.

"You need anything, John? Call me."

Fox turned to his condo. The unmarked car pulled away.

Smokey was waiting inside the front door. The cat meowed and rubbed against Fox's legs. "Hello. Smokey," Fox said softly. He stood there for a long moment. The house was quiet. A pendulum wall clock ticked rhythmically in the living room. How could she be gone, he questioned? Her home was here. The flowered pillows on the couch. The plants. The paintings. The only thing missing was Pam. He bit his lip until he tasted blood.

He stripped his soiled bloodied shirt off in the garage and the tossed it into a trash can. He gathered a dustpan and broom and headed for the bathroom. Walking into the bathroom Fox could smell the scent of her.

Cosmetics and brushes lined the countertop. He looked at his image in the mirror. He was a naked, haggard man... and, he was alone.

He tuned, tossed the dustpan aside and began sweeping the broken bloodied glass on the floor. The cat sat silent in the doorway and watched.

The reality of Pam's death wasn't just a matter of cleaning up the bathroom where he had found her. Calls had to be made. Pam's father was a retired Judge who lived in Orange county south of Los Angeles. He and Fox were less than close. Nevertheless, the call had to be made. "Judge, I'm sorry," Fox stammered after the man answered his cell. "Pam is dead."

"Dead! What! the hell are you talking about?" The Judge did not take the news well. "Suicide? Bullshit!" Angry at first, he wanted the name of the officers at the scene and the name of the doctor at the hospital. Fox had few answers. "Where is my daughter?" The Judge demanded. Again, the answer was difficult, but the question told Fox that Pam was still his wife and he was still responsible for her. The conversation with Pam's father was painful and difficult for both men. Finally, after an extended silence on the line the Judge took a deep breath and forced the words. "All right, John, Karen and I will be out in the morning."

After the tense conversation with the Judge Fox found a telephone book and searched for mortuary services. Palm Springs, he found, had many. He made a call to the Hall Mark Mortuary. He had only to tell them his wife was dead and at Palm Springs Memorial. They asked few questions. After offering a professional assurance they would pick up Pam from the hospital they asked Fox to call or visit their office when he was ready.

Ready? Fox wondered. Ready no longer seemed to be a possibility, he concluded sitting silent in the darkness of his living room. Palm Springs seemed ready to move on. They wouldn't want the news of the suicide of a beautiful young woman. Pam Fox may be dead, but the city's persona would cover it. A proliferation of safe deposit boxes and savings accounts bulged with old money in Palm Springs. Snowbird money, money awaiting an army of would be inheritors, tax assessors and thieves. An elephant burial ground. Palm Springs was what the FBI bank men called an "orchid", easy pickings. More money, less violence, than robbing banks in L.A. You may get caught, but not likely you'd get shot.

The gangbangers, the take-over artists and the lone wolves had discovered Palm Springs. Los Angeles bristled with cops eager for a shooting. Palm Springs was different. It had far fewer cops with an effective philosophy of service, not confrontation. The Crips, the Bloods, the Big Dogs, the White Fence Boys, they all came calling. Banks without guards, customers whose average age was seventy-two, served by mature silver-haired tellers, were far more attractive targets than an L.A. branch where the young black cashier may be a cop with a twelve-gauge shotgun waiting beneath the counter.

Fox had learned Palm Springs with its combination of wealth and celebrities, had something else L.A. didn't. Influence. Staggering under an onslaught of robberies and violence, the gray-haired board members and bankers called their Congressmen. The politicians dedicated to the well-being and contentment of their powerful constituents quickly passed the buck to the FBI. Thus, twenty-four months earlier Fox and three other experienced L. A. bank men were assigned to task force CAT, Catch-A-Thief, and transferred to Palm Springs.

At first, Fox was both disappointed and angry. Palm

Springs wasn't where you built a career, it was where you ended one. But that was changing. The town, once little more than a quiet retreat for Hollywood's old guard, was fast becoming the option of new money. Brokers, writers, artists and an eclectic mix of young professionals, no longer tied to a metropolis moving to the desert. In the Springs you could walk the streets at night, sleep with your windows open and still find your car in the driveway in the morning. Fox found himself responding to the desert heat. The seeds of his youth in Arizona, he decided. The smog and traffic of L.A. was easy to leave behind. After eight months, he and Pam bought their condo. He allowed a smile thinking of her. Pam loved the heat, the sun and the small-town feel. Remodeling and tennis became their off-duty passions. Life was good. Collectively they made nearly two hundred thousand dollars a year. Fox carried an American Express Gold Card. He was married to a beautiful woman. He owned a two-year old BMW and he loved his job and his identity as an FBI Agent. He was, Fox decided, like many of his neighbors a member of an exclusive club, but membership in his club couldn't be bought. Influence couldn't get you in and membership was very limited. Carrying the badge of the Federal Bureau of Investigation was key to many things. Prestige, self-esteem and pride among them, Fox's thoughts about tomorrow and the day after were fleeting. He could see yesterday. Yesterday, when his Indian heritage had him standing in front of the President of the United States. The fact he was half Indian wasn't important, the fact he was one hundred percent FBI was, but what lay ahead for an agent whose wife had just committed suicide? An agent who had no explanation seemed to be an agent with no future.

5   TURNING OVER STONES

> *"The outline of the stone is round, having no end and no beginning; like the power of the stone it is endless. The stone is perfect of its kind and is the work of nature, no artificial means being used in shaping it. Outwardly it is not beautiful, but its structure is solid, like a solid house in which one may safely dwell."*
>
> **Chased-by-Bears—Santee-Yanktonai Sioux**

Fox couldn't bring himself to lay on a bed he had shared with Pam. Although numb with a grief that near paralyzed, he forced himself to shower in the guest bath. He tried sleeping in the guestroom, but it was futile. He returned to a chair in the living room. Smokey joined him. Finally, exhaustion captured him. He was still asleep when the door chime surprised him when it sounded just after eight o'clock. Fox was surprised when he opened the door to find Tom Roberts, the Special Agent in Charge of the Palm Springs office of the FBI and another man dressed in a suit and tie carrying a briefcase. "Sorry, John. I called several times. You didn't answer."

Roberts' look and tone told Fox this was no courtesy call. "Sorry," Fox offered opening the door wider. "I may have been in the shower." He had no idea what he had done with his cell phone. He did remember leaving the kitchen phone off it's hook after talking with Pam's father. He didn't want the man calling back, and didn't he feel he was obligated to explain to these two. "Come in,' Fox said with an awkward glance at his naked feet. He hadn't put on socks or shoes after his shower hours before.

Fox lead the two to the living room. "Please, sit down." Fox gestured as he opened several blinds. The two men sat on a couch. Fox sat down in a chair across from them. A coffee table divided them. Smokey the cat busied himself by carefully smelling the man's briefcase that set on the carpet. Fox waited; he knew he didn't have to initiate talk. It was obvious the two men were on there on business. Fox sensed it was serious. "John, this is Tim Griffin. He's the US attorney for the southern district which covers Palm Springs."

The man made no effort to stand or offer anything other than a sober look as Robert's introduced him. Fox's pulse quickened. He was on the edge of being really annoyed. He waited for Roberts to continue. "I invited Tim to join me this morning because a situation has developed subsequent to your visit to Washington and the..." Roberts hesitated to straighten himself and take a breath knowing he was on sensitive ground, "the unfortunate death of your wife."

Fox's annoyance now showed on his face as he

studied the two. "Don't talk to me as if you're conducting an interview, Tom. What's going on?"

The man at Roberts' side answered for him. "After you returned to Palm Springs, Agent, did you talk to anyone about your trip to Washington or who you met while you were there?"

Fox glanced at his bare feet before answering. They were beginning to feel cold. He raised his look to the US Attorney. "I was a little busy after I got home," Fox answered sarcastically.

"Perhaps during your time at the hospital?" The attorney pressed.

"I talked to no one," Fox added.

"John, someone talked to the press," Tom Roberts offered, "The Washington Post. They claim to know of your native American heritage and the fact you were flown in to speak with one of the men involved in the White House invasion, and then your speaking the president."

"I'll say it again, Tom. It wasn't me. I didn't even tell you about it."

"Okay," The attorney granted, "Let's say it wasn't you. The attack on the White House by three Indians wearing warpaint is still big news. A horde of reporters will be looking for more. Which means you—an FBI agent who is part Indian. If they haven't found you yet, they will."

"So, my native American heritage is the issue?" Fox questioned.

"No," the attorney answered quickly. "The President of the United States is the issue. He has the right to privacy, and his privacy has been violated."

"You want me to say it again. It wasn't me."

"The press is going to find you, agent. That's why I'm here. You, like it or not, have been drawn into this by the fact of your heritage. The press won't be far behind us.

And once they find you there are quickly going to find the news of your wife's' death."

Fox bristled at the accusation. "My wife's death is none of their goddamned business."

"John," Tom Roberts plead extending a hand as if to ward off Fox's anger.

"Here's the issue. Three Indians climbed over the fence at the White House in the darkness. They're all shot. One killed."

"I fucking know that, Tom."

"Let me finish," Roberts continued, "Then it's leaked to the press, an FBI agent, reportedly an Indian, is flown in from Palm Springs to meet with the surviving chief and then the President."

"And the story ends, right there," Fox declared.

"Not quite," the US attorney added. "The press is going to find you here in Palm Springs and when they do find you, they're going to, as I said before, find the mysterious death of your wife."

Fox bolted to his feet. Smokey the cat bolted from the room. "Get the fuck out."

Roberts and the US attorney stood. Roberts again extended his hand again as in an effort to restore calm. "John, this has reached the Director's Office, and the President's chief of staff. They're both sensitive about the press. The reputation of the White house and the Bureau are both on the line."

"None of it has anything to do with my wife." Fox warned.

"Let's cut to the chase, agent," the US attorney warned. "Your wife's death, although a reported suicide, will be investigated by the Palm Springs Police department and the US Attorney's office. You're a federal agent. While this investigation moves forward you are ordered onto administrative leave until findings are reported and a federal grand jury renders a verdict."

Fox stood speechless, stunned by the warning.

"John," Roberts added, "None of us could foresee this. As the agent in charge, I have to ask you to turn in your badge and identification. I also have to warn you this is an active investigation. You are prohibited to discuss with anyone."

"Get out of my house," Fox said in a slow deliberate tone. The two men moved for the door. Fox sank to his chair as the door closed behind them. He lowered his face and covered it with is trembling hands. Smokey returned and rubbed his whiskers on Fox's closed hands.

The Palm Springs Police were less than enthusiastic when the US Attorney advised he would be joining in the investigation of the apparent suicide death of an FBI agent's wife. The uniformed officers who had responded to the scene had conducted a cursory investigation. They took pictures. Collected evidence in the form of the ligature the woman used around her neck. The scene had suicide written all over it. The fact the victim was the wife of an FBI Agent made it sensitive but not a mystery.

The rank and file of Palm Springs PD were unanimous in their collective pity for Fox. What the hell was there to investigate? Seemed the Justice Department and the FBI had a warped system of caring for their own. Tom Roberts, the man who would have to answer all the questions, the man who took his responsibility as Special-Agent-in-Charge serious and the man intent on protecting his own career, was more pragmatic. He was sympathetic to Fox and the situation. My God, there was no precedence.

Nevertheless, Washington was worried. There was a leak somewhere? It could be a driver, a pilot, a nurse...anyone. He would turn every detail inside out. He would find the cause, affix responsibility and recommend accountability. Roberts already knew it was going to be messy. In the abstract, the emotional investments were not relevant to the issue of cause. Justice wasn't the issue, policy was. And, underscoring the Bureau's volumes of written policy was the unwritten, although equally as important, policy of never do anything to tarnish the image. The image had been more than tarnished, it had a dead woman lying on it.

Roberts called Terrance Bell into his office. "Go get John Fox. We tried interviewing him in his home. He threw us out. I want you to impress upon him this isn't a matter of choice. There will be a formal interview."

"Damn, Tom, this has got to be tough on him," Terrance Bell argued.

"Take Stokowski with you. I want Fox to know we're serious."

Discipline was a way of life for an FBI agent. Fox had been ordered to turn in his badge and ID, so he would do it. He was searching the suit jacket he had worn on his trip to Washington. He had it in hand when the telephone rang. He picked it up in the bedroom. "Hello."

"Mr. Fox this George Nelson from Hallmark Mortuary. You called us earlier regarding arrangements for your wife."

"Yes."

"We made an attempt for the pick at Palm Springs Memorial hospital, but we were advised her body was impounded by the county coroner's office."

Fox drew in a breath as he grasped the silver badge in his hand. He could feel it cutting into his flesh.

"We contacted the coroner's office, but they refused comment as to when she may be released. Perhaps they might be more cooperative with you?"

"Okay, yeah," Fox answered, "I'll get back to you."

Fox hung up the phone and leaned into the wall. My God, Pam was so far away. He felt powerless. He released his grip on the badge as the doorbell sounded.

He pushed the badge into a pocket and crossed to the door. He opened it to find Bell and Stokowski waiting. "John," Bell said almost apologetically, "Tom Roberts wants you to come in."

Fox studied his black partner and the broad-shouldered Stokowski who stood at his side. The tension was palatable as the trio stood silent. Fox knew the two men and even more importantly they knew him. Fox forced a nod and a shrug of his surrender. "Okay, if I put my shoes on?"

The drive to the FBI offices on North Palm Canyon was silent and quick.

Fox waited in the interrogation room alone at the Bureau office for nearly an hour. He knew he was on video and audio. Hell, he had used the room a hundred times. He never looked at his watch. Time wasn't important. Neither was what he faced. He didn't care. Nothing could threaten him. He had already lost everything. He didn't react when the U.S. Attorney and Tom Roberts opened the door.

They offered Fox a drink. He declined. They tried to make small talk. He sat silent. Finally, Brewster turned to business. He apologized for their earlier visit to his home. "These are tense times but let's remain professional. This interview is important. It is being videotaped." He paused and looked to Roberts signaling him to warn Fox of his Miranda Rights. "You have the right to remain silent," Roberts began in a sober tone. Fox tensed as he listened impassively. "If you give up your right to remain silent anything you say can be used against you. You have the right to have an attorney present before and during our questioning. Do you understand your rights?"

"Yes."

"If you cannot afford an attorney…"

Fox cut him short. "I understand my rights. I don't want an attorney."

"Are you willing to talk to us?" Roberts pressed.

"Let's see how it plays," Fox urged, crossing his arms. The two men facing him knew what the gesture meant.

"This matter is unique in that it is an administrative in nature," Brewster continued. "As an agent with the FBI you have to cooperate, and you cannot refuse to answer any of our questions. The inquiry by the Palm Springs police will be and is totaling separate when it comes to your rights."

"I got all that. Are you done talking to the camera?"

Brewster studied Fox a moment before he spoke again. "Why do you think your wife took her life?"

Fox held Brewster's look. "Because she was lonely and jealous." He offered without hesitation.

Brewster was surprised. "You were having an affair?"

"Yeah, with my assignment. You wanna guest how many hours my partner and I worked last month? You wanna guess how much time my wife and I had last week? You want to check the call out logs and see how many nights I spent in the field instead in bed with my wife? I've had maybe fours sleep in the last three days. I've traveled through three time zones twice in the past twenty-four hours. I can't remember what I last had to eat, and you wonder why maybe my wife was lonely and jealous."

Tom Roberts sat silent, his hands covering one another on the table that separated him form Fox. Brewster made notes on a pad with his blue and white government pen. They all knew notes weren't necessary.

The interview was being recorded but it gave Brewster time to plan his next question. He clicked his pen shut and returned his look to Fox." Did you speak to anyone about your trip to Washington while you were there?"

"No."

"Did you speak to anyone about it subsequent to your return?"

"No."

Brewster nodded. "Did your wife leave a note, agent?"

Fox took in a breath to steady himself. He unfolded his arms and wiped at his face before he answered. "No, she didn't leave a note, but I got the message."

Brewster added to his notes. "Let's talk about your Indian heritage. Can you explain it?"

"Pretty simple. My father fucked an Indian." Fox's answer was chilling and blunt.

"So, your mother was an Indian?" Brewster continued accepting Fox's challenge.

"My father was an agent. You know that," Fox continued. "He was assigned to Phoenix. I don't know how they met. I was five when my father transferred to Atlanta. He took me along. My mother didn't go. I know they divorced later."

"Do you know what tribe your mother was with?"

"Mojave."

"Can you tell us what she looked like?"

"She looked like my mother," Fox was annoyed. He wasn't sure why.

"And after moving away, leaving your mother behind, did you stay in touch?"

"No," Fox said returning Brewster's look. "My father remarried in Atlanta. I was raised by my stepmother. She died with him when his plane crashed. She, for all purposes was my mother."

"Do you know her ethnicity?"

"She was white, like you."

Brewster chose not to take the challenge. "How do you suppose these Indians in Washington, the one that asked for you specially, Agent Fox, how did he know of your heritage? And why did he think you would help him?"

"I haven't done Ancestry dot com, so you can hold off on wanting a pow wow, and if you want to know why he requested me, go ask him."

"You may play smart ass," the U.S. Attorney cautioned, leaning into the table toward Fox to emphasize his point, "but you have no rights in the Bureau's administrative review of your conduct in this incident." Brewster continued with a glance at Roberts as if to reinforce the intended intimidation, "Unless you cooperate fully, you may face suspension and possible termination."

Fox returned the man's look. He wasn't intimidated. "I'm done talking."

The U.S. Attorney was annoyed with the rejection of his authority. Clearly, he outranked this man. He reluctantly tempered his reaction. He clicked his pen again and made notes on the pad in front of him. "Do you understand what you've done?" he questioned, scrawling a line on the paper. "Do you know the consequence of embarrassing the President of the United States?"

"How'd I do that? By my blood mother being an Indian?" his words took him

back to the leathery, bronze face of Russell Stoner. He remembered the old man's labored breath and his words. "Life isn't always easy," Fox added from deep inside, "but it is life."

The pen clicked and again and disappeared into a pocket. The U.S. Attorney pushed from his chair and the two men left the room.

Fox was driven home by Bell and Stokowski. Tom Roberts advised he was on "administrative leave" and took his badge and ID card. "You need anything, John," Bell said when they stopped in front of the house, "Call me, okay?"

Fox nodded and climbed out.

He lay awake on the bed once shared with his wife as light faded outside. Clasping Pam's pillow in his arms, he finally yielded to exhaustion. Later the families came. Pam's parents from Orange County. Her older sister from San Francisco, and a cousin from Los Angeles. Pam's father became the anchor. He did what the grieving Fox could not. Funeral arrangements were made after the county coroners' autopsy and release of Pam's body. A viewing. A reception for the horde of well-intending friends, a combination of FBI Agents and Flight Attendants.

Although Fox was surrounded by them, he was alone, and as if sensing that, he demonstrated his appreciation by being Pam's husband one last time. On the day of the funeral, for the first time since finding his wife dead, he showered, shaved and put on a clean suit.

At the conclusion of the service at the funeral home, Fox made a final solitary walk to the open casket. The crowded room sat in reverent silence. Fox looked at his wife. She looked asleep. He reached and ran a finger carefully along the line of her jaw. A tear spilled and ran down his cheek. He didn't bother to wipe it away. "I love you, Pam," he whispered and bowed to kiss her gently on the lips. He heard her answer as a tear fell from his cheek onto hers.

The procession, the interment on a sprawling grassy knoll in Palm Desert, and the good-byes later at their home on South Palm, ran together like wet paint in Fox's mind. "She was happy being your wife, John," Jack

Sinclair told him at the door. The father who no longer had a daughter, shook the hand of the man who no longer had a wife, and drove away. Fox turned and walked into the house. Smokey, the cat, was waiting.

The telephone rang often during the first few days, but Fox never answered it. Papers collected on the driveway and the mailbox at the curb bulged with an assortment of envelopes. He ignored it all. Who was calling, what time it was, or even what day it was, were forgotten in the torrent of grief and loneliness washing over him?

In the middle of a sleepless night he called out aloud, challenging God to take his life and give it to her. But it seemed God wasn't listening. When Fox awoke, late morning, in a chair in the living room, he was still alive. Fox wasn't sure where the thought came from, but by the end of the day he knew he was yielding to it, even allowing concentrated thought about it. After deciding he couldn't stay in the condo after discovering the lifeless Pam, he now realized he couldn't even stay in Palm Springs. What he was had changed. He was no longer a husband, no longer an FBI agent. He was living among the ruins of a life that no longer existed.

It was dark once again when he picked up the telephone and called Jack Sinclair.

"Jack, it's John in Palm Springs," Fox said hesitatingly when the aging father of his dead wife picked up the telephone. It sounded as if he woke the man.

"We've been worried about you," The man's tone was sincere.

"Who is it?" Fox heard a woman asking in the background.

"It's John," the man answered.

"Jack, can you take care of this place? I'm... I have to

leave, but I don't want anything to happen to Pam's things."

"Don't worry about anything. How long will you be gone?"

"I don't know... I don't know if I'll be back."

The line was quiet for an awkward moment before the old man answered. "John, we love you like a son. You do what you have to. The house will be there when you're ready to come back. It was Pam's house too. Taking care of it will be like taking care of her."

"Smokey's here," Fox added as the cat circled his legs brushing and purring.

"Don't worry. We'll be there tomorrow."

"I'll leave a key under the matt at the front door," Fox said and hung up.

He spent several hours packing. Two suitcases and a soft hang-up bag. Ironically, he found it much like packing for the Washington trip. He didn't know what he would be doing or how long he would be staying. Nevertheless, the doing was therapeutic. After carrying the bags to the garage and loading them into the BMW, he busied himself cleaning the house. If his in-laws were going to be kind enough to look after the place, he was going to ensure it was clean when they arrived. Pam would want it that way.

After taking out trash, vacuuming and cleaning the sinks, the place looked reasonably well. He inspected each room and took a collection of dirty socks and underwear outside and threw them in the trash. It was while outside he saw the array of newspapers in the driveway. He counted six. He gathered the papers and added them to the trash. Pulling the trash cans to the curb for pickup, he noticed the mailbox standing open and the glut of mail inside. It seemed personal tragedy didn't interfere with delivery of newspapers or junk mail. Fox gathered the assortment and headed inside.

If there was any doubt regarding his departure, sorting the mail erased it. Two thirds of the envelopes were addressed to Miss, Ms or Mrs. Pamela J. Fox. Reading the name again and again was like probing a fresh wound. There were announcements of sales, advertisements and bills. Some of it he recognized, some he did not. Southern California Electric, Nordstrom's, General Telephone, Pacific Mortgage Company, the Limited, Victoria's Secret It was their paper life. It lived on with a life independent of theirs. Their marriage was over. What was the vow? Till death doth part?

Victoria's Secret didn't seem to care Ms. Pamela J. Fox had had hung herself. Ms. Pamela J. Fox was legally indebted, and the bills would continue. Fox felt inadequate and weak. He felt almost physically ill. He could face danger, he had many times, and kill when needed, but he was powerless in fending off the void, the hollow he felt deep in his soul for Pam.

Gathering the mail, he stacked it neatly on the desk in the den. Victoria's Secret, along with all the others, could go to hell. Fox was ready to leave. He opened a can of cat food and spooned it into a dish. Smokey was waiting at his feet, circling, purring. He sat the dish down and patted the cat. "Smokey, take care of your furry little ass." Fox took a deep breath and moved for the door.

Three hundred and twelve miles to the northeast, someone else was moving for a door. American Airlines flight two-twenty-six had landed in Las Vegas. Thirty-eight-year-old Dennis Milner, a certified tribal member of the Mille Lac Indian tribe in Waukon, Minnesota, was on his way to success. Milner, a second-rate contractor from

Saint Cloud had found renewed success in becoming an Indian. He was bankrupt, seven months in arrears with child support, fighting two charges of fraud and unemployed when Clyde Hanes, an attorney in Saint Cloud suggested a genealogy search may be of benefit. The only cost was fifteen percent of any revenues generated.

Minnesota was a patchwork of Indian reservations and many of the tribes had tapped into the motherlode by turning to gaming. The interstates running across Minnesota were peppered with billboards inviting passersby to strike it rich in the seemingly endless string of tacky neon lit Indian casinos. Minnesota, with its reputation for high stakes bingo, had truly become the *Under the Oh* state.

Attorney Clyde Hanes' genealogical search of Dennis Milner struck gold in the literal sense with a little help from a County Recorder for a few hundred dollars. Milner became the bastard son of an alcoholic tribal member who had died three years earlier. A dully certified birth certificate was presented to the tribe's membership committee. They met once a month, none of the six Indians were high school graduates.

Of the thirty-six applicants, many of whom had seen the dollar value in becoming a certified tribal member, only two were approved. Dennis Milner was one of them. As a tribal member he now had a voice, a vote, in all tribal business. But more important to Milner was the fact he now shared in the profits from the Mille Lac Lake Casino.

The Casino, a mid-sized operation, was modest compared to some. Its annual gross averaged around twenty-eight million dollars. Milner, tribal identification card in hand, now received forty-seven hundred dollars a month, tax free. Although his joy was short-lived. Clyde Hanes took fifteen percent and Milner's ex-wife, armed with a court order, garnished most of what remained for delinquent child support and was in the process of taking him back to court for an increase. The bitch.

Milner was left with little more than drinking money and the prospect of an entry level job in maintenance at the casino where tribal members had preference in being hired. Milner didn't mind being an Indian to share in the money, but the idea of having to work with them sent a shudder through him. He had been in the casino. It was run by white men in thousand-dollar suits. The only Indians he had seen were emptying ash trays and trash cans. There had to be another way.

Clyde Hanes, in addition to being a three-hundred-and-ten-pound compulsive overeater, was a compulsive gambler. The glut of Indian casinos around Saint Cloud entertained his compulsion, but the real action, real gamblers knew, was in Las Vegas. Hanes went there as often as his clients could afford. It was on a recent trip with a four-day stay at the Casa Grande that the contact was made.

Hanes had not fared well. In addition to the four thousand dollars in cash he had brought with him, he lost another six in house credit. When he tried to check out, the Visa Gold Card he presented for payment was rejected. He was swimming in sweat when he was escorted to the casino executive offices by two plain clothed giants.

"Sit down, Clyde," Mitch Parsons invited. A gold desk plate announced 'Operations Manager'. Parsons was a suave forty-year-old with manicured nails. He masked his distaste of Hanes' body odor as the man lowered his hulk into a cushioned leather chair. "I understand you're suffering some cash flow difficulties." Parsons was fingering a computer print out in front of him on the wide executive desk.

"I could postdate a check," Hanes suggested, wiping sweat from his neck. "Transfer some funds soon as I get home."

Parsons' eyes went to the report. "Doesn't look to us like you have any reserves left, Clyde."

Hanes wiped his meaty palm on a trouser leg. "I've got a motor home I could sell."

Parsons rocked back in his chair. "We don't want you to lose your motor home, Clyde. You're a good customer. We value our relationship. Perhaps we should consider options... Perhaps a mutually beneficial favor."

"A favor?" Hanes was puzzled, but the vice grip on his chest eased some. "What kind of favor?"

Parsons rocked forward to lean his forearms on the desk. "You're a practicing attorney. Is that correct?"

"Yes. I've been a member of the bar for fourteen years."

"And if we hired you, let's say to barter your debt for legal services, then anything we discussed, the business between us, would be privileged information?" Parsons suggested.

"Yes, absolutely," Hanes assured.

"Then consider the DePalma Development Corporation your new client," Mitch Parsons' white capped teeth smiled.

"Thank you," Hanes breathed, forcing a short-lived smile. "But what can I help you with?"

"You represent Indians, tribal members back in Minnesota, don't you?"

Hanes nodded. "Yes, many. I grew up with Indians."

"We would like to develop a relationship with an Indian businessman, an entrepreneur. A builder let's say. Someone manageable. Someone we could invest in as an insulated, silent partner. Do you think you could turn over enough stones to find a man like this?"

"Yes," Hanes assured eagerly. "I can do that."

"Good," Parsons said, relaxing in his high-backed chair again. "When you find this man, and he proves acceptable to us, we'll be more than glad to write off this token indebtedness and perhaps even establish some sort of, shall we say, royalty agreement."

"I would like that."

"But let me caution you, Clyde," Parsons said pointing a finger. "Donald DePalma takes his privacy very serious. This offer and our role in it, by your own words, is privileged. Do we agree on that?"

"Oh, yes, I understand," Hanes nodded to emphasize his acceptance.

"The man you pick will have to be equally discrete," Parsons picked up a pen and scrawled a number on a business card. "When we need to talk, call me at this number." He offered the card to Hanes.

Hanes took the card, slipped it into an inside pocket. His shirt was damp.

"It's been a pleasure talking with you, Clyde." Parsons stood.

Hanes pushed to his feet. They shook hands. "About the room charges?" he questioned hesitantly.

"I'll take care of them."

Two days later Clyde Hanes renewed Dennis Milner's expired contractor's license with the Minnesota State Department of Commerce in Saint Paul. He also registered him as a member in NIMBA, the National Indian Businessmen's Association and with the U.S. Department of Interior and the Department of Labor as a minority small business operator.

After a week of teleconferencing and exchanging faxes with Parsons' office in Las Vegas, Hanes got the call he was hoping for. Parsons was brief. "We'd like to meet Mr. Milner. Be here Tuesday."

"Ah, Mr. Parsons," Hanes pursued, sensing he was going to hang up.

"Yes?"

"The air fare... Could you?"

"The tickets will be waiting at the airport," Parsons said curtly and hung up.

The limousine waiting at McCarran International Airport in Las Vegas snaked through the crush of early morning traffic to the entrance of the MGM Grand Hotel on the strip. Hanes was puzzled. "You sure you got the right hotel?" he questioned.

"It's the right hotel," the driver answered. "Check in. You'll be called."

"Jesus!" Milner exclaimed as they walked into the expanse of the opulent, sprawling glitter and marble of the Grand's lobby.

"Shut up," Hanes ordered. "Don't act like a fuckin' tourist."

They met at one o'clock in a paneled board room on the hotel's second floor. A long conference table was decorated with fresh cut flowers and an array of finger foods. Hanes poured drinks from liquor at a wet bar. They were eating fan tail shrimp when Donald DePalma, Mitch Parsons and a shapely forty-year-old redhead arrived. Hanes guessed she was a secretary. Although he tried not to stare at the woman's ample breasts, the scent of her excited him. He silently hoped Milner wouldn't fuck up a good thing. Hanes had admonished the talkative Milner to be quiet.

Hanes had never met Donald DePalma, but he needed no introduction. He could literally feel the man's aura of power. "Let's talk business," DePalma suggested, sitting down across from Milner. He made no attempt to introduce himself or offer a hand. "Within the next month the Mojave Tribe in northern Arizona will put out bids for construction of a hundred thousand square foot casino. I want you," DePalma said with a penetrating look at Milner, "to get the bid."

"A hundred thousand square feet?" Milner questioned in awe.

"Yeah." DePalma continued, "A chicken shit little place in MFN."

"MFN?" Milner questioned dumbly. Hanes was silently cursing him through gritted teeth.

"Yeah, Middle of Fuckin' Nowhere," DePalma answered sarcastically. The redhead at his side smiled. Milner did too. He was being entertained. He liked DePalma's brash style.

"Figure seventy-five dollars a commercial foot. Factor in another ten for the MFN factor and your ballpark figure is eight-point five mill." DePalma continued, "You control labor costs with the promise you'll use all tribal, local and migrant. Your materials will be bought from Native American manufacturers whenever possible. Your money will come from a coalition of small tribes scattered over the Midwest combined with five hundred thousand of your own. You'll post a million-dollar completion bond, and using prefab components, you'll turn the key in one hundred and twenty days."

"Hell," Milner said aloud.

"Can you do it?" DePalma pressed.

"Fuck no, I can't do it," Milner answered.

DePalma smiled. He looked first at Parsons, then the girl. "I like this guy."

"But I said I can't do it," the puzzled Milner defended.

"That's the idea, you fuckin' idiot. We don't want it built," DePalma spat at him.

"Oh," Milner acknowledged.

Hanes' heart was in his throat. He felt it was all slipping away.

DePalma laid his hands palm down on the table in front of him and spoke directly to Milner. "You're a card carrying Indian, a blood brother, a fuckin' warrior. You're one of them. You've come to them because you believe in what they're doing. They've eaten dust and rabbit shit mixed with pride for the past two hundred years. You're there because you've seen what gaming can do for Indians. You've seen new schools, medical centers, housing and hope. You've seen the White Buffalo! You've tasted its meat and you're there to help them fill their own baskets."

Milner was excited. He understood and his adrenaline was surging. He leaned into the table toward DePalma, "You want me to fuck 'em into the ground."

"Promise them anything," DePalma urged with agreement, "but give them nothing."

"And why do I do all this?" Milner quizzed with a hard look. "Cause you and me are such great fuckin' buddies?"

Hanes sat frozen with fear. Parsons stiffened. DePalma studied Milner subtly for a long moment before he finally showed a smile. "You got balls. I like that. What do you want?"

Milner was ready with his answer. "A thousand a week, expenses... And her as my assistant," he said with a look at the redhead. If the woman felt anything, she hid it and returned Milner's gaze impassively.

DePalma glanced at the woman as he considered the demand. Then, pushing out of his chair, he stuck a hand toward Milner. "You got a deal." They shook hands. "Mitch, work out the details." He turned, moved for the door. The redhead got up to follow. Milner watched her ass as she left the room.

6 NATIVE SON

"A wounded animal will return to its cave."
Elias Torres—Apache

It was ten o'clock in Washington. D.C. The Director of
the FBI arrived promptly on the hour at the Attorney
General's Office. In his briefcase was the fifty-seven-
page report of what had become known as "The Palm
Springs Incident". The Assistant Director of the FBI, the
U.S. Attorney from the Southwest District, the State
Attorney General of California and two top FBI execu-
tives had spent a week reviewing the matter.

Evidence had been gathered, additional witnesses
interviewed, the events chronologically, as well as individual, expert opinions and recommendations were
made. All that remained was the decision. It was not to
be an easy one, and to avoid being accused of bias
because an agent was being judged, the Director of the

FBI asked the Attorney General for guidance. The Attorney General, no newcomer to controversy after was leery, but agreed.

They met in a third-floor conference room. The Attorney General arrived with her assistant and a gray-haired man in a three-piece, pin-striped shirt. "Louis, this is Malcom Ritter from our Civil Rights Division," the Attorney General said. "I've asked him to sit in this morning. Not knowing what your decision might be, we wanted to be prepared to address any questions."

The Director shook hands with the man, and they sat down at the conference table. The Director snapped open his briefcase. "You've read the report?" he questioned.

"Several times," the Assistant Attorney General answered. "The legal question of this being justifiable has been addressed and satisfied," the Director said thumbing the pages of the report. The Attorney General and her assistant nodded agreement.

"The more haunting dimension of your report, Mr. Director," Malcom Ritter suggested, "is not what's in it. It is what isn't in there. And what cries out in conspicuous absence is a statement from the agent involved."

"You may have noted in our psychological summary," the Director assured, "we concluded the agent is suffering from post-traumatic stress which has manifested itself in a refusal to discuss the incident. You do know it was his wife?"

"Yes," Ritter nodded, "and he has my profound sympathy, but nonetheless, don't you hold your agents to a higher standard?... My concern here is what is in this man's mind? Where has he gone? What will he have to say?"

"We deal in facts, Mr. Ritter," the Director reminded, "not supposition. This isn't a legal brief." He laid a hand atop the report. "It's the result of our investigation."

"An investigation of the conduct of an agent of the United States," Ritter countered, "and, as such, it must stand the test...."

"Gentlemen," the Attorney General said raising a hand to halt the exchange. "I think we're neglecting an important point here. When I was a student in law school, President Johnson came to address our graduating class. I don't remember much of what he said, but he did say one thing I thought profoundly wise—if you don't have to decide, don't. It pains me to quote the source, but might we be guilty of a rush to judgment? A rush fueled by the political realities of the environment we labor in. We all believe in justice and the rule of law. Isn't it those principles that have brought us here today? Isn't justice for all what we're seeking? What if agent Fox had given an interview to *Sixty Minutes*, *Dateline* or *First Edition*? It's my understanding agents had been posted near his home to keep away all the inquiring minds," she said sarcastically. "Doesn't he have a right to privacy? A right to grieve. Why are we in such a hurry? Is Pilate eager to wash his hands?

"The world now knows John Fox is the agent summoned to the White House on the night the three Native Americans climbed over the fence. How much can we ask this man to give? As the President aptly pointed out, there is the letter of the law and the spirit of the law. Fairness and justice are united. In this case I think we must be fair before we are just. It's not important we decide today. In fact, it may be more important that we don't."

Nodding at the Attorney General, the Director began gathering his report to stuff it into his briefcase. "Some days I'm glad to be part of the United States Government. This is proving to be one of them. Thank you," he said.

A flash fax went out from the Director's Office at the Hoover Building less than forty minutes later. It was addressed to the Special-Agent-in-Charge, Federal Bureau of Investigation, Palm Springs, California.

Please advise FBI Agent J. Fox the preliminary review of the unauthorized release of confidential information: Incident 2021-618-413 has resulted in a no fault conclusion by the review board and the USAG. Further review regarding civil consequences continues. Administrative and bereavement leave may continue.

"Sonofabitch," Stokowski smiled when he picked up the fax. "Hey, Tom, look at this!"

Tom Roberts, fax in hand, sat behind his desk and dialed Fox's telephone number. It rang three times before a voice answered. It sent a chill up Roberts' spine. "For your convenience," Pam Fox's sultry voice announced, "our calls are being answered automatically. If you'll leave a message at the tone, we'll return your call as soon as possible." Roberts hung up.

"What's wrong?" Stokowski questioned.

Roberts didn't answer.

Driving east on Interstate Ten with Palm Springs fading behind him and the expanse of the sprawling desert growing in front of him, John Fox remembered a quip he had heard Tommy Smothers make, "No matter where I go, there I am!" The sarcasm was proving itself true.

Fox could refuse to discuss Pam's death, he could refuse to pay bills, he could leave. He could do a lot of things, but he couldn't escape the gnawing, painful emptiness he felt deep inside. He wasn't sure where he was going, but he knew he had to go. The pain was with him. He suspected it always would be. Clinging to it was somehow an inexplicable link to her but living around those who knew him and knew his suffering was an invasion he couldn't tolerate. His grief, not so unlike the love he had for this woman, was something he refused to share. As his speed increased to seventy-five miles an hour, he was no longer just going. He was running.

Cresting the forty-three-hundred-foot Chirico Summit east of Indio, California, Fox left the last remnant of the urban sprawl behind him. Ahead lay the vast twenty-five-thousand square mile Mojave Desert. The divided six-lane ribbon of concrete and asphalt known as Interstate Ten undulated in gentle twists and turns that rose and fell into a long fine line finally disappearing at the horizon. The highway and the occasional baked, crumbling ruins of one-time gas stations and small shacks were the only blemishes on the rock-strewn face of the desert. It was vast and empty, and Fox felt part of it. He tramped harder on the accelerator.

Death, Fox was learning, also had an impact on the living. Pain for the dying, it was argued, was brief. Relief came with the end of conscious life. It was not so for the survivors. The pain of abrupt, final, irrevocable separation was searing, and agonizing and it was driving him toward thoughts of relief. Fantasy filled thoughts reuniting him with Pam in a paradise and a longing for a near forgotten mother filled his mind.

Fox realized he was closing fast on an eighteen wheeled truck laboring up a grade. Very fast! He wheeled the BMW to the left and narrowly missed the back of the trailer. The big truck flashed by in a blur. Fox took his foot off the accelerator and glanced at the speedometer. It was pegged at ninety-five-miles-an-hour. He knew he was going much faster. He tapped the brakes to slow down. His arms trembled on the steering wheel. He found himself frightened of his own thoughts.

A roadside sign read 'Desert Center 1 mile'. Fox decided to get off the hypnotic interstate. He slowed and turned toward the exit. At the bottom of the ramp he swung onto a smaller two-laned road. Desert Center, he found, was a dusty gas station with exorbitant prices and a large sign announcing '24-hour tow service'. A fleet of bleached, rusting vehicles attested to the fact the service was needed. Two motorcycles sat at a nearby yogurt stand. A duo of tattooed bikers in leather glanced at him. Another sign read 'Parker 86 miles'. Parker, Arizona.

Fox knew the place. At least some distant recess of his childhood memory did. Similar treks across the vastness between Parker and Phoenix in a van loaded with clothes and food for families on the reservation driven by an almond-eyed woman with a gentle voice. Clair Scott-Fox. A woman, a mother who seemed more a rerun than a reality. A woman left weeping with a bloody mouth the night he and his father departed for Atlanta. James Fox had backhanded her when she challenged him by standing in his path.

Fox remembered watching the road at night in Atlanta. Running to the mailbox every day after school. She never came. She never wrote. It seemed his father was right; she loved the fucking Indians on the reservation more than she loved him.

It was ironic, Fox thought following the narrow arrow- straight ribbon of asphalt across the desert in the growing heat, the two most important women in his life had abandoned him. Perhaps a greater irony was the realization that he would never get over the pain of losing either. He loved them both. He needed them both, but Pamela J. Fox and Clair Scott-Fox were both gone.

After two hours, the rolling vistas began to yield to jagged, cocoa colored mountains. The California desert was surrendering to the onrush of barren western

Arizona. The place of his birth, Fox mused. The thought provoked a smile. Was he trying to return to the womb? Was he following some deep-seated instinct to find his roots? Was his path coincidence or fate? He didn't believe in either. He was no longer sure what he believed in. He was looking forward to getting somewhere. His legs were numb, and his bladder needed relief. He had been driving for four hours.

Whatever drove him to flee Palm Springs was proving itself right, Fox decided with deliberate thought. The horror of finding Pam, the accusation of being a leaker, they were now behind him in both the literal and proverbial sense. Maybe that was it, he reasoned, the board had to be wiped clean before a new game plan was put up. Lose one game, get knocked down, get up and start over. He knew he was putting a psychological Band-Aid on his life, but he didn't care. The bleeding in his soul was slowing. A sign ahead read 'Parker 17 miles'.

Fox tried to find the images deep in the recesses of his memory. He counted the years leading to them. He would have been five or six. At least twenty-six years. Nearly three decades. He could remember a house, no, a mobile home, and dogs, lots of dogs, and an old truck sitting on blocks and the women. Lots of women. Doe-eyed, sad-faced and round. They would sit in the kitchen and talk as he brought lizards, rocks and flowers for his mother to smile at. There was little else. His mother was gone. The memories nearly were too. Innocence was lost. The flowers wilted. The rocks returned to the earth.

He could smell it before he saw it and that surprised him. He wasn't even sure what the odor was, but when the BMW crested the last rock-strewn foothill and the blue Colorado River came into view, Fox smiled with acknowledgment. The flat river valley spread like a lush green carpet reaching defiantly out into the sandy sprawling desert. Acres of aromatic alfalfa filled the warm dry air with a musty scent. A water tower, still miles away, along with a collection of Monopoly sized buildings dotted the horizon on the Arizona side of the river. Parker, Fox concluded.

He was eager to see it. It was as if the aroma of life wafting from the river had awakened something in him. He drove on, willing a motorhome towing a ski boat in front of him to go faster. It did not. He was tailgating, anticipating a break in the roadway's double line, hoping for an opportunity to pass while cresting what seemed to be an endless succession of gut tightening dips when the weathered, time weary, sign came into view. The once bold, now bleached, block lettering announced, "Welcome to the Mojave Indian Reservation—Land of many uses". In an instant the sign was behind him, but the jolt of realization it sent through Fox clung to him like a wet blanket on warm skin.

His eyes went to the rear-view mirror. The rectangular wooden frame stood on two four-by-eights. It was sagging to the right with age. The sign reminded Fox of the old leather faced Russell Stoner. It was old, fading, but it still had a message. And the message was welcome. Fox shrugged off a chill he felt building on his back and neck. He adjusted the temperature on the air conditioner, refusing to accept the feeling as emotional. It was an interesting thought, he allowed. Here he was welcome. No question of who you were or what you wanted. You were simply welcome. You didn't need an ID, a badge or a gun, you were simply welcome. Christ, Fox mused, wasn't that how the Indians lost their land in the first place?

The old man's words stabbed at his memory. "I know you, John Fox. I held you as a child." It made Fox's pulse race. He was a Mojave, a fucking Indian. His mother was a member of the tribe. He had hidden in his role as an athlete, an FBI agent, and a husband, but all that had been stripped away. He had hidden in White Man's land behind the shadow of his father, but now he was what he was. His mother's son. He wasn't in Parker, Arizona. He wasn't in the Mojave Desert. He wasn't at the Colorado River. He was home. He was the prodigal.

A psychologist could have quickly explained Fox's identity crisis as an attempt to flee the painful emotional quicksand he floundered in. He wanted to be anybody other than who he was. He wanted a clean break, a fresh start. What he didn't realize was becoming someone else could be as painful as being who he was. As the motorhome towing the boat closed on the river, Fox followed close behind studying the distant shore. The grass looked greener on the other side. The thought made him smile.

The serpentine, narrow road took it's time twisting to a long-arched bridge that reached across the placid, blue Colorado river to the western shore of Arizona. In the middle of the bridge beneath a bold sign that warned 'no loitering or jumping from bridge' hung a small, nondescript sign, "Welcome to Arizona". He was crossing more than a political boundary, Fox sensed, as the sign slid by.

For those seeking a contrast, a refuge from life in the crowded, noisy, dangerous, costly, life in Southern California, and there were many, Parker, Arizona was it. The town, growing out of an agricultural railhead in the twenties, with the advent of air conditioning and ski boats, had evolved into a blue-collar tourist town.

Twenty-seven hundred people called the small-town home. On weekends and holidays the population exploded into the tens of thousands. String bikinis, suntan oil and Bud Light filled a flotilla of sleek ski boats that turned the lazy, meandering river into a noisy, crowded freeway. It was chaos or calm. Crowded or forsaken. Rich or poor. Hot or dry. Like the desert surrounding it, Parker was a town of extremes. For now, on a sunny midday, the town was at rest.

It stood quiet as John Fox drove over its streets drinking in the sights wondering what life was hidden behind the stucco and flat boards. A line of motels stood shoulder to shoulder, driveways wide like open arms inviting weary travelers to partake of special rates, free HBO and in-room coffee. Visa or Mastercard made you welcome. The Mecca Motel yielded to a doughnut shop, a sporting goods store and then another gas station. This one surrounded with tall chain link fence and a red sign bidding prime corner available.

A traffic light sent out its red signal and Fox slowed to a stop alongside the motorhome he had followed for miles. A dishwater blond in a flowered halter top gave him an irritated look. He looked away, intimidated by her gaze. What was she annoyed with? She was alive. Her husband was at her side. They were headed somewhere for recreation. They had time. Why was she wasting it on anger with a stranger? He was relieved when the light flashed to green.

He bought gas, a bottle of iced tea, a beef stick and relieved himself. Fox felt conspicuous standing in line in the small convenience store in his pleated hundred-dollar slacks and low-cut Australian shoes. A twenty-year-old in front of him wore baggy shorts and sandals. A local behind him wore a tank top and faded jeans. Fox, feeling much like a foreigner, wondered where the Indians were.

The anchor of the town's business district was a Dairy Queen. A collection of pick-up trucks, dusty Jeeps and cars crowded the parking lot. The lunch crowd, Fox decided. The streets of Parker were wide and quiet. Tire shops, garages advertising boat and RV repairs were mixed with liquor stores, banks, an abandoned and boarded theater and a blend of small bars and nondescript restaurants. What traffic there was consisted of pick-up trucks, four-wheel drives or motorhomes. He found a major supermarket on the edge of town. It shared an L-shaped complex with a video store, an apparel shop, a hair salon and a frozen yogurt store.

As if trying to imprint himself on the town, Fox drove the dusty, narrow side streets. Many were unpaved. All were rutted and pock-marked with holes. The houses were a collection of small, barren wooden and stucco buildings with ramshackle add-ons or aging, weathered mobile homes, surrounded with weeds and abandoned cars. Cars on blocks, cars with no color, cars without windows or doors. Cars without people.

And then Fox realized what was missing. He had seen people at the market, the Dairy Queen, the banks, but they were all white. They were young, old, working middle-aged mothers with children, tanned hard bodies with ski boats and motorhomes, but they weren't Indians. Fox knew what Indians looked like. Six years with an Indian mother and then four years at Arizona State in Flagstaff had taught him that. If for no other reason than the fact he was one, he knew Indians.

It was as if fate were playing some cruel hoax. He had driven onto a reservation, a reservation his mother had once called home and into a town surrounded by the reservation to find the Indians were gone. The hollow emptiness that had filled the pit of his stomach for a week was returning.

The answer was eight miles away in what the Mojave's called the "Valley." The valley was a wide swath of irrigated river bottom that stretched along the

Arizona bank of the meandering Colorado River south of Parker. Laced with miles of deep irrigation channels and rusty locks feeding alfalfa and cotton fields as well as stands of towering cottonwood trees, the valley was divided by unposted, unnamed, and often unmapped, dirt roads. It was the heart of the Mojave Reservation. The tribe didn't need, nor want, signs or fences.

The place was known as "Big Fork." Named after a fork in an old cottonwood tree with a mushrooming canopy of green that stood at the entrance of a passing dirt road. This day the road was choked with a crush of cars and trucks. Parked on both sides of the dusty, two-laned road and in the edges of the alfalfa fields, the collection of vehicles lined the shoulders for a mile in both directions. Pick-up trucks, campers, cars of every description, especially older ones, two tractors and three motorcycles sat parked. Chief Russell Stoner's modest double-wide mobile home with its pig pen, a corral for three horses and a chicken coop, stood at the end of the rutted driveway near Big Fork. Standing silently and patiently in the stifling afternoon heat on both sides of the drive, was the tribe, three thousand, four hundred and twenty-six Mojave men, women and children.

They had started arriving just after daybreak. Slowly at first, but by midmorning the road to the fork was jammed with cars. They parked off the main road and gathered along the driveway in silence. By noon their number was in the thousands.

In Parker, classrooms were empty. Attendants were missing from gas stations. Tables weren't being bussed, fields weren't being plowed and not an Indian was to be found. Word of the gathering had spread the night before. The tribe, like any social order or group, was splintered into factions and families and political power bases.

There were the Stoners, the Tanners, the Scotts and a dozen other influential families, but today they were one. They were Mojave and they gathered because the Chief was coming home. The old, with rounded backs and slumped shoulders, the middle-aged with pot bellies and double chins, the young warriors with their shaved heads, nose studs and earrings, and the fidgety young pulling on their mothers' legs and kicking at stones and swinging at flies.

The heat and insects were increasing and relentless, but the riveted Levies and Pendleton shirts with the sweat stained Stetsons and dusty boots stood in a powerful, united silence waiting with cramping muscles and aching bladders. They flanked the driveway on both sides, ten, twenty deep, filling the yard and pushing into the alfalfa fields. The pigs and horses stared in awe, joining in the quiet, if not by reason, by the electric like aura that stilled even the warm air.

A distant plume of dust told them the car was coming. As if linked, the gathering turned collectively to stare into the shimmering distance. The call of a crow in a nearby field reverberated across the quiet. The twisting plume was moving along the horizon, turning, closing on Big Fork. The gathering waited in silence.

The old man's senses were dull with Demerol, but the bumps from the rutted road were still sending bolts of searing pain surging through his abdomen. Eleven metal clamps held the purple incision across his lower stomach together. Seventy-two-year-old Russell Stoner was four-teen pounds lighter and his large intestine was eight inches shorter. He was frail and weary, but the smell of the river stirred his senses. He had promised himself he would not die before returning to Big Fork. He was hungry for the comfort of home the companionship of his dog and the taste of his wife's fry bread.

The doctors at Georgetown warned him of his diet. He was full of antibiotics to combat the fecal matter polluting his system from the bullet torn intestine. Post-op infection was still a real threat. Watching the blue water surging through a canal bordering the road, the old man wished he were younger. The water looked inviting.

At the old man's side was twenty-eight-year-old David Rollins. His face was unshaven and the raven black hair, usually tied in a ponytail, hung uncombed. His left leg was strapped in a stiff metal brace. His knee was fused, and his leg was now half an inch shorter than the right one. Rollins looked older. The once glib, talkative, young, smart-ass warrior was now sullen and quiet.

Behind the wheel of the eight-year-old ten-passenger van borrowed from the Mojave Baptist Preschool was nineteen-year-old Dena Manygoats, one of six surviving daughters of the slain Paul Manygoats. She was secretly five months pregnant with David Rollins' child.

"Grandfather," David Rollins said as the van approached Big Fork and the endless stretch of cars lining the road came into view. It was the first any of the three had spoken since Dena had met their incoming flight at Phoenix International, a hundred miles and another world to the south.

The old man nodded. He had already seen them.

In the days following the shooting in Washington, Nightline, Primetime and a dozen other news and talk shows, along with reporters from Newsweek, Time and the Post sought interviews. A producer from Fox offered cash for the film rights. The old man refused it all. He now had what they had gone after. A letter folded carefully in his jacket pocket, from the Secretary of the Interior acknowledging the Mojave's' right to build a casino.

Paul Manygoats had bought the letter with his life. There was nothing else to say, but there was much to do. The old Chief had wondered what his people were feeling. They had taken a collection and sent airfare. Paul Manygoats was the first to come home. He now lay at rest in the tribal cemetery.

As the van reached the gathering, the old man straightened in his seat. He ignored the pain in his gut. A lump rose in his throat as his tear-filled eyes searched the passing faces. He recognized most, especially the elders. The lined, time-worn red faces of Bear-Don't-Walk, Two-feathers, Straw-Branch and others stood shoulder to shoulder with the younger men and mothers. A little girl smiled and waved a red handkerchief at him. They all wore their best. Suits, ties, vests and flowered dresses with beads. The faces were streaked with a mix of sweat and awe.

The van turned up the driveway and a big yellow dog came off the front porch of the mobile home. It ran to the van wagging its tail and barking. The van slowed and stopped. The three thousand, four hundred and twenty-six Mojave's watched in silence. Many could not see, but they were there. David Rollins climbed from the van awkwardly with his leg brace. Dena Manygoats came around to join him to help the old man. Russell Stoner slid off the seat reaching for Rollins' hand. A foot found the ground and tested it like a man stepping on ice. The gathering stared as the old man eased his weight onto shaky, thin legs.

Gaining his balance, the old man waved away Rollins' hand. He would stand on his own. The dog was whining and licking a hand. He patted its head. A graying, heavy woman in an ankle-length dress came out of the mobile. It was Sarah Stoner. She walked with a cane. Diabetes was destroying her joints. She offered a smile to the old man when his eyes found hers. Returning his attention to the wall of faces that lined the drive and the fields, the old man studied them for a long moment before he spoke. In the afternoon stillness most heard him. "It is good to be home," he said and turned to the house. David Rollins took his elbow. The old man did not resist.

The elders among the gathered tribe nodded and all began to file away. They had seen their chief and he was home. Several war cries cut through e afternoon heat and dust.

7 COUSINS

"A man must find his own place at the lodge fire."
Dark Horse—Ho-Chunk

Upriver from Parker, Fox rented a small bungalow at the Castle Rock Resort. The time-weary room smelled of mildew and insect spray, but it was clean. He felt displaced and awkward. It was too painful to look back and he had no idea what lay ahead. For a man reared in the discipline of a plan, he was a man without one. He couldn't force himself to formulate one. It was as if he had been hit and was awaiting the return of his senses before deciding what to do. Fox liked that thought. He held onto it. He didn't have to decide anything at the moment, so he didn't.

After unpacking, he changed into jeans and an open collared shirt before walking to the bank of the river. It was sunset and the western sky was ablaze with color. The clouds near the horizon were faint and flattened like distant gauze. They seemed to glow with a yellow-rose hue that reached up into the blue of the sky. The river was wide and deep at Castlerock and the placid water was like a shimmering mirror.

Fox sat on a bench near a cottonwood tree and watched swallows skim insects from the surface of the water. The river had a powerful, low voice. The passing water pulling at the rocky bank gurgled and splashed and rippled with sound. He sat and listened, watching the colors fade, losing himself in it. He was another day further from the pain.

The beef stick and iced tea Fox had eaten earlier were proving inadequate. He was hungry. More than a hunger for nourishment was an unrecognized hunger for human contact. A social individual, the self-imposed isolation Fox had sentenced himself to was wearing thin. Everything he did was social. His avocation had been one of self-sacrifice and service. He missed it without conscious recognition. He needed the company of others. He gathered his car keys from the room.

Business Route 95 twisted along the Arizona shore of the river like a discarded rope. Fox followed it looking for signs, neon and life. The darkness of the night on the river, after life in the artificial light of Palm Springs, was remarkable. It was if a black veil had been pulled across the earth. The only dimension the darkness yielded was the stark light from his headlamps. The desert night gave little back. Color was gone and stark, sharp shadows came and went. Another reality of the river Fox found, was choice. Palm Springs thrived on food and presented a thousand choices, day or night. The river seemed more Bud Light and pork rinds. He drove past several bars. They were small and uninviting.

The lights of Parker were only a few miles ahead when neon cutting the darkness announced, "Blue Water Lagoon—Fine dining and drinks". Fox doubted the integrity of the sign, but uncertain anything remained ahead other than the Dairy Queen, he wheeled the BMW into the parking lot.

The building looked more like a boathouse than a restaurant, Fox decided. It was long and low, awkwardly long, too big for the six or eight mud splattered pick-ups and cars lining the parking lot. They all had Arizona plates, he noticed climbing out. A high intensity sodium light atop a towering pole washed away the darkness with an uncomfortable orange tinted glare. A swarm of insects spun in the night in its face. Fox walked to a set of double glass doors and pulled. They rattled under his grasp. Locked. A placard read, "Use Other Entrance".

He looked. There was a smaller windowless door to the left. He trekked to it in the coarse gravel. Entering a strange bar peopled with locals who all knew on another was pushing Fox's anxiety level up. Thing to do was go in and take a seat at the bar, he reasoned. That way if he was uncomfortable, he could down a quick beer and get out. Jesus, when was the last time he had a beer alone in a bar? He couldn't remember. The night air off the river was cool and damp. He hoped it was warmer inside.

The melodic sound of country western music from a juke box reached out to greet Fox when he opened the door. It was accompanied by warm air mixed with the smell of food and liquor. He stepped inside. The persona of being an FBI agent had always reinforced Fox's self-confidence, but what life hadn't taken away he had willingly shed and now without it, he felt uncertain and vulnerable. Light inside the bar was dim. Several cowboy hats and two dark-haired women sat amidst a cluster of small oval tables. They offered a brief glance and then went back to the huddle at their table. Indians, Fox concluded. Finally, he'd found some.

There were two more men playing darts at the end of the room. They were big men. Heavy with broad shoulders and dark ponytails. More Indians. At the bar two older men with lined faces and sagging noses sat on either side of a plump, round-faced, younger woman with a blue tattoo on her neck and large breasts straining at the material of a tee-shirt. For a man who couldn't find a single Indian earlier in the day, he was now feeling very white.

Fox was relieved to see the busty, blonde bartender was white. She was in her forties, he guessed. Once attractive, now with a cigarette in one hand and a bar rag in the other, she was on the downside of cute. Although the skin-tight jeans she wore hinted at a body still supple. He eased onto a stool at the end of the bar. The bartender and the tattoo both looked at him. It was the bartender's job. It wasn't the tattoo's, so she dismissed him as another fuckin' tourist.

"Hi," the blonde's white teeth offered with a practiced smile. "What can I get you?" Her eyes were a deep blue.

"Can I get a sandwich?" Fox asked, folding his hands in front of him on the bar. The woman glanced at them. He did the same and realized he was still wearing his wedding band. Was he still married? 'Til death doth part! When should he take it off? Should he take it off? The thoughts came in a rush.

"We got a special steak and cheese with fries," the blonde said, bringing his eyes up to hers.

"Okay."

"How would you like that?"

"Well."

"Something to drink?" She was holding his look as if

it were a challenge and all he was doing was trying to follow her questions in spite of the knot in his stomach.

"Coors," he said, seeing a sign behind the bar.

The blonde turned and called to an unseen cook in the kitchen. "Hey, Tonto, kill a cow and brand it well with Velveeta."

Fox was spinning his wedding ring with his thumb when the blonde slid the beer in front of him. "You want a shoulder to go with that?"

"A shoulder?" Fox was puzzled.

"To cry on," the blonde answered. "You look like you're in a pit up to your neck. A little down."

Fox was surprised and uncomfortable. The woman was reading him. Christ, was it that obvious? He shifted on his bar stool, sipped the beer and forced a smile. "No. I'm fine, thanks."

"Uh-huh," the blonde quipped, wiping a wet ring from the bar with her towel. "And I'm Dolly Parton."

"Hello, Dolly," Fox said raising his glass. He didn't want a serious conversation.

"Sounds like a song," she smiled. "What brings you to the river?"

"Business," he lied. Then added, "How 'bout you?"

"Came out here eight years ago with a husband who couldn't take the rat race in L.A. He left two years later with a brunette who always wanted to live in L.A."

"Serves him right," Fox suggested. "Smog and freeways."

The blonde nodded, looking to a wide window across the dining room. Fox looked too. The river was out there, he knew, hidden behind the darkness and the mirror-like reflection of the bar in the glass. "You know what river that is?" she questioned.

"The Colorado," he answered.

"No," the blonde said staring, looking as if she were watching something only, she could see. "It's the river of no return."

A wave from the tattooed neck took the blonde away. The three in the center of the bar wanted another pitcher of beer. Fox was taking another drink of his when the two women from the foursome at the tables approached. He thought the girl was going to speak to him. She had dark, almond eyes and near brown skin. She smiled, averted her eyes and passed. The other followed close behind. He turned, glanced over his shoulder as they disappeared into a restroom. Indians were friendly, attractive people, he decided with another drink. Then the first cowboy hat reached him. The other one wasn't far behind.

"What the fuck you lookin' at?" the narrow-eyed, pock-marked face demanded with angry beer breath. He slammed a hand down hard slapping the flat bar top.

Fox tensed. He set his beer glass down.

The man was big and drunk. His glassy eyes and swaying stance told Fox that, but the long-sleeved shirt he wore stretched tight over big, meaty arms and a barrel chest. He looked powerful. The second man was smaller. He was staying well back. Fox concentrated on the man in front of him. He raised his hands, spread his fingers in a defenseless gesture. "I don't want any trouble." He eased off the bar stool, keeping his hands in front of him.

"Fuckin' puny white man hittin' on my woman," the narrow eyes said, clenching his fists.

The blonde bartender was quickly to the end of the bar. "Virgil, you sonofabitch, don't start it," she spat at the man.

"Fuck you, Bonnie. This asshole was staring at Tammy's ass and he's gonna apologize."

"Tonto," the blonde shouted turning away. "Call the Tribal Police!"

"I apologize for you thinking I insulted you or your lady," Fox said, lowering his right hand to offer it to the man.

The pock-marked face slapped Fox's hand away. He was intent on humiliating what he saw as a weaker opponent. "Fuckin' California surfer. Pecker-head, ball-less wonder."

"Kick his ass, Virg," the cowboy hat behind the big man urged. The two women came out of the restroom. They looked at the confrontation and scurried away.

The shock was gone now. Fox had had time to prepare himself. He had a personal credo, never start a fight, but never lose one. He burned a look at the smaller Indian. "I'm going to remember you said that," he warned with a resolve that unnerved the man.

The Indian took a step backwards.

"You ain't gonna remember shit," Virgil said, licking his palms, "you surfer fuck."

"I'm tribal," Fox announced, surprising himself. "My mother's name was Scott."

"Yeah," Virgil sneered, "well I'm tribal too and my mother's name is 'fuck you!'"

Fox saw the man's right shoulder falling. He was going to throw a punch. The clenched fist was drawn back as if he were going to throw a softball. If the sonofabitch wanted a fight, Fox decided, he was about to get one. Fox thrust out his left hand. Spreading the web between thumb and forefinger, he jammed the hand into the man's throat just above the Adams apple. Stepping forward, he followed the throat thrust with a stiff right punch into the sternum. He heard the man grunt under the force of the blow. It was a tried combination Fox had used successfully in several Karate tournaments. Most men buckled under the quick one-two designed to nauseate and disorient. This man did not.

Virgil Tanner didn't know Karate, but he did know a life of hardship, hard work and pain. He was big and he was strong and although stunned and in pain, he was far from finished. Staggering backwards, Virgil bumped into a chair, lost his balance and took a small oval table with him as he crashed to the floor.

Seeing Virgil fall, Fox closed quickly on the second man. The man tried to bolt, but Fox grabbed him by the shirt front. He felt the material tear. Swinging hard, he backhanded the cowering figure. Mucus and blood splattered. The man cried in pain. Grabbing his face with his hands, he sank to his knees. Fox kicked at the Stetson that had fallen to the floor.

"Virgil!" the blonde bartender screamed, and Fox sensed danger. He was turning when Tanner brought the chair down on him like a pile driver. He remembered being on his knees, seeing blood on his hand, hearing screams and then he fell, face down and hard.

Fox's senses returned slowly and painfully. He was disturbed by the pain in his shoulder and neck. He tried to reach for the discomfort and found his hands were shackled behind his back. Now he was fully awake. His face was on a leather seat. The sounds of a muted police radio reached him. Jesus! He was in a police car. Gathering strength, he pushed up. The handcuffs bit into his wrists. He shifted his buttocks forward to relive the pressure. His left ear was burning and ringing. His neck was canted to the left in pain. The police car was idling, the lights were on. He was in a caged rear seat that smelled of leather and sweat.

He took in a deep breath trying to clear his head, trying to remember. Suddenly the door was opened and a rush of cool, damp air engulfed him. "Come on out," a uniformed sleeve said and pulled on him. Fox grimaced and followed the grasp, not wanting to add to the pain.

The blonde bartender and a fat Indian, in a grease stained apron, stood waiting as the towering uniformed Tribal Police Officer unlocked Fox's handcuffs. There was a second police car parked at a hard angle to the first. The car's emergency lighting was sending sharp red pulses of light into the night. The light made it difficult to see, but Fox could distinguish a policewoman talking with someone in the back seat of the car.

"You wanna have your face looked at?" the Tribal Officer asked as Fox's hands came free. A hand went immediately to his left eyebrow. It was painful and swollen.

"No," Fox answered looking at his fingers to see if they were bloody. They were.

"Bonnie and Tonto tell me Virgil started this," the uniformed Indian continued. Fox looked at him. His name tag read, *Bear-Don't-Walk*. He was a man Fox's age with a square jaw, dark eyes and near brown skin. He wore his black hair pulled back in a short ponytail. "You wanna press charges?"

"No," Fox answered exploring the pain in his shoulder with a palm.

"They're gonna spend the night in the lock-up anyway. Public drunk. I'll turn them loose in the morning." Bear-Don't-Walk was studying Fox. "You gonna be able to drive? Where are you staying?"

"Castle Rock."

"I'll drive him up," Bonnie offered. "Tonto can pick me up. We owe him that."

Bear-Don't-Walk nodded agreement. "Okay by me," then he looked to Fox, "Tanner ain't all bad... 'Cept when he drinks. Problem is he drinks all the time... Maybe you should stick to Gringo bars."

"He says his mother is a Scott," Bonnie volunteered when Fox hesitated.

"Is that right?" Bear-Don't-Walk mused, giving Fox a curious look. "What's your name?"

"Fox... John Fox," he answered, irritated with the blonde and himself for revealing the secret. It was especially frustrating since it gained him nothing. He wasn't yet ready to acknowledge the gnawing deep inside to belong somewhere.

Bear-Don't-Walk granted Fox a smile. "You see Virgil Tanner over there? His mother's a Scott. Hell, you two might be cousins."

Fox wasn't interested in the sarcastic speculation. All he wanted was to lay down. His head was swimming and his ear was on fire. Bear-Don't-Walk was still studying him. It was a look of curiosity. Then he made the connection he sought. "John Fox," he said as if proud of himself for the realization. "You're the man Chief Stoner asked for?"

"Can I go now?" Fox wanted it over. It was all out of control again. Next this Goddamned Indian would be telling everyone who he was. His wife was dead. His career was over. The anonymity he had been basking in earlier was gone like the hope he could really run from it all.

"Sure," Bear-Don't-Walk said. "Sorry this happened."

Fox headed for his BMW, staggering in the gravel, hoping he could find it. The blonde followed him.

The woman didn't try to make conversation. Fox was glad of that. He was also glad she offered to drive. His eye was throbbing and nearly closed. He slumped in the seat with his head back and waited for it to end.

At Castle Rock, Fox fell into the bed after the blonde

unlocked the room. She reappeared shortly with ice wrapped in a towel. He eagerly held it to his eye. He heard her speaking with the cook who had followed them, then the door closed, and they were gone. He was alone. More alone than he had ever been in his life. He wept uncontrollably with deep agonizing sobs that convulsed his back and shoulders adding to his pain. Eventually exhaustion brought him sleep.

When he awoke, it was daylight and hot. The bed was wet where the ice had melted. Fox pushed up, moving carefully, wary of the pain. His left shoulder and neck were sore, but tolerable. He walked to the bathroom, relieved himself and looked in the mirror. The mirror was old and fading, but the reflection that stared back at Fox shocked him. He was unshaven and haggard. His left eye lid was puffy and swollen. The eyebrow was caked with blood. He pulled his shirt back from the base of his neck to find a purple, ugly bruise.

He was pleased to find the cold steak sandwich on the table beside the bed. It had been wrapped carefully. Beside it stood a Styrofoam cup of coffee. Jesus, he thought, I'm a long way from Palm Springs. He showered until there was no more hot water, letting the water pelt his eye and neck. It was a soothing balm and he imagined it washing away the pain. Thoughts of the bar fight came and went. They mixed with images of Pam and the old Indian laying in a hospital bed in Washington. It was all a blur. Fox knew he needed a focus. Something to do. Something physical.

What was it his psychology professor used to preach? Man needed a daily task, a plow to hold onto, a work to do... That was it. He was playing without a game plan. He wasn't acting, he was reacting. Act or be acted on. The principle was as old as thought itself. He twisted off the water and grabbed a towel. Before this day was over, he was going to find a plow.

Fox drove to the supermarket he had discovered the day before. The parking lot was lined with cars, pick-ups and the ever-present ski boats. He found what he was seeking. Newspaper racks. USA Today, Phoenix Sun and the Parker Pilot. He dropped in the required thirty-five cents and collected the thin newspaper for Parker. A headline announced an annual hot air balloon festival. There was a picture of a new refuse truck the town council had approved. The Phoenix library was donating used books to the local branch and the Lion's Club would be cleaning the park on Saturday. Volunteers were needed. There was no mention of crime, Fox noted. The newspapers on the Coast were filled with drive-by shootings, hostage robberies and the seemingly endless slaughter of men, women and children by serial killers, deranged employees and crackheads. Murder had become commonplace. It wasn't *if* there was a murder, the question was—how many? It was hazardous to send a child to school, drive on the freeway, or have your wife go to the bank. Life in the new century had become more than basic survival, it had become random luck. The staggering, numbing, statistics, the endless succession of bodies representing the collective mayhem of a blood-thirsty society, had been brought into a catalytic focus by the senseless suicide of Pamela Fox. Fox wished he had discovered the Parker Pilot before his wife made her fateful decision.

He was too experienced to expect Parker was Mayberry or Mister Roger's Neighborhood, the lump on his brow was testimony to the contrary, but a fight in a bar was far from a bullet in the aorta. He wasn't sure running from violence would ever solve it, but his choice to fight had cost him more than he could fathom. The battle was over. Fox had lost. All he wanted now was a place to hide. A refuge. He shuddered as he thought of a horse running into a burning stable seeking refuge.

He carried the newspaper to the BMW and turned to the classified pages. The job opportunity section was a sobering revelation. Atlas RV and Boat Repair was seeking an "experienced mechanic," Boyd Mobile Home Sales needed a "set-up helper," Davis Travel wanted a "receptionist with computer experience," Hoffman Auto Parts needed a "delivery man with reliable transportation" and Mojave Farms was looking for a "seasonal heavy equipment operator."

Fox found Boyd Mobile Home Sales on one of Parker's two main streets. Plastic banners dancing and snapping in the morning breeze promised, "Low Down" and "Easy Financing." The line of mobile homes looked awkward and displaced in the gravel lot, like Monopoly houses, Fox decided. Toy homes for those with toy lives.

Pushing the selector to park, he wondered how many people looking for work in Parker as a "set-up man" owned a house in Palm Springs. The thought brought him no comfort. It made him feel deceitful and foreign. He tramped through the gravel toward a mobile with an "Office" sign.

A big man in a sweat-stained ball cap met him outside the office door. He had a Big Gulp cup in one hand and a half-eaten doughnut in the other. "Morning. What can we sell you today?" The man had red cheeks and a full-face white beard.

Santa Claus selling mobile homes, Fox thought. "Saw an ad in the paper. You're looking for a 'set-up man'?"

The Ball cap pushed the rest of the doughnut in his mouth and looked Fox up and down. He chewed and licked his fingers before he spoke. "Got a nasty lump on your eye there, son."

"Yeah, I tripped last night putting the boat in the water." It was less than convincing, and Fox immediately regretted the lie.

The Ballcap nodded thoughtfully and glanced at Fox's car. "Boat, huh? And a BMW with California plates, but you're looking for a job as a set-up man in Parker? You got any tools?"

"Tools?"

"Sorry, son," the man dumped his coffee and spat. "I'm gonna have to pass." He turned, opened the door to the office, stepped in and closed the door behind him.

Fox, smarting with embarrassment and rejection, tramped toward the BMW. He had qualified, trained and worked in one of the world's most elite law enforcement agencies in the world, but he couldn't get hired as a *set-up man* for Boyd Mobile Homes. Fat sonofabitch. Probably looking for some know-nothing red neck kid he could hire for a part time wage. Fox was a troubled man —a troubled man with no tools.

A young Hispanic woman with a gold tooth behind the window at the Dairy Queen told Fox how to find Hoffman Auto Parts. It was across the street from the Ford dealer. Didn't everyone know that? Somehow, he made a wrong turn and missed it. He searched, trying to contain the frustration and anger he was feeling for both Santa Claus and the illegal alien. Damn them. They had jobs, lives, husbands, wives. They weren't haunted by nightmare images of loved one hanging in a shower. He braked to a stop at an intersection to find a Ford dealer directly across the street. He looked to his right. Hoffman Auto Parts. A pick-up truck behind him sounded its horn.

The auto parts store smelled of grease and rubber hoses. It was crowded with disorganized stock and aging displays. A sign above a cash register warned, "The 'C' in

California doesn't mean credit". Fox waited in line behind an elderly man with a round back buying a head gasket for his sister's riding mower. Losing interest in the discussion of what glue was best for the gasket, Fox surveyed the store. It was interesting with all of its components and parts. He wondered what it was like to run an auto parts store. How did fate choose a man's path? Why did one man sell spark plugs and another man stake-out banks? Was there any rhyme or reason to it? Who decided if life was to be in Parker, Palm Springs or Palm Beach?

"May I help you?" The forty-plus, bespectacled, balding man behind the counter asked. Fox noticed his attention was on the lump above his eyebrow. "I saw an ad in the paper for a 'delivery man,'" Fox answered.

"Sorry. Filled it first thing this morning," the bifocals said. The door chime sounded behind Fox. Another customer had entered. "Morning, Bill," the man called, dismissing Fox. Fox moved for the door wondering if he had lost the opportunity to another man or the lump on his eyebrow.

He was backing from the parking lot of the auto parts store when a dusty, sun-bleached pick-up truck went by. A sign on its door read Mojave Farms. Fox remembered the ad for "seasonal heavy equipment operators." Hell, if an Indian could do it, he could. Hell, he was an Indian. Fox pulled the BMW in gear and followed the truck.

The pick-up truck followed the river road south out of Parker into the wide spread of the valley. Alfalfa and melon fields stretched to the horizon broken only by random stands of cottonwood trees. Fox followed at a distance as the truck wormed its way over canals, past grazing beef and a herd of dirty, fuzzy sheep. The pavement ended and Fox gave the truck more of a lead. Following the plume of dust was no challenge. The dirt road passed a steady stream of mobile homes. Most had dogs and junked cars. Some had satellite dishes, others corrals and pig pens. Fox noticed the valley had no ski boats or mini marts. It did have clothes lines, bird houses on tall posts and chickens dusting themselves in driveways. It was a quiet place. There was a peace to it. It was poor by the standards Fox carried with him, but he was beginning to question what wealth was. He wasn't sure what this place had, but whatever it was, it wasn't something money bought. Studying the passing fields without fences, and the wind twisted aging cottonwoods against the azure sky, he wondered if he were looking at images his mother once saw. It was a comforting thought.

Finally, the pick-up truck turned left onto a smaller road and drove toward a collection of distant huts and equipment. Fox followed.

The huts were corrugated aluminum oxidized by time and heat. They reminded Fox of old military buildings. The six huts were flanked by a taller box-like cement block garage with no doors, full of rusty equipment. Several wooden buildings with flaking paint and warped wood stood in the shadow of a silo. A rusty water tank and a billowing cottonwood tree cast a shadow over the parking area where the pick-up truck parked. Fox pulled in as the two men got out and walked toward the open garage. They were Indians. If they saw him, they didn't seem to care.

A station wagon and another pick-up sat parked in front of one of the wooden buildings. It had a screen door. The office, Fox decided. He climbed out.

A dog laying in the shade of the building raised its head as Fox approached. The animal looked at him for a moment then, losing interest, lowered its head again.

Fox couldn't see through the screen door, so he knocked and pulled it open. The office had a musty, grainy smell to it. A long counter separated the reception area from the working office. A heavy-set Indian woman with graying hair sat at a computer terminal typing amidst a sea of paper clutter. She glanced at Fox as he entered but continued her work.

Fox leaned his elbows on the counter. A placard on the wall behind the woman read, "Tribal preference in all hiring". "Something I can help you with?" the woman asked as she typed and watched the monitor screen.

"I'm here about the heavy equipment operator position."

"Morse," the woman barked toward an open rear office.

Fox straightened his stance as the man appeared in the door of the office. Morse was big with a gut that made his jean-clad legs look skinny and bowed. A plaid shirt seemed to amplify the color of his skin. His face was lined with age. He studied Fox for a moment and then crossed toward the counter. "You drive a bailer?"

"Drove a school bus while I was in college."

"You got a driver's license?" Morse propped an elbow on the counter not far from Fox.

Fox reached for his walled. "Yeah. California."

Morse stopped him with a wave. "Day starts at first light, ends at sunset. Pays seven-teen bucks an hour plus overtime. Alfalfa ain't nothing but horse straw if its cut too late and dry. You miss a morning start, you're finished."

"Okay," Fox answered eagerly. He was excited.

Morse glanced at his watch, "You already missed five hours of the cut today, but I can have someone carry you out there, meet the foreman, look at the job."

"All right," Fox said without hesitation.

Morse pushed from the counter, headed for his

office. He glanced at the woman. "Martha, get his paper-work started."

Fox was both pleased and surprised with the casual-ness of it. "Don't you wanna know who I am?"

"We know who you are," Morse answered without turning. He disappeared into his office.

Fox filled out the single page application. It was simple. The Mojave Farms, a business enterprise of the Mojave Indian Nation, wanted his name, date of birth, social security number and address. He hesitated at the question regarding marital status and then checked married. Tribal or non-tribal? He circled tribal. Former employer. He penciled in U.S. Government.

Martha made a telephone call and shortly the same pick-up he had followed to the farm pulled up outside the office. "Bird will drive you out to the fields," she said taking Fox's application.

Neither man in the truck moved to open a door when Fox approached, so he climbed in the back and settled himself, back against the cab, sitting on an empty burlap sack.

Wind stirring his hair and the taste of fine dust in his mouth rejuvenated Fox as the pick-up truck worked its way across the patchwork of fields going somewhere. The where didn't matter. He was going and he was going because he had something to do.

The truck swung left and bumped to a stop. Fox twisted into the glare of the late morning sun. He shaded his eyes with a hand. A towering hulk of machinery, big and green with a glass enclosed cab and a vertical exhaust, sat parked on the side of a field. A maze of guides, cutters and pulleys covered the side of the big machine. The air was rich with the aroma of gasoline and fresh cut alfalfa. Fox climbed off the pick-up.

The driver of the pick-up gestured to a big man rounding the front of the bailer. "That's the boss."

Fox was looking into the sun, but the stark outline of the big Stetson hat jolted him straight. It was Virgil Tanner. Virgil closed on Fox and stopped only inches from him. His brown eyes squinted down at Fox. He wiped sweat that ran down his neck and shook it away with the snap of his hand. "Well, well," he said with a sneer, "if it ain't li'l surfer fuck."

8 X'S & O'S

"Man, scratches at Mother Earth to beg like a hungry pup, and she bares her belly to feed all."
Tall Man—Black Foot

"Bars are for drinkin' and fightin'," Virgil told Fox walking him around the big bailing machine. "Fields are for plantin' and cuttin'." The skinny man had his sleeves rolled up and he was working on the engine of the bailer. Fox would learn later his name was Cletus Spearman, but everyone called him Sparrow. "Thing is," Virgil said pointing to the alfalfa field where the mower had cut a swath, "keep 'er in a straight line. Don't look down at the cutter. Look way out there at the end of the line. Get that first cut straight and the rest is just drivin'".

Virgil and the Sparrow showed Fox how to check the oil, load the wrapper with bailing wire, shift gears and run the cabin air without overheating the engine of the big machine. Other than Virgil's greeting of "L'il surfer fuck," the bar incident seemed forgotten. The two men, who Fox a little over twelve hours earlier, had judged as typical drunken Indian do-nothings wasting their lives in beer bars, were proving to be consummate, no nonsense farmers. They talked in depth and knowledgeably about the correct moisture content of alfalfa, gravity irrigation systems, the nitrogen content of soil, insect control and weather. Fox was humbled and gratified. Gratified at his acceptance and gratified he now had his hands on a plow.

After an hour of orientation and three men riding in the cab, Virgil and Sparrow dropped off at the end of the field. "Take 'er around," Virgil urged with a wave of a gloved hand. Fox proudly pulled the big machine in gear. He drove carefully, mindful to keep his eye on the distant line, not the cutter. At the end of the field, before pushing the cutters to neutral to make the turn, he glanced in the rear-view mirror. The cut line stretched straight as a green arrow behind him. Fox swung the big machine in a tight turn, lined it up carefully and started back the other way. He was surprised when he reached the spot where Virgil and Sparrow had dropped off. The two men were gone.

The sun was low on the western horizon when the pick-up finally returned. Fox, shirt off, sweat stained, caked with dust, saw the plume of dust when it was still a mile away. He was waiting at the end of the field when it reached him. Sparrow was behind the wheel, Virgil on the passenger's side. Fox felt like a sailor suddenly awash on the shore. After hours on the vibrating machine, the stillness of the earth was strange and the quite profound. "Get in," the Sparrow cocked a thumb toward the pick-up bed. Fox climbed aboard. He was surprised to find both of his palms blistered. He wanted a well done from the two men. All he got was a ride back to the farm office. "Be here at sun-up," Virgil warned and the truck pulled away.

"You have a nice evening too, my faithful Indian friends," Fox called in loud sarcasm at the departing truck. He turned to the waiting BMW to find Martha standing in the door of the office staring at him.

The roadside sign eleven miles south of Parker read, 'Poston'. It was little more than an intersection with a gas station and a farm machinery dealership, but to the tribe it was the hub. Parker was a white man's town, a business oasis that grew up and thrived as a tourist Mecca within the bounds of the reservation and although the Indians shopped and worked there, they didn't really feel it was Indian country. Thus, Poston, deeper in the valley, became the crossroads, the social hub, the tribal refuge without the trappings of the world. Fox stopped in Poston hoping he could find a pair of gloves. He knew another day of the vibrating wheel in the bailer would turn his hands to raw meat.

The parking lot was lined with aging cars and pickup trucks. A group of teen-aged Indians were crowding around a balloon-wheeled, all-terrain vehicle. Two older youths had the hood up on a Jeep and were bending over the engine. A family with three noisy children were loading groceries into a station wagon. Perhaps it was the job on the tribal farm, the hard day's work or just convenience, Fox didn't care which. All he knew was he no longer felt like a displaced foreigner. He pushed the selector into park and climbed out.

Fox found the Indian-owned Grassman's gas station was more of a general store. In addition to a heavy pair of canvas gloves, he bought a high-topped pair of work shoes and a big blue handkerchief. Sparrow wore one and after wiping stinging sweat from his eyes all afternoon, Fox understood why. The smell of cooked meat was rich in the small store and spotting a price list for burritos, Fox bought two beef and bean and a cup of sun-brewed iced tea. Not wanting to eat the burrito cold, he sat on the edge of the store's porch and ate. He was surprised when two Indians joined him. They sat down to drink liquor from a bottle concealed in a wrinkled paper sack. They were dusty, dirt stained men like he. "Miller moths are bad this year," one of the men said watching a swarm of insects around a puddle in the rutted dirt parking lot.

"All the rain," the other man offered. "Gonna make the fish fat."

Fox, finishing his burrito, nodded agreement. The man beside him offered the paper covered bottle. Fox took it and raised it to his mouth. The whiskey was warm and sharp. Swallowing it made Fox's eyes water. He passed the bottle back to the man.

Another pick-up truck arrived. It was mud splattered and dusty. Its windshield was caked with flattened bugs swept into the wedge pattern of the wipers. A middle-aged Indian in jeans and a plaid shirt climbed out. A woman got out on the passenger's side. She went into the store. The man joined Fox and the others on the porch. "Sounds like a wheel bearing going dry, Henry," the man with the bottle said offering it.

"Think it's a brake shoe dragging," Henry speculated taking a swallow. He glanced at Fox. The other man saw it.

"Clair Scott's boy," the man with the bottle explained.

Henry sat down on the porch with the others. He aimed another glance at fox. "I heard he was back."

Fox was both amused and amazed. They were talking as if he weren't there.

"Morse put him to work on the farm, I heard."

"Yeah, he cut alfalfa all day."

"Clair Scott... Didn't she marry that Federal man that came up from Phoenix to investigate the Strawman growing that six acres of marijuana?"

"Uh-huh."

"Strawman's gettin' out this year I hear."

The fantasy of silently slipping into life in Parker and the tribe was gone, but Fox was comfortable with what seemed to be passive acceptance. He wasn't sure if these men, like Morse at the farm office, were subtly letting him know he hadn't fooled anyone, or like crows sitting on a power line, just squawking because a new bird had landed. Whichever it was, it was a lesson Fox would not forget. What was the joke? Telephone, telegraph and tell-an-Indian. The tribe had no secrets.

The physical challenge Fox was to face in the long days to follow, coupled with the serenity and solitude of the fields, literally sweated the personal anguish out of him. The images of violent human nature he carried yielded to the balance of blue skies, waving green seas of alfalfa, cool deep canals that offered refuge from the mid-day heat and birds that followed the bailer feasting on fleeing insects. It was a world he had never known. A world he had rejected. A world he now clung to.

Twenty-seven-hundred miles to the east in the Hoover Building on the District of Columbia's Pennsylvania Avenue an Epson-six thousand computer in the FBI's Special Operations Division was making a silent electronic intrusion into John Fox's world. The computer searched through seventeen million, four hundred thousand, six hundred and eighteen credit card transactions before finding a hit in Parker, Arizona. John Fox had used his Visa Card for a transaction at Woody's Shell Station where he bought forty-two dollars and seventeen cents worth of unleaded fuel and two dollars and thirty-two cents worth of miscellaneous grocery items.

A second transaction on the same date showed a room charge at Castle Rock Resort for eighty-eight dollars and fifty cents. The room charge was still open. "Would you like me to run his telephone and banking records?" the clerk at the keyboard questioned with a look at the agent studying the screen over her shoulder.

"Not now but give me a hard copy of this."

The clerk's polished nail punched a key and the print icon at the top of the screen winked.

Twenty minutes later in Palm Springs a secretary stepped into the open doorway of Special Agent Tom Roberts' office. "Pardon me, Tom," the secretary said, "the Director is on line two."

Roberts paused from his work, straightened his posture as if the Director could see him and reached for the telephone. "Close the door, please." Gathering the receiver to his ear, he said, "This is Tom Roberts."

"Good morning, Tom," the Director said from his office in Washington. He had the computer print-out in hand. "Special Ops has located John Fox. He's in Parker, Arizona."

Roberts eyes went to a wall map of the western United States. "Parker, Arizona?"

"He used a credit card to buy gas, rent a room. No reason to suspect he's in distress," the Director added.

Roberts was studying the wall map. "Looks like most of the area is a reservation."

"Mojave," the Director agreed. "You may recall it was the Mojave's that made the intrusion at the White House."

"Yes, Sir. Would you like us to make contact?"

"I don't think so. What's his leave status?"

Roberts sorted through files on his desk, flipped one

open. "Still unpaid administrative... Until the U.S. Attorney rules on the critical policy issues."

"Uh-huh." the Director said, considering. "And his in-laws are still in the house?"

"Yes, Sir. They're cooperative. As of this morning they still haven't heard from him."

"Then let's just continue to monitor. Say nothing. Keep it need-to-know. Maybe eventually he'll reach out to us. He's a good agent. I'd hate to lose him."

"Yes, Sir," Roberts agreed.

"Stay in touch, Tom."

"Yes, Sir."

"Alfalfa don't care what day it is," Virgil Tanner told Fox when he asked if they had the weekend off. "We cut until it's done."

Fox was in the mid-morning of his eighth straight workday driving the big bailer down the middle of a half-cut field when exhaustion and heat took its toll. The vibrating machine was easy to steer, and Fox's eyes kept closing. As sleep engulfed him, his head would bob, and he was awake. It was only milliseconds of sleep, but he was justifying it. He remembered an article in Newsweek claiming mini sleep was beneficial in fighting fatigue. In the heat, vibration, glare and dust even seconds with his eyes closed was a welcome relief. His head bobbed once again; his chin sank to his chest. His eyes were closed. He was asleep. This time he didn't wake up. The big machine kept going.

The wide field, for drainage and irrigation, dropped a few degrees in elevation toward the river. Fox, now sleeping soundly, didn't notice, but the six-ton machine, roaring and cutting beneath him, did. Gently at first, the bailer drifted from its arrow-straight track, turning to the left into a stand of uncut alfalfa.

The cutter blades labored, slicing a new swath through the three-foot high crop. Turning tighter and tighter until the bailer, Fox asleep in the cab bouncing like a rag doll, made a full circle. When the machine cut back into its own clear track, the engine surged and the hungry cutter blades rattled. Fox bolted awake. He was shocked, disoriented, bewildered. "Fuck!" he blurted and grabbed the wheel.

Fox had the bailer back on a straight track and was midway across the field when he spotted the pick-up truck at the end of the field. "Shit," he muttered. It was Virgil and Sparrow.

Reaching the end of the field and the parked truck, Fox shut the machine off and climbed down from the cab. Virgil and Sparrow were standing near the pick-up truck staring at the half acre big "O" cut in the alfalfa. "Maybe it's like in England," Sparrow suggested soberly. "You know, when them UFOs come down and cut big ass designs in the fields."

Virgil shook his head in disagreement. "I think it's an Indian sign... You know, like when warriors carve their names in things."

Fox's ears were growing warm with embarrassment.

"What Indian name has an "O" in it?" Sparrow questioned.

"Ox!" Virgil answered with a smile.

"Maybe Oprah!" Sparrow said and they broke into laughter, pleased with their performance.

Fox turned and headed for the bailer.

"Hey," Sparrow called, "can we stay? I wanna see how you do an X." They laughed harder.

A chalk board on the wall outside the door of the farm office announced the next day work assignments and everyone checked it when they came in from the fields. Fox arrived in the back of the pick-up along with three other bailers. Big Foot, Fleming and Wilson. Along with Virgil and Sparrow, the men climbed out and walked to the chalk board. The afternoon shadows were stretching long. Fox was looking forward to a hot shower and falling into bed. Morse was working on the chalk board when they reached him. He finished and stepped aside. Scrawled across the top of the board in irregular white lettering was "Tribal meeting tonight—Regarding the White Buffalo."

"Chief Stoner gonna be there?" Virgil asked Morse as they looked at the announcement.

"He's the one that called the meeting," Morse answered. "Expect to see all your faces there."

"This is tribal members only, right?" Fox questioned. He wasn't interested in tribal politics and meetings. He was weary and bone tired. Anything that might rob him of rest was an irritating intrusion.

Morse studied Fox for a moment before answering. "Means anybody whose mother was a member of this tribe... Unless you're just some red apple."

Fox stiffened. "I'll be there," he said, pulling off his bandanna.

Morse opened the screen door to the office and disappeared inside.

"What's a red apple?" Fox asked Sparrow as they walked to their cars.

"That's someone with red skin, but white inside."

Determined not to be a red apple, although deep inside Fox knew that's what he had been, he sped north to Castle Rock where he showered, shaved and put on fresh jeans. Once dressed, he became hesitant. What the hell did they wear to tribal meetings? Not wanting to be singled out as an outsider, he was wary of overdressing.

He looked at himself in the mirror. He was tanned dark from the days on the bailer. Better under dressed than overdressed. He decided to stay with the jeans.

The meeting was to be held at the Tribal Administrative Offices at crossroads. He had asked Sparrow for directions. "Couple miles south of Parker at the flashing light..."

"Tell me in white man's language," Fox defended.

"Come into Parker... Follow Riverside Drive."

Fox glanced at his watch. It was six-ten. The tribal meeting was set for seven-thirty. He had time for food, and he was hungry. He drove south on the river road to Blue Water Lagoon. He had not returned to the bar since the night of the fight. Pulling into the gravel parking lot in daylight, he found he felt a lot more secure. The nearby river was churning at its banks from the wake of speeding ski boats. Their engines filled the air with throaty, powerful, unmuffled roars. Damned tourists, Fox thought climbing out of the BMW.

Bonnie, the blonde bartender, was behind the bar. Fox was glad. It was almost as if she were a friend. Hell, maybe she was? He slid onto the bar stool. A big screen TV was on in a far corner. A trio of tourists in tank tops, shorts and sandals were watching a ball game and drinking beer. Two couples sat together in the middle of the room. In California they wouldn't have been served. This wasn't California, Fox reminded himself. Bonnie had been talking with two middle-aged men near the middle of the bar. They looked like locals, but not tribal. He fleetingly wondered why he was always looking for Indians. Then wondered if Indians did that. The thought provoked a smile. He was an Indian.

Reaching Fox, Bonnie returned his smile. She looked better. Maybe it was the fact he'd been in Parker longer. Bonnie was dressed in cut-off jeans that made her long legs look tan. A bare midriff, sleeveless shirt she wore was tied in front exposing a naval and the hint of a flat stomach. Her blue eyes found Fox. "Sorry, we no longer serve the steak sandwich with a chair."

"I think you did that just so you could drive me home."

Bonnie shrugged, "Never could resist a man with a lump."

Fox sensed the flirtation was taking a serious turn. He was enjoying her presence, but he was uncomfortable. He glanced at his watch. "I've only got twenty minutes."

"Are we still talking about food?" the blue eyes questioned.

Fox smiled. "Steak sandwich?"

"Tonto's been waiting on you," she looked to the kitchen. "Hey, Squaw chaser! Grill a steak san. General Custer's back."

"Is his name really Tonto?" Fox questioned, vaguely remembering the plump cook in a stained apron.

Bonnie shrugged again. When she did, it made the material over her breasts move. She saw Fox look. "He calls me the white bitch from L.A. I figure we're even. You want a beer while he picks your food off the floor?"

She was a combination of crass and cute and Fox decided he liked that. "Yeah," he answered.

"Coors, wasn't it?"

Fox nodded. Bonnie poured the beer and returned. Pushing it in front of him she said, "You know you gotta stay out of the sun. You're beginning to look like a...." She hesitated, realizing her mistake.

Fox helped her evade the embarrassment, "It's all right... White bitch."

Bonnie laughed. He liked her laugh.

Fox drove away from Blue Water Lagoon with his

physical hunger satisfied. The steak sandwich, French fries and cold beer were far from gourmet dining, but it was the best he'd had in days. But food alone wouldn't satisfy the hunger seeing Bonnie had stirred. Driving into Parker at twilight, he allowed the thought of her. Were they adulterous thoughts? Pam was dead. How long was he bound to her? Was he bound to her? The answer was quick and decisive. Yes, he was, and yes, he always would be. He loved Pam. Perhaps more now than ever in life. He tried to remember their last words, their last touch. God, how he ached for her. Like Palm Springs, like being an FBI Agent, like a mother's voice, Pam was gone. Now it was Parker, the tribe, the fields, the river and Indians with names like Sparrow, Bird and Virgil. He wondered if Pam would have liked them. He supposed so. What would she think of Bonnie? Uncomfortable with the thought, he stopped it. Pam was Pam. Bonnie was Bonnie. The two women lived in different worlds. He was no longer the man Pam was married to and Bonnie had never known that man. Perhaps that was the answer, Fox reasoned. The bond, the man, even the perception of him as Pam's husband had all died with her. All he had of Pam was past. They had no future. They were separate. Pam was gone. Her life was over. Fox's life was now on another path, living another life.

Slowing for Parker's only traffic signal, Fox considered the fact all of his thoughts might be little more than a lame excuse to get laid. Regardless, he couldn't deny the feelings the woman stirred in him. It was more than lust. It was a hunger, an aching for physical contact. The feel of a warm breath on his neck, the caress of a hand, the embrace of a warm body. All the things the mindless criminal bastard had stolen from him. A car behind Fox sounded its horn. He was sitting through a green light. He drove on wondering if Bonnie's flirting was sincere or was, she just being a good bartender? Wasn't Bonnie treating other customers the same way? It had been a long time since he tried to interpret the motives of a woman other than his wife's. His confidence was lacking, but testosterone hormones weren't. He wheeled the Explorer into a hardware store parking lot and braked to a halt beside a public telephone.

There was no phone book. Fox dug for a quarter. He dropped the coin into the instrument and dialed information. His pulse was racing. He felt a mix of excitement, embarrassment and guilt, but his mind was set. An operator provided the telephone number and he punched the buttons. In a few seconds the telephone was ringing at the other end of the line. He damned himself for not preparing a speech. He knew what he wanted. She probably knew what he wanted, but the social dance, the ageless protocol, the requisite interplay between sexes had to be addressed. "Blue Water Lagoon," a female voice said in his ear. It wasn't Bonnie.

"May I speak to Bonnie, please?"

"Sorry. She got off at seven tonight," the strange voice answered. "Would you like to leave a message?"

"Yeah," he said hesitantly, "tell her John Fox... Ah, never mind. Thanks." Fox hung up and kicked at the pole the telephone was mounted on. "Goddamnit," he growled, uncertain if the utterance came from guilt or frustration.

9 RETURN OF THE WHITE BUFFALO

"The buffalo were many...but they had no guns. The white man did. The buffalo are gone."

Thomas Elk—Comanche

Driving to the tribal meeting in David Rollins' van, Chief Russell Stoner knew he had another fence to climb. Scaling the fence at the White House had drawn bullets from the Secret Service. The fence he faced now could prove as costly. Intervention by the President had resolved the endless succession of bureaucratic obstacles blocking the approval to build a casino on the reservation. The Chief knew where the pressure was coming from. Las Vegas. In a fight you did not look for what a man had to protect, you looked for what a man had to lose. Building the casino would cause a loss. Las Vegas was about to hemorrhage millions. The Chief knew they would not give it away. There would be a fight.

He remembered the stories his grandfather told as they sat on the riverbank fishing at night, stirring embers of a small fire. "When the white man came to the river," the voice of the old man spoke in the Chief's memory with the clarity of a vision, "he did not need guns to defeat the Mojave people. The white man gave some whiskey... Others he gave fancy hats and leather boots... And to our women he gave mirrors and flowered dresses. And the Mojave people fought and argued.

"They became jealous and instead of one heart their heart was broken into many pieces, and they gave away what they had. So that they might have more, but in the end, they had less."

The Chief knew he had to be careful. The Mojave Nation had little more to give. The tactic the white man used a hundred years before was as powerful now as it was then. The wolf, when stalking its prey, never attacked from the front. It always came from the rear and it came with surprise. The challenge, the old man knew, was recognizing the wolf. A successful move in the hunt was to fool the prey. The proverbial wolf in sheepskin. Maybe, the Chief considered, the wolf would be in the skin of a Mojave. The wolf, in all probability the Chief concluded, could already be in their midst.

"Grandfather," David Rollins called from behind the wheel, "look at the crowd."

The sprawling Tribal Administrative Office complex was an aging sun-bleached single-story building in the shape of an L. Built forty years earlier by the Army Corps of Engineers, it had the look of a military barracks which is exactly what it had been. When work on the Colorado River's flood control dams, locks and canals were complete and the engineers moved to more hospitable quarters in Phoenix, the tribe bought the property. The fact the river ran through the heart of the reservation or that the barracks had been built on Indian land was never addressed. Bunk rooms became offices and the Indians moved in. Only those in their forties or fifties remembered any of it. Chief Stoner remembered it all. His eyes swept the parking lot. A sea of cars and faces jammed the crowded aisles. The Tribal Police were trying to cope with the crush. If the Chief had any doubts about interest in the casino, it was gone.

The overflow was being waved into grassy areas around the parking lots. Extended families, clans, factions, the old and the young, were arriving, gathering and moving for the council chambers. The men were dressed in brushed Stetsons, starched shirts, creased jeans and polished boots. The women wore their best. There was an air of excitement. The tribe, collectively, seemed to sense this was a memorable day.

David Rollins parked near the side entrance to the Tribal Council Offices. Dena Manygoats joined him in helping the Chief and his wife from the van. The metal clamps in the old man's abdomen were gone now, but the deep, aching soreness that hunched him as still there. He suspected it always would be.

Horace Waters, the fifty-four-year-old Vice Chairman of the Tribe, a powerfully build robust man with a sober face and a long ponytail, was standing in the office hallway with his daughter, Mara, when the Chief and young Rollins entered. Mara was a shapely, thirty-two-year-old with piercing dark eyes, raven black hair that hung to the middle of her back and a smooth, tan complexion. Like her father, Mara was an elected member of the Tribal Council. She was not a friend, fan or political ally of Chief Stoner. Mara made no secret she wanted to be the first female to head the tribe. A bachelor's degree in business from Arizona State and a relentless ambition had her well on her way. "Hello, Russell," Mara smiled with practiced charm. "Welcome back."

The Chief nodded, but he deliberately spoke to Horace Waters first. "Hello, Horace.... Glad you and your daughter could come." Now he looked to the young councilwoman. They were more than a generation apart. They were a world apart.

Mara wasn't about to let the slight pass unnoticed. She glanced at David Rollins, who held the Chief by the arm, "David, would you like some help?"

"Save your help for the vote," Rollins answered sarcastically.

"I always vote for the good of the tribe," Mara smiled without hesitation.

The Chief and Rollins shuffled on to a door stenciled "Tribal Chairman," Dena Manygoats and Sarah Stoner followed silently.

A long line of cars, all packed with Indians, made finding the crossroads and the Tribal Administrative Offices an easy task for the irritated John Fox. The frustration welling in him was sexual, but having failed in his attempt to remedy that, his anger was now focused on Morse Roberts at the farm office for coercing him into attending the Goddamned meeting. Red Apple! Hah! He wasn't a red apple. He was a rotten apple. An apple that fell too far from the tree. Whatever he was, he decided, moving at a snail's pace into the parking lot with the long line of cars being directed by a Tribal Police Officer with a gut hanging over his gun belt, he wasn't interested in Stoner or politics. All he wanted was a chance for some rest and to get laid.

Climbing out of the Explorer, Fox noticed he was the only one arriving alone. If the Indians noticed, they didn't seem to care. Then again, it wasn't an Indian trait to point out differences. He was relieved to see his jeans were appropriate. He no longer felt foreign, but he did feel alone. It was ironic. Once being an FBI agent made him feel comfortable in the presence of strange men a continent away. Now, a birthright granted by a mother who was little more than a fading memory made him a kindred spirit with these strange people. Following a family of seven toward a door to the council chambers, Fox remembered his last meeting with Chief Stoner, a world away under a slate gray sky in Georgetown and a hospital teeming with Secret Service and government officials. Feeling the last heat of the sun on his back, Fox knew this wasn't Georgetown.

Tribal Police Sergeant Bear-Don't-Walk was at the door to the council chambers. It was a spacious, spartan room bright with florescent light and crammed with rows of folding chairs. At the head of the room on a raised platform a long table was flanked by flags of the United States, the State of Arizona and the Tribal flag. The room was alive with chatter and muted conversation as the rows filled with tribal members. Fox, hoping not to draw attention or challenge, followed the family to the door. Bear-Don't-Walk's eyes found him. "Hello, John Fox," the tanned sergeant smiled. "You're looking much better than the last time I saw you."

"Hello, Sergeant," Fox answered sheepishly.

The temperature in the room was climbing as it filled with bodies. Fox sat on the left side of the room near the middle beside an old man who offered a nod when he sat down. The farm tan was working, he concluded.

In an office adjacent to the council chambers Russell Stoner leafed through a hard-backed notebook. David Rollins paced back and forth on his stiff leg marking notes on a yellow legal pad. Sarah Stoner and Dena Manygoats sat quietly.

"You have to talk about Washington," Rollins urged. "They will all want to know what happened."

"They know what happened," the Chief answered. His attention remained on the book. "Ted Koppel told them." He underlined in the notebook. "The vote on the business committee is going to be the struggle."

Rollins paused from pacing. "Then prime them. Get their sympathy. Tell the story. They'll give you what you want."

Stoner closed his notebook. "We must give them what is best... That is not always what we want." He glanced at a wall clock. "It's time."

As the Chief and David Rollins made their ways down the polished hall outside the office, the other council members emerged to join him, six in all. Horace Waters, his daughter, Mara, Morse Roberts from the tribal farm, George Manygoats, a gaunt thirty-year-old appointed to his slain father's term, Gail Burrows, a plump, round-faced, middle-aged woman, and Christine Scott, a tall, sober woman with a streak of gray hair down the middle of her dark head. The woman's nickname was Lightning Strike. The youth in the tribe believed a bolt of lightning had fried the color from her hair. An alcoholic husband was closer to the truth.

In a carefully defined pecking order set by age and questioned by none, the Chief opened the side door to the council chamber and led the way onto the platform. He straightened his stance as best he could, but the bullet wound's physical toll was obvious as he shuffled, with shoulders hunched, to his chair. A hush fell over the crowded room. The whisper of the ceiling fans was the only sound. The Chief looked at the sea of faces. He drew strength from their collective expectations. The council members filing in behind the Chief sat down at the long table.

David Rollins walked stiff legged to the front row followed by Dena Manygoats and Sarah Stoner. They sat with the elders lining the front rows.

Fox watched from the middle of the crowded room. He wondered if the Chief had seen him. He supposed not. He was wrong. He was excited to see the old man. He wanted to applaud, but the crowd sat in stoic silence, so he did too. He wondered if the old man would talk about the shooting.

"Much has happened since we last met," the old man said as his eyes drifted over the room. He used no microphone, but his voice was heard. Fox felt the old man was speaking directly to him. So, did everyone else. "Some good. Some bad. We have lost some friends.... But we have found others." Tears welled in Fox's eyes. He couldn't control it. The old man was talking to his heart. He was speaking of a pain they both felt.

"Indian people talk of the legend of the white buffalo... When the white buffalo returns, it will bring prosperity and plenty... No longer will our children die of measles and pox, no longer will our women wash the dirty clothes of white men and no longer will our elders die hungry. When the white buffalo returns there will be work for our young men, schools for our children and hospitals for our sick." The Chief reached to the table and picked up a letter. His hands trembled with age as he unfolded it. "This document has been signed by the Secretary of the Interior." He held it high. "It grants the Mojave people the right to build a casino... We will call our casino the White Buffalo!"

A young buck somewhere in the room let out a sharp yelp of delight. It broke the emotional dam welling the crowded room. War whoops, yelps and cries filled the air. The crowd was on its feet applauding, shouting, whistling, waving, dancing. The stiff-legged David

Rollins lifted Dena Manygoats high in the air. Sarah Stoner wiped tears from her eyes.

Fox was caught up in it. He pumped the hand of the old man beside him. Someone patted him hard on the back. He did the same to a woman in front of him. She turned around and hugged him. He didn't care that she smelled of sweat.

Finally, the Chief raised a hand and the jubilation subsided, yielding to a calm, then a hush. The crowd sat down. The Chief continued, "Chief Red Cloud once said the view from the mountain top is magnificent.... But you must first climb the mountain... We have a mountain to climb. There is much to be done. Sacrifice has been made... More sacrifice will be required. There are no footprints in the sand for us to follow. We must find our own way. And once we begin, we cannot turn back. We have worked on this for seven years. I would like to see the work done. If we shall begin.... Stand with me?"

Hundreds of chairs creaked and scraped the floor as the tribe, as if one, pushed to its feet. The old man allowed his eyes to search the room. Everyone was standing. "It is so," he declared and signaled them to sit. "The Tribal Secretary will now speak," the Chief said, finally lowering himself into his chair.

Davis Rollins pushed to his feet. He looked awkward and unbalanced on his stiff leg, but his face was eager. "The plan, as approved twenty-six-months ago, calls for a two-story casino of one hundred and twenty thousand square feet." He looked to his notes. "The gaming menu will include five-hundred and fifty slots, Keno, a poker room with thirty-five tables, a twelve-hundred seat bingo parlor, three restaurants, a full-service bar and a show room. We will employee six-hundred and eighteen people."

A gleeful yelp interrupted. Rollins paused. The Chief

raised a hand to silence the murmur in the room. "An estimated forty-seven-million-dollar loan is needed for construction," Rollins continued, "and now that a commitment to build has been made, tribal ordinance requires a Business Enterprise Board be formed." He looked to the Chief on the platform.

It was a cue the two had worked out earlier. The Business Enterprise Board for the casino would be a powerful force. A force that made every decision, filled every position, counted every penny. Tribal ordinance wisely required three members. The Chief could appoint one, a chairperson, who would have no greater authority than the other two. Another would be appointed by the tribal council and a third by nomination from the tribe. Each of the tribal council members had their favorites. Of the six members, only Morse Roberts and Christine Scott were likely to follow the Chief's lead. To control the board, a majority of two were needed. Chief Stoner knew that and went after it in earnest. Pushing to his feet the Chief said, "I appoint David Rollins as the Chairman of the Gaming Enterprise Board and recommend the council nominate Morse Roberts as the representative."

Horace Waters bolted to his feet. "Objection is made for conflict of interest."

Chief Stoner was silently pleased, although he was careful not to show it. Waters had taken the bait. David Rollins was really who the Chief wanted in without objection and now that Waters was objecting to Roberts, the boy was likely to be forgotten.

"Morse is the Manager of the tribal farm," Waters continued diplomatically with a glance at the tanned man beside him on the platform, "and he does a good job, but we all know it's a job that takes ten to twelve hours a day, sometimes seven days a week. I don't think it's possible for Morse to serve as Farm Manager and on the Gaming Board too. Plus, it's one business competing with another."

"How ya gonna keep em down on the farm?" a voice called from the crowd. Everyone laughed.

Morse Roberts was part of the conspiracy with the Chief and young Rollins. Horace Waters, without realizing it, was absolutely right. Morse wasn't interested in another job. He was the Farm Manager and that was more than enough for him, but in an effort to help his old friend, he had agreed to the ploy. Still playing the role, Morse pushed to his feet. "I don't wanna be in the middle of this thing. So, I'll withdraw. Thank you, Chief."

"Thank you, Morse," Waters said, still standing. "Since the councilman has withdrawn, Chief," he was being deliberately formal, "I would like to nominate an individual imminently qualified for the Gaming Enterprise Board. An individual with a degree in business finance. An individual who helped draft the gaming ordinances for the tribe, worked on the planning committee and..."

"Would that be your Daughter, Horace?" the Chief questioned, taking away the man's initiative.

"Yes, Mara Waters... Mara is..."

"All those in favor of Horace Water's daughter, Mara," the Chief said looking down the table at the other council members.

Fox, along with the entire room, was looking at the nominee. Mara sat, hands folded in front of her on the table, staring dispassionately into the distance, chin raised slightly, waiting as if a slave on the auction block. In addition to being a nominee, she was a beautiful woman, Fox decided. He was pleased. It sounded bigoted, he knew, but he hadn't seen many attractive Indian women. He suspected it was, as Morse suggested, because he was a red apple. He was using the world's standard to judge beauty, but whatever standard he used on this woman, she was attractive. Fox watched as Horace Waters, Gail Burrows, Christine Scott and George Manygoats raised their hands. It was a majority.

The Chief used the vote to slip another issue by the possible opposition. "Motion carries," he said. "Mara Waters and David Rollins are appointed to the Gaming Enterprise Board. We now need a nomination from the floor."

Across the room Virgil Tanner pushed to his feet and took his Stetson in hand. "Chief, we all think it would be nice if Paul Manygoats' boy, George, was on the Board."

The Sparrow popped up beside Virgil. "I'll second that. George is okay by me."

The Chief nodded agreement. "George Manygoats is the nomination from the floor. All those in favor, say aye."

A collective reverberating "Aye!" rattled the room.

"Those opposed?" the Chief questioned.

Silence answered him.

"George Manygoats, the son of Paul Manygoats is elected to the Gaming Enterprise Board," the Chief declared. The nomination had been spontaneous and once the Chief heard it, he knew what the emotional vote was going to be. They weren't voting for the thirty-year-old, they were voting for the father whose blood was on the grass of the south lawn. The boy, although a thirty-year-old, everybody knew, was a dimwit. His father had tried to make him a businessman by forcing him to work in the smoke shop, a family run wholesale cigarette store fronting U.S. Ninety-five just north of downtown Parker, but George was little more than a drunk. He had married a local white gold digger and together they were well on their ways to squandering the family fortune. Delores Manygoats, deep in depression since her husband's death, was doing nothing to stop it and Dena Manygoats, the youngest in the family, without her mother's support and in the absence of a will, had become, like others, little more than a spectator to her brother's excesses. The Chief hoped, as a powerful one-third of the Enterprise Board, the boy would be manageable. It was likely Virgil tanner's only motive in nominating George was the hope for free cigarettes or a cheap drunk. "David," the Chief questioned with a look at Rollins, "when is the first meeting of the Gaming Enterprise Board?"

"This Thursday. Seven o'clock to discuss financing and site selection."

The Chief pushed to his feet. "The work has begun. I move we adjourn."

"I second," Christine Scott intoned.

"We stand adjourned," the Chief ordered.

Fox moved out with the crowd. Listening, watching, he felt a real part of it. There was talk about jobs, money. He wondered how much of it was speculation and how much was bullshit. Whichever, at least for the moment, it was exciting. Following four young bucks, he listened to their exchange. "I hear some tribes give members checks every month," one of them speculated.

"Hey, the Chumash all got new cars and houses."

"All I want is one o' those big screen TVs."

"I'm gonna get me a new truck. Four-by-four by damn."

"First they gotta build the place."

"Maybe we can get a job on the construction."

"What the hell you ever built?"

"By God I can work."

Fox was worried. He knew from watching the Indian casinos pop up around Palm Springs like mushrooms in the sands, generating millions of dollars that there was a price to be paid. They had talked about it one afternoon in the FBI office. Bank robbers were averaging six-hundred dollars a hit. Bankers weren't stupid. They quickly learned not to keep cash at the tellers' windows and what was there was spiked with explosive dye-packs or recorded serial numbers. The agents wondered why the casinos weren't robbed. They had millions on deposit, security that was inadequate. Speculation had evolved into where the money went. Where were the rich Indians? Where were the big houses? The big Cars? The new schools? The Indian managers? There were no answers then. There were no answers now. Fox drove the main road north out of Parker. It was a dark moon-less night and the desert sky was strewn with stars like diamonds on black velvet. The river road would have been cooler, but he didn't want to drive by Blue Water Lagoon and stir the carnal thoughts of Bonnie. The meeting, with talk about the white buffalo, had pushed Bonnie to the back of his mind. Not forgotten, but at least postponed. Perhaps it was fate. Perhaps just rotten luck. Either way, Bonnie minus her cut-off jeans and midriff blouse would have to wait until another day.

Castle Rock Resort, in the cloak of darkness, was reduced to the glare of sodium night lights, swarms of insects and fluttering bats. The parking spaces in front of the wing of rooms stretching from the small office were vacant. Fox was the only permanent resident. It was a weekend place. The price of rooms went up sixteen dollars every Friday. "It's not fair," he had complained to Ethel Martin, the three-hundred-pound owner/manager with thinning orange hair.

"You want fair, check the weather. I'm a capitalist. I'm not a half-way house for yuppies," Ethel argued. "Plus, where else you gonna find a coke machine so close to your room?"

Pulling in, Fox noticed a TV was illuminating the park motel office. Ethel slept in front of it hoping, expecting late night arrivals. Fox parked in front of unit four and climbed out. He was unlocking the door when a voice behind him said. "John?"

It was Bonnie's voice. He wheeled to find her walking out of the shadows from the river. She had a large brown dog on a leash. He looked from the dog to her. Bonnie was shoeless in a sleeveless, low cut, brown ankle-length dress. Her hair was pinned up and she looked younger. The dog was pulling on the leash toward Fox. "How's that for timing?" she smiled, reaching him. She jerked on the leash and the dog sat obediently.

Fox was surprised. Bonnie saw it. "Julia called me at home. She said you called a few minutes after I left. I live just down river at Shadow Point. Thought Justice and I would walk over and say hi. Got here and you weren't... We were walking away when you pulled in."

Fox heard her, but the impression her nipples were making inside the sheer dress was having more effect than her voice. "You live where?" he questioned awkwardly.

She gestured, "Shadow Point. Quarter of a mile. Listen, if this is a bad time."

"Would you like to come in?" he said to the nipples. "It's not much, but I've got HBO and a coke machine."

"Thought you'd never ask," Bonnie answered, then speaking to the dog, she said, "Stay, Justice, stay." She released the leash. The dog didn't move.

Fox opened the door and cool, conditioned air from the room reached out into the warm night to greet them. "Oh, you've got air," Bonnie said brushing by. He turned on a light. A breast caressed his arm. "Can I sleep over?" she teased.

134

"Thought you'd never ask," Fox smiled in reply. He'd lock her in the room if he had to.

Bonnie's eyes swept the room and returned to Fox. "Ya know, I'd do anything for a cold diet Sprite." She laid a hand on his arm. It was as if she grabbed his crotch. He swallowed to open his throat and prayed for control.

"What if there's no diet Sprite?" he said digging for coins.

"Don't ya love living on the edge?" Bonnie teased.

"Be right back," Fox said. Coins in hand, he stepped into the night.

He felt foolish, but he prayed all the way to the coke machine. "Please, God, please." God was in a charitable mood. The machine had diet Sprite. He dropped the coins then prayed the machine wouldn't malfunction. The cold can went thud into the receptacle and Fox grabbed it. He hurried for the room.

Fox was surprised when he opened the door to the room. It was dark. "Bonnie?"

"Leave the light off," she answered stepping into him. She reached to push the door shut. He drew in an involuntary breath. She was nude. "Open the can," Bonnie whispered. Her hands found his belt buckle. She pulled, released it and jerked the belt away. He could feel her nipples and breasts through his thin shirt. She kissed him gently on the neck and ran his zipper down. He gasped as her hand massaged him. "Open the can," she whispered a second time. It popped loud in the quiet room.

Bonnie's hand left his erection to find the can of Sprite in the darkness. "This will help," she whispered filling her mouth with the cold carbonated beverage. She pushed the can in his hand and knelt in front of him. The cool air tickled his flesh as she pulled his pants and shorts to the floor. Fox was breathing hard. His mind was filled with a torrent of incoherent thoughts. Lust and love blurred as he tried to push the images of Pam from his mind. He ached for relief, ached for this woman's touch, ached for any woman's touch, but Pam's memory still held him. Or maybe it was he who just couldn't let her go. Fox closed his eyes and tried to lose himself in his passion. He failed. This wasn't Pam kneeling in front of him in the darkness. This wasn't her scent. This wasn't her touch. His lungs were about to burst. Bonnie's lips touched the head of his penis and Fox recoiled away. "I can't," he blurted into the shadows. He pulled his pants up and zipped them. "I'm sorry," he said feeling his ears and neck flush warm with guilt.

He stood staring at the faint outline of the window framed with light from the parking lot. He could hear her moving behind him. She was dressing. He wished he could think of something to say, anything! But everything he considered sounded hollow and inadequate in his mind. He could only imagine how she felt. He knew she wouldn't understand, no matter what he said. I'm sorry my wife is dead and she's all I can think of. It's not that I don't want you,...I just want her more.

Fox drew in a breath and let it out slowly. He was trembling with emotion. A hand touched his back. It was warm. It calmed him. Then it fell away. He watched Bonnie's shadow move to the door. She opened it and stepped into the night.

Satisfied she was gone Fox went into the bathroom, turned on the light and lathered his hands with soap, avoiding a look in the mirror. He twisted the gold wedding band from his left hand, laid it atop the sink, dried his hands and left the room.

He lay in bed damning himself. Bonnie and the chance to get laid were gone, but the passion was not. It was surging through his veins, capturing his every thought, filling him with lust and robbing him of reason. If only he had taken off the ring earlier. *If only...* the fuckin' *if's.* They seemed in charge of his life. In charge of the universe.

Lying in bed for over an hour, unable to sleep, Fox finally yielded and got up to walk to the bathroom. He didn't turn on the light. His fingers quickly found the cool gold on the porcelain. He pushed it onto the finger crying out for it. Pam was more than a gold band around his finger. It seemed the band was around his heart..., no, around his life, Fox allowed as he lay down in the bed again. He went to sleep praying he would not dream.

10 ONE FOR THE MONEY

"The earth and myself are of one mind.
The measure of the land and the
measure of our bodies are the same...."
Joseph Hinmaton Yalakit—Nez Perce Chief

When the alarm went off at 5 AM, Fox dressed quickly, wanting to get away from the room, the can of Sprite and the guilt. He was looking forward to the heat and solitude of the fields. There he could get lost in the dust and the sweat and the sweet aroma of the cut. There he wouldn't have to decide anything. There all he had to do was drive in a straight line.

David Rollins was also awake early. It was eight o'clock on Wall Street and word had spread among the eager money brokers that the Mojave's in Arizona were seeking a loan to build a casino. Gaming, investors had learned, was the sure bet of the nineties. A fifty-million-dollar construction loan would carry considerable commissions. By five AM young Rollins, living in an aging single-wide mobile home without air conditioning on the east bank of the Colorado River south of Poston, had received six calls from brokers offering loans. Four were willing to fly out for meetings. One wanted to meet in Las Vegas, and another offered to fly him to New York City. After the sixth call, David refused to answer any more. He dressed to drive to the tribal office.

When the sun broke over the eastern horizon, Dennis Milner and attorney Clyde Hanes were at eighteen thousand feet fifty-seven miles east of Parker on a VFR approach in a sleek chartered twin jet. Twenty minutes after the tribal meeting had ended, councilman Horace Waters made a telephone call to Las Vegas. Mitch Parsons, the Manager of the Casa Grande, took the call in his office. The fact the Casa Grande carried a gambling debt of eight thousand dollars for Waters and provided him a steady string of call girls was the insurance the call would come. "Okay," Horace Waters told Parsons, "it's gonna get built."

"Our team will be there tomorrow," the suave manager answered Waters. "You'll make the introduction."

"That's all I can do," Waters defended. He resented being manipulated.

"Perhaps your daughter could help," Parsons suggested. "Wasn't she elected to the Gaming Enterprise Board?" He was telling Waters they had other informants in the tribe. Other informants who had already reported to them.

Waters was unnerved. He tensed with the realization that the grip Parsons held on him had just tightened. "I don't want my daughter involved," Waters argued.

"Horace," Parsons offered disarmingly, "this is how

business is done. Friends helping friends. There's money to be made. If you don't broker this deal, someone else will. Why shouldn't your family benefit from this? There's no subterfuge involved. You make an introduction; our man makes an offer. The rest is up to the Enterprise Board, right?"

Waters had to agree. So, he did, hoping it meant money and not more problems. "All right. I'll introduce them."

"I'll have them give you a call."

Six hours later, the chartered jet was streaking down a rain-soaked runway in Saint Cloud, Minnesota. Dennis Milner, a certified, card-carrying member of the Mille Lac Tribe, a member of NIMBA, the National Indian Business Men's Association, a man armed with a certified line of credit letter from the Board President of Minnesota First Bank for forty-million dollars, was off to pow-wow with his Indian brothers in Parker, Arizona. Milner wondered what the Mojave Indians looked like. They had to be smarter than the Mille Lacs, he decided. At least they didn't live at the fuckin' North Pole.

The tribal administration office offered no refuge for David Rollins. By noon the hallway outside his small office was lined with men carrying briefcases and wearing twelve-hundred-dollar suits. Without a secretary, David was forced to handle calls from Thunderbird Gaming, Sodak Enterprises and IGC, all wanting to wine and dine and sell him slot machines, accounting systems, surveillance packages, gaming tables, casino tokens and consulting services. When he wasn't answering calls, he was sorting through faxes, Fed-Ex packages and telegrams. A company in New Jersey sent him an activated cellular telephone with an invitation to call anytime to discuss the White Buffalo's communications needs. He closed the door to his office and used the phone to call Dena Manygoats. The avalanche of attention was making David Rollins feel very important.

It was mid-afternoon when Dennis Milner and his red-haired, shapely assistant, Lana Casner, loaned by Donald DePalma, arrived at the smoke shop on U.S. Ninety-five north of Parker. The gaunt George Manygoats was behind the counter in the converted double-wide mobile that served as a wholesale cigarette outlet. The store, warm with the afternoon heat, was rich with the bitter-sweet smell of tobacco. "You George Manygoats?" Milner questioned, offering a hand.

"Yeah," George answered taking the hand. It was obvious he was impressed with the beauty of the woman with Milner.

"I'm Denny Milner from the Mille Lac Tribe in Minnesota. This is Lana, my assistant. I was a friend of your father's. We had been talking business about things. Can you get away? I'd like to buy you a drink."

"Nothing open probably. Not until after supper," George hedged. The truth was most bars in Parker, out of respect for his father, would no longer serve the thirty-year-old.

"I know a place," Milner smiled. "Come one, Lana will watch the store. He reached over the counter to take George by the arm. "Quick drink and we're back."

George's senses were craving a drink. He hadn't slept well. His mother's incessant weeping and his wife's whining about getting out of Parker had him up most of the night. "Okay," he agreed with a look at the woman's green eyes. "Price list is right there by the cash register. You know how to operate a cash register?"

"I know about cash registers," Lana purred.

Milner drove to Parker's small municipal airport and pulled to a stop beside the chartered jet. "Come on," he said with a glance at the wide-eyed thirty-year-old.

"Where we going?" George questioned hesitatingly.

"Vegas," Milner smiled.

"Jesus," George mouthed. He had never been on an airplane. Less than sixty minutes later they were sitting on the strip at a reserved table in the Casa Grande's exclusive LeBlanc Lounge. George stared at the heaving breasts of a long-legged cocktail waitress in a black tux costume as she set drinks on the table. "We'll have another round," Milner said picking up his glass. "Gotta fight that jet lag, right George?"

George drank and Milner talked. "Your dad had a vision for the White Buffalo," he said in a convincing tone. "I'd like to see your dad's dream come true."

"You come here often?" George asked as the tuxedo with breasts delivered another round of drinks.

Milner glanced at the girl. He saw George's interest. As she waltzed away, he said, "Only when I want something special. Her name's Bridgett. Would you like to meet her?"

George gulped down his drink.

The Gaming Enterprise Board met on Thursday evening at the tribal administrative office. It was a closed meeting. The Tribal Police turned away a broker from Chicago and a representative from ITT Gaming. The trio of Mara Waters, George Manygoats and David Rollins met in the council room. David had his cellular telephone with him. When it kept ringing, Mara asked him to turn it off. They quickly agreed the most important decision faced was the construction loan. A stack of over fifteen loan and construction proposals lay on the table before them.

They were thick, glossy, hard-bound books with colored drawings, lengthy loan agreements, detailed construction plans, marketing schemes and profit projections. Several included personally embossed copies bearing each of the commissioners' names in gold. Mara worked on hers with a hand-held calculator. She threw away several without consulting David or George. When David gave her a cautionary glance, she defended. "Eight and nine percent interest. In today's market, that's not competitive. We want five, six at the most."

George nodded agreement as if he understood.

Two hours of discussion reduced the number of proposals to four. They took a ten-minute break and returned to the task. Another was quickly dismissed when Mara found an ambiguous clause in the proposal regarding the interest cap on an adjustable interest rate. Rollins was impressed with her discovery. He had missed it.

After another hour debate over the remaining proposals, Rollins made a recommendation. "We're getting nowhere. Maybe the answer is in a vote. Let's write down who we prefer then I'll read them."

Each penciled a name on a piece of paper, folded it and pushed it to the center of the table. David gathered the papers. He opened his first. "Sodak Gaming... That's my vote," he glanced at Mara and George, then picked up the second. "Navco," he paused, looked to the two for an acknowledgment. When he got none, he opened the third paper. "Navco."

"I think that's a two-thirds vote, isn't it?" Mara suggested.

"Why Navco?" Rollins questioned, gathering the three slips into his hand.

Mara took the initiative. "Navco, an acronym for

Native American Construction Company. It's Indian owned. It draws on money from banks with Indians on their boards. The President of the company is a hands-on builder, not some executive in a plush Atlantic City office. He's here lobbying for his proposal and he guarantees Indian preference in hiring."

"I'm not sure I want a casino built by Indians," Rollins defended.

Mara laid her hands flat on the table and leaned into it compressing her breasts, her dark eyes narrowed with sincerity. The penetrating look intimidated Rollins. He had long carried a passion for this woman, but her ambition, education and family made the distance between them much greater than the table separating them. Rollins had settled for Dena Manygoats. He loved her, he was certain of that, but not with the same primal passion Mara stirred in him. "You speak with the same doubt that haunts all Mojave men," Mara spat at him with a flash of the anger she was notorious for. "What would you have us do, David? Bring in the white men that built the Luxor, or how about Trump Plaza? Let's give more of our money to the white world. Hell, all the Indians would do is spend it on themselves."

"All right," David said raising a hand. "If Navco can supervise the construction, I agree."

Mara's chair scraped the tile floor sharply as she pushed back and stood. She was still angry. "You know what, David? It doesn't make a damn whether you agree or not." Mara turned and marched from the room.

David gathered the proposals into a pile. He placed Navco's on top. A letter of acceptance would have to be prepared and sent. That could wait. He picked up the cellular telephone, turned it on and punched in a number.

"Hello," Dena Manygoats' voice said in his ear.

"I just spent fifty-million-dollars," David said to the young woman pregnant with his child.

"Could you stop and get some chips on the way home?" the voice in his ear questioned.

Thirty-five-miles north of Parker Dennis Milner sat in his suite at the Queen's Bay Inn on the shores of Lake Havasu. After seeing motel row and the limited amenities of downtown Parker, he declared, "This is worse than fuckin' Minnesota." He made the charter pilot fly the twin engine jet to Havasu. The thirty-one-nautical-mile flight cost eight hundred and seventy-six dollars. Milner, dressed in a bathrobe, was drinking straight scotch and watching the Playboy Channel. Miss July was riding a horse in the surf nude. Milner was watching the centerfold bounce, but his thoughts were on the room next door. Beyond the wall was Lana Casner. He heard her running water in the tub earlier. He was fantasizing going over, kicking in the door and raping her. The only thing that protected her from his growing lust was the likelihood Donald DePalma would cut his balls off. No, DePalma would hire someone to cut his balls off. That was even more of a horrific thought. The telephone rang. Maybe it was Lana calling to invite him over? He grabbed for the telephone. "Hello."

"Dennis, it's Clyde."

It was the fuckin' attorney. Milner hated attorneys almost as much as he hated his ex-wife. Clyde Hanes had brought Milner into the deal, but he was still a fuckin' attorney. A fuckin' attorney that thought more about eatin' than gettin' laid. Probably why he's calling, Milner speculated. Let's go get something to eat. Hanes was in the room across the hall. "Yeah, what's up?"

"Mitch Parsons just called! We got the bid! We're fuckin' rich!"

Milner bolted to his feet. "You're shittin' me!"

"No, no, I'm serious!"

"Jesus Christ," Milner stated. "I'm gonna build a fuckin' casino."

"No, no," Hanes cautioned, "remember we're not going to build it."

"Yeah, right," Milner agreed soberly. He had forgotten and now the moment was tarnished. It was akin to getting Lana from DePalma. The moment he got her was an exciting one, but then came the realization he could never have her. Only if Lana chose him and life had already taught him—Lana wouldn't.

"You wanna celebrate?" Hanes pressed. "Go get something to eat?"

In Parker, Fox was making a trip he knew he had to make. He had to return to the Blue Water Lagoon. He had to face Bonnie. Part of him, the part that cared about the feelings of others, cared about Bonnie and how she felt, but it did not outweigh his sense of infidelity. He knew there was no logic in it, but logic could not reach the bone deep conflict he was fighting. He waited until he knew Bonnie no longer hoped he would call before returning to Blue Water Lagoon. In an effort to further insulate himself, he went with Virgil Tanner and Sparrow. It was after a day of cutting and all three men were dusty and dirty and ripe with sweat. Fox even wore the blue bandanna around his forehead to add to his imaginary disguise. He followed the two men into the bar. Bonnie spotted them immediately. If she felt any insult, if she were struggling with some inner emotional pain, some sense of rejection, she seemed to be hiding it well. Dressed in the same cut-off shorts, she was at the middle of the bar talking with two tanned, muscle-bound, blond-haired tourists. "Well, if it isn't the Three Musketeers," she called.

Virgil Tanner led the way to a small oval table near the window overlooking the river. Fox liked crossing the bar with the two men. He liked the white faces in the room thinking he was an Indian. Hell, he was an Indian. It felt good.

"What's a musketeer?" Sparrow asked as they sat down.

"A candy bar, you fuckin' idiot," Virgil answered.

Bonnie left the tourists at the bar and walked to the table. "What would you like, gentlemen?"

Virgil leaned back in his chair and patted Bonnie's round buttocks. "You and your two sisters or maybe your mother," he said loudly letting the tourists know whose turf they were on. Fox glanced in the direction of the two men. They were looking. Sizing the challenge.

Bonnie took Virgil's lingering hand away. "Stop it, Virgil," she warned. "You know it turns me on when you talk dirty."

"You over there teasing them lil' sissy surfers?" Virgil chided.

"I was," Bonnie admitted, "but the minute you three smelly, low-paid, common laborers walked in, I lost all interest."

"Uh-huh," Virgil smiled. "Well, get your pretty lil' ass movin' and get us three laborers three pitchers of beer."

"I live to serve," Bonnie smiled sarcastically and turned away.

"She does have a pretty ass, doesn't she?" Virgil suggested seriously.

Fox nodded agreement. So did Sparrow. They slouched in their chairs and watched the wide river glide by. It was blue and quiet on the other side of the glass. "Cut ain't gonna last but a couple more days," Virgil said to the river. "Gettin' too hot. Alfalfa's turnin' to fireweed."

Fox hadn't allowed himself to question the end of it although he always knew it would come. Sonofabitch. It robbed him of the pleasant, relaxed feeling he had gotten into. It made him feel white. Separate. These men knew what was beyond the cut. He didn't. Anxiety made him ask. "What do you do after the cut?" He tried to make his question casual. It wasn't.

"What Injuns do best," Virgil smiled, propping dusty boots up on the empty chair at the table. "Drink and collect unemployment."

Sparrow laughed.

Bonnie returned from the bar. She set frosty brimming pitchers of beer in front of Virgil and the Sparrow then a can of Sprite in front of Fox. "Enjoy," she quipped and turned away.

"What the fuck is that?" Sparrow asked. Virgil was staring at Fox trying to figure it out.

Fox's ears smarted with embarrassment. His pulse was racing.

"Yeah, John," Virgil was reinforcing the Sparrow. "What the fuck is that?"

"It's a Sprite, you fuckin' idiot," Fox answered. He grabbed up the can and in several quick heavy swallows emptied it down his throat. Virgil and Sparrow stared. Fox slammed the empty can down on the table hard and looked to Bonnie. "Barmaid," he shouted, "another Sprite!"

Bonnie returned, but this time with the third pitcher of beer. She set it in front of Fox. "I heard you're a one Sprite man." She spoke to him as if he were the only one at the table. Both Virgil and Sparrow sensed they were listening to a personal exchange.

Fox held Bonnie's look. He wanted to tell her how he felt. He wanted to tell her about Pam. He wanted to tell her how he didn't understand any of it, but he couldn't.

"Doesn't mean I don't want another one," Fox answered not knowing what else to say.

Bonnie nodded. She understood more than he knew. "Enjoy your beer, Cochise." She moved away.

Fox poured beer into a glass. Virgil gave him an inquisitive look. "What?" Fox questioned taking a drink.

"You know," Virgil said with a look to Sparrow. "I think the white woman's right."

Sparrow's blank look told him he didn't understand.

Virgil took another heavy drink before he went on, "She called Fox Cochise. She's right. He needs an Indian name. He's my cousin. I can't have a cousin named after some skinny, little, fuckin' sneaky animal like a fox."

Sparrow nodded eager agreement.

Virgil laid a hand on Fox's shoulder and puffed up his chest. It made him look like a buffalo nickel, Fox thought. "From this day, lil' cousin, you will no longer bear the white name of sneaky lil' fox. Your Indian name will be... Sprite Man!"

Virgil and Sparrow laughed loudly. Fox took the crushed Sprite can and dropped it under the table.

They drank beer and talked about "o"s cut in alfalfa fields, their fight in the bar and the salt content of sweat. Fox, half drunk and silly, nominated Virgil as the chairman of their small group. Virgil and Sparrow didn't get the pun. Fox tried to explain. He did a poor job. Bonnie, delivering another three pitchers of beer heard the exchange. "Let me interpret," she said to Fox, with a look to Virgil and Sparrow she mocked sign language using both hands. "White man say, Indian hit in head with fuckin' chair." She played out the event.

Virgil and Sparrow starred spellbound.

Bonnie pointed a finger at Virgil. "That makes Redman... Chairman!"

The two Indians roared with laughter.

Fox was mildly annoyed. "That's what I said," he argued.

"Yeah, but you're only half Indian, Sprite Man."

Virgil and Sparrow laughed even harder.

"I gotta go home," Fox announced. Not only was he annoyed, he knew he was well on the way to surrendering his judgment to alcohol. He was irritated, for reasons he didn't understand, with the two tourists at the bar, but since his last bar fight hadn't gone well, he wasn't eager to start another.

"Where's home, Sprite Man?" Virgil questioned with a slur.

"South of Parker Dam at Castle Rock," Fox answered.

Sparrow reacted sharply with a hard look at Fox. "Don't mention the dam."

Fox was on the edge of anger with all the misunderstanding. "Fuck the dam," he shot back at Sparrow.

"Fuckin' dam ain't nothing," the glassy-eyed Virgil slurred. Fox saw the big man tense. He had seen the look before. "Let's drive up there. I'll show you the fuckin' dam."

"Forget the dam, Virg," Sparrow urged reaching for his friend's arm.

"What about the dam," Fox pressed. He really didn't care who was irritated.

"I gotta piss," Virgil said pushing out of his chair with effort. "Watch the level of the river go up two inches." He grinned and staggered away.

Sparrow waited until Virgil was gone. Then with a look at Fox, he explained. "Virgil had a twin brother... Damon. He jumped off the dam two years ago. Didn't find his body 'til a week later. Virgil thinks the dam wants to kill him too."

"Kill him? Why?" Fox asked.

"Because he was screwing Damon's old lady. That's

why Damon jumped. He had to kill Virgil or himself. That's what the note said. He put it on the windshield of Virgil's truck."

"What the hell's the dam got to do with it?" Fox questioned.

"Virgil knows Damon told the dam."

"That nuts," Fox rejected the idea, but the thought unnerved him.

"Don't tell me. Tell the dam. It keeps calling Virgil."

An engine roared in the parking lot. Tires spun. A hail of gravel pounded the side of the building. Sparrow bolted to his feet. "Virgil!"

The taillights of the truck were disappearing into the night when Fox and Sparrow reached the parking lot. Bonnie was only steps behind them. "Virgil!" Sparrow screamed in desperation.

"Come on," Fox bolted for the Ford Explorer. Sparrow followed.

"I'll call the police!" Bonnie shouted after them.

Fox and Sparrow scrambled into the Explorer. The engine came to life. Fox jerked the vehicle in gear, and they roared out of the parking lot.

Sparrow braced a knee against the dash as Fox sped up the dark serpentine river road. The tires screamed on tight corners as the headlamps illuminated a jagged wall of rock flanking the narrow asphalt. Spiked reflectors raced at them. Fox was a skilled driver, but with his blood polluted with alcohol, he was fighting for control. He gripped the steering wheel so tight his hands ached. The taillights they had seen from the parking lot were nowhere in sight.

On a straight stretch of roadway paralleling the river Fox tramped hard on the accelerator and the night rushed at them in a blur. The speedometer climbed to eighty-miles-an-hour. Moths drawn into the headlamps slammed against the windshield leaving wet smears of pulp. Finally, two pin lights of red pierced the dark ahead. "There he is!" Sparrow shouted.

The Explorer closed the distance on the aging Chevy pick-up truck. A whirlwind was pulling dust out of its open bed. Debris swirled in the headlights of the Explorer. A fading bumper sticker on the truck read, "My family wasn't on the Mayflower." Virgil illuminated in the harsh light from the Ford's headlamps sat behind the wheel with an elbow cocked out an open window. His open shirt sleeve flapped in the seventy-mile-an-hour wind.

The speeding pick-up truck swerved onto a shoulder of the road as they rounded a sharp turn. A cloud of dust smothered the Explorer's headlamps and a hailstorm of sand and rocks hammered the front of it. A sharp bang sounded against the windshield as a large rock impacted. A jagged crack reached across the glass. Fox let up on the accelerator. The taillights raced on. "He's a crazy sonofabitch," Sparrow warned.

A sign came out of the darkness. "Parker Damn—1 mile". Fox followed a twisting s-curve, bleeding off speed. The night lights of the towering dam came into view. Built in 1938, Parker Dam stood in an eight-hundred- and fifty-six-foot concrete arch between Arizona and California literally plugging the flow of the Colorado River. The harnessed river spread behind the dam to form the seemingly endless stretch of Lake Havasu. Water surging through the dam's turbines lit the streets of Los Angeles and kept its thirsty lawns green. If the dam noticed the Chevy pick-up driven by a Mojave warrior on its face, it didn't seem to care.

Giant metal girders stood at hard angles around the illuminated face of the dam providing hangers for thick cables reaching up from the turbine generators. A two-laned road with a sidewalk on either side followed the graceful arch of the dam. Ornate streetlamps looking like icons from the thirties when they were erected stood like silent sentinels washing away the night. The roar of cascading water reverberated deep in the darkness sent a constant seismic tremor through the time-hardened concrete mass. Near the dam the desert air was cooler and ripe with moisture.

"Oh, God," Sparrow gasped as Fox drove onto the dam. Virgil's pick-up truck was parked awkwardly with one wheel up on the sidewalk near the center of the dam. The driver's door was standing open, the headlights were on. Virgil was gone. Fox braked to a halt behind it. He and Sparrow scrambled out.

"Keep back!" Virgil shouted. He had climbed over a three-foot-high concrete guard rail on the face of the dam and was hanging onto a lamp post with one hand leaning out into a black, noisy void that led to the water ninety feet below.

A police car arrived. Its flashing emergency lights sent pulses of red light washing over Virgil's face. "This is between me and this fuckin' dam," Virgil growled. "You hear me, dam? I ain't afraid of you. I am Virgil Thomas Tanner and you can't hurt me."

Two khaki clad La Paz County Deputy Sheriffs joined Fox and Sparrow to stare at Virgil. They didn't seem to know what to do. Electronic sirens were whining in the distance. More emergency vehicles were closing on the dam. "What's his name?" one of the deputies questioned.

Sparrow was staring with his mouth hanging open helplessly when he saw Virgil look down. Fox saw it too. "Virgil, no!" Fox bolted to grab him, but Virgil simply stepped away, hanging in midair for a brief second and then plummeted down into the dark void.

"Nooo!" Sparrow screamed.

Fox closed his eyes and gritted his teeth.

Two more police cars and a river rescue unit arrived on the scene. The narrow road across the top of the dam was closed. The police took pictures, searched Virgil's truck and took statements from Fox and Sparrow. Sparrow threw up behind one of the police cars.

"Why would he jump" the senior deputy asked Fox.

"I don't know," Fox answered. It was the truth, he assured himself. He knew what brought Virgil to the dam, but he didn't understand why he jumped. Plus, he didn't think it was the business of La Paz County. This was between Virgil and the dam. Fox was weary, almost sick, but he wasn't about to throw up as Sparrow had. He wanted to be alone. Away from the dam. He wanted to be on his bailer. He wanted to be in the fields. He wanted to be anywhere else other than where he was. Maybe that was what Virgil wanted. Fox silently cursed himself for mentioning the dam. He had to know. He had to question. It was difficult to grasp Virgil was gone. He knew that would change. The memory of his pain was still fresh, waiting like glowing embers. Fox was glad Virgil enjoyed being the chairman.

The cops huddled and smoked cigarettes and drank coffee from thermoses. The night air was getting cooler. Sparrow was no longer talking. He stood trembling, hands buried in his pockets near where Virgil had jumped, staring down into the noise and the night. Fox was irritated the cops wouldn't move their cars. He wanted the fuck out of there. He marched toward the knot of uniforms. They were going to move a car, Goddamnit. "County base to Sam sixty-two," a police radio called as Fox reached the men.

A deputy keyed the portable radio on his leather gun belt. "This is Sam sixty-two, go."

154

"Sam sixty-two, nine-one-one call from Dam view reports a large, naked Native American has crawled from the river into a back yard at space fourteen. Claims his name is Virgil. Can you investigate?"

"The crazy son-of-a-bitch is alive," Fox shouted with joy.

11 HUNGER AND GREATNESS

"Hear me, four quarters of the world—a relative I am!

Give me the strength to walk the soft earth.
Give me the eyes to see and the strength to
understand, that I may be like you.
With your power only can I face the winds."
Black Elk—Ogalala Sioux holy man

Virgil was bruised and battered. The leap from the dam had popped a vessel in his left eye and broke two toes on his right foot. The white of his eye, flooded with blood, added to his wild look. He was hunched under a canvas boat cover a wary homeowner had given him to mask his nakedness. "I asked where he came from," the balding sixty-year-old in a bathrobe and shower shoes said as he led the deputies, along with Fox and Sparrow, into the back yard of his mobile home. The noise and flashlights had the dogs in the trailer park barking. "Said he jumped off the dam!"

Three flashlight beams found Virgil as they converged on the figure squatting on the grassy river-bank. He was trembling and his teeth were chattering. He looked like a bewildered animal caught in the head-lamps of a car, Fox thought. Staring into the glare of the flashlights, Virgil forced a toothy grin. "The dam didn't kill me."

"You're under arrest," one of the La Paz County Deputies said, jerking Virgil to his feet. The boat cover fell away. Virgil was wearing a single, soiled, once white cotton sock.

"You lost one of your socks," Sparrow said to the naked Virgil. There were tears in his eyes.

The blue boat cover was returned to the homeowner and Virgil was wrapped in a wool blanket from the rescue truck. A paramedic examined his eye with a pen light. "He's all right."

Virgil was pushed into the back of a police car and driven away. He would be booked for trespass and disturbing the peace. By five AM his brother's widow would arrive at the La Paz County Jail in downtown Parker with seven hundred- and fifty-dollars bail. The cash was provided by Tribal Councilman Horace Waters. Indians didn't belong in white jails and the tribe seldom left them there. Calls from the Regional Director of the Bureau of Land Management and the Southern California Water Management Board to the County Attorney would discourage filing of charges. "We don't want to turn this idiot into some folk hero," Walter Adams from BLM argued. "We publicize this with a trial, Parker dam will be lined with drunken Indians."

As quickly as it began, it was over. Fox and Sparrow found themselves standing alone in the dirt street in front of Jack Mellon's mobile home in the Dam view Mobile Home Park. The police cars and rescue trucks were gone. The dogs were calming down. The only sound was the insects of the night. Fox and Sparrow stood for a moment as if trying to absorb the tranquility, then, after a glance up at the star-strewn sky, Fox said, "Come on, I'll give you a ride home."

Virgil had been the catalyst in the relationship Fox had with Sparrow. Driving south on the river road, Fox realized he had never been alone with the gaunt man before. Sparrow sat on the passenger's side staring into the night. The silence between them wasn't an uncomfortable one. Fox was learning being with someone didn't always require conversation. Afternoons on the front porch of the store in Poston had taught him that.

"Where do you live?" Fox questioned after driving through Parker. The town was quiet. Woody's all-night Shell Station was the only business open.

"First canal past crossroads," Sparrow answered.

Fox found the small dirt road. It was marked by a rusty, dented mailbox atop a leaning post. Huge mud and water-filled potholes made the narrow road a challenge. After nearly a mile of bumps and splashes, a once yellow school bus came into view. Wheels gone; the bleached hulk sat on uneven cement blocks. The windows were covered with faded curtains and a hole cut in the rounded top of the bus was smudged black with soot from a makeshift chimney. A homemade, less than high quality satellite dish, made out of scrap metal, an old gate and some wire sat atop the bus, suspended with ropes and guy wires.

"You built that antenna?" Fox questioned.

"Yeah, get four-hundred and seventy-two channels," Sparrow bragged.

A red pick-up truck, hood propped open with a pole,

windshield broken, sat parked near the school bus. The bed of the truck was heaped with trash. Two hounds came out of the darkness to greet them. They bayed and wagged their tails.

"I'm rebuilding' the engine in the truck," Sparrow said as Fox braked the Explorer to a halt. Sparrow's humble home-made Fox feel very white. He couldn't imagine choosing to live in such a place, but then he reminded himself few people here ran away seeking refuge in Palm Springs. Few people here had alarm systems and dead bolt locks on iron gates. Few people here slept with their windows locked and air conditioners running, and few people here had to find their dead wife hanging in a shower. "Six or eight?" Fox asked deliberately stopping the troubling thoughts, reaching for the precarious hold he had on his own life.

"An eight," Sparrow answered proudly. "Three-fifty-two with a four-barrel." He opened the door and climbed out.

"You want me to pick you up in the morning?"

"Virg will be by," Sparrow said confidently.

"He went to jail, Sparrow," Fox reminded.

"He'll be out by morning. Penny will get his bail."

"But they impounded his truck."

Sparrow petted the two hounds jumping at him. "Jim Speers will release the truck. He doesn't, we won't let him fish the canals."

Fox nodded. He was learning not to question such matters. He was in their world. "See ya at the farm."

Sparrow was off with his dogs toward the door to the school bus. Fox pulled the Explorer in gear.

After the drive to Castle Rock, Fox lay on the verge of sleep thinking about Virgil and the dam. It was more than an Indian with beer in his belly trying a stupid stunt. It was a man facing death. A man realizing, he couldn't live without conquering the fear of his own mortality. A man with nowhere to run but into the abyss. Fox wondered where his dam was. He knew he had to find it. He also knew what he had to do when he did.

True to his credo of bars were for fightin' and fields were for cuttin', Virgil was at the farm at sunrise. There was no talk of the dam. The only testimony to the event was Virgil's bloody eye and slight limp favoring the broken toes squeezed into his narrow western boot.

A chalk message scrawled on the work assignment board pushed thoughts of the dam aside. "Cut ends in two days." The handwriting was Morse Roberts'.

"I was hoping for another week," Virgil complained, spitting tobacco juice in the fine dust. "Need a couple tires."

A smaller message at the bottom of the board concerned Fox. It was terse. "J. Fox—call 4112/6:30" Fox was studying it when Virgil patted him on the shoulder. "Last in, first out," Virgil smiled. "Lil' something we learned from the white man."

"Shit," Fox muttered. The others were climbing into the trucks. He looked to Virgil and Sparrow. "How do I call a four-digit number?"

"All the river bottom is 669," Sparrow answered.

"But the office doesn't open 'till seven," the irritated Fox complained. "Where the hell can I make a call?"

The trucks were pulling away "Weren't you FBI?" Sparrow said sarcastically.

"Weren't you an asshole?" Fox called into the dust the departing truck left behind.

Fox drove to Poston. There was a public telephone at the gas station. He dialed the number. He expected Morse Roberts to answer. Morse would tell him the cut was over. He was being laid off. The voice that answered was that of an older woman. An Indian woman. "Hello."

"This is John Fox. I had a message to call this number."

"One moment, John," the voice was gentle. The woman spoke as if to a friend. Was it the memory of his mother's voice stirring in him? Was it his imagination?

"John," an older male said in his ear. "This is Russell Stoner. Thank you for calling."

Fox straightened his stance. "Good morning, Chief," he said uncertain what to say. He was puzzled. Apprehensive.

"I am going to Buck Point this morning," the Chief said. I'm told the bass like the shallows there. Would you like to come along, John?"

"Ah... Yes, I'd like that."

"I will see you there," the Chief said. He hung up.

Fox asked for directions at the farm machinery repair shop across the road from the store. They were vague. "Buck Point," an oil-stained old mechanic pondered. "Yeah, down the road to Ehrenberg... Maybe eight, ten miles. You'll see two palms on the right... I think that's it."

"You think?"

"Pretty sure."

Fox was filled with doubt, but nine miles down the road two stubby palms appeared in the distance. They stood in knee-deep grass beside the road like a silent testimony to the old man's accuracy. Fox smiled, slowed and turned right at the trees.

The road twisted across the field. Following it, Fox sent a covey of doves into flight from grass lining the narrow-rutted path. Amidst a stand of twisted creosote trees on the bank of the river he spotted the car. It was an old boxy four-door Fiat. The sight of it made Fox smile. There was something amusing about an Indian Chief driving an Italian sedan in the Arizona desert. He parked and found the old man hunched on the muddy bank of the river working a waterdog onto a fishing hook. "So, this is Buck Point," Fox said to let the old man knew he was there, but he already knew.

The old man stood. He was taller than Fox expected. Dressed in a green plaid Pendleton shirt, he examined his work on the hook. Satisfied, he let it swing free, flicked the tarnished rod he held and watched as the water dog and the line arched forty feet out to plop into the placid water. "A hundred years ago, the story goes, a Mojave warrior watched a great buck emerge from the water here on the point," The old man was looking at the river as if he could see the animal. Fox looked too. "The warrior drew back his bow to send an arrow into the prize, but the buck paused and looked at him." The Chief turned his eyes to Fox. "If you kill me, the buck warned the warrior, you kill what is great and if you kill what is great, you are killing yourself."

"What did the warrior do?" Fox questioned.

"He killed the buck," the old man said matter-of-factly breaking away his look. "It is hard to think of great things when you are hungry."

The Chief squatted down and concentrated on the line in the water. Fox hunched down not far from him. "The Mojave people have been hungry for many years," he mused. "It is difficult for them to have great thoughts. Perhaps the white buffalo will quench their hunger."

Fox said nothing.

The old man looked to him again. "I called you here to thank you for giving us hope."

Fox nodded his appreciation. "I did little."

"What you did made it possible," the Chief added. "Life has no minor roles."

"I'm glad I could help," Fox said sincerely.

"Will you be staying here, John Fox?"

"I was working on the farm. The cut is almost finished."

"There will be other work. The casino will soon be under construction. We need security. Money will bring problems."

Fox nodded agreement. "I'm not sure I'm part of this. This was my mother's home. Does that make it mine? The world I know is many miles from here."

The Chief nodded. "But the casino will bring your world here. We need your experience." He pointed at the river. "If I took a bass from this river and put it in a river in another land, would it not still be a bass?"

"It would," Fox agreed.

"And if the bass returned to the river where it was born, would it not belong with the other bass? We are not seeds of the earth, John Fox. We are men. We follow many trails, and who we are," the old man touched his heart, "is not determined by where we are, but by what we are. You are Mojave. You are welcome here... But only you can answer the call of your heart. I heard of your troubles in Palm Springs. You know a pain suffered by few. I have lived many years, but even I must guess at why you are here. I only know I would be pleased if you stayed."

Fox pushed to his feet. The old man's words were touching wounds that were still raw. He was uncomfortable. Thoughts of family and loyalties and responsibilities came and went in a rush. His mother, his wife, his career. It all had once been organized and logical. Now it was splattered like a broken window and the sharp shards were painful and impossible to put back together. "I'll think about it," Fox answered.

"Learn to think with you heart, John Fox," the Chief suggested. "Life has taught me the heart is more trustworthy than the mind."

"Was it your heart that told you to go over the fence at the White House?"

The Chief considered the question carefully before he answered. "Yes...," he nodded. "My mind finds no logic in it."

Fox smiled and turned to go. "Good luck with your fishing."

"And, good luck with yours," the Chief answered.

Fox trekked up the bank to his waiting Explorer.

Hunger was not a problem for attorney Clyde Hanes. Management of a fifty-million-dollar building fund had kept him awake all night. Factor in secret financial links to Las Vegas billionaire Donald DePalma, gambling debts at the Casa Grande and Dennis Milner as a casino developer and Hanes' gastronomical tract had become ground zero.

Following six hours of hotel room channel surfing mixed with a half dozen diet Pepsis, two Snickers bars, a bag of Beer Nuts, three beef sticks, a fudge brownie with walnuts, a cup of blueberry yogurt and a chocolate Wittman's Sampler—all from the suite's honor bar—Hanes was on his knees in the bathroom with one hand braced on the porcelain rim of the toilet bowl. He was forcing a finger down his throat in an effort to relieve the burping, bloating, gassy swelling in his stomach. He gagged and his stomach convulsed as it had been taught to do. It was his third trip to the bathroom since returning from dinner.

Much to Hanes' surprise, Milner had agreed to dinner in celebration of the bid being accepted by the Mojave's. The fact Lana Casner joined them added to the evening's enjoyment. Hanes could see Milner's lust for the busty, attractive forty-year-old. He was certain Lana saw it too. Milner was like a dog around a bitch in heat. Hanes was worried it would eventually evolve into a serious problem with DePalma, but he was powerless to do anything about it. Plus, a result of Milner's less than tactful amorous advances on Lana was her subtle but growing dependence on him for protection.

As they dined at the Anchor Inn on steak and lobster, Lana had inched toward him away from Milner in the curved, cushioned booth until her thigh was touching his. It was like the heat of a warm blanket. Excited, Hanes ate three baked potatoes and an extra chocolate mousse. Lana had to know. Perhaps it was exciting for her too, he fantasized. As soon as he got back to the room he masturbated. In his sexual fantasies he wasn't a fat man.

Pushing from the toilet bowl, Hanes flushed it and washed his face and hands. This wasn't bulimia he assured himself. Bulimia was an addiction of young, obsessive, adolescent females. He was simply a successful middle-aged man controlling a weight problem. He toweled his hands and walked out of the bathroom. Maybe he'd have an orange juice before going down for breakfast. Maybe Lana would want to join him.

Dennis Milner hadn't slept much either, but his restlessness wasn't linked to baked potatoes with butter or even Lana Casner's breasts. Excitement had adrenaline surging through his veins. A mere telephone call had transformed his life. Yesterday he was like a thousand other wannabe contractors. He had business cards, a resume, an office in Saint Paul with an answering service, an expense account. He had everything but a job. That was then.

Now he paced, telephone in hand, yellow notebook in the other as he gave orders. Orders that people listened to. Orders that would change lives. Orders that would transform dust to dreams. Milner was intoxicated with the thought of it. Christ, it was almost as good as sex! He listened to his words as he spoke into the telephone.

They were ripe with power. "I understand you're the Regional Manager of Avis. I'm building a major casino in Parker. I'm gonna need a fleet of cars, Jim. Maybe ten, twelve for at least four months. I want big cars. Some Lincoln's, couple Cadillac's, two, three luxury vans. A good mix. Can you handle that?... Uh-huh, just call First Bank of Minnesota in Saint Cloud. Ask for Dick Snyder. He'll handle the details." Milner hung up, redialed. He paced waiting for an answer. "Dick, it's Dennis. Avis is gonna call you... Okay, good. Dick, I want to transfer a quarter of a million to the Bank of Arizona in Parker. I need access to operating capital. Uh-huh... Get me a Gold card too... And how about cellular. Get me five or six cellular. I can't run around with a fuckin' pocket full of quarters. This morning, Dick. Like quick, okay?" He hung up, glanced at a number and dialed again. He resumed his pacing as he awaited an answer. "Arizona Builders' Supply? This is Dennis Milner. I'm building the White Buffalo in Parker. I need some portable office trailers. I want some nice VIP double-wide, some mid-management types and a half dozen others... And I want 'em today."

Milner, although pumped with delusion of self-worth and importance, was following a carefully detailed fifty-eight-page construction operations agreement between Navco and the Mojave Indian Nation. Twenty-four articles described the announcement of bid assignment to opening day activities. The agreement had been reviewed by the Bureau of Indian Affairs, the Nation Indian Gaming Commission and the Department of

Interior. The principal endorsees had undergone background checks by the FBI

The Mojave Indian Nation was in what Donald DePalma called a National Geographic black hole. They were minor leaguers. "This is gonna be like shootin' buffalo from a fuckin' train," he had laughed sarcastically after the deal was made. DePalma used a brokerage firm in New York to assemble the finances. First, the fifty million was transferred to a trust account in Singapore, then to a venture fund in Brazil, followed by a short-term loan for precious stones in the UK which generated a profit. A cash-out in Sterling was transmitted to an offshore account in the Caymans and then back into a venture capital fund in Chicago where it was converted to a tax-free minority business loan for Navco.

In the eight days it took to complete the transaction, the brokers netted eighteen percent in commissions and profits while Donald DePalma's net worth increased slightly and his corporate tax burden decreased. All in an effort not to build something. "This is a great fuckin' country." DePalma smiled when Mitch Parsons brought him a fax informing him the transaction was complete.

It was early afternoon when the driver from Avis delivered the silver four-door Lincoln Town Car to the Tribal Administration office at Crossroads. "Could you tell me where to find David Rollins?" The man was a Branch Manager from Phoenix. He was dressed in a suit and tie.

The plump, dark-eyed receptionist dialed Rollins' office. "David, you have a visitor."

"Yes?" David was puzzled when he met the man in the lobby.

"Your car, Sir," the driver offered David a set of keys. "Courtesy of Navco. If you have any problems, please give me a call." He pushed a business card into David's hand.

David dared a glance into the parking lot after the man was gone. A group of five Indian men were examining the big Lincoln. Keys in hand, David pushed through the door and headed for the car. The men clustered near the Lincoln all knew David. Two were from accounting, one from tribal housing and the other two from maintenance. Seeing David approaching, they backed away. It surprised him. He had known these men since boyhood. They were friends. Never-the-less, a yet to be recognized aura of power was settling over David. "You want to go cruise downtown?" he teased reaching the driver's door. None of the five answered. They just stared in awe, envy and silence. Several young women from the tribal offices arrived to join the men.

The intoxicating aroma of new leather reached out to greet David as he opened the driver's door. He had never smelled it before. David stared spellbound at the instrument panel and dashboard. The carpet was rich and clean. He reached and carefully touched the leather seat. It was smooth and soft. He eased himself in behind the wheel as if expecting someone to order him out. His eyes were wide with wonder. His hands caressed the steering wheel.

"Start it, David," one of the females urged from thirty feet away.

David slid the key into the ignition. A chime began to sound. He twisted. The engine came to life and idled silently. He ran the power windows up and down, adjusted the air conditioning, turned on the radio, opened the trunk, tried the turn signals and adjusted the seat in eight different positions. His heart was racing with excitement and wonder. He pictured himself pulling up to the Manygoats' house. Dena came out the door. She was awed to find him behind the wheel of the big car that cost more than the house they lived in. David moved a leg to the accelerator to race the engine and his stiff knee reminded him of the price of the car. He quickly turned off the ignition and climbed out.

"Aren't you going to drive it?" a voice called from the knot of spectators. David tossed the keys through the open driver's window onto the smooth leather seat. He turned and walked with a limp towards the administrative offices. He did not answer the question.

Fox drove north from Buck Point. Passing the turnoff for the tribal farm, he could see distant plumes of dust rising from the field. Virgil, Sparrow and the others were out there driving, sweating, lost in their work. Nothing lasts forever, Fox told himself when regret started to settle over him. He drove on. The fields of the valley, he had found, were much like Bonnie. They were a diversion, not a solution. The agony of his loss, he was learning, would never go away. He was simply learning to live with it.

The work on the farm was over and Fox knew he was facing a decision the old man had put to words. "Will you be staying here, John Fox?"

12 THE WINDS OF CHANGE

"When living things gather in herds.
Confusion and stampedes often follow."
Limping Horse—Pawnee

The Parker Chamber of Commerce had worked for thirty years trying to sell sand and heat. It wasn't an easy task. There were successes, but they never outweighed the failures. What the Parker Chamber of Commerce couldn't do, boat builders in Southern California did. Hordes of Californians equipped with needle-nosed, fiber glassed bullets powered by gas guzzling engines descended on the river town every weekend and holiday. They bought gas and beer, but little else. They left in their wake beer cans, used tires and resentments. The locals, whose wages averaged twenty-eight-thousand-dollars, could only look and dream of ski boats, Sea-Doo's and ninety-mile-an-hour twin hulls. The ski bunnies with their tawny bodies wore bathing suits that cost more than most locals earned weekly. The Californians had money. And they spent it, but seldom in Parker. Parker was the proverbial cheap date. It was fun, it was quick, it was goodbye.

Business in Parker was like mold on bread; it only grew around the edges. Parker wasn't a destination. It was a place to drive through, a pit stop. A place to buy gas on your way to Laughlin or Vegas. A place to repack your ice chest, a place to scrape the bugs off your windshield.

The Indians, on whose land the small town stood, were not a factor. They were invisible to the casual observer. Tribal members could be found bagging at the local market, driving trash trucks, repairing roads, but everyone knew Indians didn't have business savvy. They had no entrepreneurial spirit. No appetite for success.

It went unsaid, but the locals, those who really felt they were the backbone of the town, had been embarrassed by the fiasco at the White House. Indians climbing over the fence at the White House. What the hell did they expect? There were no white faces at Paul Manygoats' funeral. No one really expected them to build a casino. They heard of the hope, the rallies, the meetings. They had heard it all before. If the white buffalo was returning, the Parker Chamber of Commerce was betting it would be the Wal-Mart they were lobbying for.

Walter Boyd from Boyd's Mobile Home Sales was the first to see it. The site was just up 95 from his sales lot. He called Ray French at Auto Liquidators. Heavy equipment, survey crews, trucks carrying building supplies and a fleet of mobile offices had begun arriving at the junction of U.S. 95 and the river road. The site was a natural, a sprawling mesa that stretched from the interstate to the banks of the Colorado River. It was prime, it was choice and it was Indian owned.

The growing crowd of awe-stuck, curious whites watched as a crew erected a sign: "Coming soon—The White Buffalo Casino—Fun, food and gambling. An enterprise of the Mojave Indian Nation".

"Jesus," Jim Hoffman from the auto parts store muttered. "They're gonna build it."

The local branch of the Bank of Arizona on Third Street already knew it. The Branch Manager, Frank Leeper, was giddy. His A.O.D., assets on deposit, in the eleven years he had worked at the bank had never been higher. He had called Havasu requesting additional cash. They didn't have enough. An armored car was being sent from the main branch in Laughlin. Leeper was eager to get home and tell his wife.

The Stardust and the Desert Flower Motel knew too. Two advance men had arrived and booked every room for the next sixty days. Francis Watson, the sixty-year-old owner of the Stardust took the for sale sign off her property.

By nightfall Parker was a town ripe with excitement and anticipation. Few knew what to expect, but they all knew Parker would never be the same.

The economy was kind to casino builder Dennis Milner. Arizona, the alleged miracle in the desert had been on its economic knees. Downsizing, belt tightening and profit taking had wilted the flower in the desert. Phoenix, once a sunny Mecca for the unemployed armies fleeing the northeast, had grown fat with excess and was now as much a troubled place as Los Angeles. Skilled construction workers stood in line for jobs at Burger King and usually didn't get them.

The unemployed programmers from Apple or A T & T had better people skills. Thus, the evening broadcast on local CBS affiliate KPNX announcing the construction start of the White Buffalo, the first major casino in northwest Arizona, was more than just local news. It was hope. Hope for masons, electricians, carpenters, plumbers and more. Pick-ups and vans were gassed, and road atlases were pulled out. Where the hell was Parker? The desert night was soon a train of headlamps pointing northwest toward Parker. The genie was out of the bottle.

In Parker, the Mojave Gaming Enterprise Board was having its first meeting with Navco's CEO, Dennis Milner. They met in the executive construction office, a handsomely appointed double-wide, sixty-foot mobile with a board room and a wet bar. Milner offered champagne after attorney Clyde Hanes made introductions, but when David Rollins and Mara LaSalle declined, George Manygoats reluctantly did the same. Eyeing the chilled bottle sitting in ice, George silently wished he had taken time for a drink before the meeting.

"This is a memorable day for all of us," the buoyant Milner said from the head of the table. He gestured to the wall where detailed blueprints and an artist's rendering of the casino hung. "The White Buffalo is no longer just a dream."

"The White Buffalo is also not a Lincoln Town Car," Mara interjected, pushing her keys across the smooth table towards Milner. Hanes stiffened and straightened in his chair. "Keep in mind, Mr. Milner," Mara's dark eyes warned, "you work for the Gaming Enterprises Board... Unwarranted budget indiscretions will not be permitted."

David Rollins, toying with a ball-point pen, silently breathed a sigh of relief for deciding not to accept the car. He watched as Milner, turning red-faced, bristled with anger. "The fuckin' cars were meant only as a token of good will," he defended.

"The fuckin' cars," Mara answered matching his tone, "were bought with our money. We don't want your good will. We want your good management."

Milner glared at the dark-haired woman. He was regretting admiring her ass and long hair when she walked in. The boots and long dress didn't hide the figure masked beneath them, but he was wary of the woman. Smart women unnerved him, yet she excited him. What her attitude needed was a good fuck. He wondered if there was a man in her life. Milner tried to find a compromise, a way out of the confrontation. He burned a look at Hanes. "Clyde, you arranged for these cars. Goddamnit, make sure they're charged to our operating expenses and not part of the tribes loan repayment."

"Yes, Sir," Hanes answered sheepishly. He made awkward, meaningless notes.

"Now, let's talk about getting a crew together," Milner said, trying to regain his shaken confidence and control.

"All skilled and unskilled construction labor will be given tribal preference," David announced. "Then Indian preference, then all qualified; section three, paragraph A of the agreement." He stabbed at the document in front of him.

"No argument," Milner granted, "but the site bosses, the lead men, have to be experienced and qualified. I don't wanna build a shit-house just to be a job corps for a bunch of Indian wannabes."

"Most wannabe's drive Lincolns," Mara said sarcastically.

George Manygoats shifted nervously in his chair. The keys to the Lincoln Town Car he drove to the meeting suddenly became an uncomfortable lump in his pocket.

Milner ignored the dimples Mara's nipples were making under her white blouse as well as her remark and pushed a stack of resumes toward her. "My selection for the site boss, survey crew, trenchers, iron men, framers, concrete specialists and Chief of Security are in there."

Mara passed the collection on to David without looking at them. It irritated Milner. "We'll review them and let you know by eight AM tomorrow."

"Tomorrow?!?" Milner protested, "I wanted to get trenching and footings in tomorrow."

"The contract gives us twenty-four to seventy-six hours to consider candidates for key positions, Mr. Milner," Mara cautioned. "Will eight AM tomorrow be all right?"

Milner pointed a finger at Mara; he was no longer trying to mask his anger. "You want the Goddamned casino built on time, you're gonna have to get off your ass."

Mara wasn't shaken. She answered with restraint, choosing her words carefully and matching his challenge without anger. "Get off our ass, Mr. Milner, we take the contract serious. If you fail to meet the one-hundred-twenty-day construction schedule, you will forfeit one half of one percent interest for every day extended. Isn't that correct, Mr. Hanes?"

"Ah, yes... I think it is," Hanes granted awkwardly, wanting nothing to do with the exchange.

"I'll build your Goddamned casino on time," Milner grated through tight jaws.

Mara wasn't finished. "And in respect to the Director of Security, the contract specifically grants the tribe the right to appoint that position."

"Well, have you?" Milner demanded. "I've got a hundred-thousand-dollars' worth of hardware on site and more on the way. I don't want this town without pity carrying everything away."

"I'll ask the Tribal Police to watch it tonight," David said in an attempt to get back into the meeting. "We'll start interviews in the morning."

"I want Hanes sitting in on the interviews," Milner demanded.

"I'm starting at six AM," Mara said with a glance at Hanes.

"Six AM?" Hanes questioned.

"He'll be there," Milner assured.

The meeting continued another ninety minutes. The friction between Milner and Mara also continued. It was controlled, but it was there, waiting, smoldering. As they discussed signature approval on operations accounts, control of petty cash, permit approvals and waste disposal, David wondered what its roots were. What was Mara seeing in this man that he hadn't? Where was the threat? What was the irritation? David concluded it was sexual. Perhaps more chemistry than sex, but still it was the spirit between man and woman. Either it was right or one of the other sensed a threat; an uninvited will to seduce. Physical or not, the spirit didn't care. It was there. Maybe that was it. Mara knew this man wanted to dominate her and she was rejecting him. The conclusion was less than comforting for David. If he was right, Mara felt no threat from him. He needed to be more dominant. Wasn't that one of the classic complaints about Indian men? They were dominated by Indian women. Christ, it was true. He was letting Mara run the meeting. Three men were being pushed around by a pair of tits. Hell, David told himself, he had climbed over a fence at the White House. He sure as hell could climb over Mara. "We've gone far enough tonight," David announced forcefully, propelling the collection of resumes to Mara.

He had little interest in the talk about lighting in the non-public corridors. Mara looked surprised. "Go through these, make your recommendations, pass them on to George," David pushed to his feet to confirm the meeting was over. He looked to Manygoats who had hardly spoken. "George, I'll need them in my office by seven AM."

Milner and Hanes both pushed to their feet as David rounded the table. He offered Milner a hand. "I think it's important we maintain momentum," he said with a firm shake. He was using a phrase he'd heard the President use on CNN. He wasn't sure what it meant, and he didn't really care. "I'll give you a call in the morning as soon as I get through the resumes."

"I appreciate that," Milner said with sincerity.

David shook Hanes' hand but gave Milner a look. "Dennis, these Lincolns... I think it's important we do not lose sight of your intent. What if we gave one to the Tribal Council for general use, another to Tribal Admin. and the third we reserve for casino use. We're gonna have a lot of VIPs making courtesy calls. I think it's time we give up our pick-up truck mentality." He moved his look to Mara, "Don't you agree, Mara?"

Mara seemed at a loss for words, but hesitantly offered, "Yes, I...."

"Thank you," David quipped, cutting her short. He moved for the door.

The phenomenon began shortly after midnight. Parker, like most small towns, was asleep. Only the usual nocturnal players were on the stage. Two Tribal Police Officers, the dispatcher and station Sergeant at the La Paz County Sheriff's Office, Penny Collins, the cashier at Woody's twenty-four-hour Shell and Mini-mart, a nameless, long-haired trash roach pushing a shopping cart full of aluminum cans and Lamont Palmer, the town drunk. They watched in awe as a seemingly endless string of vans, cars and campers mixed with backhoes, pile-driving machines, flatbeds loaded with long steel beams, motor homes and eighteen-wheelers converged on the casino building site north of downtown. Seeing the growing crush of traffic, Penny Collins checked her calendar. She was convinced it was some sort of holiday. In a sense, it was.

The Tribal Police turned a nearby sunbaked, dusty field into a parking lot for job seekers. It was soon lined with pick-ups with camper shells—many without—as well as station wagons, vans, cars and motorhomes. Bonfires were built. Ice chests were pulled out and the blue-collar crowd gathered like moths around the flames. Stories of hardship and hope were exchanged as several hundred yards away the hardware of their collective dreams was off-loaded under the glare of truck headlamps. The White Buffalo was stirring fine dust and diesel noise into the desert night.

They began lining up an hour before sunrise and when it was full light, four-hundred and sixty-three men and women stood in the warm, shade-less sand outside the construction trailer with a personnel placard on its window. The line of hopefuls snaked in a lazy S away from the steel steps to the office. At the head of the line was Terri Nelson, a twenty-three-year-old single mother of two from Yuma. She was employed as a desk clerk at Comfort Inn where she earned two-hundred and eighty dollars a week. She would apply as a plumber's helper. Her ex-husband was a plumber. He earned twenty-two dollars-an-hour and refused to pay child support. Four-hundred and sixty-one souls behind Terri Nelson stood sixty-seven-year-old Jose Pineda, an illegal Mexican alien who had been in Arizona for seven years. Jose was a skilled carpenter. With a seventy-five-dollar counterfeit driver's license and social security card in his wallet, Jose had until recently worked a housing tract in Phoenix. Most of his employees knew he was an illegal, thus, all of his withholdings went into their pockets.

"Jesus Christ!" Dennis Milner exclaimed as the construction site came into view. He was behind the wheel of one of the rented Lincolns. Attorney Clyde Hanes was at his side. Milner, fearing Hanes wouldn't arrive at six AM for interviews as Mara Waters had dictated, chose to drive the man. The sight of the waiting string of applicants, the sea of parked cars, the collection of construction equipment, all fueled Milner's excitement. "Can you fuckin' believe this?"

Clyde was staring at the array of activity, but he didn't share Milner's excitement. It frightened him. He felt a growing nausea deep in the pit of his bulging stomach. "This is getting out of hand," he warned.

"Out of hand?" Milner challenged. "This is fuckin' exciting." He wheeled the big car in near the main office trailer enjoying the curious looks from the line of applicants.

"What's going to happen when all this stops?" Hanes' voice was edged with anxiety. "Look at them."

Milner pushed the selector into park. He looked first to the crowd through the tinted side window, then to Hanes while considering an answer. "Who gives a fuck? Enjoy today. They are."

After seeing the crowd of applicants, Mara telephoned David Rollins and George Manygoats. She needed help. David was already dressed. He'd be there in fifteen minutes. George Manygoats, having arrived home drunk the night before and unable to sustain an erection, was now reinforcing his faltering male ego by remounting his wife. He was saved by the bell. "I have to go," he said to his young white wife. He was secretly relieved.

"Asshole!" the girl snarled as George stepped into his pants. "My girlfriend's right, Indians ain't worth a fuck."

The three of them passed out applications to the waiting throng. Mara suggested a two-stage screening process. David and George, working at a card table set up outside the trailer, would conduct an initial interview. Those endorsed for hiring would be sent onto Mara and Clyde Hanes inside for a second interview and a decision. It was to be a bitter-sweet experience. The reality was hundreds of idle, unemployed men and women were about to get badly needed jobs. On the other side of the coin was the sobering realization that many would likewise be turned away. It was to be a first for David Rollins and George Manygoats. Neither man had ever had a white face ask anything of them. Now, some literally begged shamelessly baring their souls. The white world, David was learning, wasn't the silver lined trouble-free paradise he imagined. "I haven't worked in sixteen months... I had to borrow gas money to get here... I got six kids... I don't get this job; I'll lose my home... My wife's in the hospital... My mother has cancer... I'll work for anything... I can do anything."

The whites pleaded. The Indians did not. The tribal members among the waiting stepped one by one to the table and presented their applications. Indians did not complain. Perhaps it was because hardship, unemployment and disappointment were a way of life. Those who were turned away as drunkards, slackers or trouble-makers went quietly. Indians had long ago learned to expect nothing.

Dennis Milner came by occasionally—usually talking on his cellular telephone; once to introduce the site boss who was a broad-shouldered, muscular black man by the name of Amos Moses and once to compliment the two men on how well the job line was moving. He patted each on the shoulder. "Good work, fellas." David knew Milner was basking in his role. He was annoyed when Milner went into the trailer behind him.

David's thoughts were still on Milner when the next applicant stepped to the card table and laid an application in front of him. David scanned the boxes on the form. He had processed a hundred or so. The faces and names were all beginning to blur. His eyes went to the box indicating tribal preference. It was checked. He looked to the name. Fox, John Douglas. It wasn't a name David recognized. His eyes lifted to the man standing in front of him. He looked Caucasian although his eyes and hair were dark. He was dressed in an open collar pullover shirt and pleated slacks and there was a gold and silver Seiko watch on his left wrist. "You checked tribal preference. That means Mojave." David had concluded the man was from another tribe.

"My mother was Mojave," Fox answered. "Clair Scott."

David made the connection immediately. He straightened in his chair feeling a bit foolish for not recognizing the name. He knew Fox was in the valley, knew he was working on the farm, knew he had spoken to the President on behalf of the tribe and knew his wife had killed herself in Palm Springs. David hid his embarrassment by scanning the application. "Do you have any experience?" Now David felt completely stupid. He knew Fox was an FBI agent. He did not look up.

"Some," Fox answered. The question hadn't seemed to annoy him.

David scrawled a note on the side of the application. "Take this inside," he pushed the paper to Fox and allowed his eyes to find him. "Good luck, John Fox."

"Thank you," Fox answered.

Fox recognized the woman immediately. He couldn't remember her name. Perhaps he had never heard it, but he did know she was a member of the tribal council and that she had been elected to the Gaming Enterprise Board. He did not know the heavy man with jowls beside her. He did not look tribal, Fox decided. The woman was more attractive than he remembered. Perhaps it was because he was closer now. Her black hair was pulled back into a long tail that disappeared between her shoulders. It framed dark, penetrating eyes and smooth tan skin. Her nose was slim and arrow-shaped above full lips. She was dressed in a man's starched white shirt. The cuffs were rolled up. "Application?" Mara said, extending a hand when Fox hesitated.

Fox offered the papers. Dark polished nails pulled them away. He watched as her eyes swept over the page. "Sit down, Mr. Fox." The man beside her was doodling on a yellow tablet. Fox sat down.

Mara read both sides of the application and placed it in front of her before allowing her eyes to find his. "I am Mara Waters, Mr. Fox. Until we hire a human resources director, personnel decisions are our responsibility. Mr. Hanes is assisting me."

"Thank you for the opportunity to interview," Fox answered, matching Mara's professional tone.

"I'll be blunt, Mr. Fox," Mara said holding his look. "The tribe is embarking on an endeavor that could result in substantial financial reward for legitimate members. Is that what's motivating your newfound interest in Indian affairs?"

"No," Fox answered without hesitation.

Mara quickly added another question. "You indicated on your application you worked for the Federal Government."

"That's correct."

"In what capacity?"

"Law enforcement." He was now being deliberately evasive. Her question annoyed him. He no longer cared about the job. She may be an attractive woman, but she had ice water in her veins.

"The FBI?" Mara pressed.

Hanes quit doodling and straightened in his chair to look at Fox.

"Yes, the FBI," Fox answered flatly.

"And you've decided to give up a career with the FBI to become a security officer in the White Buffalo casino?"

"I left the FBI before hearing of the White Buffalo Casino," Fox defended.

Mara challenged him. "Aren't you the John Fox that met with Chief Stoner and the President in Washington?"

Hanes eyes went from Mara to Fox as if he were watching a tennis match. The revelation had his full attention.

"Yes," Fox agreed,

"And your appearance here is simply coincidental?" Mara countered.

"I don't believe in coincidence," Fox answered candidly.

"If you were Director of Security for the Casino, Mr. Fox, how would we know you weren't reporting wrongdoing to the FBI?"

"I wouldn't allow wrongdoing," Fox replied.

"Are you a white man or an Indian, Mr. Fox?" Mara questioned leaning back in her chair.

"I'm an applicant," Fox answered. "My qualifications and experience, should have greater relevance."

"It is my responsibility to the tribe to hire an individual who has a vested interest. An individual who will be here more than six months," Mara pronounced.

"Do you have a degree?" Fox questioned. Her demeanor and vocabulary told him the question was safe.

"Yes," Mara's pride answered.

"Then why am I a greater risk than you? You left the reservation and returned."

"My family roots are here," Mara answered.

"So are mine," Fox said. "My mother lies in the tribal cemetery."

"You'll be notified of our decision," Mara announced picking up his application. She avoided a look at him.

Fox pushed out of his chair. "Thank you for your consideration. I enjoyed talking with you." It was a lie. He knew it, she knew it, but he was proud of the sincere tone. He turned and moved for the door.

When the door closed, Hanes looked to Mara. She was making notes on the application. " He's the one that met with the President of the United States?"

13 ECHOES FROM THE PAST

"*From Wakan-Tanka, the Great Mystery, comes all power.*

It is from Wakan-Tanka that the holy man has wisdom and

the power to heal. Man knows that all healing plants

are given by Wakan-Tanka; therefore, they are holy.

So too is the buffalo holy, because it is the gift of Wakan-Tanka."

Flat-Iron—Ogallala Sioux Chief

Fox drove to Castle Rock after the interview. The encounter with Mara had been unsettling. It seemed not every Mojave saw him as "the prodigal". Mara's suggestion he was an opportunist was particularly offensive. Weren't the callousness and blisters on his hands evidence of his willingness to work? Fox wished he had shown them. She hadn't even acknowledged his work on the farm. Mara was a female Russell Means. Anti-Federal Government, anti-FBI, anti-John Fox. She was blind with bias and anger. It was the curse of Indians with education, Fox decided. Their enlarged egos deluded them into becoming self-appointed spokespersons for poor and downtrodden Indians who obviously needed the benefit of their leadership. Real Indians called them "bird shit". Birds relieved themselves on the wing and their waste fell to earth with a splat. Thought of the insult was comforting to Fox. He was confident he stood shoulder to shoulder with working Indians like Virgil and Sparrow. The aristocrats in the tribe could go to hell. Maybe, Fox thought with a smile, what he saw in Mara was the equivalent of a Jewish/Indian Princess.

The gulf between Chief Stoner—who had recommended he apply—and Mara puzzled Fox. His decision to stay was rooted in the bond he felt with the Indian men he had met and grown fond of. Virgil's noisy bravado was anchored in real courage and he was a brave in the truest sense. Sparrow's timidity was contrasted with an inbred kinship with the fields. He could read crops, soil and wind as readily as most men read a morning paper. And Chief Stoner's quiet wisdom and gentle spirit epitomized masculinity.

Perhaps that was it, Fox thought. His link to Indian men. Perhaps the clashes were true. Indian women wanted to dominate. Perhaps they were driven to it and once in a position of authority, as Mara was, they had no choice. Fox liked the thought. It allowed his ego an escape from Mara's rejection, but memory of his mother made him reject the idea.

Clair Scott had been a gentle woman as well as a gentle spirit. She didn't submit to James Fox because she had to, she submitted because she loved him. Fox wondered if the abandonment killed her. James Fox claimed she died of diabetes. Fox suspected in was a broken heart. "Jesus," he muttered as the thought swept over him. He had abandoned Pam much like his father had abandoned his mother. Both he and his father loved their jobs more than their wives, and the wives of both men knew it.

The blend of anger, emotion and logic stirring in Fox led him to a conclusion he was ready for. Women were women. Red, white or black, their attitudes were as different as their bra sizes and seldom did it have anything to do with the color of their skin. Perhaps what was more important than the application he put in front of Mara was where she was in her menstrual cycle. The decision on his employment with the White Buffalo Casino may have fallen victim to a cramp in the uterus of the woman interviewing him. That was it, Fox decided. The fact Mara was an Indian didn't really matter. Being a "bitch" cut through all racial considerations to become a basic, common denominator understood by all men.

The thorn in Fox's ego was painful. But ego was among the few intact facets of his being, and to protect it, he was twisting logic to cloak himself in it and to keep the cloak from being pulled away by truth, he would leave. Staying meant he would have to accept the rejection. Leaving would, at least in the cloud of emotion driving his thoughts, demonstrate their mistake. He was the best goddamned candidate they had. Eventually they would realize that, but he sure as hell wasn't going to wait. He'd show these Goddamned Indians. He was beginning to think coming to Parker was a mistake.

Wheeling the dusty and mud-splattered pickup into the Castle Rock parking lot stopped Fox's thoughts. A

187

green four-door Ford sedan sat parked in front of his room. It was FBI. Behind the wheel was Terrence Bell.

Bell, jacket off, tie loose, climbed out of the government car as Fox pulled in. The two men met in front of the pickup. They hugged each other, slapped backs. It was a warm reunion. The two had been partners for nearly two years in the FBI's operation CAT in Palm Springs. Their trust ran deep and had been demonstrated time and time again as they dealt with seasoned harden armed criminals intend on enriching themselves by robbing a bank. When their hug ended, they pumped each other's hands. "Been waiting long?" Fox questioned.

"Couple hours. I took a nap," Bell smiled. "Jesus, look at you," he admired Fox's bronze tan. "You look like a fuckin' Arab."

"Bet you tell all your white friends that," Fox mocked. "Come on in."

Bell followed Fox to the door of the motel room. The glare of the afternoon sun was hot. Bell wiped at his sweaty neck. "Is it always like this?" he questioned.

"Naw," Fox smiled unlocking the door. "Sometimes it's really hot."

Bell's eyes surveyed the humble room as Fox led the way. The wall air conditioner was running. The room was dark. Fox turned a light on and swung the door shut. Lifting a pair of jeans from a chair, he glanced at Bell. "Sit down."

Bell eased himself into the padded, fading chair while glancing at a placard on top of a television set. "HBO and Showtime... Now I know why you're here."

"Remote too," Fox sat down on the edge of the bed. "You want a beer?"

"Got anything non-alcoholic?"

Fox reached bedside to dig in an ice filled Styrofoam cooler. He lifted a can. "Sprite okay?"

"Sure."

"How's business in Palm Springs?" Fox asked passing the can to Bell.

Bell popped the can open. "Been quiet for a few weeks."

Fox didn't want to talk about banks in Palm Springs of America. "How's Robin?" he asked.

"She's fine. Still fighting the daily battle with second graders," Bell took a swallow from his can. Fox waited. He knew where the conversation was going. Bell took it there. "You ready to come back, John?"

"I don't know, Terrence. Maybe."

"The director and the attorney general made a decision," Bell offered. "They reached out to Tom Roberts. Said they found the leak at the bureau. Fired him. Pam's autopsy came back. Cleary a suicide. No cubo, conduct unbecoming an officer on your part.

"Clearly a suicide," Fox offered sarcastically. "Damned nice of them."

"I miss having you with me, John," Bell answered.

Fox studied Bell for a moment. "You ever thought about walking away, Terrence?"

"Yeah."

"I loved what we were doing but look at what it did. I...," Fox couldn't finish. It was too painful.

Bell allowed the quiet for a moment before speaking again. Turning the Sprite can nervously in his hand he said, "Look at this place, John. Think of where you are, what you've left behind."

Fox looked to Bell. Held his look. "It's peaceful here, Terrence. Is it peaceful there?"

"I'm FBI, John," Bell answered. "That's what you are."

Fox nodded. "This isn't about what we are. It's about what we should be."

The exchange was proving awkward for both.

Neither man wanted a confrontation. Sensing Fox was on an emotional edge, Bell decided to end it. He pushed to his feet. "I gotta get back, partner. You need anything?"

"No, thanks. I'm okay."

Fox followed Bell to his unmarked car. Bell took a final look at the nearby, jagged, rock-strewn hills. "Tom, said he'd like to have you back, John. They've been carrying you on an administrative leave. I'd like you back too, Partner?"

"Thanks," Fox answered. He was uncertain how he felt.

Bell climbed in the car. "Take care of yourself, asshole."

"You too, dick face."

Bell cranked the car to life and backed away. The telephone in Fox's room rang. It was an old black instrument with a bell. Fox had never received a call in the room. He was betting it was the manager bitching about tenant parking. He had to find another place to live. Maybe Palm Springs was the answer. Maybe Terrence Bell was right. Maybe it was time to go home. Fox waved to Bell as the car pulled away and then hurried into the room to gather up the receiver. "Hello."

"John Fox?" a female voice questioned.

Fox recognized the voice immediately. It was Mara. "Yes," he answered.

"John Fox, you applied for the position of Director of Security at the White Buffalo Casino. We are prepared to offer you employment at a salary of seventy-seven-thousand-dollars plus benefits if you're available to start immediately."

Fox's pulse was racing. The salary wasn't a concern. "What do you mean, immediately?"

"Tonight," Mara answered.

"The terms are acceptable," Fox said, restraining his excitement.

"The Gaming Enterprise Board would like to meet with you at seven o'clock at the job site. Is that convenient?"

"I'll be there."

"Thank you," Mara hung up.

"Yes, fucking yes!" Fox shouted slamming down the receiver. Thoughts of Palm Springs, the FBI and a life that was becoming more a memory than reality were quickly washed away with the excitement.

Fox was backing the pickup out when Ethel Martin emerged from the motel office. Her orange hair was rolled in tight curlers and she was wearing a tent-like flowered muumuu. "Need next weeks," she shook a finger as Fox rolled by. He nodded. The excitement surging through his veins wasn't about to be contained in a small room at Castle Rock Resort. Fox knew he needed a better place to live. People stayed in motels, people played in motels, but nobody lived in a motel. He applied as much logic to finding a permanent residence as he did in finding Castle Rock. He drove the river road looking for vacancy signs.

Fate was in a charitable mood. A "Furnished trailer For Rent" sign lured Fox into Branson's River Resort. River resort seemed to be a synonym for aging trailer parks with faded, oxidized coaches, abandoned boats on trailers with flat tires, sunbaked grass and weeds. Branson's was no exception, but the park was quiet and on a stretch of the river that was wide and deep. Fox found the coach with a for rent sign in a window. It was a forty-eight-foot single-wide with a covered, raised porch and swamp cooler. The trailer's aluminum skin was tarnished, but to Fox it looked perfect. He drove to the park office. "The coach down the street. The one..."

The gray-haired, once attractive woman behind the counter cut him short. "Four-twenty-five a month plus a fifty-dollar deposit for cleaning and butane."

"I'll take it."

"You got a dog?"

"Not yet."

"You smoke?"

"No."

"You party?"

"Only on my birthday."

"Where do you work?"

"The new casino. I'm the Director of Security," Fox said it with a sense of pride.

"You gonna have Bingo?" the gray hair questioned.

Fox filled out the single page rent application. He was amazed at how simple it was. No references. No credit history.

"When do you wanna move in?" the woman asked.

"Tomorrow."

"I'll turn the water and the swamp cooler on," the woman said, accepting his cash. He had spent little of his wages from the farm. "It's gonna be hot. You need anything, you come see me. Ask for Jeannie." Bony fingers pushed keys to him.

Fox was surprised when he arrived at the casino site. Earlier in the day the site was little more than a cluster of office trailers, a line of applicants and a survey party driving stakes in the dusty earth. Now the stakes and strings had yielded to sharp, deep trenches lined with wooden forms, black plastic pipe forming intricate plumbing networks and temporary poles carrying thick, black wires. The site teemed with an army of laborers. A pile driving machine shook the earth as a huge hydraulic cylinder hammered an iron beam into the ground.

Brown syrup spewed from the nozzle of a cement

pump as its long crane-supported arm reached out into the middle of the rectangle that formed the expansive floor of the building. Fifteen men in high rubber boots waded in the wet cement looking like fishermen in mud. They worked with broad, flat shovels, hoes, bull floats and sweat. Fox, like others, stared in awe as the mounding puddle of cement deposited by the powerful pump transformed dirt into form-filled, slick, wet, jelled slabs.

A catering truck promising cold drinks and hot sandwiches was parked nearby. It served a steady stream of sweaty workers and excited spectators. The excitement of the activity was contagious, and Fox had it.

It was early evening and interior lights in the office trailers told Fox he wasn't the first to arrive. He was crossing toward the personnel trailer when a familiar voice cut through the construction noises. "Hey, Sprite Man!"

Fox turned, looked. Sixty feet away Virgil Tanner stood in wet cement that reached halfway up his knees. He wore a splattered tank top and a ball cap. Virgil labored through the thick, sucking soup to the edge of a plank frame. Fox walked to meet him. "Virgil, what the hell are you doing in there?"

Virgil leaned on his shovel and scratched his head with a muddy glove. "Is that a trick question? On the farm I earned sixteen bucks an hour. Here I earn nineteen."

"What do you know about cement?" Fox questioned.

Virgil glanced down at the gray, lumpy mire engulfing his rubber boots. "I've been wadin' in shit most my life. What're ya doin' here, Sprite man?"

"Like you, wading in shit," Fox smiled.

"It's open," David Rollins called in response to Fox's knock on the door of the office trailer. David sat at a conference table with Mara, George Manygoats, Dennis Milner and Clyde Hanes. Before them was a blueprint, an array of paper plates, cups and a collection of work orders scrawled with marginal notes. Milner was talking. Fox's arrival drew little more than a glance. Milner pointed a pen at the blueprint. "This is a bearing wall. The columns have already been pile driven in. Even with the floor curing we can proceed with the tilt-up walls. Welders should have the interior superstructure ready in four to six days."

Fox waited inside the door not wanting to interrupt. When Milner paused, David pushed from his chair and stood up. "This is John Fox, our Director of Security."

Fox stepped forward. Milner reached out a hand. Fox reached across the table and took it. "Dennis Milner... I hear you like talking to Presidents."

It was a subtle challenge and Fox understood that. He matched Milner's firm grip and penetrating look. "It's what I had to do at the time."

"And now you're working with us," Milner continued positioning himself as a superior. "You have any problems, you let me know."

Clyde Hanes reached out his hand. "Clyde Hanes. Attorney for Navco." Hanes' hand was damp with sweat.

"George Manygoats."

Fox remembered who the gaunt man was. He had a perpetual sad look about him. "Nice to meet you, George."

"Miss Waters," Fox said acknowledging Mara. She did not stand or offer a hand. Her look was sober, but not hostile. She was a difficult read. Fox wondered if she had been forced into hiring him. Even if she had, he was determined to prove he was the right choice. It was important to him to please this woman, although he didn't understand why.

"Mara," the dark eyes corrected.

"John," Fox suggested in return.

Milner gathered the blueprint. "Come on, Clyde. Let's allow the Mojave Social Club to get on with its meeting." Fox looked to Milner. He decided he didn't like the man. There was a shallow, counterfeit, phony, smart-ass dimension to him that Fox knew well. It was an inherent trait of a con man. He saw what Milner was. Studying him, thinking about Milner's remarks, told him Milner knew what he was too. Very quickly lines had been drawn.

David Rollins softened the moment by offering a hand to Fox. "David Rollins."

"Hello David." They shook hands.

Milner and Hanes moved to the door. "Keep an eye on my trailer, John," Milner said further reducing Fox to a security officer.

Fox chose not to challenge the remark. When the two men were out the door, Mara spoke. "Sit down." When Fox had, she glanced at George Manygoats. "Get him the security applicants."

George gathered a stack of forms from atop a file cabinet and set them in front of Fox. The applications, like everything in the mobile, were crisp, clean and new. The room smelled of carpet glue, fresh paint and Mara's subtle perfume. Giorgio, Fox guessed.

"There's one hundred and thirteen security applicants," David said. "Retired cops, fired cops, wannabe cops, shouldn't be cops."

Fox ran a thumb down the edge of the stack. "How many do I get?"

"How many do you need?" David countered.

George Manygoats lit a cigarette with a butane

lighter and exhaled smoke toward the overhead florescent light. Mara gave him an annoyed look. "Do you have to smoke?"

"I run a smoke shop," George defended as if his habit were required.

"Open construction site. Lots of material around," Fox said in answer to David's question. "Office trailers with computers, parking control... initially, six men per shift, twenty-four-hour operation," Fox did the calculating silently. "Plus, an admin assist. At least eighteen men during construction."

"Are you excluding women?" Mara questioned. It was close to an accusation.

"No," Fox defended.

"Do you understand tribal preference?" Mara explained.

Fox studied her face. "If I have two equally qualified applicants, one tribal, one non-tribal, preference dictates I hire tribal."

"The key phrase is qualified," Mara cautioned. "There are many who oppose Indian casinos. If the White Buffalo earns a million dollars, someone else loses a million. I'm sure your experience with the FBI has taught you those who run Las Vegas and Atlantic City do not take losing a million dollars lightly. Our market survey predicts, done right, the White Buffalo will gross between forty to fifty million dollars a year." Fox was impressed, not only with the dollar value of the operation, but by Mara's grasp of how brutal gaming was. "If we see this, they do too. Blood has already been spilled. We don't want any more."

Fox was relieved. Mara understood security went far beyond protecting spools of coaxial cable and tools on a job site. She was talking about meeting the subtle threat from what Mara had kindly called those who ran Las

Vegas and Atlantic City. She was talking about a multi-dollar business birthed in greed and corruption; a business once nurtured, groomed and run for decades by organized crime. A business that thrived where no other business could, in the middle of a hostile, unforgiving desert. A desert that bloomed with neon, flashing lights, bulging silicon-filled breasts and the illusion of easy money. It was not a business of survival of the fittest. It was survival of the toughest. Crime families had been pushed aside by multi-national corporations. Smoke filled poker rooms yielded to family theme parks. Enforcers with muscle gave way to asset liens and TRW reports, but the motive remained the same, money, lots of it.

"I'm going to need help," Fox said trying to assess the complex challenge.

"Hire the men you need," David said with a glance at Mara. Fox could read something between them. David, he concluded, was going to be an ally. Mara's role seemed more forced. She said all the right things, but her words were sharp edged like broken glass. She had a wall. Fox wasn't sure if it was to keep others out or Mara in.

"Tribal is preferred," Mara cautioned, "but qualified is mandatory."

"Will you allow security be armed?" Fox questioned.

"We want real security," Mara answered, "not fat retirees with beer guts and empty belts... Do you own a gun?"

"No," Fox said. His service automatic hidden in the back of a closet in Palm Springs. He didn't want it back. Nor did he want the small automatic kept in the house for Pam. They were icons from a past life.

"Tell me what type of guns you need," David suggested. "I'll get a purchase order written up."

"What about permits?" Fox thought aloud.

"You're not in Arizona or California," Mara answered. "You are on the Mojave Federal Indian Reservation. By treaty we are a sovereign nation. Finger Mountain is our northern boundary. Blythe is the southern. That's an area roughly the size of New Jersey. Here we make the law. We operate our own government. We elect our own officials. We have our own courts, police and schools. We did not worry about Miranda Rights, Constitutional searches or drive-by shootings."

"I guess that means no," Fox smiled.

Mara didn't return his smile.

"We will need a policy and operations manual. Can you create one?" David asked.

Fox gathered a notebook and pen that lay on the table. He opened it, made notes, "Yes, thirty to forty-five days. Can you give me access to a computer? I'll need two desktops and three laptops. I'll also need the password to what I assume is your tribal net. For security, I'll set up a separate net for Navco construction. We don't want them on ours. I'll also need the combination to any and all tribal safes as well as the location, amounts, and name of all the tribes accounts. I'll get a locksmith on property tomorrow. As we rekey, you'll sign for a new key. I'll also need the telephone number for all your cells. Let's initiate a log for all visitors to this office and I'll need a list of all your employees and their assignments."

"We'll have this to you tomorrow," Mara suggested curtly.

"We also need to get a fence up, control access. Some lookie-loo gets his foot smashed; we're going to be paying out our first jackpot. I'll try to get ID cards and parking passes ready in a couple days." He was thinking aloud.

"ID cards?" George Manygoats questioned.

"We've already got a hundred employees. Within a few days we'll have two hundred. Next week three. By opening day, five hundred. You gonna remember them all?"

"No," George agreed.

"What about background checks?" Fox questioned with a look to the three. "I know National Indian Gaming requires them."

Mara, David and George exchanged a look. It was obvious to Fox that he was getting into an area where they had no experience.

Fox led them. "There are a number of data bases that provide service. All I need is the computer and a modem." He added to his notes.

"What do these data bases show?" Mara questioned. She tried to mask the apprehension in her voice. It was subtle, but Fox recognized it.

Fox looked to Mara. "From the moment of our birth to the moment of death we create records, a paper trail. Some public, some private. Birth certificates, school diplomas, marriage licenses, social security withholdings, tax records, credit applications, real estate transactions, medical records, driver's licenses, automobile licenses, court appearances, gun permits, passports and more."

"And you will look at these records?" Mara pressed.

Fox nodded. "It's important we know who we're hiring and who we're doing business with."

"Will we be included in this background stuff?" George asked.

"The regulations from National Indian Gaming dictate who's included," Fox answered, "but as I recall, it's required of everyone involved in a gaming operation."

"Then you would be included," Mara suggested.

Fox looked to her. "And as you would," he answered.

"We think it important to be informed," David said after an awkward moment between Fox and Mara. "We will meet once a week. You will report directly to us. You will not be an employee of the casino."

"It is important you are not under the authority of the construction company or the casino manager," Mara added. "We have given you significant power and trust."

"And I thank you," Fox answered.

Mara looked to the others. "He has much to do."

David took the initiative away from her. "I agree," he said pushing to his feet. George followed the lead. He was eager for a drink.

Mara studied Fox for a moment. "You drive the pickup you bought from Howard?

"Yes."

"Get a new four-wheel drive SUV. No, get two of them. One for yourself and the other for your team." She pushed out of her chair and moved for the door. "We will pay for them," she assured. "She stepped out the door. George nodded to the two men and followed her.

David hesitated for a moment at the door. "Good night, John Fox."

"Good night, David."

David stiff-legged himself out the door and down the metal steps before the door swung shut.

14 FOX'S ARMY

"Everything on the earth has a purpose, every disease an herb to cure it, and every person a mission. This is the Indian theory of existence."

Mourning Dove—Salish

The Colorado River, forming the serpentine western boundary of Arizona, forged change. The water with its relentless surge had carved the deep chasm of the Grand Canyon. Water cut through rock. It also cut through lives. A reporter from the Arizona Republic in Phoenix had spent the weekend in Parker water skiing. She was looking for refuge from traffic, smog, noise and the blight of contemporary urban life. Parker, small and quiet, had offered a convenient retreat for years, but as the rocks in the river's path changed, so had Parker.

Motels with no vacancy, gas stations with empty tanks, supermarkets with empty shelves, convenience stores without beer and restaurants with lines shocked the weekenders. Their worst fears had been realized. Their hidden paradise had been discovered, not only discovered, but overrun with blue-collared, hard-hats with attitudes and dirty pick-ups. Men who ogled and cat-called the ski bunnies. Men who hadn't come to ski, but to work. The White Buffalo not only returned, it brought change with it.

The annoyed reporter set the chain of events in motion. Her pen became a sword in the literal sense. A sword that would draw blood. A burly construction worker at Burger King suggested the reporter had a nice ass. The remark became a three-column article entitled "Paradise Lost". The text decried Parker's loss of innocence. The reporter, earning fifty-nine-thousand-dollars a year plus expenses, did not consider, nor care, about the positive economic impact the casino's construction was having on a local populous long paralyzed by poverty. Poverty the weekenders found quaint. A quaintness that made them feel superior, secure, dominate. Parker was a refuge where the middle class could gather with their trappings of ski boats, motor homes and spa-toned bodies and, at least for a weekend, feel more than they were. The reporter felt this, but what she wrote about was the pandering of a small town. A small town that lived only in her imagination. A small town with quiet nights, safe streets and neighborhood parks. A small town with friendly faces, old cars and an ageless morality. Parker, at least in the reporter's subconscious, became the husband that would never leave her, like her's had.

An editor, favorably impressed with the prose in the story, sent it out over the AP Network. Two hours later it became the subject of a news director's production meeting at the ABC television affiliate in Phoenix. The station was doing a week-long series on the sagging economy and sky-rocketing unemployment. In Arizona, a story one hundred and fifty miles away was a local story. Especially if it related to jobs. "Dinah," the news director said to a twenty-nine-year-old field reporter, "take your crew and get up to Parker. I think they've got an airport. Get me four minutes for the prime broadcast. I want construction. I want noise. I want faces. Get me some sound bites, where the laborers are from, what this means to their families. See if you can get a time frame... Weeks, dollars, you know the real stuff."

"Do you want some Indian color?" Dinah Carlson asked. She had been in Phoenix three weeks. A recent arrival from an independent in Cleveland, she had never met an Indian.

"Naw," the news director answered. "Indians don't play well on video tape. They're too flat, too introspective. Find some white faces."

It was mid-morning when the television news crew arrived at the casino construction site in Parker. Fox, having spent the night screening applications, surveying the physical layout of the job site and the morning setting appointments for afternoon interviews, was seven miles away asleep in his recently rented mobile home. Dennis Milner would step into the gap.

Diana Carlson, in heels and a short skirt, was welcome among the army of iron workers, plumbers and concrete men. A sound man and a camera man shadowed Dinah as she worked her way around the site. She spoke with a trucker from Yuma who had driven in a load of support beams, a rebar laborer from Phoenix who hadn't worked in three months and a female electrician who wanted to become a poker dealer. It was Amos Moses, the big, powerful black site boss who trekked to the executive trailer to complain about the reporter that brought Milner onto the scene. "You let this pair of tits with a camera around here much longer and someone's gonna get hurt."

"I'll take care of it," Milner said checking his hair in a mirror.

Dinah and her crew were talking to a knot of lookie-loo locals seeking reaction to the idea of a major casino in a small town when Milner reached them. "Hey, who authorized this?" he barked.

The crew deferred the question to Dinah who looked to Milner. She hesitated, studying him, then, "Aren't you Doug Mitchell?" Dinah was new to Arizona, but not the male ego.

"Who's Doug Mitchell?" Milner questioned, deciding how the girl would look naked.

"The anchor on channel twelve," Dinah answered. "You have the same square shoulders, sandy hair, friendly eyes." She used her on air smile.

"People think I'm somebody all the time," Milner said holding his stomach in. "I'm just the guy spending fifty million to build this place."

Dinah signaled her camera man. The sound man moved the boom over Milner's head. "Mister...?"

"Milner. Dennis Milner."

"Mr. Milner, some people are calling the building of the White Buffalo the miracle in the desert. You're betting fifty-million-dollars it is. Why?"

Milner reached for his best Clint Eastwood look as his eyes reached into the distance. "I guess I'm just a dreamer," he mused. "A man who likes making dreams come true."

Fox was back in the mobile office conference room by mid-afternoon. After four hours sleep, he was rested and eager for work. He knew he needed more than enthusiasm. He needed help. A skilled army was outside transforming a significant piece of the desert into a multi-faceted, complex gaming casino. A casino that would employ over six-hundred people. A casino that would offer a wide menu of games. Games he knew nothing about. The challenge sobered Fox. He had to find men who did know. He would manage them, and they would manage the games. He was betting in the literal sense he could do it.

In a sense, Fox was back in the fields. Once again, he had a plow in his hands. A task. A work to lose himself in. A task so demanding, responsibilities so plentiful he would have no time for his own life. Because, in reality, although he wouldn't allow the thought of it, he had no life. His life had stopped. It was as if fate had grabbed his heart and choked the life beat from it. Now the life he had wasn't a personal one. It was tribal. His goal, his purpose, his labor was for the tribe.

Earlier on the edge of sleep, Fox wondered who they were. Who was the tribe? A tribe wasn't singular. It was plural. Tribal members were never alone. Family extended into the tribe. You couldn't lose them all. Chief Stoner was aging and nearing the end of his journey but was following a path worn smooth by a line of men stretching back over hundreds of years. Maybe that was the allure of tribe Fox considered. Maybe after having his life pulled from its roots like a bloody tooth he was seeking something bigger: something that didn't depend on a single individual; something that wouldn't die with a single bullet; something that could throw itself off the face of a dam in the dark of night. Whatever it was, Fox hoped he had found it. Now he was determined to lose himself in it.

Paper, Fox had learned in his FBI training, was more reliable than the spoken word. A man was far more apt to write the truth than speak it. Perhaps it was the simple fact it was easier to speak than write. An FBI psychologist had suggested writing down an untruth, a lie, took two conscious acts; thinking it and writing it, which compounded lying in the conscience of the liar by producing a record of the act. Thus, the written word was usually fifty percent more accurate than the spoken word.

Fox used this knowledge in selecting candidates for hire interviews. He had studied the applications for hours. He knew the paper was more reliable than the candidates who would sit across the table from him. He was an experienced interrogator, but he didn't delude himself into believing he had become, as some cops did, a reliable lie detector. Fox was skilled in reading body language, eye movement, breath rate and speech patterns. Nevertheless, experience had taught him a good liar was difficult, if not impossible, to detect with human perception alone.

The casino proposal developed by Navco called for twelve security officers during casino construction. They would be under the direct supervision of Navco CEO Dennis Milner. The Tribal Gaming Commission, recognizing the inherent conflicts in surrendering security ops to the builder, excluded it and left the number of officers to the discretion of their security director. Reporting to a triad reduced the odds of corruption at the highest level. In casino operations, that was critical.

The first phase of casino construction was the foundation. It had to be done right or all that followed was in jeopardy. Fox knew it was the same in casino security. He was building a foundation. He had to get it right. He was about to set the moral compass for all that followed. He, and the individuals hired for security, would be the moral barometer for the White Buffalo. Mara was right, they had entrusted him with great power. He hoped he wouldn't fuck it up.

Perhaps it was Mara's sarcastic remark about excluding women, but even without it, Fox assured himself he would have interviewed Jill Cox. On paper she was solid. A divorced, single parent and former Dallas Police Officer with three years' experience, Jill, according to her application, was seeking a stable position to provide income and allow her to continue her education. Her handwriting was uniform and concise. Fox decided with a name like Jill she would be a petite, sandy-haired blonde. She was the first interview with an appointment at four PM. A knock sounded on the office door. Fox glanced at his watch. It was exactly four PM. He wrote punctual on the margin of the application. "Come In."

The woman opening the door wasn't blond or petite. She was a buxom, leggy, five-foot-ten-inch brunette with green eyes, an hour-glass figure and an attitude. Dressed in heels, a mini and a sleeveless top, she gave Fox the impression she had just walked off stage. When he didn't speak, the girl did. "John Fox?" she questioned.

Fox stood. "Yes, you must be Jill Cox."

"Uh-huh." She had a firm, near masculine handshake and a sincere smile.

Standing near eye to eye with the woman unnerved Fox. Her perfume engulfed him. Her beauty was a distraction, a liability. It wouldn't be easy to manage, he decided. She would be a problem with employees and customers alike. He would be accused of hiring a bimbo. "Sit down, please."

Jill sat and crossed her long legs. It was modest and ladylike, but damn it was difficult not to stare. "I've studied your application, Jill. Tell me about Dallas PD. You said your resignation was linked to a divorce."

"My husband was a cop too," a toe danced nervously, swinging a high heel. "He met this little cop sucker in Records. Six years of marriage and an eleven-month-old lost to Generation X."

"And that made you resign?" Fox was shocked with her candor.

Jill twisted a gold earring. The move lifted a breast. "Texas is not exactly user friendly for women. The dickhead I worked for put me on graves. You ever try to find day care for an infant between midnight and dawn?"

"I suppose that could be a problem."

"You suppose right."

"And after Dallas PD," Fox glanced at the application in front of him, "you worked at King James as a hostess. Is that a restaurant?"

Jill's green eyes smiled, "Could say it was home of the Big Gulp. It's a topless joint. I danced. Worked days. Made more money and took less shit than I ever did as a cop."

"A topless dancer?"

"Just long enough to show every dick swinging friend of my ex what they weren't going to get... And save enough to move back to Phoenix." Seeing Fox's sober reaction, Jill added, "It's a legal profession you know. What's worse, my ex getting head in Records on-duty, or me playing Born Free?"

"I get your point," Fox agreed.

"Is that a pun," Jill smiled.

"Jill," Fox warned, "Indians by nature are conservative. In a casino the presence of a former topless dancer as a security officer could be criticized."

"You know how many Indians have stuffed wampum down my pants?" Jill defended uncrossing her legs. "Where do you think all those little Indians come from? They're like rabbits. And who's going to know what I was? She placed a hand between her breasts. "You think I tell everyone? I was a street cop for three years, a dancer for one. You won't find anyone who put up with more shit... And, I handled it. You touch me without invitation,

208

and I'll hand you your balls. I can do this job and if you don't hire me it's because you're like the guys I danced for. Love looking', but a little short on nerve."

It was quiet. Fox held the green eyes, considering the consequences. His mind raised warning after warning, so he went with his heart. "Can you type?" Jill smiled and raised her polished nails. "Do birds have feathers? Do fish swim in the sea?

"I take it that's a yes." He returned her smile.

"Windows, Microsoft Word, Word Perfect, Excel," Jill answered. "You think Arizona Electric pays me seven and quarter for nothing?"

Fox rocked forward to rest his elbows on the desk. "Well, to avoid the accusation of being a little short, you're hired."

"When do I start?" Jill was eager. Her face was radiant.

"Tonight," Fox answered. "Next candidate will be here in ten minutes."

A succession of candidates followed. One every twenty-minutes for the next five hours. There was Luis, a rotund Hispanic who had failed a annual physical from Barstow PD, Parsons, a disabled Yuma Fireman with two scar-fused fingers on his left hand, Two Feathers, a recently discharged Marine from the tribe, Adam, an overweight Tribal Police Officer who, at forty, was eager to give up family disputes and bloody automobile accidents, Curtis, a young LAPD cop terminated for excessive force—he had two kids -, Jerkins, a thirty-two-year-old black woman who worked the La Paz County jail, Clark, a karate instructor from Blythe, Stevens, a retired Arizona Highway Patrolman, Peters, a fish and game warden from San Bernardino, Holman, a retired sailor who had worked military criminal investigations and Scott, a tribal member from the farm. He was a young, unqualified high school dropout, but Fox hired him because he had the nerve to apply.

Jake Collins was the final candidate. Fox had seen on the application that Collins was a former Palm Springs patrol officer. At first, he considered eliminating Collins simply because he may know him, or perhaps more importantly, that Collins knew him, but need overrode fear of the past and Fox had called him to set an interview.

Collins was a surprise. He was a thirty-two-year-old with long wild hair, a full beard and an earring. "You don't look like a cop," Fox suggested as the man sat down to face, he and Jill.

"Dope," Collins answered.

"Why did you leave the department in Palm Springs?" Fox questioned, thinking of the irony of his question.

"I told a judge to stuff it where the sun doesn't shine," Collins explained. "Lieutenant told me I had to apologize."

"And?" Fox pressed.

"I told the Lieutenant to stuff it where the sun doesn't shine."

Jill giggled. Collins thanked her with an admiring smile.

"That's called insubordination, isn't it?" Fox suggested.

"That what they said," Collins answered. "I called it principle. I could stay as long as I did what they ordered me to, or I could resign and tell them to stuff it."

"What's going to make you different in Parker?" Fox questioned.

"I was hoping Parker was different," Collins answered.

Fox hired the man. They talked to three others. In spite of the paper screening he had done, they were rejected. Questions about raises, benefits, vacations, sick time, shooting policy, gambling off duty, tribal preference and more made Fox wary. He would rather be undermanned than have a malcontent in the ranks. Those hired, he ordered back the next morning.

Jill stayed to help fill out the paperwork required for each new hire. David Rollins had left detailed instructions, withholding forms, declarations of right-to-work, citizenship statements, personnel action forms, payroll forms and more. They finished near midnight. "I really appreciate your help."

Jill sat massaging a nylon-clad foot. "You think this is going to work? A casino in the middle of MFN?"

"I don't know," Fox answered. "Maybe. Vegas is in the middle of a desert."

"I don't wanna shock you, but this isn't Vegas. There aren't many Indians on the strip."

"What do Indians have to do with it?"

"They're not exactly party animals, are they?" Jill suggested.

"Do you know any Indians?"

"C'mon I grew up in Phoenix," Jill pointed her foot at the ceiling stretching her leg and baring the thigh to near buttock. It was done without inhibition. Fox decided Jill didn't realize how attractive she was. "I know lots of Indians."

"Name one."

Jill dropped her leg and thought about the question. "There was this girl in seventh grade. Wore two pigtails. Becky Townsend. Yeah, Becky Townsend. She was an Indian."

"I didn't ask if you remembered an Indian. I asked if you knew one."

Jill worked at smoothing a wrinkle from the nylon

wrapping her leg. "Okay, so I haven't sleep in a tee-pee. So what?"

"Indians are like topless dancers," Fox said. "You gotta know 'em before you judge 'em."

Jill's green eyes studied Fox. "You an Indian missionary or something?"

"No, I'm an Indian."

"Kiss my ass!"

"Whatever turns you on."

Fox walked Jill to her car. It was a ten-year-old Toyota with bald tires. He saw a suitcase on the back seat. "Where are you staying?"

"I'll find a motel." She unlocked the car door.

"Were you planning to drive to Phoenix tonight?"

"Job comes first," Jill forced a smile.

Fox dug out his wallet, pulled out a credit card. "Charge a room and gas. The Casino reimburses me."

"I can't," Jill balked.

"You want another Indian stuffing wampum down your pants?"

Jill took the credit card. "Thanks."

Fox watched the taillights of the Toyota as it bumped across the rutted, dusty parking lot to U.S. Ninety-five. The lights of Parker were a short half-mile away. The fresh night air was cool and tinged with humidity from the river behind him. Fox was tired, but it was a comfortable weariness. He was pleased with the work accomplished. Not only had he assembled the nucleus of the security team, he had made a friend. Jill was a paradox. She was a bundle of sensual surprises. She was Frederick's of Hollywood with Jimmy Kimmel's wit. She was candid, sexy, provocative and savvy. He wasn't sure if he had been hustled or humbled. Either, Fox decided, was okay.

He liked her. She was satin and lace with balls. He

could sense she would work well in a casino environment. He hoped he could control her. Fox turned to walk back to the mobile office. Mara would be happy. He had hired a female. The thought of the two meeting, the sober Indian princess and the perky topless dancer, made Fox smile even more.

Fox was almost to the mobile when he saw the figure near the middle of the slab of curing cement that would be the casino's first floor. The hard, yet green cement was spiked with capped pipes and sharp metal post anchors. Lit with sparse night lighting, it was hardly a place for a lookie-loo. Stepping over plank framing onto the cement, Fox headed for the man. He wished he had a flashlight. He made a mental note to buy a dozen three-cells. This would be the last night the casino would sleep alone. This was his turf and from now on it would be under armed guard.

As Fox closed on the man, he saw he was frail, elderly. Another desert vagrant looking for brass fittings or wire to convert into a bottle of cheap wine. He was thirty feet away when the man heard his approach and turned. Even in the heavy shadows Fox recognized the hawk-nose and rounded shoulders. "Hello, John Fox," Chief Stoner said.

"Hello Chief... Thought it was you," Fox lied. He couldn't see the old man's eyes.

"I thought I would come see how a buffalo sleeps."

"The buffalo won't sleep at all after tonight," Fox said. "Night lighting comes in tomorrow. Then the plumbers and electricians will work nights, masons and framers during the day."

"I hear you took the job, John," the dark shadow said.

"Took?" Fox chuckled. "It was more got, than took."

"Anyway, you are here and that is good," the old man declared.

"I wish I understood it as well as you," Fox said. The darkness was allowing him a mask to hide behind while asking questions that nagged for answers.

"A leaf cannot pick where it falls," the chief intoned with a look toward the river, "but it does not fall without a purpose."

"Never dreamed I'd work in a casino," Fox confessed.

"Twenty years ago, there were no Indian casinos. Now there are many."

"Is it good?" Fox wanted reassurance.

"Good wears many faces. If you win, it's good. If you lose, it's not."

"If the White Buffalo makes money, you win," Fox speculated.

"We've looked at the world and its wealth and told ourselves if we had money, we would be happy. I've met wealthy men and they are not all happy."

"But you nearly died getting this started," Fox reminded. "If you didn't believe in it..."

"The people think it will work. It gives them hope. It gives them work. It will give them what the white man is born with... a chance. My responsibility is to feed their hunger, not only their bellies, but their spirits and the spirit of our tribe needed a challenge. They were beginning to think of themselves as waiters and gas station attendants. The young people were leaving. This is more than green cement beneath our feet. It is hope."

"Maybe it will become the best Indian casino in the west," Fox suggested trying to be upbeat.

"I hope not," the chief said.

"I don't understand," Fox was puzzled.

"There are no Greek casinos," the chief's silhouette answered. "I've never seen a Mexican casino. In Las Vegas there are many casinos, but none are Jewish or Italian or black or white. They are only good or bad. I want the White Buffalo to be a good casino. I want people to come and go and not even know this is Indian land. I want the best dealers, the best waitresses and the best slots. Business, I have learned, is color blind. The winner wins and the loser loses not because of his color, but because of the rules. We must play this game by the rules."

"What are the rules? Who will tell us? Las Vegas isn't going to send volunteers to help us. There is no book on casino security. I've looked. How do we find the help we need?" Fox's questions were sincere. Thoughts of it had robbed him of sleep earlier in the day.

The chief nodded in the darkness. "It is a difficult question. It brought me here instead of to sleep. I found you. Maybe we'll find others. Good night, John Fox." The rounded shoulders turned and shuffled into the darkness.

Fox watched him go, almost ghost-like, fading into the darkness. The river air was cool on his neck, almost chilling.

15   THE SPARROW FALLS

"A hawk does not know the day it will fall."
Stonehead—Ute

In Las Vegas, Donald DePalma was back on his perch. It was morning and the ritual was in process. Dressed in a silk robe and cushioned slippers, the Don was on his second-floor balcony of his Lakes estate enjoying a cup of Amaretto, the Wall Street Journal and the TV tuned to Good Morning America. It wasn't wealth that gave the Don his leisurely mornings. It was choice. The self-discipline requiring fourteen to fifteen-hour workdays dictated pacing. Start easy, finish hard was the Don's personal credo. Wealth, he had learned, wasn't the gift of fate; it was the fruit of perseverance and hard work.

The Don checked the Dow averages, NASDAQ and a new offering from Seaborn Gaming. Fuckin' Arabs were in a big push to expand casinos on cruise ships. Assholes!

It was fly shit competition, but he knew if they succeeded, the money they made wouldn't be ignored by their ports of call. Soon tie-up gambling would be legalized, then port casinos would follow. Everybody wanted a piece of the action, especially Indians and Arabs. Next the fuckin' Arabs would be dumping money into Indian casinos.

The threats were an irritant, but secretly, he fed on them. They kept him focused, centered on success, driven to maintain his position as top dog. That's what he told himself and others, but in reality, he was a frightened man. A man who lived and traveled with bodyguards and guns. A man who could not shake the fear hammered into a frail fourteen-year-old by a gang of neighborhood toughs who stole his watch, his bicycle, his lunch money and, perhaps most importantly, his pride.

Fear made the Don a dangerous, paranoid opponent and it was about to be fueled. Laying the newspaper aside, he sipped his Amaretto, scratched and adjusted his testicles while thinking of Lana Casner. His wife's suspicions had led to the exile of Lana. He really liked the sultry Lana. It was "style" to have her as an assistant. Hell, people expected him to be with a beautiful woman. Could he make an entrance at the Casa Grande with his three-hundred-pound wife on his arm? If it wasn't for the kids, he'd dump her fat ass.

He turned his attention to an attractive reported on TV. "The emerging theme of the Presidential campaign continues to focus on jobs and the economy," the reporter said as DePalma imagined the comfortable set of Good Morning America as a Las Vegas stage with hot white light and a black background. "With the downsizing of cooperate giants and the shrinking of the defense industry, Americans are finding themselves forced into following opportunity." Maybe, the Don considered, the hook for the act like he imagined could be the girl next door. The reporter had that all-American quality about her.

"Dinah Collins from our affiliate in Phoenix recently visited a remote area of western Arizona. A small town where a miracle in the desert is taking place... Dinah."

The Don made a mental note of the phrase, miracle in the desert. He liked the sound of it. Maybe it could be used with his Gold River development in Laughlin. Gold River, the Miracle in the Desert. It worked, but it would soon be forgotten.

The reporter's image yielded to Dinah Collins standing in front of an active, noisy construction site. An army of sweat glistening men labored in the background. "I'm in Parker, Arizona, Jean," the reporter announced. "It's here the miracle in the desert is taking place. Three hundred construction workers, six hundred permanent jobs, fifty million dollars. What are they building?"

DePalma was stiff with shock. The blood was draining from his face. He knew the answer. His knuckles turned white as they gripped the arms of his chair.

"The White Buffalo," the perky reporter continued. "An Indian casino. A casino with hundreds of slot machines, restaurants, lounges, show rooms and a water park for the kids."

"Jesus Christ.... It's a commercial!" DePalma cried in angry protest.

"I spoke with the builder, Jean," the enthusiastic reporter smiled. "Here's what he had to say."

DePalma stared at the TV screen in shock as the tape of Dennis Milner began to run. "We're building more than a fifty-million-dollar casino," Milner beamed confidently. "We're building a future. A future for thousands of people."

"You back-stabbing sonofabitch," the Don growled, reaching for a cellular telephone.

"How long before the future is here?" the reporter questioned.

"As a developer, I've learned you can only estimate... And hope. But I would say four to six months, " Milner answered.

"Developer!" DePalma hissed through clenched teeth. He punched numbers on the cellular. "You couldn't develop a shit house."

Two-hundred and fifty-miles south in suite twenty-two-oh-six at the Queen's Bay Inn in Lake Havasu, Arizona, the telephone rang. Lana Casner, dressed in bra and panties, was sitting on the unmade bed painting her toenails. She paused and gathered up the receiver. "Hello."

"Lana!" the Don barked. "Where is that sonofabitch?"

"Which one? I'm with two of them." She cradled the receiver between shoulder and jaw and continued the work on her toes.

"Milner," DePalma ranted. "I just saw him on television. He's going to build the Goddamned place. I knew it."

"Time for plan B," Lana suggested matter of faculty, dipping the brush for more polish.

"I'll take care of that. You take care of Milner. Suck his dick if you have to, but I don't want him out of your sight."

"Do I get paid by the inch?" she questioned sarcastically while painting a small toe.

"Don't fuck with me, Lana. Where is he?"

"Breakfast with the Parker Chamber of Commerce. Would you like me to blow all of them too?"

"Goddamnit, Lana."

"You know you love it, Don," she purred. "Ask me what I'm doing. Ask me what I'm wearing."

The line was silent for a moment, then he spoke. "You really are a slut... What are you wearing?"

In Parker the walls of the White Buffalo were casting their first shadows. The pre-fabbed, tilt-up, massive slabs had been trucked in under escort during the night. Now a towering crane was lifting them like graham crackers to positions along the sprawling floor. Shouts and commands filled the air as construction workers teemed around the vertical slabs like hungry ants.

Fox and his returning new hires were pushed out of the Gaming Commission's mobile and into a lesser trailer. "We have interviews pending," Mara told Fox. "Take your guards and meet somewhere else."

"They're not guards," Fox defended. "They're security officers."

"And a chicken isn't a bird, I suppose," Mara countered sarcastically.

"What's that supposed to mean?" Fox demanded.

"It means we have to hire a Human Resources Manager, a Director of Food and Beverage, a Maintenance Engineer, a Payroll Operator and sixteen other key positions... Which means we need the space."

Fox went. It wasn't that he was resenting women. The Special Agent in Charge of the Miami office had been a woman. He had no problem being Mara's subordinate. What he had a problem with was her attitude. The fact she was attractive seemed to amplify it. What Mara needed, Fox decided, was a large dose of tact.

The real irritant for Fox was the grim reality of the assembled security force. It was one thing to see them on paper, even the hire interviews weren't that discouraging, but now as they gathered for the first time, Fox's anxieties were running wild. A recent refugee from the epitome of professional law enforcement agencies, the FBI, he had learned to take high performance and excellence for granted. Every agent had a four-year degree or more. Every agent had been through the grueling, demanding FBI Academy. Every agent met the same standard.

It was not so with the new hire nucleus of the White Buffalo's security force. They were young; a twenty-two-year-old tribal member and they were old; a forty-eight-year-old retired sailor. They were skinny, obese, tall, short and generally uneducated. Two had high school GED's, one an associate degree and four were police department rejects or resignees. Jake Collins was wearing an earring, Jill Cox a mini skirt with heels, the young tribal member had a long ponytail, the female jailer was wearing Star Trek sunglasses and the fireman from Yuma failed to show.

None had worked in a casino. They were an eclectic mix and Fox was having serious doubts about his ability to lead them. Even if he could, he wasn't sure where they were going. It was a sobering thought to realize he and the little army before him were all that would stand between the White Buffalo's millions and the horde of professional thieves and cheats, he was certain would descend on them. It was sobering to realize only four hours away was a job he once loved and wanted, a job commanding respect, a job with professionals, a job he knew he could do. Maybe the Parker sabbatical, the work on the farm, the warm, fuzzy flirtation with the tribe were all just some needed respite, a time to mourn, a time to heal. Maybe, as Terrence Bell suggested, it was time for him to get back to work.

Jake Collins brought Fox out of his cloud of doubt. "Hey, John, Jill tells me you're an Indian. Is it true?"

Collins' brash candor brought a smile to Fox's face. "I prefer the term tribal member." The confession of the link to the tribe eased the self-doubt some. What was it Chief Stoner had said? A leaf couldn't choose where it fell, but it did not fall without purpose. Doubt or not, Fox knew he couldn't walk away from the challenge. It was time to go to work.

They gathered in what was to become known as the Security Trailer. It had a desk, a telephone, file cabinets, a computer, a wipe board and folding chairs. Fox made everyone stand and introduce themselves. It was awkward and difficult for some. Jake, he found, had an easy, polished style hidden beneath his beard. He exuded a quiet, confident command presence Fox didn't ignore. Jill had to be interrupted and told it would have to wait until another time when she started rambling about dating in high school.

When it was Fox's turn, he talked about his FBI experience and his mother's Indian heritage—although he skirted the trail of events bringing him to Parker. "The reasons each of us are here now become subordinate to the task at hand," he warned.

A hand went up. It was the young tribal member with the ponytail. "What's subordinate mean?"

Fox explained and went on. He talked about the fundamental ethic of honesty and fairness. "Honesty and fairness will be our credo. Use it to measure all you do. Ask, is it honest? Is it fair? If it's one, it's usually the other. Our motto will be, "Integrity knows no compromise.""

He talked about basic observation, looking beyond human character for furtive moves and reaction to authority. He found he was lecturing and enjoying it. The enthusiasm and interest he was reading in their expressions told him they were following; not only following but trusting. Maybe he could make this thing work after all.

Orientation ended when David Rollins delivered the guns Fox ordered; Brand new blue steel Browning nine-millimeter automatics. The new hires crowded around the box like kids at Christmas. After the serial numbers were recorded and the weapons examined and toyed with, Fox warned, "Unless your life or the life of another casino employee is under immediate threat, this gun stays in your holster. We don't shoot thieves or cheats. This is Parker, not Tombstone."

"Where do we carry these?" Jill pushed the barrel of the flat automatic down into the waistline of her mini skirt over her stomach.

"I'm not wearing mine that way," Jake Collins teased.

"You'll get leather gear," Fox advised, "including a holster. When we finish here, Jake's going to take you to A-1 Uniform Supply in Havasu. You'll all get uniforms. After that, you're going out to the Tribal Police pistol range for a live-fire orientation. By the time you get back, I'll have the shift assignments ready. From this day forth, we're a twenty-four-hour-a-day operation. Any questions?"

"Can Paula and I wear nail polish?" Jill said with her hand in the air.

"The key word is uniform," Fox answered. "We all dress the same, and I don't plan on wearing nail polish."

"All dress the same?" Jill questioned.

"That's what I said."

"What size bra would you like?" Jill smiled.

The others laughed.

Dennis Milner left the Chamber of Commerce breakfast at Kline's Cafe feeling Parker wasn't so bad a place after all. It was hotter than hell, but there were far fewer mosquitoes and ex-wives than in Minnesota. Here he was a multi-million-dollar developer building a casino in a town full of enthusiasm and hope. There he was a bankrupt, small-time, out-of-work contractor. These people were interested in what he had to say. The believed the bullshit he offered as an assurance that the casino wouldn't bring crime and corruption to their small town. "Orlando, the home of Disney World, has a higher crime rate than Las Vegas," he had told them. He hoped it was true. After the meeting, he had been approached by a local banker and a realtor. "There's going to be an influx of people," the realtor suggested. "Parker's got a real housing crunch. Maybe we could sit down some time and talk about mutually beneficial development." The man pushed a business card in Milner's pocket.

Maybe, Milner thought making the drive to the casino construction site, he'd call DePalma and talk to him about finishing the White Buffalo. Managed properly, it could be a real cash cow. Wasn't DePalma in business to make money? Hell, Milner reasoned, maybe he should apply for the position of Casino Manager. If things went well and he finished the job early, he'd be a hero. Maybe he could even bring it in under budget. They'd love him. After all, he was a fuckin' Indian. The tribal identification card in his pocket proved that, didn't it?

Milner parked the rented Lincoln Continental not far from the executive mobile office. He ran the windows halfway down to keep the interior from overheating in the afternoon glare. He was heading for the office when a leggy brunette in a mini skirt caught his attention. She was with the dick-head ex-FBI agent and some others. He made a mental note to find out who she was. Maybe she'd like to work for the CEO of Navco. Lana Casner, instead of a Vegas party girl, had become an expensive accessory, a hood ornament, a speed bump. A copy of Penthouse was a better deal. At least you got to see someone's ass. Girl with a body like the brunette had to be a player. Shit, she looked like a dancer or something. Wham! Milner, his attention on Jill Cox, walked directly into a big construction worker. He staggered awkwardly. The gloved man, sweaty and covered with cement splatter, grabbed Milner by the upper arms. "Careful, buddy," Virgil Tanner said.

Milner pushed Virgil's gloves off his arm. "Careful, shit. Get your gloves off me." He brushed at the transfer of sand and grit the gloves left behind.

"Next time fall on your ass," Virgil quipped.

"What's your name?" Milner demanded. He was masking his awkwardness in anger and authority.

Virgil balked at answering. He knew who Milner was. He had no fear of the man, but what he was intimidated Virgil.

"Either you tell me or you're outta here," Milner warned. "I own this fuckin' place."

"Stoner," Virgil granted reluctantly and convincingly averting his eyes. "Russell Stoner."

"Well, Stoner," Milner brushed at his sleeves, "yesterday you mud slingers splattered my car," he gestured to the Lincoln, "today you fuck up my jacket. I come out here later and find one spot on that car, you're fucking outta here. You got that?"

The big Indian stirred the toe of a boot in the dust. Milner's ego relished in making the man cower. "Yes, Sir... I understand," Virgil muttered without looking up.

"Then get back to work,"

Virgil shuffled away.

Milner's new-found mastery of fate seemed to continue when he opened the door to the executive trailer. Lana's scent reached out to engulf him. It was flower-like and intoxicating. Lana was at a drafting table with Amos Moses, the foreman, studying a blueprint. She was dressed in a sleeveless, cotton blouse and form-fitting jeans. She surprised Milner with a smile. "Dennis, Amos says you may pour the second level balcony tomorrow."

Milner had been paying little attention to details of the construction. It was much more exciting to meet with local officials, the press or lunch with the Rotary Club and drink at the VFW. But he wasn't about to admit it. "Yeah, it's going pretty good, isn't it Amos?" He pulled his jacket off and loosened his tie.

"Sure is, boss," Amos agreed, pulling on a cap. "Better get out there."

"Keep me posted, my man," Milner urged, rolling up a sleeve.

Amos nodded and was out the door. Milner walked to the drafting table to join Lana. She slipped an arm through his as she looked at the blueprint. The warmth of a breast compressed against his arm was like a branding iron. The heat quickly found its way to his groin. "All this building and erection," Lana purred. "It's a real turn-on."

"I'm glad you like it," Milner said with a glance at the breast against his arm.

Lana raised her eyes and found his. She had seen his look. "You know, Dennis, at first I wasn't sure you could build this place... I'm impressed." She moved subtly and a nipple jolted him.

Milner wet his lips. "Not only can I build it. I could fuckin' run it."

"I'm sure you could." Lana released his arm and moved away. Walking to a desk, she massaged the back of her neck as she turned and sank into a high-backed chair. "It's hot, isn't it? Wanna take off noonish and go find a spot on the river for a swim?"

"I don't have a suit."

"Neither do I," Lana smiled.

The mud gang, the cement workers and masons, were on the construction site at first light. Fresh pours and the harsh heat of day weren't allies, so start early, finish early became the norm. Afternoons and nights were left to plumbers and electricians who, cooked brown, had learned to live and work in the searing heat.

Milner labored through a stack of purchase orders, check authorizations and delivery requests. Lana, waltzing around the office, proved a significant distraction. He was puzzled by her new-found interest in him, but his lust wasn't allowing logic to ask serious questions. Anyway, he reasoned, Lana was right, this was exciting. Spending fifty-million-dollars building anything was exciting. Add in the fact it was a casino and you felt like fuckin' Steven Spielberg. No wonder Lena was turned on. Maybe together, Milner chuckled to himself, they could fuck Donald DePalma.

"Something funny?" Lana questioned from near a window.

"No," Milner answered, scrawling his signature across a final document. "I'm done. Let's get out of here."

Milner tossed his jacket over his shoulder and followed Lana toward the parking lot. She had a coke bottle figure and a gorgeous ass. He was imagining his hands holding her bare buttocks when Lana stopped abruptly. "Oh my God!" she blurted.

Lana pointed. "Look at your car!"

Milner stared. His mouth hung open in shock.

Twenty feet away the polished Lincoln Town Car sat with wet cement oozing out of its open windows. The interior of the car was an enormous slick puddle of watery concrete. It had been filled with gray, colorless cement.

"Ahhh... That sonofabitch!" Milner screamed, shaking his clenched fists.

Fox, at his desk in the Security trailer, heard the scream. He bolted for the door.

In the Gaming Commission trailer, Mara, David Rollins and George Manygoats were interviewing a plump, forty-six-year-old candidate for Personnel Manager. "I think decorum is important in any workplace," The woman was telling the three when Milner's scream reached them.

George Manygoats shot to his feet. "What the fuck was that?"

"I want the sonofabitch arrested!" the red-faced, angry Milner demanded as he marched around the cement filled car. His shoes and cuffs were soiled with the ooze that ran down to puddle on the ground. "I want him put in jail."

"Who?" Amos Moses asked. He was the first to reach Milner and Lana. Others were arriving. Electricians, plumbers, the driver from the catering truck, George Manygoats, Fox, Mara, David Rollins and the candidate for Personnel Manager. They stared in shock. Some laughed, others whispered and pointed.

"Russell Stoner," Milner answered. "He's the sonofabitch that did this."

Several construction workers laughed. Milner burned them with a look. "Next bastard that laughs is fired."

"Why do you think Russell Stoner did this?" Fox asked.

"Because he's an asshole," Milner growled. "I told 'im to stay away from my car... And where the fuck were you, Mister Security Chief? You gonna handle this or do I call the FBI?"

The angry Milner left in Lana Casner's car. Fox asked Amos Moses' help in getting the area cleared and people back to work. Mara gave Fox a look and followed the others back to the office. After calling a tow truck, Fox took off his jacket, rolled up his sleeves so he looked a little more like one of the guys and went out on the job site. He tried all his tricks, sympathy, humor, intimidation, persuasion and promise. Nothing worked. He talked to eighteen men: framers, electricians, plumbers and laborers. He got nowhere. Fox had his own suspicions, but he needed something to reinforce them; hearsay, an eyeball witness, anything. He knew this would be a test. Milner had justifiably pointed a finger. Security on the construction site was his responsibility. Maybe, he reasoned, that was what Mara's look was about.

The temperature was in the nineties. Fox was feeling the heat. After an hour of talk he needed a drink. He turned toward the catering truck and realized the answer. The catering truck, although several hundred feet from the cement filled Lincoln, sat directly in line with it. The view the caterer had was unobstructed. Fox knew what he had to do. "Sprite," he said, reaching the drop window counter. The caterer, a balding, no neck forty-year-old with a gold earring, set a cold can in front of Fox. Fox pushed coins toward the man "How's business?"

"Good. Business is good." The man busied himself behind the counter. He knew who Fox was.

"I'm going to ask you one question," Fox warned soberly. "I don't like your answer, business isn't going to be so good. As a matter of fact," he paused to take a drink from the can, "this could be the last thing you sell here."

"You wouldn't do that."

Fox studied the narrowed, hard eyes. "We're building a casino. You wanna make a bet?"

"I'm fucked either way," the no-neck complained. "I tell you, they ain't gonna buy shit from me no more. I don't tell you; you throw me out."

"Cruel world, isn't it, but nobody's going to know what you say to me. Now who was it?"

The no-neck wiped at the drop countertop with a rag. "Big fuckin' Indian. I don't know his name. He's a mud slinger. Wears his cap backwards."

Fox walked away. He knew it was Virgil.

He drove to the gas station in Poston, bought a beer and joined three tribal members sitting on the porch. The afternoon shadows were stretching, it was beginning to cool. The taste of the beer was refreshing. Fox savored it as he remembered the fields. They seemed a long time ago. He missed them and the time on the porch. "Anybody seen Virgil today?" Fox questioned, breaking the silence.

"Saw a truck out near Harry Patch's place. Next to the canal," one of the leather faces answered and then spat tobacco juice into the dust. He wiped his mouth with a plaid sleeve.

"Was it Virg's truck?"

"Maybe."

"Boys like to go canaling out there after work," the other man suggested.

"Canaling?" Fox questioned.

"Water skiing in the canal," the man added.

"You can't get a boat in the canal," Fox argued.

"You can get a pick-up alongside."

Virgil knew Fox would come. Maybe that was why he drank more than usual. What the hell! Maybe Fox would have a beer with them. They'd fight and then he'd go to jail. Shit, it wasn't like he hadn't done that before. He'd lose the mud job, but he'd find another. Fuckin' Minnesota Indian got his. Virgil chug-a-lugged the remainder of a beer, crushed the can in his hand and tossed it away. "Get me another beer, Sparrow!" he bellowed. "Then I'm gonna ski board fuckin' fifty-miles-an-hour."

Eight of them—all Indian—in cut-off jeans, BVD's and one nude, lounged in the crushed cool grass on the inclined bank of the wide irrigation canal. The area around them was littered with empty cans, wrinkled potato chip bags and scattered cement-soiled work clothes, shoes and boots. Atop the embankment on a narrow-rutted road bordering the placid canal sat Virgil's pick-up truck. Attached to a hitch on the truck was a coiled and less than cooperative—forty-foot-long, pencil-sized steel cable. The end of the cable was nailed to a make-shift ski board fashioned out of heavy plywood salvaged from the construction site.

Sparrow, looking bony and awkward in wet boxer shorts, scrambled up the grassy bank and into the bed of the pick-up. "Mojave missile," he yelped and launched a shiny aluminum beer can high into the air. The can climbed, arched and plummeted. Virgil opened his hand and the can smacked into it. "Fuckin' luck from the white side of your family," Virgil said sarcastically.

"Luck, shit," Sparrow defended. "C'mon that buys me the next ride."

"Shit," Virg slurred pushing to his feet. He staggered up the grassy bank, falling, splashing beer from the can in his hand. "Fuck!"

"Virg," another of the men called, "maybe you should let me pull 'im."

"I can fuckin' drive," Virgil protested. "Who's gonna spot 'im?"

Two men got up and followed Virgil up the embankment. Virgil climbed in behind the wheel and cranked his truck to life. One man climbed into the bed of the truck. The other slid in across from Virgil. He twisted to look out the rear window.

Behind the truck Sparrow stretched out the thin, coiled, stainless cable until it was taut. Then wading into the canal, he floated onto the plywood ski board. The man in the truck bed slapped the roof of the cab. "Hit it."

Virgil tramped on the accelerator. The truck engine roared and it jumped forward.

In the canal the stainless cable snapped straight, and the ski board sent out a surging wake. "Yahoo," Sparrow cried with delight.

The pick-up truck, gaining speed, crashed, bumped and roared as it raced along the edge of the canal kicking up a swirl of dust. Forty feet behind, the ski board was hydroplaning, plying a curling wake, sending ducks and birds scattering. Sparrow was on his knees. His face was bright with excitement. He gave a quick thumbs-up.

Faster," the man at Virgil's side yelled above the roar of the engine.

Virgil glanced at the speedometer as it climbed; thirty-five, forty, forty-five. "The lil' sonofabitch is gonna do it." Virgil looked to the outside mirror for a glance at Sparrow. What he saw startled him. A quarter of a mile behind was a white Ford pickup. "Shit," Virgil knew it was Fox. He lifted his foot off the gas pedal.

Immediately there was slack in the tow cable. Sparrow's momentum carried him into a coil of the cable. Irritated with the loss of speed, Sparrow stabbed a thumb in the air.

"Faster," the man at Virgil's side yelled.

Virgil tramped on the gas and the truck responded. The slack in the stainless cable cut through the water like a knife. The unseen steel garrote closed with deadly speed. There was a bump and the ski board spun into the air. Sparrow was gone. "He's down," the spotter shouted. Virgil slammed on the brakes.

The pick-up truck slid to a dusty stop and the man in the bed stood up. His eyes searched for Sparrow. A leg popped to the surface. Then another. They were not attached. "My God!"

Fox braked to a halt. Virgil's truck was sixty feet ahead. A man on the back of the truck pointed toward the canal, screaming. Virgil and the passenger were scrambling out, running toward him. Something was wrong. Fox looked to the canal. Sparrow popped to the surface like a cork. He was face down. The water around him was crimson.

Virgil ran and dove into the canal. He was quickly to Sparrow. Grabbing Sparrow by the hair, Virgil pulled the limp form to the bank. Fox and the others joined in pulling them from the canal. Fox grimaced. "Ahhhh," the man at Fox's side cried. Both of Sparrow's legs had been severed just below the knee. The bloody stumps were spurting crimson arterial blood with every heartbeat.

"Jesus." Virgil, kneeling at Sparrow's side, clamped a two-handed vice grip on an upper thigh. Virgil's face was a mask of horror. "Don't die, you little fuck, don't die!"

Fox fought an urge to turn away, but he knelt and pulled off his belt to cinch it around Sparrow's right thigh. He jerked it tight puckering the flesh. The spurting decreased to a pulse. The grass around them was syrupy and slick with blood. Sparrow's eyes stared aimlessly at the sky. His face was ashen, and his lips were colorless. "Get a rope, a belt, anything!" Fox ordered in desperation. His hands were bloody to the wrists.

"Don't die, Sparrow!" Virgil pleaded. Tears streamed down his face and off his chin. "Please don't die."

They tied a belt around the stump Virgil held and then carried Sparrow, arms flailing, to the rear of Fox's pickup. Tee shirts and pants were wrapped around the bloody stumps and Sparrow was pushed into the bed of the truck. Virgil cradled Sparrow in his arms. He was covered with blood. Fox scrambled for the driver's door. "Get the legs!" They were floating in the canal.

Fox drove hard. Virgil braced himself and held Sparrow. It seemed forever to Fox, but they finally reached the river road leading to Poston. Swinging the pickup from the bumpy dirt road onto the asphalt, Fox accelerated rapidly. When they flashed through Poston and by the gas station, it was at well over eighty-miles-an-hour.

Approaching the hospital in Parker, Fox laid on the horn. When he braked to a halt at the emergency entrance, they were met by a doctor, two nurses and an orderly. The four were quickly onto the bed of the pickup. Virgil was pushed aside. An orderly arrived with a wheeled gurney. One of the nurses started mouth to mouth resuscitation. Their actions were quick, tense and practiced. Sparrow was pulled from the pickup's open bed onto the gurney and rushed inside. The CPR continued. Fox wondered if Sparrow was dead.

The two men sat in the hospital's small waiting room. Virgil was sullen and quiet. He sat, elbows on knees, staring at the floor. The antiseptic smell, muted voices reverberating in the hallway and the sporadic ringing of telephones took Fox back to another hospital. The memory of it was so vivid, his heart raced with fear. He tried to control his breath. Saliva filled his mouth. He felt faint, ill. He had to move, had to escape it. He pushed to his feet.

Fox found the restroom in the hallway. He washed his bloody hands with a yellow liquid soap, then his face. The water was calming. He rinsed his mouth and drank.

He tried rinsing the blood from his shirt cuffs. It was futile. He felt better, but not well. He wished he could leave but knew he couldn't. Waiting hadn't saved Pam's life. He didn't think it would save Sparrow's either. Death didn't care about those who waited.

Six men were in the waiting room when Fox returned. They were dark, long-haired, young men, tanned and muscled, dressed in shorts, tee shirts or bare chested. Fox recognized most from the construction site. Looks were exchanged, but no one spoke. There was nothing to say. Most, like Virgil, stared at the floor in silence.

A call from the hospital brought Sparrow's family. His mother was a frail, stooped woman with gray hair and sad eyes. An aunt and a young cousin breast feeding an infant comforted her. Chairs in the waiting room were surrendered to the women. As word of the accident spread across the reservation, more of the tribe arrived. The waiting room filled, spilling into the hallway. Chairs were brought in. Mara and her father, Horace, arrived. They were followed by Morse Roberts and the secretary from the farm. Someone brought home-made burritos and iced tea. Although the number waiting increased, they remained quiet and still.

Sergeant Bear-Don't-Walk from the Tribal Police arrived. Clipboard in hand, he began calling the men that had been at the canal. Fox noticed each time Bear-Don't-Walk returned from an interview with one of the men, he would straighten his posture and pass close to Mara.

Fox was annoyed when Bear-Don't-Walk pointed a pencil at him and gestured. Submitting to the man's authority in front of the tribal members, humbled Fox. His ears burned with embarrassment as he followed the uniformed sergeant into the hallway.

Bear-Don't-Walk compounded the humiliation by

continuing to walk in front of Fox in the corridor. Fox understood the inference. This wasn't man to man, peer to peer. This was cop to suspect and embarrassment gave way to anger. If this Indian wannabe wanted to play cat and mouse, he was ready for it. The sergeant led the way into a small coffee room. Fox guessed it was an employees' lounge. "Sit down." Bear-Don't-Walk slid onto a chair at a small table.

Fox sat down across from the man. Bear-Don't-Walk was making notes on his clipboard. Fox wondered if the men he had interviewed over the years resented this as much as he did. "Tell me what happened," the dark eyes ordered soberly.

"I didn't see the accident."

"Who said you did? I asked you to tell me what happened."

Fox stiffened. The man was no idiot. He thought about the question before answering. "I saw Sparrow in the canal. There was a cable. It looked like Virgil had been towing him. Everyone was in a panic. Sparrow was floating face down. Virgil went in after him. We applied tourniquets. I drove him here."

"You have anything to drink out there?"

"No."

"How about the others?"

"I don't know."

"You don't know, or you won't say?" the sergeant pressed, studying Fox.

"Listen, Sergeant," Fox straightened in his chair, "I don't know what your problem is, but aim that badge at someone else. I've told you what I know."

It was a challenge and Bear-Don't-Walk didn't ignore it. Leaning both elbows onto the table, he glared at Fox. "I'll tell you what my problem is, Fox. You keep showing up on the fringe of things. The shooting at the White

House, the fight at Blue Water, the accident at the canal. Is that what happened in Palm Springs? ...or don't you know?"

Fox's reaction was quick and blind with rage. He wanted to bloody the man's face. He hit the table with both hands, propelling it into Bear-Don't-Walk's chest, sending him backwards crashing to the floor. "You sonofabitch," Fox growled and went after him.

The sergeant rolled, pushed an overturned chair toward Fox to slow him and scrambled to his feet. Fox kicked the chair aside and closed on the man. Bear-Don't-Walk blocked the right hand aimed at his face with a raised forearm, but he missed the left Fox slammed into his stomach just above the gun belt. The punch pushed the breath from him with a grunt. He felt the fluids in his stomach rise up into his throat. He bent forward and sank to a knee when the other failed.

Fox grabbed the front of the sergeant's uniform shirt and jerked. He felt the material tear. He drew back a punch, but Bear-Don't-Walk wasn't waiting for it. He delivered one of his own, driving a fist into Fox's groin. Fox groaned and turned to stagger away.

Bear-Don't-Walk pushed to his feet and followed. Fox leaned against a wall in agony. The sergeant grabbed him by the shoulder, turned him and struck him hard in the mouth. Blood spewed from a split lip. Fox staggered backwards, hit the swinging door and fell crashing into the hallway.

There was a mix of fire and salt in Fox's mouth. Blood, he realized just before the sergeant grabbed him again. Fox knew another punch would end it. He was still stunned, still disoriented, but when Bear-Don't-Walk jerked him to his knees, Fox shot up with all of his might and slammed his forehead into the man's nose. Something cracked and Bear-Don't-Walk reeled away.

The sergeant clutched the searing pain in his nose. Blood poured from between his fingers and down the front of his uniform. He leaned against the wall to keep from falling.

"Help, someone get in here!" a nurse yelled when she discovered the two bloody men in the corridor.

Mara was the first into the hallway. She stared in disbelief.

16   ALL THE KING'S MEN

"It is the general belief of the Indians that after a man dies his spirit is somewhere on the earth or in the sky, we do not know exactly where, but we are sure, that his spirit still lives.

Chased-by-Bears—Santee-Yanktonai Sioux

Fox was hustled into a treatment room. A nurse swabbed away the blood, dabbed an antiseptic on the inside of his lip. It was swollen and numb. The green curtain masking them was pushed aside. It was Virgil. "Goddamn, Sprite Man, I can't leave you alone for a minute."

"You'll have to wait outside, Sir," the irritated nurse ordered.

"Come on," Virgil pleaded, "this is my cousin. He didn't have open heart surgery. He got punched in the mouth. I promise I won't kiss him."

"You'll have to leave when the doctor comes."

239

"I know this doctor. Trust me, I'll leave."

The nurse stepped out and jerked the green curtain closed. Virgil looked at Fox's lip, grimaced. "Lucky you didn't lose some teeth."

"That sonofabitch," Fox muttered, wiping saliva from the corner of his mouth.

"You broke his nose." Virgil sat down on a stool beside the treatment table.

"Too bad it wasn't his neck," Fox slurred, his lip thick.

"I don't think Bear-Don't-Walk wants you around Mara," Virgil suggested.

"That's his problem," Fox countered.

Virgil nodded. "Has been for a long time."

"This wasn't about Mara."

"Maybe you don't think so."

"How's Sparrow?" Fox wiped his mouth again. The numbness was yielding to a sharp burning.

"Doc says they can't put Humpty-Dumpty back together again. His heart stopped a couple times. Shock, they say. Whatever, he's in too bad a shape to operate."

"Will he live?"

"They say the first couple hours were the worst. He got by that. Guess I'm gonna be his legs. Owe him that."

"Wasn't your fault."

"Wasn't the fuckin' Easter Bunny drivin' that truck."

"Could have been you."

"But it wasn't," Virgil said sadly.

"What's Bear-Don't-Walk gonna do about it?" Fox questioned.

"He won't do nothing. Hell, he skis the canals too. He's just doing what he has to do."

"I'm not on his 'to do' list," Fox warned.

"Figure he understands that now." Virgil smiled.

"How much bail am I going to need?" Fox was beginning to regret his outburst. The price was likely going to include his job. As the Director of Security, it was less than a stellar example to commit battery on a tribal police officer.

"Bail?" Virgil questioned. 'You're not gonna need bail. Bear-Don't-Walk and his bent nose already left. He won't put you in jail for bustin' his face. People would say he arrested you because you kicked his ass. Big loss of face. Looks better for him to let it slide."

"Jesus," Fox said, shaking his head. "This sure ain't Kansas, is it Dorothy?"

"And ain't we glad of that. Listen," Virgil whispered, "Harry Lafoon knows the head nurse. He's gonna get us Sparrow's legs. We're gonna get a case of beer, go down to Sparrow's and bury 'em. You wanna come along?"

Fox grimaced. "You're going to bury his legs?"

"What the hell do you wanna do, have a barbecue?"

It was dark when they gathered at Sparrow's school bus trailer. A bonfire was built, and the men stood around it in a wide circle. The fire sent embers dancing into the night and lit the faces. A shaman in a brown Stetson, a heavy man with big hands and a low voice, danced slowly around the fire, shaking a dried gourd that rattled like a snake. He held an eagle feather in the other. Fox, like the others, stood and watched in reverent silence.

Twenty feet away, near the pick-up truck Sparrow had been re-building for three years, Virgil and the six men from the canal were digging a deep trench. Beside the trench lay two elongated bundles wrapped in soiled hospital sheets.

David Rollins appeared at Fox's shoulder. They exchanged a look. David made no mention of the swelling or bloody cut on Fox's lip. They listened to the shaman and watched his dance. Three other men joined in the slow dance and the soft chant. The firelight gave it a surreal, dreamlike quality. Fox was watching a glowing ember lift and spin in the heat of the fire when he saw the uniform. Directly across from him stood Sergeant Bear-Don't-Walk. Their eyes met and held. Bear-Don't-Walk wore a swath of white tape across his nose. Finally, he looked away. Fox exhaled without realizing it. He had been holding his breath.

Virgil shouldered his way through the circle of men around the fire. He was glistening with sweat and covered with grit and mud. He moved to the shaman and spoke close to his ear. The man nodded.

The circle parted as the shaman's dance led him toward the trench. The others who had joined in the dance followed. The chanting increased as more and more of those encircling the fire joined in. Fox moved shoulder to shoulder with the others in a shuffle as the circle undulated like a large snake and re-formed around the trench.

The shaman climbed awkwardly into the fresh hole. Loose dirt spilled in around his feet. He stood waist deep. The chanting stopped. The only sound was the crackle of the bonfire and the incessant hum of the night insects. "Great Spirit, we offer the legs of the Sparrow... We are thankful you took only his legs. We ask that you care for them... And that you heal the Sparrow's wounded spirit so he may know it takes more than legs to make a man stand tall."

Virgil lifted the sheet-wrapped bundles and passed them to the arms of the shaman. The old man laid them carefully in the bottom of the trench. He shook his gourd rattle and waved the eagle feather over them and then pulled a handful of dirt into the trench. He gestured to the others to do the same and the circle closed as each man pushed dirt into the trench. The sheets disappeared beneath the fresh soil and the hole filled quickly. The Shaman danced atop it signaling the others to join him. The chanting resumed, louder than before. Fox had no idea what the words were, but he was caught up in it. He mouthed sounds and danced in circles like the others.

When the last truck pulled away and the fire was little more than a dying bed of orange coals, Sparrow's yellow hound appeared from beneath the fading school bus. Walking with its tail tucked between its legs, the dog crossed to the fresh packed earth where the legs were buried and laid down atop it.

It was nearly two AM when Fox reached the casino construction site. It was dark and moonless and the stark lighting on the site gave it an eerie shadow-filled look. The barren tilt-up walls stood linked with a network of naked beams supported by smooth, round metal columns. Near the front, the metal framework of the second story silhouetted itself against a curtain of darkness. Fox parked and climbed out. The smell of curing cement burnt welds and sawdust mixed with the cool air off of the river reached out to greet him.

Stepping over a wooden frame onto the cement, Fox walked under the canopy of open girders toward the center of the floor. He paused trying to orient himself with the blueprints and diagrams he had studied. A voice in the shadows spoke. "Thought I had a scavenger there for a moment."

Fox turned, looked. Jake Collins stepped out of the shadows. He was in uniform and wearing a gun. Fox was surprised. The man looked official. Jake crossed to him. "I heard you ran into a little delay, so I made up a schedule."

"The uniform looks good," Fox complimented.

"Got our shooting done too," Jake said, patting his holstered gun. "Everyone did pretty good."

"You put yourself on night watch?" Fox questioned. He was impressed with Collins' sacrifice.

"Someone had to do it," Jake said modestly.

"I appreciate you getting things done," Fox said sincerely.

"Thought I heard voices," Jill Cox smiled as she reached the two men. Her uniform shirt was snug and pulling at the buttons. It did little to hide her beauty.

"Hello, Jill," Fox said, offering a knowing glance at Collins.

"What do you think of my uniform?" Jill questioned like an excited teenager. She turned, showing it. The pants fit like a leotard, a second skin.

"It's uniform," Fox granted.

The stop at the construction site was a stall and Fox admitted that as he pulled in and parked beside his trailer at Branson's. Days could be filled with work and legitimate diversion, but the nights, especially the moments before sleep, were a deep, lonely chasm. A chasm steeped in the painful memory of Pam's scent, her touch, her voice, her breath. It was a chasm with no escape.

Lying on edge of sleep, exploring his split lip with a tongue, Fox thought of the ironic bond with his father. He too had experienced the loss. James Fox chose to abandon his wife. Did that make the loss any less painful? Weren't his nights as empty? What wedge had been driven between husband and wife to separate them forever? Was it the formidable spiritual gravity of the tribe that held Clair Scott? Was it the drive of an ambitious man that pulled James Fox away? It seemed the sins of the father had befallen the son. Perhaps, Fox reasoned, Bear-Don't-Walk's painful accusation was rooted in reality. Perhaps he was unknowingly walking through life with an albatross around his neck, some fateful curse that tainted the lives that came too close to his. Why else would Pamela Fox take her own life? What God would choose such a plan? It had to be an abomination; some unrecognized demon, a demon that severed Sparrow's legs like dry twigs. A demon Fox knew he must find; not only find, but face.

Maybe, Fox reasoned, if he could find a sacrifice, some meritorious unselfish deed that would please God, it could all be made right. What he needed was a chance to think, to concentrate. A walk along the river would help. There it was pure and quiet. There, maybe the answer would come to him.

The grass was cool under his feet. There was a mist hanging over the surface of the water. He was nearing the bank leading down to the water's edge when he saw her, and his heart stopped. It was Pam. He recognized her silhouette instantly. She was standing knee-deep in the water. The folds of her long hair glistened even in the faint light. "Pam!" Fox called. She turned, looked. Her face was radiant, alive. She was wearing a long, sheer white dress. It was damp and clinging from the river and the mist. Her nipples were erect in the chill of the night. Fox ached with passion and anticipation. He slipped and fell on the grass.

She looked startled, bewildered. "Pam!" he said reaching out for her, but she turned and waded deeper into the water. "No," he cried, trying to get to his feet. The water was engulfing her, spilling over the nape of her neck, her shoulders, into her hair. He watched in horror as she disappeared beneath a succession of ripples. Fox dove and grabbed at the water. Suddenly he was awake and gripping an empty, wrinkled sheet. He was swimming in sweat, breathless and shaken. An illuminated bedside digital clock read four-fifty AM. He drew in a breath to calm himself and swung his feet to the floor.

Pushing off the bed, Fox wondered what was more painful, burying your legs or burying your wife, either one made it difficult to walk.

Eight miles away an ICU nurse in Parker Community Hospital nudged the form sleeping on the floor beside the legless man. Virgil Tanner stirred and sat up. He was stiff and sore from the hard floor. "It's nearly five," the nurse whispered.

Virgil wiped at his face and climbed to his feet. He looked at the frail form in the railed hospital bed. Sparrow was hollow-cheeked and ashen. A green plastic mask over his nose and mouth hissed with the flow of oxygen. An IV line taped to his wrist led to a bottle hanging bedside. Fine lines traced from monitors on his chest to a cluster of electronic scopes above the bed. Sparrow's pulse and breath were transformed to green images. Virgil's eyes moved to the sheets covering Sparrow's form. The impression from his legs stopped above the knees. It made him look even smaller. Virgil laid a hand carefully atop Sparrow's. "I gotta go to work," he whispered. "Don't go anywhere, Sparrow. I'll be back." He turned and moved for the door.

Fox formulated the plan while he shaved. It was simple. He would ask Amos Moses to send Virgil to the Security trailer when the mud crew took their first morning break. They started a first light. It would be over by the time Dennis Milner arrived. Although neither man had spoken of it, Fox knew Virgil understood why he came to the canal. Virgil had to know he couldn't get way with cementing the car. He had to know the consequence was losing his job. Fox liked Virgil, but there were dimensions to him that were wild and unpredictable.

He could be a dangerous opponent, Fox decided. Filling the Lincoln with cement was another jump off a dam. A choice. Virgil knew that. Fox was certain he'd take it like a man. Maybe with time available, he could be with Sparrow. What was it Virgil said, "I'll be Sparrow's legs?" Rinsing his face, Fox made a mental note to remind Virgil of that. Maybe it would allow him to leave with face.

At the construction site the first light of day was spreading. A rebar crew was working on the framework of the second story laying heavy paper atop a wire mesh that would reinforce the cement poured to form the second floor. Amos Moses chewed a cigar butt in the corner of his mouth. Sleeves rolled up over muscled arms, hard hat in place, he roamed the framework like a busy moth unable to decide where to land. He looked at welds, I-beams, bolts, expansion joints. The floor would become a link to a bearing wall making it vital to the integrity of the structure.

The burly mud crew gathered near the catering truck. They drank steaming coffee, ate doughnuts in two bites, smoked and pissed on sand piles. Virgil was among them. They were awe-struck when the Barbie Doll dressed as a security officer marched into their midst with a three-cell flashlight. "Next one of you people," Jill Cox warned soberly and, in a tone they understood, "I see pissin' in the dirt is gonna be pissin' in the wind. Use the portable johns."

The cement trucks began arriving. Six of them. Mixers spinning their heavy loads, they parked to idle and wait.

"Let's do it," Amos Moses barked and the mud crew tossed their cups and cigarettes. The wheeled cement-encrusted pump and its long nozzle crane was muscled into position beneath the second floor. Virgil and six other men pulled on heavy rubber boots and gloves, gathered shovels, hoes and bull floats before climbing up a ladder to the wire mesh floor awaiting the pour.

The safety alarm on the first cement truck pinged loudly as it backed slowly to the mouth of the cement pump. Construction workers teemed around it like ants around a fat bug. Soon the rotating mixer was spewing gravely, wet mud into the cement pump. The pump's long nozzle, suspended by a jointed crane, snaked high to the second story where Virgil and the mud crew stood ready. Jill, standing with Jake Collins not far away, watching, thought the pump with its long trunk looked like an anteater.

Diesel engines growled with labor as they belched smoke into the morning air. On the second floor the cement nozzle vibrated, coughed and spewed out its heavy stream of mud. The mud crew skillfully spread the widening puddle across the wire mesh. Virgil, the nozzle man, held the powerful shaking hose with both arms, directing the powerful flow of cement as if he were a man watering a garden.

The first cement truck was followed by the second, then the third. "Let's hustle," Amos Moses encouraged with a shout after a glance at his watch and a look at the sunlight growing on the site. "We gotta beat the heat."

Fox arrived and parked near the Security trailer. He had deliberately driven through the employee parking area. Virgil's truck was there. The mud crew were busy with a pour. They would be taking their first break in an hour. Pushing the selector to park, he looked to the executive trailer. Lana Casner's rented car hadn't returned, which Fox hoped meant Milner hadn't either. He wanted Virgil off the site before Milner arrived. Fox did notice Mara's open Jeep CJ was there. The woman worked more hours than he did. Fox was climbing out when Jill

Cox spotted him. "Better put your windows up," she teased. "They're pouring cement."

Fox smiled and headed for the security trailer. He wondered how the woman looked so good after spending all night on the construction site. He hoped she wasn't going to be intimidated by the construction workers.

The fifth mixer truck was at the cement pump and nine tons of fluid mud was spread eight inches deep over the second story floor. Virgil knew from experience the truck's load was nearly spent. "One more and we get to take a piss," he shouted to the splattered, sweaty crew.

"Be careful where you go," a hard hat warned. "That lady cop down there'll be all over your Indian ass."

"I'm always careful when I pull it out," Virgil answered. "Attracts women like a big bulb attracts bugs." His smile vanished with the tremble he felt beneath his boots. The wire mesh had moved. His first thought was the rebar crew had fucked up, but then the entire floor sagged in the center and the mud crew stood frozen, transfixed with fear.

"Jesus Christ!" someone muttered aloud.

Cement continued to spew out of the nozzle Virgil held.

"Turn the mud off!" another frightened hard hat yelled. The liquid mud kept coming.

The liquid floor groaned like an old wooden ship and sagged deeper. "She's leaking," someone below shouted. The cement continued to jet from the nozzle. "Get out," Virgil barked. He could feel the rebar moving beneath his rubber boots.

The mud crew scrambled for the ladders. Tools were thrown. They labored through the thick, sucking cement like men in slow motion. Something cracked. The floor shook and a sink hole appeared in the middle of the fresh cement. A river of mud poured down through it. Tools and deep footprints were swept toward it. Below voices were shouting in panic. Above Virgil's head, an I-beam groaned and twisted. Virgil dropped the cement nozzle and reached up to jam both arms against the sagging beam. Virgil knew if the overhead came down on the already sagging floor, the entire structure would collapse. He locked his elbows and braced his back. The weight and strain were enormous. "Hurry!" he shouted at the men near on ladders. The veins on his forehead were bulging. His arms trembled.

Tons of wet cement poured in a deadly cascade down through the rupture near the center of the second floor. The crew below scattered like frightened rabbits as the mud spread in a wet wall sweeping all that was loose with it. Shouts of alarm and panic filled the air. The abandoned cement pump continued to deliver additional weight to the sagging second floor depositing it at the feet of Virgil Tanner.

"Virgil's up there!" a mud slinger cried as he jumped from the ladder and ran. The I-beams were groaning like wounded animals.

"Get away... Get back!" Amos Moses was screaming and waving. Electricians, framers and plumbers were all running for the safety of the parking lot.

"Sonofabitch, she's is gonna come down!" someone shouted.

Jill didn't know what was wrong, but she heard someone was still on the second level. She ran to the ladder and climbed. The rungs were wet and gritty. She slipped twice but was quickly at the top. She saw Virgil twenty feet away. "My God," she mouthed. His trembling arms and neck looked like they were going to burst. His face was beet red, jaws tight.

Someone grabbed Jill from behind. Jerking her hard, Fox shouted, "Get down!"

"But..."

"Get down, Goddamnit!" Fox pushed by her. Jill, filled with fright, obeyed.

Fox looked at the sagging overhead beam. It hung to where Virgil stood and under its enormous weight he was beginning to bend. Mud continued to suck toward the hole in the floor. The ominous groaning of stressed steel continued. Fox's mouth was bitter with the taste of fear. Holding onto an upright beam, he stretched and extended an open hand toward Virgil. "Virgil," he called, "come, grab my hand!"

Virgil squinted an eye open at Fox. His face was a mask of agony and sweat. Strain had burst a vessel in his eye and the white was blood red. Trembling, Virgil forced an answer. "Get away, Sprite Man!"

"Goddamnit, take my hand," Fox pled.

The floor groaned and sagged more. The flow of wet cement into the hole became a torrent. It was pulling at Virgil's legs. "I showed that fuckin' dam, didn't I?" he gritted through clenched teeth.

"Virgil, please!" Fox cried, stretching to reach a few more inches.

The collapse came suddenly. The second story floor and the superstructure above—a combination of steel I-beams, rebar, wire mesh, pipes and wet cement—fell into the center of the ruptured floor as it came apart like torn paper. The noise was a thundering wet thump as tons collapsed twenty feet to the floor below. Fox felt himself falling and then he was engulfed in a wet, suffocating, heavy blanket of cement. The caustic lime burned his eyes and his nostrils. He tried to move and could not. He held his breath, knowing the moment he opened his mouth, he was a dead man. He could feel the ooze pushing up into his sinus cavities.

He was frightened. The weight on his chest was increasing as the cement squeezed him. He was amazed at the silence of it all. Lights began to dance in front of his eyes. His lungs were crying for relief. The lights grew brighter and a hand touched his face. Grabbing him behind the neck, the hand pulled him up into the light. His face burst free of the cement and he gasped at the air he felt on his face. Jill and Collins, covered with cement, pulled Fox into the light. "It's okay. It's okay," she said softly hugging Fox in her arms.

The muddy Jill, Jake Collins and three construction workers drug Fox away from the debris of the collapse. Fox coughed and gagged and threw up. One of the hard hats brought a hose and Jill washed his face, hair and arms. She ran her hands over his face and neck like a mother feverishly bathing a child. Fox continued to gasp in air. "It's okay. It's okay now," Jill kept repeating as if to assure herself. When Fox opened his eyes, he saw she was crying. She continued to wipe cement and grit from his neck and jaw. A siren whined in the distance. "Virgil?" Fox questioned, finding his voice was faint and strained.

Both Jill and Collins heard the question. Neither answered.

Fox felt weak and his knees were shaking, but with Jake's help, he got onto his feet. Jill unbuttoned his shirt and pulled it away as she continued to rinse him. The water was cool and refreshing and helped wash away his fear. He watched the search for Virgil as Jill knelt and pulled his shoes off. He glanced at her. She was almost as much a mess as he. She caught his look. "You owe me," she sniffed, rinsing his feet.

Dennis Milner and Lana Casner were arriving as the

ambulance pulled in. "Something's wrong," Lana suggested. Milner was out of the car and gone.

"What the fuck happened?" Milner demanded when he found Amos Moses standing, staring as the search for Virgil continued.

"I don't know," Mosses shrugged. "Fuckin' thing just fell down."

"Fell down?" Milner was shaken.

"Yeah, fell down," Moses repeated, burning Milner with a hard look. "Make matters worse, there's a fuckin' Indian in there."

"You're fired!" Milner barked in anger. He was only inches from Moses' face. Lana Casner reached the two men. She folded her arms and watched the rescuers.

"You're not in charge of jack shit, asshole," Moses growled, sticking a gloved finger in Milner's face. He turned and marched away.

"You better get control, Dennis," Lana warned and followed after Moses. Milner felt a sinking sensation in his stomach. It was all slipping away. He turned back to the rubble. It was as if he were looking at the ruins of his life.

An agonizing twenty minutes passed before one of the hard hats digging in the drying mass of steel and concrete found a hand. It was clinging to a beam. Shovels, hoses and hands quickly excavated the body. Virgil's limp form was pulled free and the waiting paramedics went to work. Communicating with the local hospital by radio, they tried CPR, shock paddles and finally a shot of adrenaline directly into his heart. Nothing worked. After twenty agonizing minutes, they stopped.

A stretcher was brought out and Virgil was covered with a sheet. Muddy men helped load the body into the ambulance. It departed without lights or siren.

Fox sat shirtless on a cement block on the fringe of the spectacle watching. No one needed to tell him what he saw. Jill stood at his side with a hand on his shoulder. When the ambulance was gone, he pushed to his feet. The temperature was in the eighties, but he was cold. He looked at his, his arms and his soaked stained pants.

"I need some clothes," he said feebly.

"I'll drive you," Jill offered, gathering up his shoes and socks.

"I can drive," Fox defended.

"Jill will drive you," Jake Collins said firmly. "I'll take care of things."

Fox didn't have the energy to argue. He was weak and drained. He nodded and turned to walk toward the parking lot. Jill followed. What the fuck did it matter? What the fuck did anything matter?

He didn't notice Mara. She stood on the steps of the Gaming Enterprise trailer watching.

The seven-mile drive to Branson's Trailer Park went quickly. "Turn here," Fox said. He was in no mood for small talk. His shock was yielding to anger. The succession of carnage and fear flashing through his mind was numbing and thoughts of it were filling his bloodstream with adrenaline. His arms and legs trembled. Blood pounded in his ears like a drum. "Turn the air off," he ordered with a glance at Jill behind the wheel. She switched off the blower for the AC. His trembling was increasing.

He gave terse directions to the trailer and climbed out as soon as Jill parked. Fox waited at the door while she unlocked it. "Maybe we should get you checked." He did not look well.

"I'll be all right," Fox said stepping by her and into the trailer. "I need a shower to get this shit off me."

Jill followed. "I'll make some coffee."

254

Fox stripped off his pants and wet shirt in the small bathroom. They were cold and stiff with grit and cement encrustations. His skin was sandy and blanched with lime. He turned the shower on, adjusted it to hot and climbed in.

Jill found the coffee and brewed a pot. She cleaned her nails in the kitchen sink. There were dark lines of cement under each nail. She noticed her own hands were trembling. She washed her hands, her arms and the front of her uniform shirt. She took off the heavy leather belt and gun. Sand and grit fell to the floor. "Shit." She pulled her pants out from her stomach and grimaced as a finger dug sand from her navel.

Jill had her blouse unbuttoned and was wiping sand and grit from beneath bra straps when the shower turned off. She rebuttoned her blouse and was pouring coffee when something crashed in the bathroom.

Bolting down the narrow hallway, Jill paused at the bathroom door. She heard sobbing on the other side. "John!" She was frightened.

Fox didn't answer.

Jill's heart raced as she listened. The sobbing was muffled. She pushed the door open to find Fox standing in front of the sink. He was nude. A towel lay at his feet. He had his hands clasped over his face. His back and shoulders hunched as deep emotional sobs shook him.

Jill stepped and drew him into her arms. He buried his face on Jill's shoulder and wept. The emotional dam welling in Fox had broken. Jill held him, stroking his neck and rubbing his back. He was warm and smelled of soap. "It's okay," she whispered into his wet hair. "It's gonna be all right." She could feel his tears on her neck. Her own spilled and ran down her cheek and under her jaw.

When his sobs began to subside, Jill lifted his face

from her shoulder and took his hand. She led him from the bathroom into the bedroom. It was a small room filled with a bed that left little space around it. The mini blinds were closed, but sunlight filtered in around the edges. Jill pushed the sheets and blankets aside and Fox sank to the edge of the bed. "I made coffee," she said running a hand along his cheek. He looked like a frightened adolescent. "Cover up. I'll be right back."

Jill turned to leave but Fox took her hand. "What?" she questioned with a look and saw the answer. He had an erection. Fox pulled on her arm drawing her face down to his. He kissed her. At first, she just allowed it. It was a hungry, passionate kiss and Jill finally willingly yielded to it. She felt him push between her legs. She squeezed his erection with her thighs as a signal of approval. He unbuttoned the front of her uniform shirt, pulled a bra cup aside and covered her breast with his mouth. She gasped in a breath. Holding the breast in his mouth, Fox unbuttoned her pants and pushed them down taking her panties with them. Jill reached and unhooked her bra as much for comfort as passion. It was twisted and stretched. Fox pulled the bra and blouse away and moved his mouth to the other breast.

Lifting her, he turned and dropped her onto the bed. He was quickly atop her. His tongue found hers as his erection probed. Jill adjusted her buttocks to accommodate him. Fox pushed into her with a hungry lust-filled thrust. Jill moaned, hugged him and bit into his neck.

The bed squeaked and thumped against the thin wood paneling of the trailer as Fox hammered at the supple body beneath him. Jill arched her back. Fox's pace was quickening. She could feel the muscles in his back and neck tightening. The breath in her hair was rushed and shallow. She wrapped her legs around him. Fox groaned and bit her shoulder with restraint. The spasm of climax shook his body. Jill knew it was important, so she tensed, gripped him tight and raised her buttocks. Biting him softly on the neck, she moaned.

speared and on her shoulder with a second. The pain
terrified her close blackout, although knew it was important to
be around, helped him relax and raised her furiously
fully in securely until she moaned

17   CURVES AHEAD

"Those who save the life of another
living thing become its caretaker."
Mojave Legend

Fox slept and Jill showered. She had much to think
about. She had heard the story of why Fox left the FBI,
what brought him to Parker, his link to the tribe. She
understood—perhaps more than he—the desire, the
need to seduce her. It reinforced a shattered male ego.
An ego battered and shaken with lost love and tragedy. It
wasn't so unlike her drive to dance nude in front of
other men after being betrayed by a husband in love
with a younger woman. Jill didn't mind making love
with John Fox. She had even enjoyed it. What she hoped
was that she hadn't been fucked. Screwing the boss
usually meant getting screwed by the boss. She was

uncertain what lay ahead. How should she act? How would he act? She had no answers, just serious fears.

The search for answers was also underway at the casino construction site. Sergeant Tom Bear-Don't-Walk and two patrolmen arrived shortly after Virgil Tanner's body was taken away. Amos Moses already had a crane and cables hooked to the twisted, fallen mass. "Gotta get this cleared before the cement sets," he told Bear-Don't-Walk, "otherwise we'll have to blast the shit outta here."

"What happened?" Bear-Don't-Walk questioned.

Moses shrugged. "It fell down. Shit happens! Lucky there wasn't more hurt."

Chief Stoner, several council members and David Rollins drove to the double-wide trailer in the valley where Virgil's mother and dead brother's wife lived. Mary Tanner, a tall, heavy Mojave woman was pinning laundry to a sagging clothesline in the back yard when the two pick-up trucks arrived. She stopped to stare as the men climbed out. Chief Stoner led the group to her. A chained dog was yapping with anxiety. "Mary, can we talk inside?" the Chief said.

"Is it Virgil?" the woman questioned.

The Chief nodded. The clothes on the line snapped and flapped in the heat and wind. "I'm sorry," he said.

"Both my sons," Mary Tanner sniffed. Her eyes were welling with tears. "Just like their daddy. Just lived too hard."

"We'll take care of things," the Chief assured. "There will be insurance."

Mary nodded. "Guess we'll know what to name the baby. Ruth Ann is pregnant."

"Virgil would be proud," the Chief suggested.

"Would you help me tell the girl?" Mary questioned, wiping a tear.

The Chief nodded and the woman led the way to the house.

Dennis Milner paced in the executive trailer like a caged bird on a perch. He was angry and desperate. His mind was filled with a rush of schemes and ideas. All of them trying to piece together his shattered fantasy. It was DePalma. He had no doubt about that. Amos Moses and Lana were his puppets. Moses was right. He wasn't in charge of jack shit. They only let him think he was. It was all smoke and mirrors to fool the Indians. He was stupid enough to think DePalma would let him build it. That's why Lana had stroked him. Lured him away so the asshole could sabotage the superstructure. Cocksucker! He'd show them.

He pictured himself meeting with Mara and the gimp fuck, David Rollins. He'd lay it all out. They're not going to build it. Not now, not ever! Just gonna bleed you out with stalls, accidents and fuckups until the White Buffalo is nothing but a big pile of bankrupt cow shit! Maybe together they could fuck DePalma. Maybe they could bury his ass in cement. Milner's fantasies stopped when Amos Moses opened the door. The big man was sweaty. His black skin glistened. Stepping in, he closed the door and pulled off his hard hat. "You know what's worse than a fuckin Indian?... A fuckin' Indian cop."

"They're gonna find out what happened," Milner warned. He moved behind his desk as if that would protect him from the man.

Moses sat down on a stool in front of an inclined drafting table covered with blueprints. "I'll tell you what happened," he said with restraint. "Me and that badge with a ponytail dug in that pile of shit out there and found the beam that failed. It was a thirty-six inch. Should've been a forty-eight. Guess who signed off on it... You."

"You're not blaming this on me," Milner exploded.

"Not unless you don't shut your mouth. It's a fuckin' accident. That's all. You got that?"

"I'm not gonna take responsibility for...," Milner stopped when the door opened. It was Lana Casner. She looked at the two men, sensed the tension.

"I just spoke with Don," Lana announced. "He's worried about this. He wants a full report," she said with a look a Milner. "He'll call you tonight at seven... In your room."

"We're not supposed to call him from here," Milner warned.

"I used my own cell," she defended. "He wants you to assure the Indians everything's on track. A tragic accident, but you'll get things back on schedule."

Milner wanted to believe it. Maybe it was just an Indian fuck-up. "He said that?"

"That's exactly what he said," Lana was convincing. "I think he's beginning to realize this place can make money."

"About Goddamned time," Milner suggested.

"I gotta get back out there. Maybe we'll only lose three days." Moses grabbed his hard hat.

"Make that two days," Milner urged. "I'll pay the overtime."

"You just take care of the Indians." Moses pointed a finger at Milner as he crossed to the door.

"Haven't you heard?" Milner smiled sarcastically. His confidence was returning. "We're blood brothers. I'm the reason you got this fuckin' job."

"Uh-huh," Moses said, stepping out the door.

Milner looked to Lana. "You wanna go get a drink or something?"

Fox slept soundly for two hours. He awoke to the scent of her. He pushed up on an elbow and listened. She was in the bathroom. He could hear movement on the countertop. Brushes, combs, he wasn't sure what. It had been a long time since he had awakened to a woman. He flushed with guilt realizing he had seduced an employee, a subordinate, a woman who had done nothing more than offer sympathy and help. He tempered his guilt by remembering the heat of their passion. Hell, it wasn't planned. It just happened. He savored the memory. God, she was beautiful. A centerfold. She was as beautiful as... He stopped the thought. There was no need to compare. Jill was Jill. He was confident she was as eager for it as he had been. He thought about her responses, her moves, the touch of her skin. Feeling a stirring in his groin, he was suddenly aware of his nudity. He swung his feet to the floor.

Pulling on pants and a shirt, Fox expected to find Jill in the bathroom. He was wrong. She was in the kitchen pouring coffee. "Hi," she said without turning. She had heard his approach. She was dressed in panties and one of his tee shirts.

"Hi," he answered admiring the legs, remembering their embrace.

Jill carried two mugs to a small table that sat against a wall beneath a window. Everything in the trailer seemed small and scaled down. Fox sat down across from her. Their knees touched. "Sorry," he said accepting the mug.

Jill smiled. "Let's see, you've got a mole on your lower back and you know I sunbathe in the buff, but when you touch my knee under the table, you say sorry."

"Sorry," Fox said matching her smile.

"Well," Jill said raising her coffee mug, "here's to moles, tans and better days."

Fox touched his mug to hers and they drank. "Where's your shirt?... Not that the tee shirt looks bad."

"Let's see," Jill said raising her chin in mock serious-ness. She had a slender nose and pouty lips. Her hair was gathered and pinned up. She had washed it, Fox thought. "Last time I saw my shirt; it was with your pants... Now where could they be? I hate when this happens."

Fox studied Jill as she talked. Intense blue eyes. Flaw-less complexion. White, perfect teeth. He decided he loved her. Not in a romantic sense. Hell, he hardly knew her, but what he did know, he liked. She had taken what could have been an awkward, difficult after-encounter and turned it into pleasure. That was it, he decided. Jill had turned pain to pleasure. She was doing it with inno-cence and grace. The only way it could be done.

Jill was relieved to see Fox smile. It was a sincere smile. He wasn't playing the role of boss or seducer. He wasn't playing a role at all. God, there was a concept for manhood. She knew anxiety was making her a motor-mouth. She fought the urge to tell him more, to assure him she wasn't easy: To tell him she hadn't been with a man since her husband. To tell him the pain of being naked but lonely in a room full of cat calling rednecks. To tell him of the fear of being a thirty-two-year-old woman without enough money to buy her child food. To tell him she was sorry he hurt.

Fox held Jill's look for a moment then, after a glance into his coffee, he found her eyes again. "Seriously, Jill, I'm sorry for today. I need to..."

She reached across the table and pressed a finger to his lips. "Shhh," she warned, "don't fuck it up."

Fox smiled. "Your choice of words is interesting."

Jill pushed to her feet. "What you see is what you get... Come on, I wanna go home and go to bed... Alone."

They dressed and Fox drove to the construction site. He was surprised at the level of activity. The debris from the second story collapse at the front of the casino's skeletal frame had been lifted away by crane and laid in a nearby twisted heap. The spilled cement, dried into a lumpy, gray mass, was being scooped up by two diesel-powered skip loaders to be dumped into waiting trucks. The rebar crew, framers and plumbers were busy working, repairing the damage, looking like spiders mending a torn web. There was little evidence a man had died. Fox wasn't surprised. It would take much more than one dead Indian to stop the money machine.

Fox parked near the security trailer, turned off the engine and looked to Jill. She was dressed in wrinkled and cement-stained pants and shirt. "Okay, so I don't look good in concrete," she said, catching his look.

"You saved me twice today. Thanks."

"My pleasure," Jill quipped and climbed out. "But now I have to go chisel my pants off. See you tomorrow."

A weary Jake Collins was at the desk in the security trailer. He got up to yield the chair when Fox entered. "How are you feeling?"

"Fortunate," Fox didn't want to talk about his four-hour absence. Collins was a streetwise, savvy cop who could quickly discern bullshit. "Who's on duty?"

"Martinez and Two Feathers," Collins answered. "Schedule's on the desk. Tribal Police showed up. Took pictures. Asked questions."

"Bear-Don't-Walk?"

"Yeah," Collins smiled scratching his beard. "Hear he may be changing his name to Bear-don't-smell."

Fox ignored the remark. He sat down behind the desk.

"Bear-Don't-Walk and Moses found the problem," Collins continued. "Wrong support beam. Couldn't handle the weight. Collapsed under the stress."

"Who's responsible?" Fox questioned.

"Didn't ask" Collins answered. "Figured that was your business."

Fox nodded. "You've had a long day. I appreciate your covering for me.... But now go get some rest."

"Gladly," Collins agreed, moving for the door. "Jill okay?" He paused.

"Yeah. She just went home."

"Ballsy girl, isn't she? Climbing up that damned ladder, pulling you out of the cement."

"She gets my vote," Fox agreed.

"She's not married, is she?" Collins asked.

Collins knew Jill was divorced. He was probing, staking a claim and Fox recognized that. "I don't think so."

"Well, glad you're okay. See ya in the morning." He stepped out the door. Fox picked up the schedule. He was going to separate Collins and Jill.

Mara, David Rollins and George Manygoats were searching through copies of the construction contract when a knock sounded at the door. Fox opened it. "Got a minute?"

Mara was relieved to see him, although she said nothing.

"Sure, come on in," David Rollins said. "Are you all right?

"Fine," Fox assured. "Shower and a clean shirt were all I needed."

"We're looking at who's responsible for accidents during construction," David advised. "It appears to be Navco's."

Fox glanced at Mara as he moved to the conference table where they sat. He could feel Mara evaluating him and it made Fox self-conscious. It was as if she were some silent Indian sex detector. His ears warmed with guilt. These three people had lost a life-long friend, a fellow tribal member. They hadn't run away to hide and weep in a crowded, humid trailer bathroom or get laid. They were worried about the consequences. They were taking care of business. What had happened to his life? Where there had once been order, pride, drive, direction and purpose, there now seemed to be only doubt and guilt. Maybe he had become Sprite Man.

Maybe Virgil's nickname for him was more than a tease. Maybe it was some intuitive spiritual insight Indians had. Maybe Virgil understood that like some human compass that had lost its bearing. Fox was now thinking with his dick instead of his brain. It was late in the game and he was losing. And to make it worse, Mara knew it. Her look told him that. He looked at her. "It's that responsibility I have a question about," he said reaching for an official tone.

"What is your question?" Mara asked holding his look. It was as if her dark eyes were searching his mind.

"We need to determine responsibility," Fox answered. "To make sure it doesn't happen again and to make sure it was an accident."

"Do you have any reason to believe it wasn't?" Mara questioned.

"No, but a man lost his life. That demands we consider all possibilities."

"Do what you must," Mara said looking to David and George for agreement. They nodded.

"I think this must be done quickly," David added. "Delay could bring suspicion."

"I'll make it a priority," Fox turned for the door.

"The girl," Mara questioned. Fox paused, looked to her. "...the one in uniform?"

"Jill," Fox answered.

"Is she all right?"

Fox nodded. "Getting some rest. She tried to save Virgil's life... Did save mine."

Mara held his look. "There is a Mojave saying that warns those who save a life become responsible for it."

She knows, Fox thought. Not only did she know, but she was taunting him with sarcasm. "She's not Mojave," Fox answered flatly. He stepped out the door.

Dennis Milner had it back. He had put Humpty-Dumpty back together. A morning filled with doubt and fear like the debris from the second story collapse was being swept away. Fate was being kind. He had even laughed aloud when he learned the fuckin' Indian that filled his car with cement was the one that drowned in it. Now, with a Mexican lunch and two margaritas in his stomach and Lana at his side, he was returning to the construction site to finish the afternoon. Lana had even played footsy with him at lunch while he talked about his plans for managing the White Buffalo. "Tits 'n' ass," he had proclaimed. "That's what the place needs. Sex sells. Good lookin' babes to bring em' in." Now all he had to do was sell the idea to DePalma. And, like Lana said, even he was beginning to come around. Hell, he was almost looking forward to tonight's call. As he drove, Milner reached and laid a hand on a nylon-clad leg above Lana's knee. As he slid it higher exploring the inner thigh, Lana's hand stopped him. "I have my seatbelt on," he said with a glance at her.

"You still have to watch for curves," Lana warned.

"You gonna come over tonight?... Be there when DePalma calls?"

"Call me afterwards," she suggested. "Then we won't be interrupted." She lifted her hand off his and he slid it higher on her thigh.

"Why don't we go back to the trailer and lock the

door?" Milner pushed his fingers into the nylon web between her legs.

Lana closed her eyes, leaned her head back and sighed. "Promise you'll tell me what we do if Don says no?" She forced the words.

Milner's pulse pounded with excitement. He probed the nylon with his fingers while watching the road ahead. "What we do?" He laughed. "You want in, don't you?"

"Well," Lana smiled, reaching to grasp an erection swelling beneath Milner's pants. "Isn't in what you want?"

Fox walked the construction site. It was unnerving to stand where the tons of wet cement had cascaded down from above. It was difficult to imagine Virgil dying. The dam buster may have died, but his Samson-like act likely saved the lives of others. The sanitized site revealed nothing. Fox went to the pile of twisted I-beams lifted from the collapse. They lay curled and bent like discarded leather belts. He compared a thirty-six-inch beam to a forty-eight. The difference was significant. Someone had made a reckless mistake.

He was brushing his hands, walking back onto the construction site when Milner pulled in with Lana Casner. Fox walked into their path as they headed for the company trailer. He had already thought about the tactic to use. In the Bureau they called it bold and cold. A harsh verbal slap in the face. "We've got to talk," Fox said, blocking Milner's way. He deliberately avoided a look at the woman. She was to be ignored. It was part of the ploy.

Fox read apprehension on Milner's face. When he opened his mouth to speak, Fox took the initiative away from him. "It's important and it's now," Fox declared.

The woman did what Fox trusted her instincts would

force her to do. Avoid confrontation. "I'll be inside, Dennis." She squeezed his hand and moved away.

Again, Fox took the initiative. He turned and walked to the center of the construction site. It was late afternoon. The temperature was in the mid-nineties. Most of the hard hats were gone. Two electricians worked atop a ladder pushing conduit through a remaining network of girders. An unseen laborer hammered somewhere. It was cooler inside the stark shadows of the tilt-up walls. Milner followed. "All right, what the hell is it?" he demanded in his best CEO tone.

Fox took a step toward him crowding the normal space between two men. It was meant to be 'in your face' and Fox made it that. "I'll tell you what it is! It's an order from a Federal Court declaring this construction site unsafe and shutting it down! It's an order seizing your cash assets and it's an order for you to appear in front of a Federal Grand Jury in Phoenix."

"Whoa, whoa," Milner urged. "We can work this out," He was shaken. "This was nothing but an accident. We're sorry about what happened, but we can get things back on track." Sweat was beading on his forehead.

It was a subtle mistake, but Fox caught it. Milner referred to we. Before, his ego had always spoke of I. Now under threat it became we. The threat had worked. He was in business with someone. He was, as Fox suspected, a stooge. A front man. A throw-away. Fox came at him again. "They put you out here and said they'd take care of you, didn't they, Dennis?" He didn't wait for an answer. "Give you money, a title, good looking woman."

Milner's Adam's apple moved as he swallowed. He was listening.

"But they didn't tell you what was gonna happen when shit went wrong, did they. They didn't tell you whose balls were gonna get crushed, did they. Well, it's time, Dennis. The line's been drawn, and your ass is on it. You can tell me what happened, and we'll sit down with the tribe and make a deal.... Or the party's over. Which is it?"

Fox knew an innocent man would answer without hesitation. An innocent man would tell him to go to hell and walk away. Milner did neither. His face was a cloud of doubt. Fox deliberately backed off a step allowing the man room. It worked. "I need... I need some time to think."

"We don't have time, Dennis." Fox walked around behind him. "A man has already died. People want answers. People are angry."

Milner turned to him. He glanced at his watch. "The workday's over... How about morning? I need some time."

"Seven o'clock, Dennis," Fox warned. "You fuck me, and I'll stick the court order up your ass."

Milner raised his hands, opened them. It was a clear sign of submission. "I'll be here... I'm sure we can work things out." At first Milner had been frightened, but these people wanted to make a deal. If DePalma wouldn't buy into his scheme to build the fuckin' casino, he'd simply defect to the Indians. He now had an option. "You got my word," Milner added. "I'll be here.

Fox walked away from him without comment.

"Fuckin' Fed-ex," Milner muttered sarcastically. If he made a deal with the Indians, he promised himself, Fox was going to be the first asshole fired.

Fox was elated. Finally, something had gone right. He had to fight to restrain his excitement until he was inside the security trailer. Closing the door, he cocked an arm and growled, "Yes!" In a little over twelve hours he'd have answers for the Enterprise Board. He was aching to know too. Who the hell was the we? Who was Milner in business with? Was the collapse an accident or sabotage? If it were sabotage, Virgil's death would be murder.

In the meantime, Fox had a hundred things to do. Collins had been at the helm in security. Fox appreciated that, but he wanted things done his way. He had to revise the schedule. Jill deserved day watch. Her heroism earned her that. Perhaps he'd make her a sergeant or lieutenant. None of his considerations had anything to do with their lovemaking, he assured. There were also post assignments and responsibilities. There were two armed men on duty. They knew they were casino security, but what were they supposed to do and when were they supposed to do it? Who was in charge? A watch log had to be organized. Reporting policy defined. Employee ID cards and parking passes had to be created and issued. Inventory controls established. Vendor access defined. A security fence and night lighting had to be installed. Detention and arrest policy had to be established, written and incorporated into an operation manual. The casino surveillance plan had to be reviewed and approved. Personnel files and training had to be organized and implemented. Hell, he had people working for him he had only spoke to during their hire interview.

In addition to the internal administrative mountain he had to climb, Fox faced a similar challenge with National Indian Gaming and the Arizona State Gaming Commission. A stack of unopened mail from both organizations demanding attention laid on his desk.

Tackling the formidable task was like working on a car with the engine running, Fox thought. Eventually a finger would get caught in a fan belt, and one had. The collapse of the second story that took Virgil Tanner's life demanded an investigation. Comparing support beam sizes wasn't exactly an in-depth investigation. Who selected the beam? Who inspected the welds? Who approved the pour?

Shaking Dennis Milner by the roots brought a momentary rush of satisfaction, but unless it evolved into something more, he knew he was facing a tough investigation. An investigation that would demand time, concentration and effort. An investigation that would have to share its demands with a hundred others. Christ, he was beginning to have doubts about his ability to do it. Especially in the short sixty days that remained. Could it be that being an FBI agent was easier than being a Director of Casino Security? Pulling the watch assignment schedule in front of him, Fox picked up a pen. He really understood why men farmed. He missed the clarity of the work, the fields and Virgil's simple admonishment... "Just keep it in a straight line."

"I hope I can, Virg," Fox whispered. "I hope I can."

Dennis Milner's stomach was in a knot. Returning to the executive trailer, he went to his desk and dug for a roll of antacid tablets. Lana locked the door and followed him. She massaged his neck and shoulders as he crunched three of the chalky tablets in his mouth. "What's wrong?" she questioned. "What did he want?"

Milner ignored her and pushed up to cross to a bottled water dispenser. "Fuckin' Mexican food," he complained downing two quick cups.

Lana settled her buttocks on the corner of a desk. Keeping her feet on the floor but separating them, she tightened her mini skirt across her thighs. Milner noticed. He crushed a paper cup and discarded it. Lana dug in a pocket on her shirt and slowly pulled out a pair of panty hose.

"You took them off?" Milner was surprised.

"Weren't they in your way?" She tossed the panty hose

at him. Milner grabbed them in the air and pushed them to his face. He inhaled. "You smell good enough to eat."

"Want dessert?" she smiled, sliding her bottom back atop the desk, raising her feet off the floor. She inched the mini skirt up. Milner crossed to the door locked it and returned to Lana. He went down on his knees. To push face between her legs. She grabbed the sides of his head. "Business first," she warned, "pleasure second... What did the man want?"

"He's making bullshit threats," Milner said, looking up at Lana from between her legs. His face was flushed with excitement. "Talking about a Grand Jury investigation." He lowered his face and pushed. Lana slid her hands to the back of his head. She closed her eyes and drew in a breath as his mouth found her. Milner's head bobbed as he licked at her. She swayed under his touch for a moment and then pulled him away. "What is it he wants?" she questioned with effort.

Milner looked up, licking his lips. "Wants to know who I'm in business with."

"Did you tell him?"

"No, but if DePalma fucks me around, I can make a deal with them. I know I can."

Lana smiled at Milner and pushed his head back into her. "You're a clever man, Dennis."

Jill did all the things she had to do. A ritual that usually led to sleep; a hot shower, shave the legs and underarms, a quick call to mom in Phoenix, Scotty was fine, yes, she would give him a kiss, close the blinds, set the alarm. But sleep hadn't come. She was beyond tired. She was exhausted. The images of John Fox kept her awake, more than images, the vivid memory of his touch, his hunger, his kiss, his vulnerability. She wished she had been more relaxed, more honest. Jesus, being Jill Cox wasn't easy! Why could some women, even dumpy women, marry attorneys, doctors, brokers and have one point six kids, drive Volvo station wagons, go to country club dances, while she went to fuckin' Parker, Arizona? Money. She'd come because of the money. Now even that was muddled with the ache she had for this man.

At thirty Jill had planned on having her life firmly under control. It wasn't. The best laid schemes had taken on a disturbing sarcasm. Her life, any woman's life she decided, was half over. Half over and less than half done. Instead of a married professional she was a single parent starting over. More than an ex-cop or an ex-anything she was a topless dancer. And if you bared your tits in public everyone knew you had to be an immoral nymphomaniac. Everyone wanted to see them, everyone looked, but then everyone judged. Flat chested women didn't know how fortunate they were.

Love, faithfulness and hard work had brought her nothing but a stinging betrayal. Jill was hungry for love, wanted to believe in it, but no longer could trust it. How many times could a woman fall in love? How many times could a life be rebuilt? She had no time to waste. Life it turned out was much like the tank of gas that brought her to Parker. It cost a lot and it would take her only so far. The lesson was you had to be damned sure where you were going.

Jill wanted to believe John Fox was the man he seemed to be, but even if he were, she had little hope the former FBI agent and widower would be interested in an ex topless dancer. He had even said as much. And, now they had crossed the line into intimacy, all of his sensitivity could be little more than regret. Life was a bitch. When sleep finally came she had tears in her eyes.

Seven o'clock came and the anticipated call from Donald DePalma didn't. Dennis Milner paced in his room at the Queen's Bay Inn in Lake Havasu City.

Straight scotch in hand, he was mildly drunk, worried and pissed. It was now twenty minutes to ten. He considered calling Hanes in the room next door, but what could that fat fuck do? Shit, by now he hoped to have Lana Casner sucking his dick in celebration. He thought of calling her, but he was afraid using the telephone might mean missing DePalma's call. The Sonofabitch! He had planned on everything but his not calling. What the hell did it mean? What the hell could he tell that Fed-ex bastard in the morning? The ring of the telephone stopped Milner's thoughts abruptly. He took a gulp of scotch and grabbed up the receiver. "Hello."

"Dennis, this is Mitch Parsons in Vegas. How are you?"

Parsons was the Casino Manager at the Casa Grande. Hanes had introduced them. Milner was annoyed. "Busy. I'm expecting a call from DePalma."

"I'm calling on Don's behalf," Parsons explained. "He's tied up. He wanted me to ask you to be available tomorrow night. Same time. Can you do that?"

"Fuck!" Milner complained. "I'm under a lot of pressure."

"Mr. DePalma appreciates that, Dennis. You're a resourceful man. It's just one more day."

"It better be fuckin' tomorrow," Milner warned, "or the shit hits the fan!"

"Goodnight, Dennis." The man hung up.

"Cocksucker," Milner growled and slammed down the receiver.

Two more glasses of scotch and two hours of HBO had Milner asleep on the bed. Curled in a fetal position, he held a pillow with one hand and his testicles with the other while two TV detectives tracked a cat burglar. The ring of the telephone again and again finally brought Milner out of his alcoholic stupor. Once he realized it was the telephone, Milner struggled to clear his mind. Shit, it was DePalma. Parsons had found him, told him how important it was and now he was calling. He stretched and gathered the receiver. "Hello." A bedside clock radio read three-twenty-two.

"Dennis?" It was Amos Moses.

"Yeah." Milner recognized the voice.

"Something's wrong at the job site," Moses said. "I need you and Hanes down here right now."

"Wrong!?! What's wrong?" Milner was alarmed. He was in a fog. He wished he hadn't drank so much.

"Just get your ass down here, man," Moses urged. "We can't talk on the phone."

Milner swung his feet to the floor. "Okay. Okay."

"I called Hanes. He'll meet you at the car."

"The car... Okay."

"Hurry, man." Moses hung up.

"Fuck," Milner complained, reaching for his pants.

Milner ate a mint left by a maid to fight the aftertaste of sleep and scotch. He had trouble finding his socks and discovered he was still wearing them.

The obese Hanes, hair in disarray, a worried look on his face, waited beneath a cone of light from an overhead parking lot lamp near the car. Milner appeared out of the shadows. "Did Moses say what was wrong?" Hanes questioned apprehensively.

Milner tossed the car keys at Hanes. "No. Let's get going." It was a thirty-five-mile drive and Milner was hoping he could get some sleep.

"You wanna stop and get a doughnut or something?" Hanes asked unlocking the car.

U.S. 95 south of Lake Havasu City followed the eastern shore of the massive, man-made inland sea. The first fifteen miles of the route was nearly arrow straight with only gentle dips. Even in the cloak of early morning darkness, median stripe paint and cat-eye reflectors made the road user friendly. Hanes maintained an easy seventy-miles-an-hour while Milner slept. The high beam headlights reaching far ahead had dimmed only twice for northbound traffic. The desert was at rest.

At the midpoint of the drive to Parker, the wide, straight interstate started downhill to reach almost water level at the Bill Williams River, a minor tributary of the Colorado. A half-mile-long arch bridge stretched low across the point where the river met the lake. Hanes glanced at a "bridge ahead" sign appearing out of the darkness. He knew Parker was now only fifteen miles away. In Parker he would be able to get a pastry and hot chocolate. The doughnut shop opened at five AM. He glanced at Milner slumped on the passenger's side. He was snoring and filling the car with his foul alcoholic breath.

Hanes slowed as he approached the bridge. He knew from making the drive before that there was a gentle turn to the right. A set of bright headlamps was closing fast from behind. He hoped it wasn't the Arizona Highway Patrol. Hanes glanced at his speed. Sixty. A truck pulling a boat had passed him earlier. Tourist trying to beat the drive in the heat. He was betting it was another one. Whatever it was, the lights were closing fast. Bastard. Must be going eighty or ninety, Hanes speculated. They were onto the bridge. Jesus, the idiot was going to pass on the bridge. The glare was blinding now. Hanes averted his eyes from the rear-view mirror concentrating on the road ahead. As soon as the bastard passed, Hanes was going to switch on his brights.

The impact was severe. The Lincoln surged ahead. In panic, Hanes jerked on the wheel. The car swerved to the left and struck a three-foot-high cement rail. Chrome and glass sprang into the night. The dual air bags exploded. Dennis Milner tried to move and couldn't. Sparks sprang into the night. Metal dug savagely into the bridge rail as the car slid along it. Slamming into a support post, the big car cartwheeled like a toy. A heavy splash spewed up as the Lincoln hit the water. It sank quickly. Eight feet below the surface, light shimmered up from the car's headlamps. Again, the desert was quiet.

18 THE WHO

> *"Among the Indians there have been no written laws.*
> *Customs handed down from generation to*
> *generation*
> *have been the only laws to guide them."*
> **George Copway—Ojibwa chief**

Fox worked in the security trailer at the construction site until nearly three AM. He was dead tired when he fell into bed, but it was a good tired, not unlike a day cutting alfalfa. Although the backlog of work wasn't done, he had a game plan. The task was organized. Jill was now the Security Administration Manager. Manager sounded better than secretary and he really intended for her to manage the routine business. Plus, with Mara's subtle but sarcastic inquiry regarding Jill's wellbeing, he was certain making her a secretary would have drawn more criticism.

Watch assignments were made. Teaming the experienced with lesser experienced. Posts were assigned. Responsibilities defined. Logs initiated. Fox's Army, such as it was nick named by Collins, was on the field. Fox sought sleep, trying not to remember the desperate look on Virgil Tanner's face just before the collapse or his own fear after being swallowed by the cascade of cement. Remembering, Fox had learned, did little but extend the pain.

A thump awoke Fox at five-fifteen. He looked at the clock. The alarm was set for five-thirty. His last thoughts before sleep were of the seven o'clock meeting with Dennis Milner. He considered being late. It could give him a psychological edge, but his own eagerness dismissed it. He wanted to know. Fox swung his feet to the floor and grabbed for his slacks. Probably some weekend weenie from California at the wrong trailer. The plague of Parker was the desert rats that descended on the river every weekend like a horde of lemmings with boom boxes and beer. Fox tramped to the trailer's front door intent on having a piece of some muscle shirt's ass. He opened the door to find Bear-Don't-Walk waiting. He was still wearing a swath of tape across his nose under the brim of his Stetson. "Lana Casner may be dead. Thought you might be interested."

Fox was interested. A few minutes later he was strapped into the Sergeant's Tribal Police car as it sped north on U.S. 95 at over a hundred-miles-an-hour. Fox discretely tightened his seat belt as Bear-Don't-Walk lit a cigarette and talked. "Other day when Virgil cemented Milner's car, I took down a few license numbers. Figured they might be good to have."

Fox nodded wondering wishing he would have thought of that.

"Heard Department of Public Safety dispatcher,"

Bear-Don't-Walk pointed at a bank of radios mounted between the two of them on the floor, "talking about a Lincoln going off the Bill William's Bridge.... Couple bass fishermen spotted it. License number matched Lana's car."

The bridge was easy to find. It was ablaze with flashing emergency lights. A heavy-duty tow truck, two Arizona Highway Patrol cars, an ambulance and a La Paz County Sheriff's car jammed the northbound lane of the low bridge. An arc of burning flares lying on the road hissed out acrid, sulfur-laden smoke and ominous red-tinted light. Several uniformed officers with flashlights directed what little traffic there was traffic. A heavy, cable stretched from the tow truck's crane to the surface of the dark water where several men in wet suits stood in an aluminum boat shouting commands and waving lights.

Bear-Don't-Walk parked at the end of the bridge. Fox walked with him to a knot of officers near the tow truck. A veteran of crime scenes crowded with uniformed officers from a variety of jurisdictions, Fox expected Bear-Don't-Walk to be greeted with the proverbial nod of acknowledgment dictated by the unwritten protocol of the badge. They got nothing except curious glances. It bothered Fox. Bear-Don't-Walk didn't seem to notice.

They stood on the fringe of the group and watched as the thick cable groaned and creaked lifting its find from the shallow water and muck. Hooked around a rear bumper support, the cable lifted the car into the air. Water poured from around the doors in a showery spray. The headlamps were still on. The car spun on the cable like a slow top as water cascaded down.

The crane on the tow truck groaned and the car swung over the rail, rocking and swaying. "Keep clear," the operator ordered. Flood lamps on the cab of the truck covered the hulk with stark white light. Water continued to jet from every crack and crevice. The crane operator pushed a lever and the front bumper of the car inched toward the pavement. The Lincoln seemed to sigh as it settled onto its wheels. The top was slick with muck from the muddy shallow river bottom.

The officers surrounded the car. One opened the driver's door. Water spilled out. The door chime began its faithful warning. The air bag had deflated and looked like a large, wet condom. A gloved hand pulled it away from the form behind the wheel. Hanes sat strapped in the seat, arms limp at his side. Fox recognized him but said nothing. The air bag was torn away from the figure on the passenger's side. The man had twisted completely around beneath the seat belt. His arms were tangled in it and his face was pushed sideways against the leather seat. He had not died without a struggle. Water drained from his nose and mouth. Dennis Milner was dead. A team of paramedics began searching for signs of life they did not expect to find. Fox and Bear-Don't-Walk exchanged a look and turned away.

"Did you see the damage to the taillights?" Bear-Don't-Walk questioned as they walked to the patrol car.

"No," Fox answered, sorry that he hadn't.

"It was bumper level. All the way across."

"Who will investigate this?" Fox questioned.

"Out here?" Bear-Don't-Walk speculated, "Nobody."

Lana Casner had spent an hour packing. The flight from Lake Havasu Municipal Airport, such as it was in some sort of no-service, ten-passenger something, was scheduled for seven-forty and she was going to be on it even if she had to throw someone off. She was sick of pizza and beer and construction sites. If Don ever sent her on another assignment like this, she'd tell him to stuff it. This was whore work and she wasn't a whore. In

Vegas she worked the Premier Escort Service. Fifteen hundred a night. Five hundred more for anything other than straight sex. She had never walked a street in her life. DePalma's money wasn't worth this. She agreed to become his assistant because it was a rush to be seen with the most powerful man in Vegas, not to get sent to the edge of hell. Indians and assholes. She had seen enough for a lifetime. It was back to Vegas and straight to the spa at the Casa Grande. She longed for an oil bath, a full body massage and a facial. Instead of Lake Havasu City, it should be Sand City. A rap sounded on the door. She had called for a cab and a bellman. "It's open," she said, applying lip gloss.

Lana stared as the two men stepped in. She recognized Fox from the casino construction site. She didn't know the man in uniform. He looked like an Indian.

Fox and Bear-Don't-Walk saw the three bags on the floor. "Not coming to the casino today?" Fox questioned soberly.

"Casino?" Lana quipped, sticking cosmetics into a handbag. "Is that what you call that broken chicken coop?"

"What about your car?" Bear-Don't-Walk asked.

"Dennis has my car. What the hell is this? I'm not on your reservation."

"Dennis is dead," Fox said bluntly. "So is Clyde Hanes. They were found in your car."

Lana was shocked breathless. She raised one hand to the middle of her chest and braced the other on the counter.

"Where are you going?" Bear-Don't-Walk pressed.

"Las Vegas," Lana answered and then regretted it. "I... I have family there." It was feeble.

"Thought you were from Saint Cloud?" Fox questioned.

Lana's mind was in a panic. After calling the Don to tell him Milner was going to make a deal with the Indians, he became livid. He told her to get out of Lake Havasu, not to talk to anyone, just leave. Now she wished she had gotten in the car and drove. Fuckin' desert. She hated driving in the desert. And this place with no regular air service! What the hell could she do? She never thought anyone would be killed. Jesus! Was he calling her back to Vegas to kill her? This was worse than when a fucking evangelist died on top of her in the penthouse at the Tropicana. "Maybe it was an accident," Lana said with a worried look at the two men.

"Just like at the casino." Fox suggested.

"I.... I don't know anything," Lana defended. Her hands trembled as she stuffed her purse.

Fox moved closer to her. She refused to look at him. "Vegas isn't a very big town. We can find you there... That is if you don't have an accident first."

Lana gathered courage and burned Fox with a look. "If you don't get out, I'll call the police."

Bear-Don't-Walk crossed to the side of the bed, picked up the telephone and carried it to Lana. Offering it, he said, "Go ahead."

Lana knocked the telephone from his hand. It crashed to the floor. "Get out!" she ordered.

"You better be sure what you're running to is safer than what you're running from," Fox warned.

"Get out!" Lana screamed a second time. Tears were streaming down her face.

The two men moved for the door.

News of the deaths shocked Parker like a California earthquake. The business community reeled under the word of it like a man struck with a ball bat. Someone had killed the Golden Goose! The telephone lines hummed as local merchants tried to reassure one another. It was of little help. Liquor orders were put on hold. Gas prices jumped a nickel and motels demanded cash only. Rumor quickly spread that Navco's capital assets, with the death of its two executives, would be withdrawn by noon. The local markets suspended cashing payroll checks and local banks were all seeking advice from their main branches. No one was really surprised. However, they were all angry *The Indians* had "somehow fucked up a good thing".

The Indians were much more philosophical. Two leather-faced old men sitting on the porch of the store in Poston put it in its proper perspective. "You hear about the wreck?"

"Yup," the second answered. "Death usually comes in threes."

Amos Moses had scheduled more cement pours at the construction site, but the worried driver of the mixer refused to dump the load until he had a signed check in hand. Construction checks required two signatures: one from any of the three members of the Gaming Enterprise Board and one from Navco. The only one authorized to sign Nevco checks was dead and seemingly the world knew it. Dennis Milner's body was being examined in Flossman's Funeral Home in Lake Havasu City by the County Coroner. After forty minutes of haggling, the mixer drove away. The pour was canceled. Eighteen masons were sent away. The driver of the cement truck stopped six miles away and dumped his load alongside a desert road. "Fuckin' Indians," he complained.

Forty minutes after the mud crew walked away, the electricians followed. Then the plumbers and framers. Rumor was payroll checks due in two days had been canceled. By mid-morning the job site was quiet. Work on the White Buffalo had ground to a halt. The caterer finally closed his truck and left. Business was dead.

The two security officers on duty were arguing with Jill Cox when Fox and Bear-Don't-Walk pulled in. "What's the problem?" Fox question when he reached them.

"Everybody's saying there's no checks this week." It was Sanchez, the ex-cop from Barstow. "I got two kids. I can't work for nothing."

"That's bullshit!" Fox countered without hesitation. "You think a fifty-million-dollar deal is going to stop because someone drives a rented car off a bridge? Ever hear of force du jour? It's a clause in the contract that gives the tribe power of attorney in a case like this."

"Well, okay," Sanchez agreed, "but everyone else was saying...."

"We get paid to be smarter than everyone else," Fox snapped. "Now get back to work."

Jill followed Fox and Bear-Don't-Walk toward the security trailer. "What's force du jour?" she asked.

"I have no idea," Fox admitted. He was proud of the loyalty he had seen in her, but in Bear-Don't-Walk's company he said nothing about it.

They paused outside the door of the security trailer. The sprawling construction site was quiet. The outside walls were up. The interior was divided with skeletal framing laced with plumbing and electrical lines. A network of girders crisscrossed the open ceiling. Stacks of stainless ducting, lumber and insulation sat on the now hard floor. "Yesterday an Indian died here, and nothing stopped," Bear-Don't-Walk mused. "Today two white men drown fifteen miles away and everything stops."

Amos Moses didn't have much in the executive trailer. A tool belt, a slide rule and a pair of leather gloves. It was quickly stuffed into his tote bag. He found nearly four-hundred-dollars in an envelope in Milner's desk marked petty cash. He took it. Expenses, he justified. The telephone on the desk rang constantly. Amos ignored it. His work in Parker was finished and he was glad of it. He was tired of being the only black man within fifty miles. He was tired of third-rate motels, redneck bars and fat women. Shit, this fuckin' place didn't even have full-time whores.

By mid-afternoon he'd be back in Vegas. Air conditioning and lights. Maybe he'd have the twelve-ounce fillet at the River tonight. There were always good lookin' babes at the Riv. He pictured himself with a good-looking woman on his arm while he played craps. Steak, a big ass and craps. A trio any man could enjoy. Maybe with his bonus from Mitch Parsons he'd try his craps system. Hell, he could afford it and if it worked, he could afford anything. Amos was stuffing a silver pen from Milner's desk into his pocket. Milner sure as shit wasn't gonna need it anymore. The office door opened. It was the fuckin' Indian that thought he was a cop. He was a quiet, nosy sonofabitch and he made Amos nervous.

Bear-Don't-Walk looked out from under the brim of his Stetson. He glanced at the tote bag sitting on the desktop, then to Amos.

Amos saw the look. He no longer needed to restrain his contempt. He didn't like cops and he didn't like Indians, so disliking this man was easy. "Well Bear-don't-squawk, maybe you and your Indian brothers can turn this place into a Wal Mart."

Bear-Don't-Walk crossed his arms and leaned his back to the wall. "You're quitting?"

Amos zipped the tote bag. "Friend of mine said don't go to work for Indians. They never finish a fuckin' thing they start."

"I'm not the one quitting," Bear-Don't-Walk answered.

"Maybe you're used to working for pinto beans or whatever the fuck you use for wampum," Amos shot back at him, "but I get paid cold, hard cash for what I do and since you've never been anywhere or done anything, let me tell you what's gonna happen. Before the day's over, some attorney representing Milner's estate is gonna stick a court order up some Indian's ass and all this is gonna be tied up in court for the next three to five years. Sorry, my red-skinned brother, but your dream's gonna have a little rust on it." Amos smiled confidently. It was payback. Bear-Don't-Walk had worried him with questions after the collapse.

"Is that what you told the driver of the cement truck?" The dark eyes under the brim of the Stetson questioned.

Amos stiffened. He was surprised at the accusation. The Indian had balls. "If I had time, Cochise, you and I could go outside and settle matters."

Bear-Don't-Walk didn't react to the challenge. Arms still folded, he said, "Maybe while we're out there we could look at the bumper on your truck."

Amos' nostrils flared. "You better watch what the fuck you say. I was nowhere near that fucking bridge when they crashed."

"Who said anything about a bridge?"

Amos grabbed the tote bag and marched for the door. Bear-Don't-Walk unfolded his arms and stepped into his path. Amos, three inches taller and forty pounds heavier, glared at him. "You better get your ass outta the way, Indian."

"Where would you like us to send your final check?"

"Use it to buy a new rug for your fuckin' wigwam," Amos snarled. His face was a mask of anger.

Bear-Don't-Walk knew the talk was over. He saw the

288

muscles in the man's neck tighten. He stepped aside. Moses was quickly out the door. It slammed behind him, rattling the walls.

Amos' dual-wheeled pick-up truck roared out of the parking lot throwing dirt and dust. Bear-Don't-Walk stepped out of the executive trailer. He stood watching as Fox appeared from the corner of the trailer. Fox was carrying a camera "Did you get the pictures?" Bear-Don't-Walk questioned.

Fox shook his head. "You didn't stall him long enough."

"Not long enough?" Bear-Don't-Walk complained, "You had enough time to change the tires. I was about to get my ass kicked."

"Okay," Fox smiled, raising the camera, "maybe I got a few."

"Any fresh damage?"

"Think so."

The three members of the Gaming Enterprise Board were the first tribal officials to arrive at the construction site. They were followed shortly by Chief Stoner and the tribal council. They came in a collection of pick-up trucks and old sedans. The chief's faded Fiat was smoking badly.

A terse call from Mara had both Fox and Bear-Don't-Walk waiting in the security trailer. "The council has questions for both of you." Fox paced, glancing out windows on each circuit, checking his watch. Bear-Don't-Walk sat with his arms folded, Stetson low over his eyes. "You sleeping?" Fox questioned.

"Not now."

"What questions could they have for us?"

"I don't know."

"How about if I go get some coffee and doughnuts?"

Jill volunteered. She had been at a computer inputting personnel data. Fox's pacing was making her nervous.

"Chocolate buttermilk," Bear-Don't-Walk said from beneath his Stetson. His face was hidden.

"And you look like a glazed," Jill said with a glance at Fox. She pushed out of her chair.

"In the FBI we didn't have time for doughnuts," Fox answered, "but I'll take a jelly-filled."

"My favorite." Jill smiled. She gathered her purse and moved for the door. "Be right back."

"And she types too," Bear-Don't-Walk said after the door closed.

"What's that supposed to mean?" Fox questioned wondering if Bear-Don't-Walk was reading something in his relationship with Jill. Since the encounter at the trailer, he had been deliberately cool and business-like.

"Doesn't mean anything," the Stetson answered matter of factly.

Fox studied the sergeant. He was making a much better friend than an enemy. Bear-Don't-Walk had a casual, no-nonsense approach that Fox admired. Among the ranks it was known as command presence. Bear-Don't-Walk exuded it. He didn't have to tell you of his authority. It was his invisible aura. The shoulder patch of the Tribal Police and the badge told you what he was. A quiet, authoritative demeanor told you who he was. Time and fate had drawn a line between them, Fox decided, but it was a thin one.

Mitch Parsons was in the executive board room at the Casa Grande Casino with the staff of gaming managers. It was a weekly meeting and they were reviewing the weekly slot drop. "We're down in quarter slots by eighteen percent. That's a net loss of twenty-two for the calendar month," the rotund, balding slot manager said as the group of eleven suits around the table studied copies of a computer printout. "Some of this we can attribute to the usually warm weather and the increasing price of gasoline, but if it continues, we won't make our end-of-quarter goal."

"What if we gave away a car a day?" marketing suggested.

"The Rio did that for a month," accounting offered. "They lost their ass. Nobody cares about cars. Most slot players are over fifty and already own two point six cars."

"Dollars we took a bath too," the slot manager continued soberly. "Down eleven percent. Nickels, eight percent."

"What do you recommend, Tommy?" Parson's questioned from the head of the table.

"Choke the chicken," the slot manager answered without hesitation. "Crank up the jackpots by two, three hundred percent. Choke off the pay outs. Promise them everything. Give 'em nothing but free drinks and more bells and whistles."

"We could do a big promo on increased jackpots," marketing suggested.

A shapely secretary entered through a discreet door in the dark wood paneling. She leaned to Mitch Parsons' ear and spoke softly. Parsons pushed to his feet. "I have to take a call. Tommy, crunch some numbers. What do we need to stop this hemorrhaging? Talk about it. I'll be right back."

"This is Mitch," Parsons said sliding into the high-backed executive chair at his desk. The panorama of the Las Vegas skyline filled the window behind him.

"Mitch, we did it!" DePalma shouted gleefully into the telephone. "I just got a call. The fuckin' White Buffalo is dead. Everything has stopped." DePalma was on a car phone in the back of his chauffeured Rolls-

Royce. "I'm not gonna forget you came through for me in this."

"I'm glad I was able to help," Parsons answered smoothly, "but I would still recommend follow-up. Send in the legal team. Freeze the assets with a court ordered escrow. Keep them on their knees."

"Do it," DePalma said. "No wonder Wild Bill liked shooting buffaloes from a train. It's fuckin' great."

"I would also recommend closure on the matter," Parsons continued. "Cut the line that puts any possible connection in jeopardy."

"Good point," DePalma agreed. "We still have other assets if needed. Can you make the arrangements?"

"I'll take care of it," Parsons assured.

"You're one step closer to becoming a partner," DePalma intoned.

"Thank you, Don. I appreciate your gratitude." Parsons hung up. "Italian asshole," he muttered in disgust. He had nothing but contempt for DePalma. He wasn't the boy-faced billionaire entrepreneur the world pictured. DePalma was in fact a deviate who spent the majority of his time not managing his fortune but pursuing fantasies about seducing stars and celebrities. Parsons had a fantasy of his own and it was him at the helm of DePalma Gaming. A partnership would bring him the chance. Then he could expose DePalma as the whore-chasing, panty-sniffer he was and seize control. If it took more lives and careers, so be it. Business was business. Parsons picked up the telephone and dialed.

Fox and Bear-Don't-Walk spent nearly two hours fielding questions from the Tribal Council and the Gaming Enterprise Board. It was a tense, candid exchange. Emotions were running high. The Indians knew their individual and collective dreams were on the line. They

292

were dressed in plaid shirts, dusty boots and cotton dresses. But the fate of a fifty-million-dollar gaming venture was in their hands. "So, if I understand," Councilwoman Gail Burton said to Fox, "you expected Dennis Milner to tell you who he was in business with?" They were sitting in folding chairs around a long table. Copies of the construction agreement lay in front of each member.

"Yes," Fox answered. "And I think it's someone opposed to the building of the casino."

"Las Vegas?" Morse Roberts speculated.

"Both Lana Casner and Amos Moses left for Las Vegas. We think they're part of it. So yes, Las Vegas is a likely connection."

"But you don't know who?" Christine Scott questioned.

"No, I don't know who," Fox admitted.

"And the who is still out there?" Chief Stoner reminded.

"Yes," Fox agreed.

Mara, who had been pacing back and forth behind the chairs leaned on the back of one and said, "Why do you care who it is?"

"Because three lives have been lost," Fox defended. The question annoyed him.

"But if you had the name of the individual responsible, what would it change?"

Fox balked. He didn't have an answer.

"We are talking about who," Mara suggested, "but we need to talk about how. How do we save the White Buffalo?"

"Money," Morse Roberts quipped.

"Right," Mara agreed. "Money solves everything. The masons, the framers and the electricians didn't walk away because Dennis Milner was killed. They walked away because they thought they weren't going to get paid."

"And they were right," Horace pronounced. "The money is gone. The contract requires all checks, transfers and drafts be signed by the tribe and the CEO of Navco. He's dead. End of deal. You can't do business with a dead man."

"And we can't touch the money," Morse Roberts complained, massaging the hair on the back of his neck.

"Why not?" Mara challenged.

"Probate," Horace warned. "The court will freeze all the assets of the deceased, decide the legal debts and distribute everything left to rightful heirs. You learn these things with experience." He was annoyed with Mara.

"Where is the money right now?" Mara demanded. Her dark eyes were bright with excitement.

"In the bank," Horace answered flashing her a disapproving look.

"And where's the bank?"

"Bank of Arizona. First Street and Riverside Drive."

"In Parker?" Mara added.

"Yes," Horace snapped making little attempt to hide his anger.

"And Parker is on the Federally recognized reservation of the Mojave Indian Nation... A sovereign nation with its own government, its own laws and its own courts. We have jurisdiction over the money!"

The council members exchanged looks. The air was electric with a mix of anxiety, doubt, fear and hope. Fox's heart was racing with excitement. He wanted to stand and declare Mara right. He hoped she was.

Quickly attention turned to the Chief. The old man had listened attentively. All had given their opinions. Now it was time to weave opinion into consensus and consensus into action. Fox literally held his breath waiting for the old man to speak.

"When we chose this path, I warned there were no footprints to follow... We had to find our own way. I am sorry three men have died: one, a son. I am sorry, but I am not surprised.

"We once fought to keep from being put on a reservation. Should we now be surprised that we must fight to escape it? The reservation that holds us is not only a line on a map, it is also an economic line. We are slaves of poverty. Slaves seldom go free without a fight.

"The sons and daughters of those who put us here offer a hand of sympathy... And their old clothes. It is when we say we want their clothes that the hand is withdrawn.

"The world that wished us well will now say they are sorry to learn of our failure, but they will not help. We must win this fight ourselves. Perhaps that is the lesson Mara has already learned. She is a young woman, but she has the spirit of an elder."

19 REDIAL

"Men and women talk to each other, but seldom do they listen. Much more is understood when they do not talk."

Good Eagle—Dakota Sioux holy man

In its seventy-year history, the Parker Chamber of Commerce had never met with tribal officials. The joke was 'you could tell and Indian a mile away, but up close you couldn't tell him a damned thing'! Local business leaders knew the Indians had no business savvy. Hell, they owned the best property on the river; prime river front that could be lined with condos, marinas and water parks. Instead, the Indians used it for family swimming, bar-b-cues beneath shade trees and fishing. It was a waste and now, when it looked like the impoverished tribe was about to climb out of its financial abyss, the man that led them was dead.

The Indians couldn't do it themselves. Milner's death proved that. Construction stopped immediately. The movers and shakers of Parker's Chamber of Commerce had little concern for any Indian's loss. Their concern was much more personal. They were concerned with empty motel rooms, vanishing lines at gas stations, empty grocery stores, idle banks and over-stocked liquor stores. Parker's sagging tourist economy had been stimulated with a shot of cold, hard cash. Construction of the White Buffalo Casino had brought an influx of six-hundred workers. Men and women with families, appetites and money, but as quickly as they came, they vanished. The desert flashflood of money was gone. The Chamber of Commerce hoped they could bring another green rain.

The call to Chief Stoner's office at the Tribal Administration Office came from the President of the Parker Chamber of Commerce, Judge Jacob Drum. In addition to being judge of the local Justice Court, the judge also owned an auto parts store, a yogurt shop and a video rental shop. Start of construction on the casino had generated a three-hundred-percent increase in his business profits. The judge wasn't about to let it slip away without a fight. After a four-hour emergency meeting with the Chamber, a plan had been formulated. The judge, appointing himself Chairman of the React Committee, decided he was best suited to sell the plan to the Indians. "Hell, I know more Indians than anybody else in this town," he had bragged. "Most of them have stood in front of my bench one time or another."

The meeting was held at Sand Point Landing three miles north of Parker. It was one of the few restaurants large enough to facilitate a private meeting and it also belonged to the Judge's son-in-law. Eleven o'clock was the appointed hour. The judge, along with Ted Brookshire, a local attorney and bar owner, and Ray Wilson, the owner/manager of the River Bend Motel, were waiting when Chief Stoner, Mara Waters and David Rollins arrived. They sat around a large table in a banquet room with a view of the river. The judge introduced himself and his associates. He was disappointed the only Indian he recognized was Chief Stoner. It would have given him an edge, he thought, if they had been among the many, he had sent to the county jail or work farm. The woman was attractive for an Indian. The white she wore amplified her dark eyes and hair, but this meeting was likely a little deep for an Indian woman.

The chief introduced David and Mara. The Judge signaled a waitress to pour coffee. Mara and David both declined. It was a small irritant to the Judge.

"I'll be direct, Chief," the judge warned, straightening his back as if he were on the bench. "We're aware of your problem with construction. Dennis Milner's death must be a great loss to you, but we don't want to see you lose it all because of a single tragic accident. We represent considerable business experience that's underscored by my legal background on the bench. For an equitable share, a percentage of the casino operation, we will find you a qualified construction manager and additional financing if necessary."

The judge paused to study the trio of Indians. They were a tough read. Lack of emotion, he had long ago decided. It was an Indian trait. He wondered if they understood the offer. He probed more. "I think you should also know I have a reputation for being a pretty damned good poker player. I've played in Vegas and Atlantic City. The Card Room Manager at the Aladdin always comps my room. I'm no novice in a casino."

"He's good," Ted Brookshire smiled, patting the judge on the back.

The Indians sat stoic.

The judge exchanged a look with his two associates. His patience was near the limit. In court he wouldn't tolerate such silent contempt.

Finally, the old man spoke. "We appreciate your concern, Judge, but the casino is not for sale."

"Sale," the Judge countered, "we don't want to buy it. Hell, man, we're simply trying to help you save it... I doubt you could find a buyer for it."

"If it has no value, then why are you here?" Mara challenged.

"Because you people need help," the judge quipped.

"You mean us poor, dumb Indians?" David Rollins bristled.

The chief raised a hand to stop the exchange. "Our turn for bluntness, Judge," then with a glance at Mara he added, "Explain what is needed."

"The CO-principal in the construction agreement between the Mojave Nation and the Native American Construction Company is dead," Mara explained. "There is no provision in the contract for such an event, so the agreement is null and void." She aimed the statement at the judge.

"Agreed," he granted grudgingly.

"Which results in financial assets being held in escrow for probate by an appropriate court," Mara added.

"John Doe or Howard Hughes," the judge agreed with a nod. "The result is the same."

"In your experience on the bench, Judge," Mara said playing to the man's ego, "have you seen instances where debtors or surviving family members have submitted petitions of relief for financial hardship?"

"Yes," the judge answered firmly as if it were a ruling.

The woman was smarter than she looked. It surprised him.

"Would you not agree the loss of revenues caused by the stoppage of construction has caused immediate and grave financial hardship for both the Mojave Nation and the Parker Business Community?"

"No question about it," the judge said reinforcing Mara. "That's why we're here."

"Then a petition of exception and financial hardship will be prepared and presented to the court to allow us access to the cash... With a provision to guarantee all other contractual obligations are met to protect unidentified investors."

"And no one gets hurt," the judge smiled. "It's goddamned brilliant! Do it. I'll sign it."

Mara paused. She knew she was facing the same challenge the judge faced earlier selling the idea. "We would like to present it to another court first."

"Another court?" The judge was puzzled. "I'm the law in Parker," his ego declared.

"That's true," Mara conceded. "And that's the reason we would like to hold your authority in reserve. For the real challenge."

"I don't understand," the Judge was amazed.

"Allow me to explain," Mara said in a condescending tone. "We prepare the petition and present it to the Tribal Court."

"Tribal Court?" the judge huffed. He didn't really consider the Tribal Court part of the legitimate judicial system. Hell, the Tribal Judge was an Indian appointed by the Tribal Council. The current Indian judge was a Goddamned farmer. Grew cantaloupes for Christ' sake! "I really don't think this is a Tribal matter," he said spreading his hands before him on the table. "The Tribal Court's jurisdiction is limited to Indian affairs."

"That could work for us," Mara suggested. "The Tribal Court will rule in our favor. Any appeal regarding jurisdiction will come to your court."

"Correct." The judge was listening.

"When the appeal comes, and you take it under submission..."

The judge raised a hand halting Mara. "It would be ill advised to try and influence my decision, young lady."

"Judge," Mara assured, "I agree your reputation for fairness and impartiality wouldn't allow it... But regardless of your decision, researching the matter will take time."

"Granted." The judge's ego had been restored.

"All we ask is consideration in not allowing a temporary court order to stop us. If your final decision is against us, we will appeal. All of this takes time... And all we need is forty-five days."

The judge considered, weighing the possibilities.

"The case will come to your court, Your Honor," David Rollins added, hoping another voice would add weight. "It could go all the way to the Supreme Court."

"It does have complex aspects to it," the judge agreed. He pictured himself talking to Mike Wallace after a final ruling was made.

"We came here today needing help from one another," Chief Stoner said. "We cannot do this without you... And you cannot do it without us."

"How soon do you think construction would resume?" Ray Wilson asked. Only three rooms in his forty-room motel were occupied.

"Tomorrow," Mara answered confidently. "The more time we lose, the more money we lose." She knew the trio of white businessmen weren't there out of benevolence for the Tribe's welfare. It was a matter of color, but the color was green.

301

The judge pushed his chair back and stood up. He was stone-faced. David Rollins felt his stomach muscles tighten. The judge surprised him by sticking a hand across the table to Chief Stoner. "You got a deal, Chief."

The chief grasped the hand.

Mara exhaled softly. She had been holding her breath.

John Fox wouldn't bet on the courts. Experience had taught him not to. He'd seen too many kidnappers, rapists and robbers walk out of courthouses free men. Justice, he had learned, was much like history. The winner decided what was just. Even when convicted, some men would spend their lives watching television, eating well, enjoying free health and dental care, conjugal visits and free legal services for an endless succession of appeals. An eye for an eye. It was the only answer. It worked in football. It worked in the FBI and Fox believed it would work now.

After the meeting with the Council, Fox went to the chief and warned. "We have to find out who Milner was in business with. Do you think he's going to give up just because Milner's dead? He's the one that ordered it."

"And when you find him?" the Chief questioned.

"Turn it over to the FBI," Fox answered.

"You may find things different now that you are here," the old man warned.

"I have found things different," Fox agreed.

"Then do what you must," the Chief said.

Fox needed help, and realizing it was an annoyance. As an FBI agent, he had a vast store of resources at his call. He had learned to take the might and power of the federal agency for granted. It was always there when he needed it. That had changed. Now, as Director of Security for a skeletal, maybe someday casino, he was learning if he couldn't find a pen or a stapler, it was because he hadn't ordered them. What was it Terrence Bell used to say, "It was hard to remember you came to drain the swamp when you're up to your ass in alligators." Fox felt he was up to his ass in alligators.

Jill had pulled him out of the fire before. Maybe she would do it again. He had mixed emotions about asking for her help, but hell, he was the boss. What he didn't realize was that dependence, needing help, meant vulnerability. He had depended on his wife. He needed her, yet she abandoned him. Now if he needed help from another woman, especially one he had shared intimacy with, wasn't the threat of betrayal renewed? Yet need, as is often the case, outweighed fear.

Fox found Jill in the Security trailer. She was kneeling near a file cabinet. Damn, she had a nice ass. It was difficult for him not to remember her physical beauty. Her touch. Her passion. He wondered if she thought of him. He supposed not. He really didn't believe women had those thoughts. More love and romance than get naked and do it. He thought about how long it had been. Obviously long enough. He pushed the thought aside as Jill stood up. At least he tried to. Her uniform fit well. "Got some work for you," he said.

"Good," Jill said sarcastically dropping files onto her desk. "I'm just killing another ten hours with policy guidelines, payroll, personnel files and background forms."

"I'm sorry, that's not what I meant," Fox offered sitting down at his desk.

"If you don't always mean what you say," Jill speculated, "do you always mean what you do?"

Fox studied Jill. He wondered why attractive women had a psychological edge. Perhaps, he reminded himself, it was because he'd been in bed with this one. If that was the case, he understood what she was asking. It seemed he wasn't the only one with anxieties. He granted the answer he thought she wanted, but it was also sincere. "I always mean what I do."

"Good," Jill smiled. She began organizing the files taken from the cabinet. Neither of them regretted the sexual encounter. It had been said. Subtly, but nevertheless said. The matter no longer hung between them like an unanswered, awkward question.

The irony of intimacy, Fox reasoned, was it could create bonds or destroy them. In this instance, it seemed to create, and although it was between a man and a woman, neither seemed eager to declare it romance. Perhaps because both knew its roots were elsewhere, something deep in the human character that when crisis struck, cried out for the reassuring touch of another.

"So, what is this challenging assignment you're bringing me?" Jill questioned. "Remember, I don't do windows."

"We're going to find out who Milner was in business with," Fox answered.

"We already know," Jill suggested.

"We do?"

"The Indians," Jill answered.

"I'm talking about his money. He had a fifty-million-dollar line of credit and he wasn't fifty-million smart."

"Lana Casner knows."

"She's gone. Vegas."

"Amos Moses?"

"Same."

"Do you think they were working together?"

"More value in having them separate, but I think they both worked for the same man."

"And they caused the collapse and put the car in the river?"

"Maybe."

"And we're gonna find them?"

"Right, but first we gotta get you out of that uniform."

"Why John Fox, you little devil," Jill teased."

"I'll take a look around the executive trailer. You go change into something.... else."

"What would you like?" Jill questioned. "Fredericks, Victoria's Secret or Sears?"

"What I'd like," he answered pushing from the desk, "hasn't got much to do with what we need... Let's go with Sears, the softer side, of course."

"I'll be back in thirty minutes."

"If I'm not here, I'll be in the executive trailer."

The executive trailer was typical of construction offices. Tubes of blueprints, a drafting table, desks, file cabinets. Artists renditions of the completed casino lined the walls as if to inspire completion. The desks were cluttered with papers. The only sound was the steady hum of a wall air conditioner. Fox stood inside the door and searched the room with his eyes, left to right in a full circle. Nothing seemed out of place. No ransack. No evidence of a hasty departure. Milner, dying unexpectedly, would have taken nothing. Amos Moses, if he were Milner's killer, had ample time to sanitize it. Fox made a mental note to talk to the grave watch security team. They might be able to pinpoint Moses' arrival at the construction site. If he got lucky, it may even be in a log.

Fox started with the trash cans. Evidence of the last business, criminal or legitimate, was often found there. Crushed water cups, a discarded Styrofoam coffee cup, an adding machine tape. He saved it. A pair of panty hose, charcoal—Lana Casner's, he guessed. Junk mail. Vendors trying to sell smoke detectors, carpet, lighting, trained dogs and poker tables. Candy wrappers, a soiled Kleenex, an ATM withdrawal slip for three-hundred-dollars. Fox pushed it in a pocket.

He washed his hands in the small bathroom and went to Milner's desk. In the center drawer he found a collection of business cards. He thumbed through them. Lake Havasu City Cement, the Queen's Bay Inn, First Bank of Minnesota, Arizona Electric Supplies, the Casa Grande Casino in Las Vegas, Mitch Parsons, Casino Manager, Budget Rent-A-Car, Tri-State Building Supplies.

In a side drawer Fox found a torn envelope marked "petty cash—$400.00". It was empty. In another drawer he found a wallet-sized photograph of Dennis Milner and two children. The trio was smiling. Fox turned the photo over. "Todd, 14. Cindy,8." was scrawled on the back. Milner had a life. Two children had lost a father to the Arizona desert. Everyone weeps for someone, Fox thought. He put the photo back.

He searched the other desk, the file cabinets folder by folder, the bathroom and then the mail. He found nothing. He would ask David Rollins to keep the trailer locked. Maybe in the meantime he would find something to make a second search relevant. Fox was moving for the door when he thought of the telephone. He crossed to Milner's desk. It had the same four-line telephone console as in his office. He picked up the receiver and punched the redial button. The electronic chime of the autodial played in his ear. The number rang. On the second ring a pleasant female voice answered, "Thank you for calling the Casa Grande Casino. How may I direct your call?"

Fox hung up and dug in a pocket. Pulling out the business cards, he studied them. A gold embossed card read "Casa Grande Casino. Las Vegas, Nevada. Mitch Parsons. General Manager." He pushed the card back in his pocket. Lines were beginning to cross. A pattern was emerging. It was called circumstantial evidence. He moved for the door.

Fox was following a makeshift gravel walkway from the executive trailer to the security trailer when Mara approached from the parking lot. Their paths would cross. Fox felt boy-like and silly as his pulse quickened. What the hell was it about this woman? A white dress down to the tops of her black boots was hardly a fashion statement. Maybe it was the white. A representation of purity, virginal suggesting. He realized he had never had a private conversation with her. What could he say? What should he say? They were closing on each other. He remembered a psychology class at Quantico that taught women would break eye contact with a lone male at about forty feet. This woman was breaking the rule. Wasn't that shocking? He was still far enough away to avoid being accused of staring. Why did she have an attitude? She was close now. "Hello, Mara."

"Hello." It was devoid of expression.

Fox paused.

Mara was almost to him. She carried a briefcase. "Did you have your meeting with the Chamber of Commerce?" he asked.

"Yes." Mara studied him. She didn't seem to be concerned about staring. "Have you started work on backgrounds?"

"I've been busy on other things," Fox defended. Where in the hell did that question come from?

"Yes, I understand," Mara said pronouncing each word in a distinct Indian manner.

Fox couldn't think of anything other than how clear her eyes were and how smooth her skin was. Mara brushed a sweep of hair away from her eyes. "Is there something else?" she questioned.

"No," Fox said dumbly.

Mara walked on. "Shit," Fox muttered softly.

"Just got back," Jill said as Fox stepped into the security trailer. His mind was still on Mara. The woman was a pain in the ass. She stirred a bewildering mix of emotions in him. What the hell was the question about backgrounds? Was she inferring he wasn't doing his job? "Earth to John," Jill added. "Hello." She had read his preoccupied look. "Did you find anything?"

"Maybe," Fox answered. He pulled out the Casa Grande business card and offered it. He looked at Jill as she took the card. She had pinned her hair up and changed into a matching dark jacket and skirt. The skirt was cut an inch above a nylon-clad knee and the heels she wore were moderate. She didn't look Sears, he thought, she was more Saks. She had transformed herself from a Barbie Doll in khaki into a demure, none-theless attractive, businesswoman. She could easily pass as a female agent. Fox thought of the paradox. He was supervised by an Indian princess with an attitude and worked with a topless dancer turned security guard.

Those who wished they could work with attractive women usually didn't know what they were asking for. When Pam was alive—sharing his life and filling his needs—Fox seldom felt attraction to other women. Now as a widower in his thirties, he found he was feeling like an adolescent with constant thoughts of breast size, skirt length, perfume and when or if he would get laid again. Both Jill and Mara had a know-it-all sarcasm. All he had was a thick tongue. Fox remembered the admonition from his father when he failed a geometry class that could have kept him from college. "Quit thinking with your dick." That was it, Fox decided. He was thinking with his dick. He had to change that.

Jill didn't help when she held the business card up with polished nails, "You want me to call and make us a reservation?"

Fox took the card from her.

"You watch the right. I'll watch the left," Fox ordered as he drove the Explorer from the casino construction site. "We're looking for public telephones."

"Why not use the phone in the office?" Jill suggested.

"We're not going to use them" Fox answered. "We're going to get their numbers."

"I knew that." Jill smiled.

They found the first public telephone a half mile from the construction site at Parker's only shopping plaza. It was a wall-mounted telephone just outside the entrance of the Anchor Store, a supermarket. Fox got out and jotted down the number.

The search continued as the Explorer crisscrossed the small town concentrating on commercial locations: motels, gas stations and liquor stores. They found six more. The telephone search complete, Fox headed the Explorer north on U.S. 95. "Next stop, Lake Havasu," he said with a glance at Jill.

"What's there?"

"Queen's Bay Inn," Fox answered. "Milner, Lana and Moses all stayed there."

"And what do we hope to find?" Jill questioned.

"I don't know," Fox confessed.

"And these?" Jill held up the list of public telephone numbers they had collected.

"They'll tell us what long distance calls were made from each phone."

"You can do that?" Jill was surprised.

"I hope so."

As Fox drove, Jill talked. She decided if this man was to know her naked, the term was not going to simply mean not wearing clothes. John Fox, she resolved was going to get more than a topless dance. He was going to get it all. Rejecting or accepting was his call, but it wouldn't be because he didn't know her. Jill talked of her worries about being separated from her child. Worries about the long-term impact of her mother's influence on the child. Worries if she would be able to find day care in Parker after finding a place to live. Worries about her aging car making the long drives to Phoenix. Listening to her, Fox felt fortunate. Jill's trek to Parker brought with it a web of tentacles that clung to a life elsewhere. Fox had none. It was as if his life in the world had ended and started anew in Parker.

Jill's talk brought about another realization. She spoke of a child growing up, of buying a new car, of someday driving to Disneyland. She was looking ahead, making plans for the future. Fox was shocked to find he had none. He had been living day to day. There had been no thoughts of love, marriage, children, a home, career, or a future. The man who prided himself on meticulous planning, the man who knew the importance of planning, found he had none. He was a man with no future. He was a man riding other men's dream.

Hell, the White Buffalo wasn't his dream. He hadn't planned on becoming the Director of Security. What was it Chief Stoner had said, "A leaf doesn't fall without purpose." Fox felt he was a leaf that had fallen into a surging torrent. Now he was spinning, turning, drifting with the current with no idea where he was going. It unnerved him, but he found himself envying Jill. She was alive. She was vibrant. She was happy just because she was alive. Fox had to admit he was glad she was with him. She was becoming his candle in the darkness.

The lobby of the Queen's Bay Inn was cool and shadowed. The two of them—Fox in an open collar and jacket and Jill in the two-piece business suit—looked displaced with the others in the lobby. Most wore tank tops, bathing suits, shorts and flip-flops. The air smelled of suntan oil and liquor from a nearby lounge. They stood in line behind two couples checking in. Both of the couples were burdened with luggage. "What are you going to say?" Jill asked, leaning close to Fox. One of the couples, keys in hand, moved away and the line inched forward.

"We want to see the telephone records. The room, if possible," Fox answered quietly.

"And why will they show them to us?" Jill pressed.

"Trust me," Fox urged.

"You sound like my ex."

The remaining couple soon departed the long reception counter. Fox and Jill stepped to the clerk. "May I help you?" a thirty-year-old brunette in a tailored jacket questioned. She had already decided the two were not tourists. Her name tag read Carol.

"Carol," Fox said with a glance around as if to assure the conversation was private. "Some of our associates may have been in earlier." He dug in an inside jacket pocket and pulled out a small notebook. Jill could see he didn't open it. The clerk could not. "Concerning two guests... Milner and Hanes."

"Oh yes, the two in the car accident," the clerk answered. "Sergeant James was in. He looked at the records."

Fox nodded. "James was one of the officers on the scene." He glanced at the notebook a second time. "We've since learned the two victims... And, this must remain confidential..."

The clerk nodded assurance.

"....were connected to two other guests," Fox continued. "Lana Casner and Amos Moses."

"I believe I checked them out," Carol said punching

information into the computer in front of her. "Yes, Ms. Casner first and then... Moses about two hour later."

"Have their rooms been serviced?"

"Let me check." The computer keyboard rattled; eyes searched. "Ms. Casner's has not."

"We'd like to take a look at it," Fox announced.

The girl hesitated.

"It will only take a minute," Fox assured. He stretched out an open palm.

The clerk reached for a key.

The door to the room swung open. Fox searched and found a wall light switch. Jill was behind him. They stepped in and closed the door. The bed was unmade. A room service tray and dirty dishes sat atop a dresser. A coffee cup bore smudges of lipstick. A bathroom light was on. Fox's eyes searched the room. Jill sniffed the air. "First," she said.

"First what?" Fox questioned.

"The perfume. It's First. Expensive."

Fox crossed to a bedside table and picked up the telephone. Jill moved to his side. "Get you in a motel room and what do you do? Make calls." She smiled.

Fox punched the redial button. "If this works, someone might get screwed." The redial tone sang in his ear. He listened. The number rang once, twice.

"Hello," a male voice answered.

"Let me talk to Lana," Fox said without hesitation.

"Lana's not here. Who's calling?" the male questioned. He was irritated.

"She told me to call her at this number," Fox countered matching the irritation. He thought it sounded like a cellular connection. "Who the hell are you?"

"Don DePalma," the male barked. "Now who the fuck are you?" The line clicked and a dial tone sang in DePalma's ear. "You, sonofabitch!"

20 BLOOD, SWEAT AND TEARS

"The American Indian is of the soil. He fits into the landscape, for the hand that fashioned the continent also fashioned the man for his surroundings. He belongs just as the buffalo belonged."

Luther Standing Bear—Ogallala Sioux Chief

In the "get-it-done" inner circle of Las Vegas they were known as the Bear and the Weasel, although the brass plaque on the wall next to their second-story office on Flamingo Road read simply "Howell and Long". Three-hundred-fifty-pound Jimmy Howell and his tall, chain-smoking, gaunt partner Walter Long were retired police detectives from Chicago. Rumor had it they did as much work for the mob in Chicago while cops as they now did as security consultants in Las Vegas.

Las Vegas, not unlike most business, had debt collectors. The majority of the major casinos had their own sophisticated and legitimate debt collection services. The courts had long ago ruled gambling debts were legitimate. Thus, collectors operated with liens, seizures and court-ordered garnishments. It was usually effective. The days of crooked-nosed Vinnies showing up on your doorstep were gone for the most part, but when a problem casino deadbeat ran or evaded and the usual failed, unusual tactics were required. The Bear and the Weasel were experts in the unusual. When Donald DePalma called, they dropped everything.

DePalma was waiting in his eighth-floor executive office at the Casa Grande Casino when Mitch Parsons escorted the Bear and the Weasel in. They had come in through the subterranean parking area and up on a private elevator. "Don, I'd like you to meet James Howell and Walter Long."

The Don pushed to his feet and reached across the wide desk to extend a hand. "The Bear and the Weasel." He smiled "Pleasure to meet you, gentlemen." After he shook their hands, he gestured to chairs. "Sit down, please."

The two men sat down drinking in the opulence of the office. It was extravagant even by Vegas standards. Mitch Parsons followed suit and sat down in a third chair to the Weasel's right. "Mitch, thanks for bringing them up," DePalma smiled. "That'll be all for now."

The usually suave Persons was shocked. He balked at being dismissed. "Don, I think it's important that..."

DePalma, still smiling, cut him short. "Mitch, please. I know you've got other business."

Parson submitted without argument. Pushing to his feet, he forced a smile. "Of course. If you need anything, please call." He nodded to the two men and marched for the door. He was livid, but he hadn't lost his composure.

As the big oak door swung shut with a thud like a

castle gate, DePalma walked around the desk to be closer to the two men. "My office is secure, whatever is said, stays among the three of us. Understand?"

"If it wasn't," the Weasel said while lighting a fresh cigarette from the tip of a smoldering butt, "you wouldn't have called us." He exhaled smoke.

DePalma acknowledged the remark with a nod and leaned against his desk. "I only invite one kind of man into my office," he told the two, "and that's a rich man. If you weren't rich when you came in, then you get a chance to be rich going out."

"You got my attention," the Bear said as pudgy fingers dug in a candy bowl.

"You might find this hard to believe, but there seems to be a smart fuckin' Indian in Parker."

The Bear and the Weasel exchanged a look. "Where's Parker?" the Weasel questioned exhaling smoke out his mouth and nose.

"Arizona," the Don answered. "It's a fuckin' wide spot in the road about ninety miles south of Laughlin. They're building a casino there. The White Buffalo."

"What did this smart Indian do?" the Bear asked pushing candy into his mouth.

"Called me on my private cellular. Nobody's got that fuckin' number. I checked the records. He called me from the Queen's Bay Inn in Lake Havasu. I want you to find out who he is, and I want him to regret it."

The Weasel drew on his cigarette. "We don't like going out of state. It ain't cheap."

"Neither am I," DePalma countered. "I want this asshole found."

"We can find him," the Bear assured.

"And when you find him, I want him humbled."

"We can do humble," the Weasel smiled.

"Sometimes, we've heard," the Bear explored, "people want a deeper humility... If you know what we mean."

"Find 'im, ...humble 'im".

Fox waited until nearly midnight before doing what he hadn't done in a long time. He dialed the FBI office in Palm Springs. It was a weekday night and at the late hour he hoped the office would be unmanned. He was relieved when on the third ring an answering machine with Tom Roberts' voice announced, "You've reached the Palm Springs Office of the Federal Bureau of Investigation. We are unable...." Fox hung up. If the telephone was hooked, programmed to electronically trace all incoming calls, as sometimes was done to locate anonymous threats or informants, he was screwed, but he had to know the office was vacant before dialing into the computer.

In an effort to expand the resources of agents in the field and make them less dependent on the office, each agent had been assigned a PIN number enabling them— with the use of a modem and code access—to dial into the NCIC, the National Crime Information Center computer network. NCIC was a vast pool of criminal and intelligence information: names, personal and corporate addresses, telephone numbers, criminal and civil records, credit histories, banking, military service, education, birth, death, marriage, tax histories and more.

Users required careful identification and access was limited to a need-to-know. Browsing was prohibited and policed. Codes providing access were changed and routinely challenged electronically. All Fox could do was hope. His link would be by modem from Parker to Palm Springs, Palm Springs to Washington, D.C. If it worked, it would only take seconds to make the access. If it failed, the attempt would be recorded with an electronic hook and the consequences of hacking NCIC were grim.

Terrence Bell's visit while he still lived at Castle Rock gave Fox hope. No agent ventured three-hundred-miles from a field office without authorization. Bell's seemingly solitary mission and invitation to come home had undoubtedly been carefully plotted and approved. If Fox was right, then there was still a chance he was on the access list and his PIN would be accepted by the computer. He had not resigned and the bureaucracy for an involuntary termination took time. Time that he hoped was still on his side.

"You wanna tell me how you're going to do this?" Jill asked as Fox sat down at the computer terminal in the security trailer.

"Isn't it time for you to go home?" Fox questioned as Jill pulled a chair close beside him.

"Sure," she answered sarcastically. "Three people dead. You swimming in cement. I'm just a woman. Why would I be interested in this when I could rush back to my motel room and catch the last twenty minutes of Jay Leno?"

"That's not what I mean," Fox defended.

"Let's not go down that road again," Jill cautioned.

Fox studied her. "I don't want you to have problems because of me."

Jill looked at the list of telephone numbers and names lying beside the computer keyboard. "You don't have to be a rocket scientist to figure out you're going to hack your way into some computer system. Is it, NCIC?"

"If you don't know, you'll have deniability."

"Isn't that right up with 'respect me in the morning'?"

Fox smiled. "Does everything in your life relate to sex?"

"Doesn't it in yours?"

"All right," Fox agreed, "if I get in, you read the numbers to me."

"And if you don't?"

"We get a visit from our local Feds."

Fox turned his attention to the computer. He typed in the modem telephone number for the Palm Springs FBI Office. When an acknowledge showed on screen, he drew in a breath and added his Personal Identification Number. The computer gave an electronic beep. "Access granted" appeared on the screen. "We're in," he whispered in relief.

They started with the telephone numbers—both the public numbers and the ones obtained from the hotel records—after Fox selected the public utilities file. He requested all long-distance records both made and received.

Record checks followed the telephone numbers. Fox requested all intelligence and criminal records information on Dennis Milner, Clyde Hanes, Lana Casner, Amos Moses and Donald DePalma. He asked for a cross reference and association search on all five individuals.

The final category was business and corporate. Again, Fox requested all records and cross references on First Bank of Minnesota, Queen's Bay Inn, the Casa Grande Casino and any or all of the businesses or individuals queried.

"How long do we wait?" Jill questioned after Fox punched the Enter key.

Immediately a nearby printer came to life and began spewing out information.

"Not long." Fox smiled.

The sound of jet engines over Parker was rare. A sleek corporate craft appeared in the sky shortly after nine AM. It circled high and wide as the pilot oriented himself with the short runway and winds. There was no control tower. Finally, the circling jet lined up with the runway and made a long, low approach. The rubber tires yelped as they grabbed at the warm asphalt.

Sixty-seven-year-old Herb Thompson, a stooped man in gray coveralls, met the craft as it taxied to the mouth of the airport's main hangar where he worked on the engine of a Cessna. Herb paused to wipe his hands on a rag as the howl of the jet turbines fell. A door opened and two men in three-piece suits, carrying briefcases stepped out. They squinted in the sun, shading their eyes. Spotting Herb, one of them pointed and they walked to him. "Do you have cab service here?" the older of the two men asked.

"Nope." Herb spit tobacco juice on the pavement.

"How do we get in town?" the other questioned.

"What's your cruise speed in that thing?" Herb was looking at the, two-engine aircraft.

"I don't know," the older man answered. "You'll have to ask the pilot."

"Is it a rental?" Herb asked.

"Yeah. Is there a car we could rent?"

"Rent you my truck, I suppose," Herb speculated.

"How much?"

"Hundred and fifty."

"A hundred and fifty?!?" the younger man complained.

"You can afford that plane," Herb defended, "you can afford my truck."

Forty minutes later the sun-bleached, twelve-year-old Dodge pick-up belonging to Herb Thompson arrived at the office of Justice Court Judge Jacob Drum. The storefront court was located next to Hoffman's Auto Parts and only four miles from the airport, but the two men renting the truck had gotten lost twice.

They were sweaty and irritable when they entered the office.

The court clerk, Judge Drum's thirty-three-year-old daughter-in-law Shirley was at a desk behind the courtroom bar when the two suits came in. The younger of the two men offered a business card. "I'm attorney Martin Hummel and this is my associate, Lee Sheldon. We represent the estate of Dennis Milner. We would like to present a petition to seize capital assets for the Judge's signature."

The girl studied the business card. "You're from Las Vegas?"

"We were retained by a firm in Saint Clair, Minnesota representing Mr. Milner's family. We're both members of the Arizona Bar."

"Have a seat, please."

The two attorneys waited in the small, warm courtroom for ten minutes before the girl returned. "The Judge will see you now."

"Sit down, gentlemen," Judge Drum invited as the two were escorted into a rear office. The paneled walls were decorated with mounted bass and antelope trophies. Hummel noticed there was an open copy of Field & Stream on the Judge's cluttered desk. "Clerk tells me you got a petition to seize assets."

Sheldon snapped open his briefcase. "I think you'll find everything's in order, Your Honor." He lifted out a thick brief.

The Judge raised a hand. "This is in regard to Dennis Milner?"

"Yes."

"He was the general partner of the Mojave's in building the White Buffalo Casino?"

"That's correct."

"Can't help you."

320

"Pardon me?"

"Casino is on Indian land," the judge said rocking back in his chair. "You'll have to present it to the Tribal Court."

"Tribal Court?!?"

"Think they've got legal jurisdiction."

The two attorneys exchanged a look of irritation. Sheldon stuffed the papers back into his briefcase "And where is this Tribal Court?" Hummel questioned.

"About three miles from here," the Judge answered. "But it won't do you any good today."

"Indian holiday or something?" Sheldon questioned.

"Funeral," the Judge answered.

The Tribal Cemetery stretched along the river road in the valley. It was deep in the heart of Indian country. Row after row of modest headstones and weathered monuments decorated with plastic flowers and potted plants withered by the heat attested to the fact that for the Mojave's, this was holy ground. The Tanner family plot was in the northwest corner not far from a canal that bordered the cemetery on its path to nearby alfalfa fields. Virgil would like that, Fox decided as he stood in the midst of the nearly three hundred that had come to see a native son laid to rest.

There were farmers, construction workers, Bonnie and Tonto from the Blue Water Cafe, Bear-Don't-Walk and half dozen others from the Tribal Police. The Tribal Council, David Rollins, George and Mara from the Enterprise Board, Chief Stoner and his wife Sarah and a leg-less Sparrow looking pasty and frail wrapped in a hospital gown and sitting in a wheelchair with a nurse at his side.

They were dressed in their best: suits and hats, coveralls and boots, flowered prints and black crepes. Virgil's mother, his sister-in-law/lover and young nephew clung to one another at the mouth of the fresh grave. The flower-laden coffin hung suspended by straps, ready to be lowered as Leland White feather, a round-faced, three-hundred and seventy-pound Baptist Minister spoke to the sky with a worn dog-eared bible in hand. "God, you will enjoy the company of our son and brother, Virgil Tanner.

"He has a strong back and a strong heart. If you have fields to cut, he'll cut 'em. If you got something to build, he'll build it. You need a friend; he'll be your friend... Look at this, Lord." He gestured to the crowd encircling the grave. "He had friends. And Virgil wasn't just a sunshine friend. He was there when you needed help. He helped us pour the foundation of the White Buffalo." The big man's eyes went back to the sky. "And now, Father, we lay Virgil in your foundation and the lives we live will be stronger because of it. Thank you, Great Father." He raised his hands. "Thank you for sharing this man with us... He is now with you."

The nurse was wheeling Sparrow to a waiting ambulance when Fox pushed through the departing crush to reach him. "Sparrow."

The nurse paused and Fox knelt beside the wheelchair. Sparrow's eyes were rimmed with tears. His cheeks were sunken, and his once tan skin looked pasty. "Hey, Sprite Man," Sparrow forced a short-lived smile.

"Maybe we should go up to the dam tonight. Throw beer cans off the top," Fox said. "Virgil would like that."

"Yeah," Sparrow reminisced. "That was quite a night... But I don't get around much."

"How are you feeling?" Fox questioned.

"Two feet shorter," Sparrow coughed sarcastically.

"When do you get out of the hospital?"

"Week. Ten days, they say."

"I need help in surveillance," Fox explained. "Setting

up camera positions, the monitors, switchers, cable tracks, computer matrix and VCRs. Figured since you built that dish in your back yard, you might know something about closed circuit TV, VCRs and things."

Sparrow brightened. "I did all the closed-circuit stuff at Tribal. The Council Chambers, the Tribal Police.... I installed a couple satellite dishes."

"Think you could help me?"

"You mean a job?"

"Ten, twelve hours a day getting things set up. If you can't...."

"Hey," Sparrow said, cutting Fox short, "I can do it." His voice was weak but edged with determination.

Fox stood up. "Come see me when you get out."

The nurse smiled and Sparrow and his chair moved on. He twisted to look back at Fox. "I'll talk to the doctor soon as I get back."

It was time to go, Fox decided walking to the parked Explorer. No need to tell Mara, David or even Chief Stoner. The work was done, and it was time to go back to a world he had once known. He glanced at his watch. Jill would be in the office soon, if she wasn't there already. Even she wouldn't miss him for several hours. They had worked until nearly two. He thought about telling her, but there was the need-to-know. It was easier not telling her. Just do it. It felt good to have a plan again, Fox thought as he dug for his keys.

Mara was on the telephone in the Enterprise trailer when David Rollins and George Manygoats arrived. "Thank you, Judge," Mara said and hung up. "That was Jacob Drum. The attorneys are here. They wanted him to sign an order to seize. He told them the Tribal Court had jurisdiction."

"Casino's already a success," David quipped. "We got a white judge screwing white attorneys."

"You need to be less of a bigot, David," Mara warned gathering her purse and a file folder.

"And you need to be more of an Indian," David shot back at her.

Mara ignored the remark and moved for the door.

"We need to talk, Mara," David said taking her by the arm.

Mara asked, "About what?"

"About the new construction foreman," David answered. "George and I have made a decision."

"Without me?" Mara was angry.

"It's called two-thirds majority," David defended. "It needed to be done. We must get back to work."

"And who is it you didn't want me to object to?" Mara questioned.

"Me," David answered.

Mara was shocked. "You?!? What have you built? How are you qualified?"

"What have I built?" David growled pointing a finger at an office window. His face was an angry mask. "I've built a dream." He pounded on his fused knee with a fist. "My knee holds the walls up and my heart will fill the empty space with hope. I can build this place. We have the plan. We have the money. What would you do, Mara? Bring us another hireling? Another white man to save the ignorant Indians. If you don't think I can do it, don't mock me, help me! George's father and I had to join hands to get Chief Stoner over the fence at the White House. Join hands with George and me and we'll get this done."

The silence roared in the room when David finished. George stood looking awkward and uncertain. David's chest heaved and fell as he held Mara's penetrating look.

Finally, Mara spoke. "I will help you, David Rollins,

but I will not settle for less than best... And if you fail, I will fill you with regret."

"You will have no regret," David said with resolve.

Mara wheeled and stormed out.

"I need a drink," George Manygoats exhaled.

Fox could see the veil of smog hanging over the city when he was still fifty miles west of Phoenix. He was eastbound on Interstate Ten driving at seventy-five-miles-an-hour. The divided interstate stretched ahead in an arrow-straight line to disappear at the horizon. He drove amidst a trio of eighteen-wheelers that out-paced him every time the highway yielded to a downgrade. He thought about Phoenix trying to remember the last time he was there. Nearly two years. A brief overnight visit to pick up a bank robber who had fool-heatedly tried a demand note in a mini-mart. His demand got him a gun pushed in his face. Fox tried to remember living in Phoenix. It was vague. There were images of a play-ground at an elementary school, a tree in the back yard, an above-ground pool, but nothing of life, just places. He tried to imagine James and Clair Fox. It was difficult to picture James Fox as a husband. Even more difficult as a lover. A roadside sign rescued him from the thoughts. Phoenix—32 miles.

The traffic surprised Fox. He found he was gripping the steering wheel and driving slower than most as he navigated the maze of freeways crisscrossing downtown Phoenix. After weeks of refuge in Parker, the reality of the metropolitan inner-city was shocking. The Civic Center, the Federal Court House and the high rises of downtown stood stark like rectangular monoliths, monuments to man's conquest of a hostile environment. Phoenix was a paradox. It had no reason to be where it was. Hot, barren desert had yielded to air conditioning and a lifeline of water surging through the Arizona aqueduct from the Colorado River to sustain a million sun seekers. The white man was still drinking Indian water. Exiting the freeway near the Federal Building, Fox thought of the irony of the drive. It had taken over twenty years, but now the circle was complete. Maybe the leaf wasn't lost in the torrent after all.

A security officer in the lobby of the Federal Building glanced at Fox as he walked toward the elevators. He expected to be challenged, but the jacket and tie he had put on for Virgil's funeral eased the man's concern and all he said was, "Good morning."

Fox shared the elevator with a crush of others. Men with pasty, white skin, briefcases and copies of the Arizona Republic. Men talking on cell phones, and women with handbags. Women smelling of roses and gardenia and shoes shiny with patent leather. He looked at the sharp creases in the men's' slacks, the nylon-clad women's legs. None wore boots. Except himself.

"My name is John Fox," he told a sober forty-year-old receptionist with long acrylic nails inside the double-doors marked Federal Bureau of Investigation. "I'm from the Palm Springs Office. I'd like to see the Special Agent in Charge."

"You're an agent?" The woman was suspicious. She looked Fox up and down.

"Yes."

"May I see your identification?"

"I'm on administrative leave." Fox felt awkward and foreign. His ears were growing warm with embarrassment.

"Do you have an appointment with Special Agent Clark?"

"No, but he'll see me."

"May I tell him what this is in regard to?" She was making notes.

"It's private.

"I see. Please have a seat, Mr. Fox."

Fox sat in the spartan reception area while the woman talked on the telephone. He deliberately avoided a look at the camera dome on the ceiling. He pretended interest in a copy of Arizona Highways, a month-old Newsweek and dog-eared copy of People magazine. Five minutes passed before an agent appeared from a door near the reception desk. The man was Fox's age. He had dark hair and a bushy mustache that wouldn't have been allowed in Palm Springs. "John Fox," he said as if announcing the next name on a list.

Fox stood. They studied each other. It was a quick professional evaluation. The man finally offered a hand. "I'm Agent Hodge... Are you armed?"

"No," Fox answered as they shook hands. It was perfunctory.

"Follow me please."

Fox expected to be escorted into the agent's squad room, offered a cup of coffee and given a chance to say hello to familiar faces. He knew four or five of the men assigned to the office. He'd been there before, but instead, Agent Hodge led him down a nondescript hallway and into an interrogation room that smelled of stale nicotine and body sweat. "Have a seat," Hodges said. There was a worn wooden desk, three straight-backed chairs and an opaque camera dome.

Fox sat down. He was disappointed and surprised. This was hardly a reception for a visiting agent. Hodges stepped out and closed the door. This was isolation and suspicion and Fox didn't like it. He had given the Bureau a dozen years of his life. He had paid his dues with blood, sweat and tears. Hell, the President of the United States had shown him more respect. What the hell was their problem? What was this bullshit about being armed? Fox waited, growing angrier by the minute. Ten minutes passed before the door opened again. Agent Hodges returned with an older man. He had gray hair and wore glasses. Both men had their jackets on. It was a signal Fox understood. This wasn't casual. This was raw suspicion. "I'm Special Agent Lang," the gray-hair with glasses said as he sat down across the table from Fox. "I'm the second in command here in Phoenix. What is it you need, Fox?"

Hodges sat down beside his older partner. Fox swallowed his anger. He sensed revealing it would only add to the chill already in the air and he needed their help. "Do you know who Donald DePalma is?"

"Yes," Lang answered flatly.

"I've been working in Parker. Three men have been killed up there in the last forty-eight-hours. I've got evidence that points to a conspiracy involving Donald DePalma."

"You say you've been working in Parker. Are you on assignment there?" Lang questioned.

"No, but..."

Lang raised a hand to stop Fox. "Wait.... If you're not on assignment but you're working there, who are you working for?"

"The Mojave Tribe. They're building a casino. At least they're trying to. DePalma doesn't want it built."

Agents Lang and Hodges exchanged a look. Lang returned his attention to Fox. "You're working for Indians."

"Yeah, I'm working for Indians," Fox defended. "You got a problem with that?"

"Why didn't you go to Tom Roberts in Palm Springs with this?" Lang asked avoiding Fox's question.

"Because your office has jurisdiction," Fox answered.

Land nodded. "True, but we usually let the tribe

handle their own business. Until we're invited in or there's a serious crime, the Bureau doesn't get involved.

Fox's patience was wearing thin. "I'd call three deaths pretty damned serious."

"Were these deaths reported?"

"Of course. The Highway Patrol is investigating two of them. The Tribal Police the other one."

"So, the authorities are involved?" Lang pressed.

"Yes."

"But you're conducting your own investigation?"

"With twelve years in the Bureau I just might have an edge on a Highway Patrolman assigned to Parker," Fox snarled.

"True," Lang agreed, "but he's got something you don't have."

"What's that?" Fox asked stepping into the trap.

"A badge."

"That's why I'm here," Fox argued. "You've got the badge and I've got the information... Remember the concept?"

"I think you've lost your perspective, Fox. You're too close. You're personally involved. This is an Indian matter. We have to prioritize our cases. The best advice we can offer," Lang suggested, "is take your information and give it to the local authorities. They're investigating... If they want or need our help, all they have to do is pick up the phone."

Fox burned the man with a look of contempt. "You're kissing it off."

"Not at all," the gray hair answered. "I'll make a full report... And the bottom line will be, the matter is being handled by local authorities."

Fox pushed out of his chair. Hodges also stood. Fox silently willed the man to challenge him. His pulse pounded in his ears. Every muscle in his body was tight with anger and contempt.

Lang saw the tension and pushed to his feet. "Lemme give you some advice, Fox... I've seen other agents get involved with Indians. It never turns out good. It's messy. They're an incestuous, immoral people. Indian gaming is a cesspool... You can't help those who aren't willing to help themselves."

"Will that be in your report?" Fox challenged.

"Look at you," Lang continued. "Boots, long hair. Hell, if it gets any longer, you'll...." his voice trailed away.

"I'll what," Fox questioned, "...look like one of them? I am one of them."

21 SAVAGE GAMES

"Never bring shame on another human being, it is like allowing your enemy to live after a battle. He will hunt you down and kill you. Shame turns him into a savage."

Simon Pokagon—Potawatomie

By sunset, David Rollins had the majority of the crew back on the construction site and working. Sergeant Bear-Don't-Walk was at his side when he withdrew seventy-five-thousand-dollars in cash from the Bank of Arizona. The Branch Manager was pale as he counted out the twenties, fifties and one-hundred-dollar-bills. "Get more cash," David warned, giving the man a copy of the Tribal Court Order. "I'll be back."

"Money talks," David told Mara after spending two hours on the telephone begging contractors and workers to return. "We're paying cash," he told each of them.

"Every day, and we're paying overtime. We're going on twelve-hour shifts. Around the clock." He was using daily cash payments as bait, a way to restore confidence, a way to demonstrate the Tribe had the money. He hoped they would come. They came. And when they came, David assembled the lead men and supervisors in the Enterprise Trailer. "I want this place lit up," he told the electrical contractor. "We're going to work night and day. I'll pay each of you a hundred dollars a day for every day you cut off the completion date, and, if you can beat it by ten days or more, I'll pay you each a thousand dollar bonus."

As the shadows stretched long, the lights came on. The construction site looked like an ant hill. Plumbers, drywall men, electricians, heating and cooling contractors and an army of laborers teemed over the framework, filling the night with sounds of high-speed saws, hammers, welding generators and pipe cutters. Spartan, framed walls became smooth, fresh corridors. The kitchen took form with stainless sinks, grills and huge exhaust ducts. Cashier counters and bars and restaurants began to take form.

The cash withdrawn from the bank was stored in the Security Trailer where two of Fox's security officers guarded it with shotguns. In the midst of the expectant organized clamor, the catering truck returned. A line quickly formed and the aroma of sizzling hamburgers, bean burritos and fried onions filled the night.

The glare from the White Buffalo attracted more than the swarms of bugs spinning in front of every light. It also attracted hundreds of lookie-loos. Cars, trucks towing boats, motor homes, pick-ups and Jeeps jammed both sides of U.S. 95 in front of the construction site. The crowd lined up shoulder to shoulder to stare and watch and speculate. It was the best late show Parker had ever had. Among the spectators were Judge Drum, the members of the Chamber of Commerce, tourists, truck drivers, housewives and two sober faced attorneys from Las Vegas. "By damned, it looks like they're gonna get it done." Ray Wilson, the owner of the River Bend Motel, beamed. His face was bright with excitement. The two men in suits he spoke to turned and walked away.

Fox's return drive to Parker was in the darkness. He was glad of that. It was as if hiding the humiliation in the night eased its sting. He may have sat in an interview in the Phoenix office of the FBI listening to an admonishment from a senior agent, but Fox had heard the speech before. The words were different, but the message was the same as when the eight-year-old stood in the principal's office being berated for acting like an Indian.

The circumstances were different, but the consequences were the same. Indians didn't have problems. Indians were the problem. There was no logic in it. It was akin to blaming a woman for her own rape. It was the abusive spouse blaming the beaten wife for causing the anger. It was the winner pointing to the history he had written. The Indians didn't lose their lands. They didn't deserve to have them. And now a century later, they didn't deserve help. Maybe a billionaire was blocking the construction of an Indian casino.

Maybe three men had died. Weren't the local authorities investigating? Why would the FBI get involved? It was David versus Goliath, but the stone in the sling was missing. The help Fox hoped for, the faith he had in the Bureau, the plans he had formulated were all gone. Gone as quickly as the life he once had. Staring into the glare of his headlights as the Explorer raced through the night, Fox wondered what was lasting. It wasn't love. It wasn't loyalty. It wasn't justice. He found it easier to identify what wasn't than what was. Why had other men found what eluded him? Where was his peace? Where was his joy?

His life, he found, was like the car he was driving, it was speeding down the highway in the darkness. He didn't know where he was going. Parker lay sixty miles ahead, but what was there for him? What was the allure? What was he doing? He knew it was more than a job. Just as bank robbers robbed for more than money, he knew he had become Chief of Casino Security for more than the job. Was its purpose? Was its excitement? The sense of tribe? The need to belong. The collective hope? The acceptance? In Palm Springs he was an FBI Agent. In Parker he was John Fox. Who he was had become more important than what he was? Was that the answer? Was that what he was seeking? Was he in search of himself?

If so, he had found who he was. He was Claire Fox's son. He was Tribal. That too seemed part of the answer. He was John Fox, but John Fox was part of the Tribe. That could not be taken away. The Indians had proved that. They had lost everything. Lands, lives, pride, but never what they were. There was conflict in it, Fox found. Phoenix offered insult, humiliation and rejection. Ahead Parker waited with understanding, acceptance and reassurance.

Fox was beginning to understand the frustrations Chief Stoner faced in Washington. He could have given up and drove home empty handed, but he chose to climb over a fence. The price was both high and bloody. But the problem was solved, the logjam broken, the casino started. Fox knew he had to find his own fence. Find it and climb it. He had looked to Phoenix and the FBI as a quick fix, a hand-off, someone else to carry the ball. The ball was now back in his hands and he was determined to find a way to the goal. Donald DePalma had wealth and resources, but he was just a man. A man who had already made mistakes. He would make more, and Fox would be waiting.

Flashing red lights in the rear-view mirror and the yelp of an electronic siren brought Fox's thoughts back to the drive. He glanced at the instrument panel. The speedometer hung near eighty-miles-an-hour. "Shit!" he muttered, lifting his foot off the accelerator. Insults from the FBI and a ticket for speeding. End of a perfect day.

The Explorer slowed and eased onto the soft shoulder. the police car, lights flashing, stopped close behind. Fox pushed the selector to park and reached for his wallet. The days were gone when he could pull out his badge and identification, offer a smile and an apology and drive on. The interior of the Explorer was bright with light from the police car. Fox ran the window down. He heard the door thump shut on the patrol car, footfalls in the gravel and sand.

"Figured it had to be some half-breed driving that fast," a familiar voice said.

Fox squinted into the light. Bear-Don't-Walk looked at him from beneath the brim of his Stetson. Fox offered a smile. "You out here terrorizing white people?" He opened the door and climbed out.

"You've been on the res. for the last forty miles," Bear-Don't-Walk advised. "I was down in the bottom. Johnny Sandman got drunk and kicked the shit out of his wife again."

"Find him?"

The Stetson nodded. "Yeah, took a while. They don't call him Sandman for nothing. Part Apache. Real asshole."

"Every tribes got 'em, I guess."

"So, I hear. What are you doing so far from home?" Bear-Don't-Walk asked.

"In Phoenix," Fox answered. "Trying to do some follow-up on Milner and Hanes."

"Any luck?"

"Just bad."

"Not much help out there, is there," the Stetson speculated. Bear-Don't-Walk was reading the disappointment in Fox's tone.

"Not much," Fox agreed. He knew the sergeant understood.

"David Rollins got construction going. Place looks like Disneyland."

"He found a job boss?"

"Yeah... In the mirror."

"At least we know who he is," Fox smiled.

"He'll be there if you stop by."

"Tomorrow," Fox said. "I'm going home and get some sleep.... You've heard of that, haven't' you?"

"Had some last week... Gotta get Johnny to jail. Drive easy." Bear-Don't-Walk turned to the idling patrol car.

"You too."

Bear-Don't-Walk was right. Fox could see the glare from the casino night lighting when he reached Parker. The town was asleep. The streets bathed in warm, chalky night lighting were quiet. The glare got brighter as he turned north on 95. A mile north of Parker he found both sides of the road lined with cars and spectators. The construction site was shadowless. Bathed in bright light from light stands, spot lamps and newly erected parking lot lamps, it became an oasis of light in the desert night. An oasis teeming with activity. A jumble of vehicles crowded the fenced employee lot. A line of customers stretched from the catering truck. Drinking it in as he passed, Fox could feel the energy from it. He glimpsed Collins and One Feather in uniform. They were dependable men, he decided. The crane and cement pump were working on a re-pour of the second story. Jesus, it was beginning to look like a casino. If Virgil Tanner could see it, he would be pleased.

"Keep it moving!" a Tribal Police Officer with a flashlight barked. He was standing in the center of the roadway urging traffic on. Fox wasn't the only one to slow and gawk.

Leaving the lights of the construction site behind, Fox drove on into the night. Seven miles north was Branson's Trailer Park and the waiting comfort of his bed. Thoughts of his bedroom brought memories of Jill. Naked, sensual, exciting Jill. He savored the memory of her touch. He passed Riverside Drive where the road turned toward the river and Blue Water Lagoon. The cafe would still be open. Bonnie would be behind the bar in her shorts. He pushed the thought from his mind as he remembered Mara catching him studying Bonnie at Virgil's funeral. Mara was a candidate for his passion too. He wondered if it was just curiosity of an Indian woman or was, he really attracted to her?

It was attraction, Fox decided. Indian or not, she was a desirable woman. He wasn't sure what it was about her, but the allure was real. Reaching the turn-off to Branson's he pushed the thoughts aside before they became an annoying distraction. After the comfort and routine of marriage, going to bed alone wasn't easy. Being tired would help. His legs and buttocks were aching to be out of the Explorer.

The trailer park was at rest. Streetlamps and yellow night lights cast shadows over the lines of coaches. Cars, pick-ups and boats sat nestled next to the trailers like sleeping partners. A jackrabbit darted through the headlamps as Fox turned onto his street.

The night was warm. Unlocking the door of the trailer, Fox welcomed the rush of cool air that reached out to greet him. He turned on a light and pushed one boot off with the toe of the other. His foot enjoyed the freedom. He pulled the other boot off and walked to the kitchen. The refrigerator offered limited choices. He damned himself for not shopping more. He took a swallow from a bottle of cranberry juice and headed for the bedroom.

Fox was at his desk in the Security trailer when Mara opened the door. He was shocked. Mara was topless. Her breasts were large, melon-like and firm. She stepped in and walked to his desk, seemingly uninhibited by her nakedness. "As you can see," Mara said defensively, "contrary to what you think, my breasts are not too large."

Fox stared in shock. He was torn between talking to her eyes or her nipples. "I never said they were too large."

Someone banged on the side of the trailer. The noise alarmed Mara. She cupped her breasts in her hands. The banging grew louder and then Fox was awake. Someone was knocking on the door of the trailer. "Shit." He swung his feet to the floor. He pushed his legs into his pants in the darkness and headed down the narrow hallway to the living room in his bare feet. The knocking continued. "Coming," he called.

Reaching the living room, Fox paused and opened a space in the window mini blinds beside the door. A tall, gaunt man with stooped shoulders waited outside the door. He drew on a cigarette and the glow illuminated his face. Damned wayward tourist, Fox concluded when he didn't recognize the man. He unlocked the door. The thoughtless bastard was going to get told. He was irritated for losing Mara's jelled breasts to a lost smoker. "What is it?" Fox got out before the aerosol spray hit his face. His eyes were on fire and he couldn't breathe. He reeled away, choking, coughing and gasping for breath.

He knew it was pepper spray. Fox sank to his knees, blind and helpless.

The Bear and the Weasel were quickly into the trailer. The Bear closed and locked the door as the Weasel continued to douse Fox with the spray. "Enough, Goddamnit!" the Bear complained. Fox was on his hands and knees coughing mucus and saliva onto the floor. He knew he was in serious trouble. The Weasel grabbed him by the hair on the back of his head. Fox kicked backwards like a horse and flailed an arm. "You sonofabitch," the Weasel snarled and drove a clenched fist hard into Fox's kidney. He gasped and collapsed.

The trailer floor creaked as the heavy Bear moved about the living room and kitchen twisting the mini blinds shut. He switched on an overhead kitchen light when he finished. The Weasel pulled the disoriented Fox into the kitchen and set him down hard in a chair. Fox continued to cough and spit. His eyes were clamped shut in pain. It was if they had been filled with hot, jagged sand. Saliva flowed from his mouth and ran down his chin. Mucus hung from his nose. The Weasel, cigarette dangling in his mouth, pulled a roll of silver duct tape from a jacket pocket and quickly taped Fox's right wrist to the upper front leg of the chair. He wrapped it tight again and again and then tore the tape off. The Bear held Fox's left arm. He kicked feebly when the Weasel grabbed his ankle.

The Bear slammed an elbow into the back on his head. The resistance stopped. The Weasel, his cigarette now only a burned stub, taped Fox's ankles to the bottom of each chair leg. Standing, he tore a long swath of tape from the roll and ran it around Fox's head covering his mouth. Fox, his nose clogged with mucus, fought to breathe. "Calm down, calm down, you can breathe," the Bear assured holding Fox's left arm atop the low counter that divided the kitchen from the living room. "We don't want you to die on us... Not just yet."

The Weasel wet a towel in the kitchen sink and wiped Fox's face with it. "Does that help?"

The Weasel repeated the process twice more. 'Your eyes feeling better?"

"Good we used the spray," the Bear said. "I didn't know the sonofabitch was this young." He was holding Fox's arm with two hands.

"We charge more for young," the Weasel laughed as he rinsed Fox's face a third time.

Fox's eyes were swollen and painful, but the rinsing enabled him to blink, to try and focus. He fought to control his breathing. His nose was full of fluid and he kept swallowing the saliva that filled his mouth. His mind was in a panic. He willed himself calm. His left arm still hadn't been bound. If he could break it free of the man's grasp and get the tape off his mouth, he could shout, scream, maybe get help, maybe break a window. Shit, he didn't want to die tied up.

The Weasel pulled a chair in front of Fox and sat down. Lighting another cigarette, he coughed and said, "Look at me."

Fox tried. He couldn't keep his eyes open. It was as if they were on fire.

"Come on," the Weasel prodded. "It's a little fuckin' pepper spray. You can handle it." He swung a hand and slapped Fox. "Come on, look at me. Open your eyes."

Fox did it, not to please the Weasel, but because he knew he had to see to help himself. He held one eye open, then the other, then both.

"Good, can you see me?" the Weasel exhaled.

Fox could see the man.

"So, you're John Fox, huh? We hear you're rude on the telephone, John." The Weasel puffed as he talked.

Now Fox understood. DePalma sent these men. The redial in the motel room was a mistake. As an FBI agent, Fox seldom considered personal reprisal, but as Special Agent Lang had pointed out, he no longer had a badge. To Donald DePalma he was just another minor irritant to deal with. He had underestimated his opponent.

"Hear you work in a casino. The White fuckin' Buffalo or something," the Weasel continued. "That makes you a gambler, right."

"I'm sure it does." The Bear chuckled.

"Well then, what say we gamble," the Weasel suggested digging in a trouser pocket. He came out with a silver dollar. He held the coin between thumb and forefinger.

Fox strained to focus on it, blinking, shaking his head. His vision was improving.

"What should we play?" the Weasel questioned. "Bear, you got any suggestions?"

"Yeah, since he's a rude fuck on the phone," the Bear chuckled, "let's play 'let your finger do the walking'."

"Excellent choice." The Weasel sucked on his cigarette and exhaled. "But we can't play that. We don't have any wire cutters."

"Yeah, we do." The Bear dug in a pocket and tossed a set of steel wire cutters to the Weasel.

"How fortunate," the Weasel mocked examining the tool. "All right, here's the rules."

Fox's chest heaved and fell as breath rushed in and out his nostrils. He was listening. He knew time was short.

"I flip the coin," the Weasel smiled holding it in Fox's face. "Heads, we cut your phone line... Tails we cut your fuckin' finger off!"

Fox stiffened. The Bear felt it and leaned on the arm

he held atop the counter. "Go for it," he said to the Weasel.

"Show time!" The Weasel flipped the coin in the air. It spun and he caught it. He smiled and flattened it on his leg. "Whadaya think?"

Fox strained. The Bear tightened his grip on Fox's arm.

Fox's heart raced. The Weasel lifted his hand. "Heads," he announced.

"The poor phone line," the Bear moaned. "Maybe we should make it two outta three."

"You're right," the Weasel agreed and flipped the coin a second time. Fox jerked. The Bear had been expecting it. He easily restrained the attempt. His grip on Fox's arm was vice-like. The Weasel flattened the coin on his leg. He raised his hand slowly, peeking. "Uh-oh." He smiled uncovering the coin. "Tails... You lose."

Fox closed his eyes and relaxed his body. It was a play and the Bear fell for it. Fox jerked with all of his might. His arm came free, but the Bear quickly had it and slammed it down hard on the counter. "Cocksucker," he growled.

The Weasel stood. "Time for that finger to go walking." Stepping to the counter, he pressed the heel of his hand down hard on the back of Fox's hand. The Bear held the wrist and elbow. Fox thrashed his head and body in a futile attempt. The Weasel pushed the open steel blades over Fox's little finger just forward of the first knuckle. "Next time you call Vegas, think of this!" The Weasel snapped the sharp blades shut. Bone crunched and the finger bounced off the kitchen wall. Fox bolted stiff giving a muffled cry. Blood jetted onto the smooth countertop from the stump of his finger.

The Bear was chuckling with delight when a crash sent the door inward. It swung and banged the wall.

Bear-Don't-Walk, gun in hand, filled the doorway. "Move, assholes, and you're dead men."

His tone was convincing. The Bear and the Weasel raised their hands. Fox's head slumped to his chest.

Bear-Don't-Walk pulled a portable radio from his belt. "Dispatch, Sam-twenty-eight requesting Lincoln-three meet me at Branson's, code two. First street from the river."

"Roger, Sam-twenty-eight," a filtered female voice answered.

"Now both of you on your faces. Side by side," Bear-Don't-Walk ordered. "And you, spit out the cigarette and drop the wire cutters."

The Weasel balked, exchanging a quick look with the Bear. Bear-Don't-Walk saw it. He took a quick step toward the big man and slammed the barrel of his gun into the side of Bear's head. The Bear went down like a sack of potatoes. He swung the gun back toward the Weasel. "Do it!" he barked. The wire cutters thumped to the floor.

The Weasel got down onto the floor beside the Bear. The two men covered the kitchen floor of the small trailer.

"Keep your hands where I can see them," Bear-Don't-Walk warned, "or I'll kill you where you lay." Kneeling, he picked up the wire cutters and used them to cut the circle of duct tape around Fox's head and mouth. When he pulled the wide silver tape from Fox's mouth, he gasped for air. His free arm hung at his side. The stump of his severed finger fed a growing pool of blood beneath the chair. Holding an aim on the two men on the floor, Bear-Don't-Walk cut at the tape holding Fox's right wrist. When it was free, Fox grabbed at the pain in his left hand. His face was a mask of anguish. Bear-Don't-Walk snipped at the tape holding Fox's ankles. Fox jerked and was free. He bolted from the chair and staggered away toward the bathroom leaving a trail of blood.

A set of headlamps washed over the interior of the trailer as a car arrived. A door slammed and a huge Indian with a ponytail in the uniform of the Tribal Police filled the doorway. He looked at Bear-Don't-Walk then the two men on the floor. "Cuff 'em, Merv."

Fox washed the stump of his severed finger under a flow of water in the bathroom sink. He looked at his image in the mirror. His eyes were bloodshot and puffy. He grabbed a washcloth, soaked it and wiped at his face. A wave of nausea swept over him. His stomach convulsed, but he clamped his mouth shut to fight it. He rinsed the washcloth and wrapped it tight around his severed finger, grimacing with pain. Bear-Don't-Walk appeared in the doorway. "Who are they?"

"I don't know," Bear-Don't-Walk was looking at the washcloth bound around Fox's hand. "Was going to stop by and tell you what I learned. Saw the Cadillac from Nevada. Almost drove by. Figured you might be in here with some woman."

"Wish I had been," Fox answered. He cupped water in his right hand, rinsed his mouth and spat. "What did you learn?"

"Was in the Sheriff's office reading teletypes. Saw the California Highway Patrol is investigating a fatal hit and run up near Needles. Pick-up truck got run off the road, driver was killed. His name was Amos Moses."

"They play rough," Fox said holding the wrist of his left hand. Blood was oozing through the washcloth.

"How do you wanna handle this? We put 'em in jail, they'll be gone in two hours."

"Got any ideas?" Fox asked.

"Yeah, I got an idea. Can you drive their Cadillac?" Bear-Don't-Walk questioned.

Fox nodded.

He watched as Bear-Don't-Walk and Merv with the ponytail gathered the two handcuffed men off the kitchen floor. "Hey, what the fuck are you doing?" the Weasel protested as Merv wrapped a swath of duct tape around the Bear's head covering his mouth. The Bear's eyes were wide with fright.

"We got a right to make a phone call, officer," the Weasel pled as Merv stepped to him.

"You got no rights, white man," Merv snarled silencing him with another tear of silver tape. "You're in Indian country."

The big officer ran the tape around their knees and their ankles until both men were standing rigid like human posts. Bear-Don't-Walk held their wrists as Merv unlocked the handcuffs, pulled them away and applied tape. The Bear and the Weasel were trembling. Fox stood and watched in silence. He felt capable of killing both with no remorse. His pain had become anger.

Bear-Don't-Walk spotted the severed finger on the kitchen floor. Pushing the Weasel aside, he picked it up. It was curled. Fox felt strange looking at it. "You want it?" he asked with a look at Fox.

Fox shook his head. He knew there was no chance of reattachment.

Bear-Don't-Walk reached to Weasel, pulled out a shirt pocket and dropped the finger inside. Weasel winced and tried to pull away. Bear-Don't-Walk slapped him hard. Bound and unsteady, the Weasel swayed and nearly fell. "You cut the man's finger off. Have the courage to take it," Bear-Don't-Walk growled.

Merv dabbed a finger in the pool of Fox's blood on the countertop and traced a line across the Bear's nose and then his cheeks. He spoke in Mojave as a finger returned for more blood. He painted a line across the

Bear's forehead. Bear's eyes were clamped shut. He shook as if he had been dipped in ice water. Merv continued in his choppy, foreign, ominous Mojave tongue.

"What is he saying?" Fox questioned. He was cradling his wrapped left hand with the right.

"He is painting the man with the blood of his enemy. It will bring him comfort in death."

Weasel bowed his head and began to weep through his gag. Merv grabbed the man by the hair and jerked his head up to paint him with blood. The Weasel squirmed as the blood was applied.

Fox took comfort in the man's anguish. He had no sympathy for either.

Bear-Don't-Walk dug in the Weasel's trouser pocket and came out with car keys. "Follow us," he said to Fox.

Fox took the keys. He did not feel this was something the two Tribal Police Officers were doing for the first time and, although it was foreign and unorthodox, he felt it just.

Merv and Bear-Don't-Walk carried the two bound and gagged frightened men out to one of the police cars and pushed them into the back. Fox climbed into the Cadillac Seville. It was ripe with the stench of nicotine. Laying his bleeding, throbbing left hand in his lap, he followed the two police cars from the trailer park.

The train of three cars drove south along the dark river road. They passed Squaw Dam, a flood-control dam north of Blue Water Lagoon. The long dam was little more than a dark shadow stretching across the face of the quiet river. Its dark hulk was spotted with narrow cones of light and a flashing red light to warn errant boaters. A mile below the dam Bear-Don't-Walk's car led the way onto the shoulder of the road near a time-worn makeshift mud boat launch.

After they had stopped, Bear-Don't-Walk signaled Fox out of the Cadillac. Climbing in behind the wheel, he turned the car in the center of the deserted dark roadway and backed it down the slick, muddy incline until the bumper was lapped by the water from the river. Fox stood holding his bleeding wrapped hand, a silent spectator, as Merv pulled the two bound men out of the police car. Sensing their fate, both tried to resist. It was of little consequence. Fox could hear their muffled fear-filled cries as Merv handled them like rag dolls. He pushed the Bear in on the passenger's side of the Cadillac and strapped him in tight with the seat belt. Bear-Don't-Walk forced the Weasel in behind the wheel and cinched the seat belt in place.

Merv closed the passenger's door, stomped mud off of his shoes and walked to join Fox.

Standing at the open driver's door, Bear-Don't-Walk reached in and pulled the selector to neutral. The big Cadillac began drifting backwards into the dark water. The Bear and the Weasel squirmed and kicked as the water crept up over the trunk lid and spilled into the rear seat. The car's taillights shimmered beneath the water.

Bear-Don't-Walk waded into the murky waters following the sinking car. Water washed into the front seat and up over the legs of the trapped men. Their eyes were wide with terror. The Weasel's chin fell to his chest as he wept. The touch of cold water on his chin brought his head up. Bear-Don't-Walk reached in and jammed the selector into park. The car stopped. The two men were sitting with their chins high as the water lapped at their jaws. "In the morning," Bear-Don't-Walk said as he stood near chest-deep at the open door, "you will hear the loons crying. It means a new day... At sunrise they open the dam gates for irrigation. The water will rise three to four feet...., and then the sound of the loons wouldn't bother you." He closed the car door sending a surge of water to wash across the painted faces of both men. He started away, but then returned and leaned an elbow on the open window. "You should know, we must hunt down your wives and your children to cut off their fingers. Honor demands we do this. It shames a man to disfigure him and not kill him. Your families must erase this dishonor." He reached in, switched off the headlamps and waded away.

The Weasel watched in horror as the lights of the police cars winked on and drove away. The Bear, strapped neck-deep in the water beside him, was weeping. The Weasel, arms bound behind his back, shifted and squirmed testing his restraints. The tape and the seat belt allowed little movement. He was trapped. Something bobbed to the surface and touched his jaw. The Weasel twisted, squinting in the faint light to see, then recoiled away. Fox's severed, curled finger bobbed on the surface of the water.

22 A FAMILY MATTER

> *"Conversation was never begun at once, nor in a hurried manner. Silence was meaningful and granting a space of silence before talking was done in regard for the rule that, 'thought comes before speech.'"*
>
> **Luther Standing Bear—Ogalala Sioux Chief**

The glow from the White Buffalos' construction was lighting the night when the Tribal Police car sped by unnoticed. Fox glanced at the site from the passenger's side. It was comforting to see. The Buffalo had been wounded, brought to its knees, but had withstood the attack. Four men lay dead in its wake. Holding his throbbing hand, Fox wondered how many more there would be. More alarming than the deaths was the fact they seemed inconsequential. Something bigger than individual lives was at stake. Although the blood seeping through the towel in his lap was real, Fox sensed this was more than a battle of flesh and bone. The struggle he had joined was spiritual. Men, he had learned, were more than flesh and bone, more than BMWs and careers, more than husbands and lovers. More than all that, they were warriors. Warriors who had to keep the peace or steal money or build a bridge or climb a mountain or cut alfalfa. Every man needed a struggle, a fence to climb, a dam to jump off, an election to win, a casino to build. Man had no choice in joining a struggle, but he did have a choice on which side he would stand. Fox hoped he had chosen right.

"I see David Rollins' truck is still there," Bear-Don't-Walk said from behind the wheel.

"Yeah, I noticed," Fox answered. Ironic, he thought. It was as if they were out for some pleasant drive in the cool of the night when, in reality, they had just left two men to drown in a Cadillac and they were on their way to the hospital because his finger had been severed with wire cutters. Being an Indian wasn't easy, Fox decided. His stomach jerked and he threw up on the floor between his legs. Bear-Don't-Walk drove faster.

"How did this happen?" the young doctor in a green surgical gown questioned as he shot injection after injection into Fox's hand around the severed finger. Fox winced with the first several needle jabs, but then the numbing drug began to ease the pain. He was slow to answer. "Accident at home," he heard Bear-Don't-Walk answer for him.

"Look straight at the light," a nurse ordered as she loomed over Fox. He found he was looking up at the underside of her white-clad breasts. An interesting point of view, he decided just before the drops hit his eye. "This will blur your vision for a few minutes."

"This accident happen before or after the pepper

spray?" the doctor asked sarcastically as he manipulated the numbed hand and looked at the wound with a light.

Bear-Don't-Walk found a telephone in the vacant doctor's lounge and dialed the La Paz County Sheriff's office. "This is Sergeant Bear-Don't-Walk from the Tribal Police. Citizen flagged me down couple minutes ago. Said there was a car in the river maybe a mile south of Squaw Dam... No, I didn't get his name. I'd go have a look, but I'm tied up on an accident."

Eleven minutes later a patrol car, searching the surface of the placid water with a spotlight, rolled slowly down the river road south of Squaw Dam. The loons were beginning their morning calls on the distant bank. The spotlight swept back and forth. The dark waters yielded nothing as they seemed to suck at the light. Suddenly light met glass and reflection danced. The patrol car jerked to a halt. "There... There," a voice behind the spotlight shouted. The hood ornament and windshield of the Cadillac were peeking out of dark waters like a crocodile.

The patrol car swung its headlamps toward the submerged car and stopped. Two deputies scrambled out and waded into the water with flashlights. "Jesus," a deputy exclaimed, "there's two men in there!"

The Weasel had promised God he would quit smoking, get rid of his collection of pornographic CD's, give all his money to the church, attend confession regularly and open the greeting card shop in Chicago his wife always wanted if only he were spared from drowning in the cold, dark water that now lapped over his face. The Weasel's neck pained as he stretched to keep his nostrils above the water. Beside him the Bear, shorter by three inches, was blowing water like a surfacing seal every time the choppy water exposed his nose. Then the miracle occurred. Flashlights illuminated their faces. The

Weasel looked into the intense beam of the Deputy's Kel-Light. He knew he was looking at the radiance of the Holy Mother. "Thank you, Mother of God," he mumbled beneath his tape gag.

La Paz County Deputies were experienced at pulling bodies from the Colorado River. Drunken and reckless tourists killed themselves regularly with colliding boats, Wave Runners, Jet Skis, water skis, inner tubes and high dives all mixed with drugs, alcohol and the belief it always happened to the other guy. Two live men bound with duct tape in a new Cadillac was unusual. The low mud poor-man's boat launch quickly filled with a gaggle of police cars, ambulances, fire rescue trucks and curious passers-by. The roadway and the surface of the water pulsed with flashes of red strobe lights. The sound of the loons was stilled by the stereophonic blare of a dozen police radios. A small army of khaki uniforms and shoulder patches crowded around the open rescue truck as paramedics clipped away the duct tape. "What's that on his face. Is it blood?"

The Bear was a trembling, hysterical hulk unable to speak. He sat wrapped in a heavy blanket with his face in his hands weeping. The Weasel's teeth were clattering, but cloaked in a blanket, sipping a steaming coffee, he was able to speak. "Where.... Where can... Can I rent a car?"

He was bombarded with questions. "I got a right to remain silent," he defended.

"We're not accusing you of a crime," an impatient sergeant answered. "We are trying to find out who tried to kill you."

"It was an accident," the Weasel suggested.

"Bullshit!"

"Okay," the Weasel said trying a different tact. "It's part of an initiation."

"Yeah, to death."

"Listen," the Weasel pled, "We gotta get back to Las Vegas."

"You just gonna forget that Cadillac turned submarine out there?" the sergeant pressed.

"It's insured."

"Vegas, huh," the sergeant speculated. "You get caught cheating or some shit?"

"Can't we just go?" the Weasel begged.

"First we're gonna have a look at your car. Maybe there's a body in the trunk." the Sergeant challenged. "I don't know how the police in Vegas work, but down here we kinda frown on duct tape swimsuits."

"This is all just a misunderstanding," the Weasel defended. The paper coffee cup was shaking in his hand.

"Somebody really put the fear in you, didn't they?"

A tow truck made its contribution to the crowd on the riverbank. A cable was stretched to the front bumper of the Cadillac and a winch dragged its prize out of the mud, muck and water. "Wonder if this is connected to the Lincoln that took a dive off Bill Williams bridge?" the sergeant speculated as water cascaded out of the flooded car.

There was a flurry of excitement when a gun was found in the trunk. It was an expensive nine-millimeter Glock. The cops passed it around examining the action, looking at it with curious eyes. The excitement was diminished when a soggy Clark County Concealed Weapons Permit was found the glove box.

The questioning was to continue for nearly two hours. The rescued Cadillac yielded nothing. Neither did the two men. The on-scene sergeant was not a happy man. "Somebody tried to kill you tonight," he told the wrinkled and damp Weasel and Bear. "You may not want to tell me, but it's not likely they're gonna let this go unfinished."

"Does that mean we can go?" the Weasel questioned eagerly.

"Yeah, go," the Sergeant urged. "Get your asses outta my county."

"We... We're not sure where we are. Maybe you could give us a ride?" the Weasel stammered looking around at the roadside in the spreading morning light.

"And maybe you should have answered my questions."

The Weasel reached for his wallet. "I can pay."

"Get the fuck outta here."

In Las Vegas the lights of the strip were yielding to the morning sun. The city seemed to yawn as a busy night ended and a new day began. Players stayed late and slept late. It was a given in the business. As the rest of the world filled freeways, rode elevators in high-rise office buildings and crowded assembly lines, Las Vegas counted its money. All over the gaming Mecca drop teams collected money from the slots and gaming tables. Now, isolated count rooms bristling with surveillance cameras, bill counters and coin sorters were busy with an army of employees dressed in pocket-less jump suits counting the millions that passed through their hands daily. The players slept, although ninety-seven percent had lost. A comp breakfast buffet would bring them back later.

Owners and managers only slept after the count. Donald DePalma, the current King of the Hill, was no different. He was in his office at the Casa Grande awaiting a call on the daily drop. It had been a busy night. The Don had attended the heavyweight fight at the MGM Grand. The eighth-round knock-out had earned him fifty-thousand-dollars, but more than the fight and the big money flowing like cheap champagne was the opportunity to sit ringside with all the celebrities. Kimmel, Fallon, Travolta and that big-titted brunette from some shit show on ABC. He couldn't remember her name, but he couldn't forget her tits. Why the hell was it actors attracted all the pussy? He could buy or sell any of them, but few, if any of them, knew who he was. Maybe he'd produce his own fuckin' movie and not hire any of them. Except maybe the big-titted brunette. What the hell could be difficult about making a movie? You hired everybody to do everything. Try building a fucking casino. There was a ball buster!

Maybe that was why his balls hurt, DePalma mused with a smile. River Gold in Laughlin was well on its way to reality. Bigger and better than anything else on the river. He had flown in eight investors from Japan for the championship fight. The Japanese loved gambling and ached for an opportunity to buy into Las Vegas. Their money was welcome, but they weren't. The Japs were like mold; you let it get started and it soon had the whole slice. DePalma had allowed them a piece of the crust. A silent eighth of River Gold. Lana had lined up eight of her best friends for appropriate after-fight activities. A good fight, a great set of tits and a chance to invest. This was what made America great.

A market demographic report on River Gold lay on DePalma's desk. Awaiting Lana's return from tending the flock, DePalma had skimmed the grafts and charts. They were favorable, but one of the Japanese who had seen the report in an investment portfolio questioned the competitive operation paragraph on page fifty-two.

The White Buffalo, a Native American gaming operation-casino, currently under construction along U.S. 95 near Parker, Arizona, dependent on completion and subsequent curb appeal, could, the report speculated, impact significant revenues from market sources in southwest Arizona and southern California.

Fuckin' Indians! DePalma wanted to tell the investor he had the White Buffalo and those smelly Indians with dirty fingernails and yellow teeth by the balls. He wanted to say the White Buffalo was more a white elephant than any icon of the west, but he said what he had to say. "Indian casinos are aberrations. They're inconsequential, minor league, local bingo parlors," he explained. "Plus, informed sources have reported the project is in trouble. Construction has stopped. This is typical of Indian projects," DePalma suggested. "They make better blankets than they do casinos."

The Japanese had all laughed politely at his remarks.

But the marketing research company had covered its ass. It was a warning and Donald DePalma never ignored warnings. He was holding the Buffalo by the balls. But eventually he would have to let go. The White Buffalo had to be more than stopped. It had to be killed, again.

The door to the spacious executive office opened and Lana Casner came in. She crossed and moved around the desk to where DePalma sat. Wearing slacks and a jacket, she had a demure business look. "All our little Pearl Harbor friends have had their sneak attacks by now... Bonsai!" Lana smiled seductively.

DePalma marveled at Lana's insight. She was right. The Japanese, working twelve to fifteen hours a day in Japan, spending every waking moment in an ordered, stress-filled, world would suddenly find themselves capable of effortlessly seducing one of Las Vegas' finest. They would want to own part of such a world. It was star dust, it was magic. It was Vegas bullshit, but it worked. DePalma would underwrite the fantasy sex for eight businessmen, but he would net the investment capital he needed. "I feel tense," he said loosening his tie.

Lana reached and unbuttoned the front of her jacket allowing it to fall open. She was bare chested. "I've been waiting to do that all night." She scratched at the underside of her breasts with long nails.

"Me too," DePalma smiled as he admired Lana's exposed breasts.

"Might relieve that built-up tension," Lana purred, moving her nails to his leg. Her fingers walked toward his crotch. The electronic chirp of the console telephone on his desk stopped her.

DePalma reached and gathered the receiver. "Hello."

"Don, it's Mitch. I have the drop report." It was Parsons, the Casino Manager, calling from the floor below.

"Before we get to that, Mitch," DePalma said reaching into an inside jacket pocket. "I want you to make a call for me." He pulled out a note. Lana's fingers resumed their walk. Polished nails marched to the fly of his slacks and tugged at the zipper. "Here's the number," he said shifted to accommodate Lana. "Two-oh-two-two-nine-five-five-six-four-four." Lana eased the zipper all the way down and parted the material. The polished nails disappeared inside. "That's the Code Enforcement Division of the Army Corps of Engineers." Lana's finger snaked through the opening in his boxer shorts and grasped the erection. "You need to talk with Rob Peterson," DePalma glanced at his note. "Tell him it's time to review the waste disposal plans for the White Buffalo."

"Rob Peterson," Parsons said in DePalma's ear as Lana pulled the erection out of the open fly. She massaged gently with a pumping action. Pushing close to DePalma, she swung a breast and an erect nipple teased at his nose.

"Right," DePalma answered. "That's all you have to say. He'll know what to do." Lana sank to her knees between his legs, brushing the penis she held with a nipple.

"Do you want me to identify myself?"

DePalma wet his lips. It was becoming an effort to concentrate. "Mitch, what the fuck did I say? You don't tell him anything."

Lana opened glossed lips and lowered her head onto his erection. DePalma arched his back and pushed into her mouth. He gave an audible sigh.

"Did you say something?" Parsons questioned.

"No!"

"Are you ready for the drop figures?"

"Call me back," DePalma slammed down the receiver. His fingers dug into the cushioned chair arms as Lana's head moved up and down. For DePalma it was ecstasy. For Lana it was business. DePalma had succumbed to the same play as the Japanese. But he didn't think of that.

Fox, as ordered, wore his arm in a sling for a week. The stitched stump of his finger was in a metal splint and wrapped with a bandage. Fox was glad. He was in no hurry to see it. As long as it was hidden, he didn't have to deal with the fact one of his fingers was gone. "Had a cousin do the same thing with a car jack," Bear-Don't-Walk told Fox the morning they left the hospital. Fox claimed it as his story. It was much neater and cleaner than dealing with the agony of the truth. After the attack, he started sleeping with a gun, although he didn't really think the two would come back. The terror he had seen on the faces of the two men in the Cadillac was real. They would not come back for more. It wasn't their fight. They wouldn't be willing to die for it. Fox knew word would get back to DePalma.

The mention of the telephone call told Fox it was DePalma who sent the two. Maybe this would end it. Maybe DePalma, like the Department of Interior, like the United States Government, had learned the Indians weren't going to be stopped. DePalma had already exposed himself. If Fox, with the limited resources he had, could build a circumstantial case against DePalma, it proved the man was out on a limb. In that respect his telephone call had served its purpose. He had only nine and a half fingers, but DePalma had his notice. They knew who he was, and they knew what he was doing. Now the notice was being reinforced with the return of two humiliated enforcers. A rational man would stop. Fox hoped DePalma was rational.

The around-the-clock shifts continued at the White Buffalo as the construction site grew into a spartan casino. Everything was battleship gray, but the walls, the ceiling, the ducts, the wires and the pipes were all coming together like a great mosaic. Fox and Bear-Don't-Walk, knowing far more than others how real the threat was, had subtly increased security. The entire site was ringed with an eight-foot-high chain-linked fence. A security officer checked the identification of every individual coming through the gate, while others prowled the job site. Thieves in construction were not unusual. Vendors, construction deliveries and even the caterer, who now had a new truck, had to be approved by David Rollins.

David continued his cash payments. The promised overtime was paid, and the eager crews pushed feverishly for the promise bonus. Parker had its life's blood back and it was green. The metamorphosis of a skeletal frame into a recognizable casino was proving David right. He seldom left the job site and at the end of the third week he began sleeping in the executive trailer. He became obsessed with the work. The once glib, gentle, young Indian became a haggard, short-tempered tyrant. Watching him, Fox wondered if the casino was worth it, but no one could argue the fact it was getting done.

Fox was both surprised and pleased when Sparrow appeared at the construction gate in his wheelchair. Sparrow looked robust. "Hey, Sprite Man, they won't let me in," he complained when Fox met him.

"They probably didn't recognize you without your legs," Fox teased.

"You want me to give you the finger?" the Sparrow answered sarcastically after glancing at the black leather glove Fox wore on his left hand. He told the curious the black glove was to protect the injury, especially since he worked in a construction site, but the truth was John Fox didn't like the pink-scabbed, awkward stump that was once his little finger. Hiding the stump beneath the black glove was much easier than explaining it. He secretly admired Sparrow's courage for showing up in a wheel-chair. Fox wasn't certain he could have. The loss of his legs, ironically Fox thought, had made Sparrow taller.

They spent several hours on the blueprints showing the location of each of the casino's three hundred and eight closed-circuit television cameras. There were domed pan-tilt-zooms, fixed, auto-iris, black and white and color. The CCTV system would be linked to a matrix computer, monitors and a keyboard control system with joy sticks as well as real-time and twenty-four-hour VCRs and printers turning all the action into CD's to be kept in a safe. "Can you do it?" Fox questioned.

"I'm gonna need legs," Sparrow answered. "But, yeah, I can do this."

"You can have twenty-two legs," Fox told him.

"Twenty-two?" Sparrow was puzzled.

"Yeah, eleven people," Fox smiled.

"I can have eleven people to help me?"

"Yeah, eleven people you're going to educate and manage."

Sparrow was sobered by the thought. Fox saw it. "You sure you can do this?"

"Were you sure you could cut alfalfa?"

"No."

"Me too," Sparrow admitted.

As finish work began in the sprawling casino neared, the demands on the Gaming Enterprise Board increased. A horde of relentless salesmen, vendors and job seekers descended on the casino every day. David Rollins kept pressure on the sub-contractors while Mara and George Manygoats faced the army of vendors and pitchmen promising to fill their every hardware need, and there were many. Complex digital slot machines, card tables, chairs, stools, carpet, restaurant tables, booths and chairs, office furniture, bar equipment, bar stools, cash carts, safe rooms, office supplies, coin sorters, coin counting machines, coin wrapping machines, currency counters, cash registers, copy machines, computers, big screen TVs, casino tokens, uniforms, napkins, ash trays, coin cups, playing cards, matches with impounds and much more.

Compounding the hardware needs were the personnel demands. A finished casino would be of little value without an efficient experienced trusted team to run it. "You need to help us find an honest casino manager," Mara told Fox after calling him to the Enterprise Trailer.

"Are you sure there are any," Fox cautioned.

"We've had twenty-six apply. We've cut them down to nine applicants," George Manygoats added. "Could you pick the best?"

"You've got nine people that can't find a job somewhere else," Fox cautioned. "I don't think that's the best."

"We pay you for more than sarcasm," Mara warned, "You were FBI. Don't you have experience reading character?"

Fox nodded agreement. He wasn't as easily intimidated by Mara since seeing her topless. Even if it were a dream, it made him conscious of her vulnerability. She, like many assertive, ambitious women, was basically shy, he decided. A shyness wrapped in an in-your-face attitude that disguised it. "You're right. If we're going on a bear hunt, where would we go?"

"The mountains," George Manygoats blurted proudly shooting a hand in the air. Mara burned him with a look.

"Right," Fox granted. "We could sit here and wait on a bear. We could put food out and maybe eventually a bear would come, but where will the best bears be?"

"On the mountain," George answered eagerly and then offered a look of apology to Mara.

"So, if you want the best bear, you go to the mountain and get it," Fox added.

George looked puzzled. "What's that got to do with a casino manager?"

"George, shut up," Mara snapped.

"Maybe instead of a casino manager," Fox suggested, "you should start with a Director of Human Resources. Someone with gaming experience. Someone who could find qualified candidates."

"That's a good idea," Mara said allowing Fox a smile. He was surprised. Jesus, she was even more attractive when she smiled. Maybe the veil of ice between them was melting. Fox hoped so. Mara looked to George. "Do you want to drive to Vegas or fly from Lake Havasu?"

"Vegas?!?" George was puzzled. "We're talking about bears and mountains. Where in the hell did Vegas come from?"

"John," Mara smiled again, easier this time as her eyes

went to Fox. "Be careful using metaphors around the intellectually challenged."

"I'm not intellectually challenged," George defended.

"I agree," Mara answered.

Fox left the Enterprise Trailer encouraged. Mara had smiled at him twice and called him by his first name. That was a first and an important one. Maybe the dream could come true, he allowed. Maybe he would find out if beauty was more than skin deep. It was an exciting thought and Fox was comparing the form beneath the white blouse Mara wore and the memory of the dream when angry reverberating voices reached him from somewhere in the interior of the cavernous casino. They were loud, angry and profane, and they were familiar. Fox turned and bolted toward a doorless opening leading to the heart of the casino.

David Rollins, his dark hair—usually pulled back in a ponytail—hanging in disarray, stood, blueprint in hand, shouting into the face of Sparrow in his wheelchair. David's face was an angry mask. "The fuckin' wire goes in conduit!" he shouted, waving the open blueprint. "That's what the fuckin' specs demand. That's what the fuck you do!"

Sparrow matched David's anger. Shaking his own rolled blueprint, he stabbed it at David. "It might be on your print, but it ain't on mine, and even if it was, you got no right calling me an idiot."

"You're right." David leaned close to Sparrow's face. "I shouldn't call you an idiot, 'cause you're a fuckin' legless idiot!"

Sparrow swung the blueprint smacking David in the face. David kicked and Sparrow's wheelchair tipped crashing to the bare concrete floor on its side. David closed on the fallen man and kicked again. Sparrow grimaced as the boot hit him hard in the stomach, but he grabbed and held onto David's leg like a pit bull. Pulling himself up David's stiff leg, Sparrow bit hard into the flesh. David screamed and pummeled the legless form biting into his leg with both fists. Sparrow bit harder.

Fox and One Feather, coming from different sides of the wide still vacant card room, reached the two at the same time. A collection of drywall men in coveralls, electricians, plumbers and a paint crew working on a scaffold paused to watch, but no one interfered. It wasn't their fight. This was Indian business.

One Feather grabbed Sparrow by the arms and pulled. Fox grabbed David in a bear-hug and wrenched him away from Sparrow. "I want that little sonofabitch arrested," David demanded. "Lemme go, Goddamnit!"

"Fuck you!" Sparrow spat at David. One Feather helped him into his righted wheelchair. "The only thing you've ever had stiff is your knee."

David lunged at Sparrow again. Fox grabbed him from behind, twisted his wrist and shoved it high into the middle of his back. Holding the wrist and a handful of shirt collar, Fox muscled David out of the casino on his toes.

The door of the executive trailer swung wide and banged the wall as Fox stiff-armed David inside. Fox closed the door behind them. The haggard David glared at Fox and massaged his writs. "That idiot works for you, doesn't he?"

Fox crossed to confront David. "What the hell's wrong with you? The man's got no legs."

"He still has a brain."

"What's your excuse?" Fox reached and patted a pocket on David's Pendleton shirt.

David pushed the hand away, "I don't have to answer your...."

Fox grabbed David by the shoulder, spun him around

and slammed him against the wall. Holding him, Fox grabbed at the pocket and pulled out a prescription vial. He shook it. It rattled like a snake. "That's for my knee wound," David said to the wall.

Fox released him and walked to David's desk with the vial in hand. He began jerking drawers open, looking. "You have no right to do that," David protested.

The trailer door opened. It was Mara. She looked to David, then Fox. "Get out, Mara," Fox ordered.

Mara didn't move. "I'm a member of the Enterprise Board. I have a...."

"Get out!" Fox barked.

Mara stepped out and slammed the door. Fox returned to his search of the desk. David watched in stoic silence. Fox found what he sought in a bottom drawer. He jerked the drawer from the desk and dumped it on top. An assortment of prescription bottles and vials clattered onto the desktop. Pills, capsules and bottles rolled and fell onto the floor. "These for your knee too?" Fox picked up several vials and shook them. "Is this what makes David run?" David glared at Fox.

"How did it start, David? The codeine for the knee? Take as needed. Then a little something to bring you back. Twice a day. Problem sleeping. Two at bedtime. Couple in the morning. Definitely with lunch... Then you find you don't need lunch, just the pills. Sleep? That's for the weak. More pills."

David raised his hands to his face.

"I want you to go home. Go home and sleep. Do you understand?"

David, head low, stiff-legged himself to the door, wiping tears from his face. He paused, took a breath and stepped out.

When he was gone, Fox began gathering the vials, bottles and spilled capsules from the desktop and floor.

He took them into the small bathroom and emptied each into the toilet, flushing it again and again. He was pushing up from the third flushing when he found Mara standing outside the door of the bathroom. "Where is he?"

Fox rinsed his hands in the sink. "He's going to take a couple days off."

"And the drugs?"

"What drugs?" Fox rolled a paper towel from a dispenser on the wall.

"The gaming compact has a strict anti-drug policy," Mara folded her arms beneath her breasts. It was her official Tribal stance and Fox was sorry to see her reverting to it. "To have a Gaming Enterprise Member abusing drugs cannot be ignored."

Fox dried his hands, balled the paper towel and tossed it hard at a trash can. Mara's lack of compassion was irritating him. "What is your problem? Or were you born without a heart?"

The words stiffened Mara. Fox moved to her. "You come in here spewing the party line like some cigar store Indian. Haven't you ever made a mistake, crossed the line, dropped the ball?"

"What I am personally has nothing to do with what I am professionally."

"It has everything to do with it. You can't separate the two. That's psychological bullshit!"

Fox stood staring into the brown eyes. Mara didn't flinch. "I will not debate professional ethic with you. I don't have to justify my actions as long as they conform with Tribal Policy."

"Is that the same attitude I'm getting?" Fox pressed. "Is that it, or is it something else?"

"Something else?" Mara questioned.

"Let me demonstrate." Fox gave in to the impulse. He

stepped to Mara, took her face in his hands and kissed her hard. Mara tore her mouth from his. "Nooo!"

Mara turned her back and braced an arm on the desk to cover her mouth with a hand. Fox laid a hand on her trembling back. She drew away as if touched by a hot iron. "No, don't touch me!"

"Why?

Mara turned to him. Her face was a mask of anguish. Tears rimmed her eyes. "It's not what you think." Her words were ragged with emotion.

"Is it because I'm only half Indian?" Fox demanded in frustration

The question fueled Mara's anguish. Tears spilled and ran down her cheeks. "No," she shouted. "It's because I'm your half-sister."

Fox stood stunned, unable to speak. Mara bolted from the office. The door banged behind her.

23 TIES THAT BIND

---

*"It is strictly believed and understood by the Sioux
that a child is the greatest gift from Wakan-Tanka,
in response to many devout prayers, sacrifices, and
promises. Therefore, the child is considered
'sent by Wakan Tanka,' through some element—
namely the element of human nature."*
Robert Higheagle—Teton Sioux

Fox stood on the riverbank and stared into the night. He could hear the water, smell it, even feel the touch of humidity it surrendered to the breeze, but the river, like the desert beyond it was a dark void. The moon-less night sky separated itself from the blanket of darkness cloaking the earth with an array of starlight. A chorus of bullfrogs and insects filled the night with sound. Fox lost himself in it as he thought of Mara's reaction to the kiss, again and again, as if rewinding a video tape over and over. The memory of Mara's words twisted it into a thorn-filled frustration. A frustration wrapped in a frightening puzzle.

After watching Mara speed away from the casino, Fox tried to walk off his anxieties by pacing in the shell of the casino. All he succeeded in doing was pissing off a paint crew and getting tile adhesive on his boots. He had stepped in it, in the literal sense, but the idea of going home after Mara's shocking declaration wasn't a consideration. Fox had been shaken by her words. Seeing this woman of composure become a trembling emotional plea convinced him she was sincere. "I'm your half-sister," she had said. It wasn't possible. It had to be some Indian tradition, some Mojave custom he didn't understand. The hour was late but need outweighed consideration. Fox called Chief Stoner and asked him to meet at Buck Point. The old man agreed without hesitation.

The headlamps and the sputter of Chief Stoner's aging Fiat reached Fox on the riverbank as the car crossed the field from the highway. Fox's pickup was out there in the darkness. He knew the old man would find it. Soon the headlamps faded, the engine noise stopped, and a car door slammed.

"John Fox?" The stooped silhouette questioned as the old man came down the riverbank in the darkness.

"Yes."

"Let's build a fire. It will keep the bugs away."

They gathered branches from the trees and built a small fire. The smoke was sweet with the aroma of sap. The chief squatted on one side of the flames and Fox on the other. "Is this about David?"

"No." Fox was surprised the chief knew about David, but he saw no reason to volunteer more. Unless the old man asked, the details would remain private.

It was quiet for a moment. A moth fluttered in the

369

light from the fire. The old man stirred the coals with a stick. He seemed in no hurry.

Fox finally found the courage to speak. "Mara said she is my sister." His voice was unsteady and ripe with uncertainty. He watched the firelight dance on the old man's face, looking for a reaction. He saw none.

"Why did she say that?" The chief said, without raising his eyes from the fire.

"I kissed her," Fox confessed. He thought it sounded far less than the act of a warrior.

The chief stabbed at the glowing embers. Sparks lifted and spun up into the night sky. "Many years ago, your father came to this valley. He was searching for the "weed man". Your father was an ambitious young Federal man and he knew catching the 'weed man' would bring him favor."

Fox listened intently.

"But the people in the valley would not talk to your father and he grew angry. One night he found Horace Waters alone, near crossroads. He beat Horace and threatened to put him in prison unless he would tell him where to find the 'weed man'. Horace did not want to go to prison, so he told your father where the 'weed man' was."

"The 'weed man' was arrested and your father told the people it was Horace who informed. Horace was angry and ashamed. He vowed to revenge his shame."

Fox found his mouth was dry. He sat transfixed, absorbing the words.

"Horace Waters, like all the people, knew of your father's marriage to Clair Scott. Although she moved to Phoenix, she came to visit us often. She always brought her young son, John Fox."

It was as if the chief were telling a story about

370

someone else. Fox tried to find some distant memory of it, there was little.

"Once when Clair came to visit, Horace stopped her on a road near Big Fork. To shame your father, he raped her." The old man paused to add some broken branches to the flames. "Clair was a wise woman," he continued, "she knew if she told your FBI father of the rape, he would kill Horace. Your father's career would be over, so Clair said nothing."

"And Horace Waters got away with the rape?"

The chief continued the story at his own pace. "Clair discovered she was pregnant. She could not tell your father because she had not been with him for many months. Your father was with another woman, Clair knew that. Because your father had captured the 'weed man' he was promoted and transferred to Atlanta."

Now the words gripped Fox's heart in a vice. It was as if he were looking at the memory of it for the first time. The silent film now had sound. Action now had reason.

"Clair loved your father and would do nothing to bring him shame. She told him she could not leave her people, but the truth was she had to let your father go— to save him. Your father went away. He took young John Fox with him."

Fox's heart was in his throat.

"Clair lived in sorrow, alone here on the reservation. She gave birth to the child. She named it Mara."

Tears rimmed Fox's eyes.

"Clair told the people the child belonged to Horace Waters' mother who lived in Tucson with a white man who did not want it."

"So, Mara and I, are sister and brother." Fox's voice was edged with emotion.

The old chief nodded, "Clair Scott is your mother and Mara's."

"And Horace? Nothing ever happened to him?"

"Some of the people knew the truth," the old man added, he was stirring the glowing coals in the fire again. "They went to Horace and he was banished from the tribe for twenty years. Clair called me when she knew she was dying. She asked us to forgive him. She was a kind woman."

"Small price to pay for what he did," Fox said, pushing up to stand.

"What price do white men pay for rape?" The chief challenged. "Horace Waters was dating Clair Scott until your father came to the reservation. Your father took Horace Waters' woman, this his pride when he beat him. White eyes see rape. Brown eyes see justice. Your father got his promotion, but he traded his family for it."

"Why didn't you tell me this before? Why let me...?" Fox stopped the thought as it took him back to Mara's kiss.

"It was not for me to tell."

"Now what am I to do?" Fox's frustration was yielding to anger.

The old man tossed his stick into the fire. "You talk as if this were a bad thing. You knew your mother as a child. Mara and your mother are much the same. You lost a family. Now you have a sister. Make of it what you will." The chief pushed up with effort walked away into the darkness.

Fox watched the old man's silhouette until it was swallowed by the night. He was staring into the glow of the fire when he heard the Fiat's starter in the distance.

Driving to his trailer at Branson's took Fox past the casino. The White Buffalo had become the light house of the desert. He glanced at the building as he drove by. Three sets of double wide glass doors yielded illumination from the bowls of the casino. A team of carpet layers were visible in the lobby. The parking lot lamps were in and the grading complete. Soon striped asphalt and palms would surround the sprawling building. The massive head of a bull buffalo, the classic icon of the west, fashioned out of white vinyl, lit the wall above the front entrance. Beneath the big animal, in bold illuminated plastic block printing was, "THE WHITE BUFFALO CASINO."

In a few days the construction trailers would be removed. Fox, his security crew, the Gaming Enterprise Board and a host of others would be moving in. No one had picked an exact date, but all knew an opening was growing near. It was difficult to picture the site as he first saw it. Three trailers on jacks. A tangle of cars, pickups and a line of hopefuls. What was it the old man said at the council meeting? "The White Buffalo will bring us hope." Fox had seen the hope with his own eyes. He had stood in line with it. He had felt it. He had ached to be part of it, and now he was. He was no longer alone. The old man was right. He had family. He had a sister. Fox took comfort in it as the lights of the casino faded in his rearview mirror.

Emotionally drained, Fox tossed his clothes aside, set the alarm and fell into bed. He wanted to be at the casino before George Manygoats and Mara left for Las Vegas in search of a Human Resources director. No speech, no demonstration of family, perhaps not even a mention of what he had learned, but he wanted to see Mara before she left. He pictured her. Was there a family resemblance?" He decided there was. He hoped she was able to sleep. Hell, of a way to meet your sister.

It seemed he had just closed his eyes, but five hours had passed when the electronic beep of his pager woke him. "Shit," Fox muttered and reached for the phone.

"Security, Adams," a flat male voice answered.

"Adams, it's Fox. You paged me?"

"Yeah, we got a problem, boss. Two US Marshals and the FBI are here with a court order."

"A court order! For what?"

"I don't know," Adams apologized. "Something to do with wastewater."

The river, Fox thought. The two men in the Cadillac! Or maybe his illegal computer entry into N.C.I.C. Jesus, he'd made a mess of things. His mind was in a panic. "I'll be right there."

A white SUV sat parked at the gate of the chain link fence surrounding the casino. Stenciled on the vehicles front door was, "U.S. Marshall." Beside it sat a nondescript beige sedan. Fox recognized it as FBI. He parked the pickup beside them and climbed out. He was angry and the cars gave his anger a focus.

Adams, a six foot, two-hundred and fifty-pound, pony tailed refugee from the Tribal Police met Fox at the gate. The employee parking lot was lined with cars. Fox could see the carpet crew still at work inside. Others were unloading card tables from an eighteen-wheeler at a side door. "Where are they?"

"Waste disposal plant out back," Adams answered, unlocking the gate.

Fox stepped through. "Who said they could go out there?"

"They didn't ask."

"Where's the court order?"

"In the security office." Adams relocked the gate.

"How many are there?"

"Four. Two uniforms. Two suits."

"Let's find them." Fox led the way to the back of the cavernous casino.

The casino's waste disposal plant, a near half mile from the rear of the casino, sat hidden in the folds of the rolling hills leading to the river. Adding to the plants' camouflage was a stand of cottonwood trees. Two large circular evaporation ponds with rotating sprinkler arms and a maze of flow control pipes leading to a pump house was all the casual observer could see, but beneath the surface a network of leach lines stretched in every direction to carry away reclaimed water. The state-of-the-art plant had cost the tribe twenty-eight million dollars. It was designed and built by a company that installed a similar system at Lake Mead National Park.

It was nearly full light and Special Agents Lang and Hodges from the Phoenix office of the FBI were directing the uniformed Marshals. One of them was carrying a video camera. The other a digital still camera. "Get me a full shot, slow pan, left to right," Lang ordered. The uniformed Marshal moved off toward the end of the disposal plant with the video camera.

"You," Lang said to the second Marshal, "go up on the rise above the plant and shoot proximity stills toward the river." The man wore the strap of the digital camera around his neck.

"Hold it right there," Fox barked, leading Adams and Curtis out from among the cottonwood trees. He recognized Lang and Hodges from the meeting in Phoenix. Lang signaled the Marshal to wait.

Fox and the two security officers walked to confront the three men. "What was it you told me? All I had to do was pick up the telephone and call you. I don't remember doing that."

"This is official business," Lang warned. "There's a copy of a court order to 'cease and desist' on your desk. It's signed by Federal Judge William Barlew in Phoenix.

"Then what are you taking pictures of?" Fox challenged.

"He told you. It's official business," Hodges defended, he seemed eager for a confrontation.

"So's mine," Fox answered. "If you want treated with respect when you come on this reservation, show some. Adams seize the video camera from that man. If he resists, arrest him."

"Yes, Sir." Adams trekked after the man. Fox looked to the Marshall holding the digital camera. "Curtis, confiscate that."

Hodges looked to Lang for a signal to intervene. He was tense, ready. Lang shook his head subtly.

"You're going to regret this, Fox. We'll have your ass," Lang threatened.

Curtis, young and eager, quickly took the camera from the uncertain marshal.

"There's a sign at the front gate warning, 'no cameras' and 'no Trespassing'." You said you're here to deliver a court order. What happened? Did you make a wrong turn when you left my office?"

"You know we have jurisdiction." Hodges was red faced and angry. Adams returned with the video camera in hand. The humble marshal followed close behind him.

"To do what?" Fox questioned. "Are you conducting a criminal investigation?"

"You got it a little backwards, Fox." Hodges snarled. "We ask the questions."

"When you have the right to," Fox argued. "That badge you're carrying doesn't make you any taller than we are."

"Don't lecture me," Hodges defended. "I'm not some social dropout, wearing a black glove."

"That's it, isn't it? I'm out here, so I'm not connected. I'm in some black hole you want nothing to do with. That might be what your think, but it isn't the law. The law says you're on a sovereign nation. A sovereign nation that warned you not to trespass or possess cameras. You did both. We're gonna have to turn these over to the Tribal Court."

"You're finished, Fox. Your career is over," Lang warned.

"You're wrong. My career is just starting. Now you have five minutes to get off the reservation. You don't, we're going to impound your car and arrest you all for trespass."

The uniformed marshals exchanged worried looks. "We'll go," Lang granted, "but This White Buffalo's going to become a dead buffalo."

Hodges pointed an accusing finger at Fox. "And you, and a lot of others," his finger moved toward the two officers, "are going to jail for obstructing Federal officers."

"You know, Hodges, your name should be Custer. Maybe you haven't noticed, but the Indians were here long before you. And they'll be here long after you're gone."

"Come on," Lang marched away. Hodges and the two marshals followed.

"Are we in a world of shit?" Adams questioned with a look at Fox.

Fox didn't answer.

"Fuckin' Indians," Hodges muttered from behind the wheel of the FBI sedan as he backed away from the gate at the front of the casino.

"Find us a pay phone," Lang urged.

"How do we know when we're off the reservation?" Hodges questioned.

"Just find us a goddamned pay phone," Lang snapped.

Fox headed for the security trailer. Adams and Curtis were at his side. "You really told those assholes, Boss," Curtis beamed. He fondled the thirty-five-millimeter digital camera as if it were a prize seized in battle.

"It won't be that easy, Kid," Fox took the camera from him. "They'll be back. You cover the front gate."

"Yes, Sir."

"Adams, get on the telephone. Call the troops. Get everybody in here. We're gonna need help."

David Rollins was in the bathroom of his mobile home, on his knees, face over the toilet bowl, when the phone rang. His stomach convulsed into a knot and he coughed bile into the water. His face was covered with sweat, even though he trembled with a chill. His stomach was on fire and his arms and legs were sore with cramps. The night had been a sleepless, painful agony, but he had not gone back to the drugs.

At first David considered flushing the assortment of painkillers and sedatives lining the bathroom cabinet, but that was blaming the drugs. The drugs weren't the problem, they were legal prescriptions, *he* was the problem. Pain was the excuse. The irony was, David found, withdrawal from the twenty plus tablets and capsules he gobbled daily was proving far more painful than the pain in his pin-fused knee.

Initially David hid the shame in anger. Fox was the problem. Who in the hell was he to point a finger? What did he know of pain? The answer came quick. David still had a knee. Fox had lost more. So had Sparrow. David had vowed nothing would stand in the path of The White Buffalo. Drugs had. Lisa Manygoats, round faced and proud with her pregnancy, was worried when he came home early, so David lied. "I have the flu." In the middle of the night, racked with cramps and sweat, he laid his face on the swell of her bare stomach. He was resting there when the baby in her womb moved against his cheek. It was as if the child were reaching out to comfort him. David raised his face and placed a hand gently on Lisa's stomach to answer. "I will make you proud of your father."

Lisa knocked on the door of the bathroom. "David, it's John Fox."

David pushed up, wiped his mouth on a towel and opened the door.

Mara Waters had not slept well. The kiss and her confession were disturbing, and she feared the consequences of both. Her mother had spoken of John Fox for years. Mara was glad she had been born a girl because she knew Clair Scott would never share the memory of her lost son. Mara grew into a woman, feeling she knew her brother. "One day he will come," Clair had promised. When the woman lay dying, Mara pleaded to let her find him. Her mother shook her head and whispered. "He will come."

The death of her mother brought contempt and anger for the brother who did not come. Mara clung to it until the day Chief Stoner walked into her office at Tribal Administration, closed the door and said, "He's here."

Mara had lived her life trying to fill the void the missing son had left in her mother's heart. She excelled in school, graduated from college, dedicated her life to serving the Tribe, as she was told John Fox would have, and yet it was never enough. Now with Clair Scott dead, he had come. It was too late. Too late to comfort the dying woman and too late to be her brother.

Mara had nothing but contempt for John Fox, at least that was what she told herself. But seeing his humility, his hard work, his pain, as well as his face, melted her facade of anger. He was taller than she expected. More handsome too. At first, he looked white, both in manner and appearance, but time had changed that. He now had a gentle spirit. Clair Scott had promised he would. "A spirit grows. It does not change," her mother had said. "John Fox has a gentle spirit."

Working with Fox, knowing the secret had been difficult for Mara. Her father, Horace Waters, was also worried. Worried what the son of the man whose wife he had raped more than three decades earlier, would do. Mara found herself watching Fox, studying, trying to understand and know him. She longed to tell him. She believed in truth, but the truth seemed bigger than she, perhaps bigger than both of them.

Mara sensed his interest, it may have been intuitive, but she felt it was more than casual. She had few serious relationships; but she was experienced enough to recognize flirtation and romantic interest. She was seeing it in John Fox. It gave Mara a sense of power and smug satisfaction. It was exciting to see a man's interest and know secretly he could never have her. She was playing with fire. But it was not a fire of her making. The kiss changed all that. The memory of it warned how close to the fire she had come. It also shattered the wall of secrecy between them.

Now, it was all right to love this man, and she admitted to herself she did. He was her mother's son, her brother. The revelation, ironically, had come like a bolt of lightning. The clouds had been gathering, building as the powerful charge grew and then in a flash of light, released. Truth was like that, Mara decided. Truth was powerful, difficult to control and it changed things. She didn't know where the relationship with Fox was going, but she knew it would change. It already had.

Unable to sleep, Mara got up early and began to pack

for Las Vegas. Getting away for the day would give her and John Fox a chance to think. She was closing the suitcase when the telephone rang. Mara picked it up on the second ring. "Hello."

"Mara, it's John Fox."

Mara's pulse raced. She was silent.

Fox filled the void. "We've been served with a court order shutting off the casino's water. I've called Chief Stoner and David."

"I'll be in," Mara said. She was relieved to hear his voice, no matter what the reason.

"Can you call George?"

"Yes."

"Thank you, Mara."

"John..." Mara said and then she hesitated, not knowing what to say, yet she felt she had to say something. "I ...."

"It's all right," Fox heard the uncertainty. "I know how you feel ..., I promise the next time I kiss you it will be on the cheek." He hung up.

Mara placed the telephone on the receiver. "Thank you," she whispered.

They met in the gaming enterprise trailer. Fox, Mara, David, George, Chief Stoner, Sergeant Bear-Don't-Walk, Morse Roberts, Horace Waters, Christine Scott and Gail Barton. The air was tense as Mara sat and read the text of the court order aloud.

"...whereas the Code Enforcement Division of the Bureau of Indian Affairs of the Department of the Interior of the Government of the United States, finds that the waste disposal plant constructed on a tract of trust land, A270076, Map 214, Section D-3, under the treaty governorship of the Mojave Indian Nation, fails to meet the specifications detailed in U.S. Code 17, Chapter 8, 214-C as well as the U.S. Army Corps of Engineers survey dated 8/23/87: concerning contamination of public waters and waterways; and in so doing becomes a critical public hazard and eminent threat to the health and wellbeing of both human and animal life whose sustenance depends on the waters of the Colorado River, the affiant herein prays the court will order an immediate and permanent halt to any and all construction and or operation of water supply sources, water transfer systems and any and all water reclamation systems in and around the area found in violation of aforementioned sections and surveys. Affiant further recommends the court order stay until such time the Mojave Nation or its dully appointed agents, produce evidence to the court's satisfaction that the facility, referred to in attachment D-6, plan of construction: White Buffalo Casino, waste disposal plant: Is (A) moved north from its current most southern position by 152 yards; (B) demolished and removed from the site; (C) a revised plan is submitted by the Mojave Nation for review and approval by the D.O.I., and U.S.A.C.E.

Affiant warrants that the failure to comply will result in unwarranted, and possibly life-threatening contaminants, to the public waters of that body of water known as the Colorado River. So ordered this day and date. Judge William Burlew, United States Court, Southwest District."

"Goddamn them!" Morse Roberts cursed, throwing up his hands. "How can they do this?"

"The way they always have done it," Chief Stoner offered. "With court orders."

"How did this happen?" George questioned.

"Built in sabotage," Fox suggested from where he sat across from Mara. If nothing else stopped us, this was their parachute. All they had to do was have an inspector in the Bureau of Indian Affairs find it."

"Bastards," David growled as he paced on his stiff knee.

"Can we move it?" Christine Scott questioned.

"It cost twenty-eight million dollars to build!" David complained, waving his arms. "We've only got eight million left. We need that to finish the casino, and even that's a maybe."

"I take it that's a no," Mara said.

"What about an appeal?" Horace Waters suggested.

"Time and money," David answered. "Neither of which we have."

Fox straightened in his chair, looked to Mara. He was able to look at her now without being intimidated. The bond between them was growing. "What about the Tribal Court? Couldn't they issue their own order setting this aside? They did it for the cash assets."

"Do you really think a Federal Court will bow to Indians?" Mara answered.

"Would we have any less than we do now?" Fox argued.

"How much time do we have?" David questioned with a look at Fox. "You worked with court orders How long before they come back?"

"Depends a lot on attitude," Fox answered. "The judge only knows what he's told. The agents can put their own spin on it."

David pressed for more. "You talked to these people. What do you think?"

Fox looked at the two seized cameras setting on the conference table in front of them. "We don't have much time."

"And I don't think we should fuck with the Feds," George Manygoats warned. He was visibly worried.

"It's nice to know we can count on you, George," Mara offered sarcastically.

"Either this is our land, or it isn't," David complained resuming his limping. "They can't give it to us and then tell us what to do with it."

"We can't move the disposal plant. We don't have enough money to build another. Pardon me," George said "but doesn't that mean we're already fucked."

A knock sounded on the trailer door. Fox pushed up and opened the door. It was Adams, he looked shaken. "I'm sorry, but it's important."

"What?" Fox questioned.

"There's fifteen police cars out front," Adams answered. "They're all in riot gear."

Fox led the entourage to the front gate of the chain link fence surrounding the casino. Inside, nine uniformed security officers, Jill among them, stood facing the gate. Barrel-chested Tribal police officer Merv Scott, along with a smaller man, added to the ranks, but it still wasn't much. On the other side of the fence a long ominous line of police cars sat facing the fence. Their emergency lights were flashing. An army of over twenty cops were pulling on riot helmets and loading shotguns. Behind the expanding echelon of Highway Patrol and La Paz County Sheriff's cars sat a beige FBI sedan.

On the inside of the fence work stopped as paint crews, electricians, plumbers and a mix of others came to stare in awe. Among them was the caterer, who trapped inside, joined the others. "What the hell's going on?"

Fox, Bear-Don't-Walk, Mara, and the tribal officials stared in silence as Special Agents Lang and Hodges walked toward the gate. They stopped some twenty feet away. Behind them the cops, shot guns pointing at the sky, stood shoulder to shoulder, waiting.

"This is a switch," Bear-Don't-Walk whispered

beneath his Stetson. "The white guys have surrounded the fort."

"Who's in charge in there?" Agent Lang called.

"Who's in charge out there?" Chief Stoner answered from beside Fox.

"Special Agent Lang, Federal Bureau of Investigation."

"What do you want?" Chief Stoner was deliberately stealing momentum from the man.

"You have been lawfully served with a Federal Court Order to cease and desist construction, and turn off all waters," Lang paused. When there was no response, he continued. "The court has been informed you are in contempt. A Federal Judge has directed me to use what force necessary to enforce the order."

"The court has no right here," David Rollins shouted in anger.

"You have no right to poison the water we drink," Lang defended.

"You sound like an Indian," Mara called.

Lang stiffened. "You can shout through the fence like school children, but I warn you, each of you, those who refuse to surrender will be arrested and you will go to jail."

Adams stepped to a padlock that hung unlocked on the gate, he snapped the lock shut.

"Live with your decision," Lang warned and turned away. Hodges followed him.

"Live with yours," Sparrow called from his wheelchair on the inside of the fence.

24 THE SIEGE

> *"Whenever the white man treats the Indians as they treat each other, then we will have no more wars. We shall all be alike—brothers of one father and one mother, with one sky above us and one country around us and one government for all."*
>
> **Josephy Hinmaton Yalatkit—Nez Perce Chief**

The casino security force, reinforced with two tribal police officers, stayed at the locked gate staring into the swelling army of cops on the other side as more and more police cars, fire trucks and ambulances arrived. "Maybe we'll have to rename The White Buffalo the Alamo," Adams whispered to Sparrow.

Fox took Mara by the arm and hustled her to the enterprise trailer "I've got an idea."

"You're going to surrender," Fox said siting Mara

down at the conference table. Chief Stoner, David, Bear-Don't-Walk and the others were filing in behind them.

"I'll surrender when everybody does," Mara argued, "and that's never." She looked to Chief Stoner for reinforcement.

"We knew trouble would come," the old man said as he eased himself into a chair. Without his stomach medicines and special diet, he would soon be in trouble and he knew it. "And we knew we could never turn back. If they stop us now The White Buffalo will never be."

"They'll turn the water off and starve us out," Christine Scott worried aloud.

"I've gotta get back to my farm," Morse Roberts complained, "I can't be locked up in here."

"Which means we've got to act quickly," Fox said, silencing the talk. He looked to Chief Stoner.

"Tell us," the old man nodded.

"Several months ago, I was in Laughlin to pick up a bank robbery suspect. My partner and I stayed at the Silver Queen. It's the last casino on the row. I remember standing on the balcony of our room and looking at the river. Along the river was a waste disposal plant."

"There's another one in Lake Havasu," George Many-goats offered, "so what?"

"So, I'm sure it was as close to the river as The White Buffalo," Fox added. "If they can do it in Laughlin, why can't we do it here?"

"Because they're not Indians," David Rollins quipped sarcastically.

"But the President said we could," Fox argued.

"White lies may be new to your ears," Morse Roberts suggested, "but not to ours."

"But if our waste disposal is no closer to the river than Laughlin's, or Lake Havasu's, the President will see this is just another fence, and he said, 'tear down the fences'."

"And who will tell the President?" David Rollins questioned.

"I will," Fox said with force.

"Seeing the President has its price," Chief Stoner warned.

"I know that."

"Tell us more," the old man questioned.

"Mara and Christine will surrender," Fox continued. "The FBI won't be eager to arrest women. They'll be questioned and released."

"And then?" Mara pressed. She was not happy with the idea.

"And then you drive to Havasu and to Laughlin. You measure the distance from the disposal plant to the waters' edge."

"And once we have these measurements?" Mara questioned.

"You call. Give me the measurement in feet, using numbers only. Don't elaborate. By then they'll be into our telephones."

"And how will you find the President?" David Rollins asked.

"We're in the midst of an election. I'll buy a newspaper." Fox was trying for bravado, but it was thin. The others knew the plan was more desperation than reason.

"And what do we do?" George Manygoats was craving a drink.

"We wait," Chief Stoner answered for Fox.

"But this could take days," George complained, thinking of the consequence of no alcohol.

"Sobering thought isn't it, George?" David Rollins suggested sarcastically.

"What's the alternative?" Fox said. "They've turned

The White Buffalo into a prison. If anyone has a better idea, let's hear it."

Looks were exchanged among the group, but no one spoke.

"They're giving up!" a voice among the ranks of the cops shouted when Bear-Don't-Walk and Merv Scott waved a white flag at the casino gate. The cops all crouched behind their cars. A knot of six FBI agents appeared from amidst the cars. Lang and Hodges were among them. They all wore light weight vests with bold white "FBI" imprints.

"Women coming out," Bear-Don't-Walk called as Merv unlocked the gate.

"At least we can get some intel from them," Hodges suggested quietly to Lang.

"There's a paradox," Lang chuckled. "Intel from an Indian."

"Hands in the air, above your heads," another agent barked as Mara and Christine stepped through the gate. "Walk slowly toward us, do not lower your hands."

Horace Waters and George Manygoats were in the spartan casino kitchen at a large stainless-steel sink filling water bottles, cans, jugs and anything else that could hold water when the jet of water surging form the faucet sputtered, slowed and then stopped. "Fuck," George complained.

Horace was lifting a bucket from the sink when the room plunged into total darkness. "Assholes, he muttered.

A promise of paid overtime kept the work force on the job and eliminated defections, but the lack of water and power stopped all work. Crews played cards in the lobby, volleyball beside the casino and sunbathed on roof. The Fox had argued that the presence of innocent disinterested parties inside the construction force would buy them time. "They'll wait us out," he told the others.

The caterer, with a captive market, was already out of burritos and Diet Coke but he was having his best day ever. Casino security patrolled the inside perimeter of the chain link fence as if their presence were really a deterrent to the heavily armed force outside. A crowd of curious, numbering in the hundreds, continued to swell across U.S. 95 from the casino. Rumor of the siege had swept through Parker and the valley like a wildfire. The locals, as well as the Indians had much to lose, and they came to stand, stare and worry at the sight of the armed cops on one side of the fence and friends and family on the other. Curses, cat calls and boos filled the warm afternoon air when the two women came out to surrender. A television news crew from Phoenix captured the moment on video when Mara and Christine were ordered to lay prone in the dirt and patted down. Handcuffed, they were hustled into a van and driven away.

Shortly after the van departed, Sparrow appeared on the roof of the casino in his wheelchair. The crowd roared. Two surveillance technicians were with him, shirts off, the three worked assembling a long-sectioned pole with guy wires. At the command post Special Agent Hodges watched them through powerful binoculars. "Looks like they're working on a radio mast or something," he speculated.

"They must know we're going to cut the telephones off," Lang suggested, shading his eyes to watch the three distant figures. They were wrong. Atop the casino Sparrow and two others pulled on guy wires and a thirty-foot aluminum pole hoisted an inverted United States Flag into the air. A breeze caught the big flag as the pole jerked straight and the red and white folds furled open and snapped in the wind to reveal the inverted rows of the white stars in a rectangular blue field.

The crowd across U.S. 95 roared with approval. War hoops and yelps filled the air.

"The dumb fucks got it upside down," Hodges said looking through his binoculars.

"That's a distress sign," Lang corrected. He was angry. He shot a look at a nearby agent. "Hopkins, get that goddamned news crew outta there." They were near the fence shooting video of Sparrow's flag raising. Now the two technicians were flanking Sparrow's wheelchair at the roof's edge, right arms thrust rigid in the air with their fists clenched. Boos and hisses reached across the road from the crowd as two agents escorted the camera crew away from the fence.

David Rollins took the loss of power and water personal. His physical pain and discomfort were the result of drug withdrawal, but he focused the resulting anger and frustration at the forces outside. While Chief Stoner slept on the carpeted floor beneath the conference table in the shadowed enterprise trailer, David sat a nearby desk and made telephone calls. "Hello, CNN...., my name is David Rollins. I am a Mojave Indian. I'm calling because a hundred-armed cops and FBI agents have me and fifty others under siege here in Parker, Arizona. They've turned off our water and our electricity and arrested two of our women. They made them lay in the dirt like dogs. Wolf Blitzer! Yes, I know who he is. On the air? Sure, you can put my call on the air."

Fox sat in the security trailer as the late afternoon shadows faded outside. The opaque window in the door was the only source of light and it was growing dimmer. Much like their hope, Fox decided. Hope was great, but as Virgil Tanner had once reminded him, hope was a four-letter word. Thinking of the waiting forces outside, how they perceived him, the Federal court order, and the slim chance of any of it being turned around, left Fox feeling impotent and powerless, it was a paradox. He once held the might and power of the United States Government in his hand. As an FBI agent, few obstacles dared to stand in his path. Now, as a social dropout, far from the heartbeat of mainstream America, standing among the ranks of a forgotten minority, he was just another voice in the wilderness. A voice lost in the clamor of contemporary life. A voice competing with corporate downsizing, soaring fuel costs, rampant crime, shattered family values and a national government that had seemingly lost its way. The reality was, Fox concluded, the calvary wasn't coming. Help wasn't on the way. If there was a way out, they would have to find it themselves.

A decade in the Bureau and government had taught Fox one thing. Money was power. He knew he and the Mojave's were fighting the golden rule, and the man with the gold was making the rules. Donald DePalma and his billions had might and power, but the real hammer was politics. DePalma's power was limited to what money could buy. Political power was the square root of the American will and the epitome of it rested with the President of the United States.

Fox had looked into the President's eyes. They reflected compassion for the three Mojave's who had climbed over the fence at the White House. After his "Fences" speech, the President's popularity had jumped six points in the pools. The American people were agreeing with him, there were too many fences. It was ironic, Fox thought, a chain link fence was dividing some fifty Mojave's and constructions workers from an armed force of cops and FBI agents, only this time he was on a different side of the fence. Not all fences had been torn down. He wondered if they ever would be. A knock on the trailer door stopped his thoughts. "It's open," Fox called to the silhouette on the other side of the glass.

"John," Jill called as the door opened. She peered into the darkness.

"Come in, said the spider to the fly."

Jill stepped in. "You should never say 'fly' to a girl in a dark room."

Fox switched on a flashlight. Jill offered a Styrofoam cup. "Last round of coffee from the roach coach. All Mad Max has left is sunflower seeds, beer nuts and warm tomato juice."

"Thanks."

"And, this." Jill smiled, pulling a folded a newspaper from the middle of her back where she had stuffed it under her gun belt. She offered it. Her smile was bright. He could see child-like delight in her eyes. The light from the flashlight added shadow to her face. Fox found himself looking at her instead of responding. "It's a USA Today. Well, maybe a USA 'yesterday'."

Fox took the paper. "What's next my slippers?"

"Interesting thought," Jill smiled.

"Where did you get this?"

"Sheriff's deputy by the name of Hall."

"Fraternizing with the enemy?"

"You wanted a paper. He had a paper. Candy from a baby," she smiled.

Fox unfolded the newspaper and illuminated it with the flashlight. Jill moved around the desk to stand at his shoulder. She reached and took the flashlight from his hand. "You read. I'll light. Although, I can't be Bud light."

"Jill light is fine," Fox grated as her fingers slid over his taking the flashlight from his hand. Jill's touch reached deep inside of Fox as the memory of her stirred his passion. He suspected she was innocent of how sensual her touch was. He was wrong. Fox forced his attention to the headlines. "President courts California," he read aloud. "Slipping in the polls the President is trying to shore up California support with both promises and play. After promising Rockwell workers a new order of B-12 bombers worth fifteen billion dollars, the President was off for a day of golf in Palm Springs before traveling to Phoenix Sunday," Fox paused and looked at Jill. "Today's Friday."

"Very good. Would you like to take a wild guess at what tomorrow is?"

"Jesus," Fox bolted to his feet, "he'll be in Palm Springs tomorrow."

"He, who?" Jill questioned. She didn't know about the plan. "Are we talking about the President?"

"I've got to see him."

"Pardon me, but how do you plan to do that? There's a couple hundred cops out front who aren't going to let you go anywhere."

"You're gonna drive me," Fox told her.

"It was tough getting a newspaper through that fence," Jill warned.

Fox was excited. Shit, this could work. "After you're out, get a car."

"I've got a car."

"We need something fast."

"Any particular color?"

"I'm serious," Fox chided. "I need a suit and tie, some casual clothes."

"Jockey's or boxers?"

"Jill, damnit!"

"Sorry."

"After you've got everything, stay by the phone. I'll call."

"That's what they all say."

Fox called Bear-don't walk and Merv to the security trailer. "There was a tile crew working in the casino restrooms," Fox explained. "Find them. I want a can of adhesive, some caulk, a tool belt, a cap, dirtier the better."

"John, I know it's boring with the lights off and all," Jill teased, "but do you think redoing the bathroom is the answer?"

Fox ignored her humor as he illuminated her breasts with the flashlight. "What size T-shirt do you wear?"

"We're not going to remodel those either," Jill warned.

Bear-Don't-Walk and Merv smiled.

"Jill, Goddamnit," Fox snapped.

"You want me in costume? Let's go with small, and an eight and a half work shoe."

Bear-don't walk returned with the collected booty. "I know what you want," Jill said taking the collection and the flashlight to head for the bathroom. She returned a few minutes later with the visor cap on backwards, her hair pushed up under it, smudges of dirt and adhesive on her face, bra gone and breasts pushing against the taunt material of the too small T-shirt, tool belt sagging over a hip adorned with the shorts now even shorter with a rolled cuff. Jill cocked an elbow on a hip and struck a pose. "What'd'ya think?"

"Does she have to go?" Merv asked.

"Woman coming out," Bear-Don't-Walk called into the glare of intense portable flood lights that washed away the shadows inside the fence. They were white hot orbs that masked the world beyond them.

Lang, Hodges and now, the Special Agent-in-Charge of the Phoenix office, Dan Clark, stood behind the lights watching as Merv Scott unlocked the gate. "Those Mojave's are big, aren't they?" Clark commented as he studied Merv. He had decided to take over as the on-site tactical commander after an Indian called CNN's Don

Lemon Live. Now a hoard of press was descending in Parker and The White Buffalo. Local motels were sold out. The small airport was lined with a squadron of chartered turbo props, jets, and news helicopters.

"Don't confuse big with bright," Agent Hodges chuckled as Merv swung the gate open.

Sixty feet away Jill, in her tile workers costume stepped into the light. A wolf whistle followed by a cat call came from amidst the line of police cars. A half dozen news camera crews inched closer.

"Where in the hell did she come from?" Lang questioned as he stared at Jill's coke bottle form.

"She's got everything but a staple in her navel," Hodges added.

"Raise your hands above your head and walk forward," an unseen voice hidden among the glare ordered.

Jill slowly raised her arms. Pushing them skyward caused the taunt T-shirt to stretch even tighter. Jill's nipples were to make the front pages of the Arizona Republic, The Los Angeles Times and USA Today.

"Walk toward the light," the voice ordered after an awkward pause.

"Please," another voice quipped.

Laughter rippled through ranks behind the police cars. Jill had heard it before. This wasn't so different than the club.

Fox and Bear-Don't-Walk walked a circuit of the fence. Teams of security officers had been doing it since the gate was padlocked so they drew little attention. Away from the glare at the front of the casino, night vision was easier. The fence bordered the casinos rear parking lot, designed for deliveries and parking for passing truckers, stretched into the darkness toward the distant river. "They've got five or six officers out here,

"Bear-Don't-Walk said. "Think they're rotating them every two hours."

"I don't suppose they expect anybody to break-out." Fox speculated.

"Probably not."

Two flashlights winked on. Fox and Bear-Don't-Walk raised hands to shield their eyes and squinted into the glare from the other side of the fence. A dog began growling and barking.

"You didn't tell me they had dogs!" Fox whispered.

"I didn't wanna worry you."

"My dog eats nothing but red meat," a gruff voice warned from behind the lights.

Bear-Don't-Walk stared into the glare on the other side of the fence. "I'm really sorry, officer. I heard some of your men were having problems like that with their wives."

"Fuck you, Indian asshole!" The gruff voice answered. "Get 'im Wolf." The dog hit the fence hard, snarling and slobbering.

"Yeah, that's her," Bear-Don't-Walk mocked.

Fox took Bear-Don't-Walk by the arm and pulled him away into the darkness.

"Fuckin', ball-less Indian," a voice called after them.

George Manygoats found religion. On the verge of tears from his alcoholic drought, he prayed God would provide him relief as he rifled through drawers in the Executive trailer. He didn't really expect to find anything and doing it reminded him of his father as he searched for bottles, he had hidden but forgotten. He found two sticks of spearmint gum in a top drawer and pushed them into his mouth. He pulled open a bottom drawer and saw the bottle. His heart stopped. It was a quart of twelve-year-old Red Label scotch. George picked up the bottle. It was cool to the touch. The seal was unbroken.

"Thank you, God," he mouthed, studying the liquid in the bottle. It was as if it were some life-giving nectar and to George's alcohol deprived system it was. He twisted the sealed cap like a chicken neck, spun it off and took one, two, three heavy swallows of the liquor. "Thank you, Jesus," he said as the warmth spread in his stomach.

The trapped workers, reveling in no work and double time, built a bonfire of scrap wood in the casino's yet unpaved front parking lot. Several tribal members found discarded empty five-gallon paint cans. Inverted they became drums and the night was filled with the ominous rhythmic thump of tom-toms. Shirts were pulled off, bodies were painted with stripes of Navajo latex flat wall paint, duct tape and mud. Soon the fire was ringed with chanting dancers. The chief, along with Morse Roberts and Horace Waters came and sat cross-legged near the flames. They canted and bobbed and clapped with the beat of the drums.

The news crews lined the fence with camera and soundmen. The cops and FBI watched in silence from the shadows. It wasn't long before the light of a bonfire punctured the night across U.S. 95 where the spectators gathered. They now numbered in the hundreds. Agent Hodges wanted to take a platoon of cops and clear them out arguing, "Indians in front, Indians behind. I don't like this Little Big Horn shit." But Clark, the site commander, denied the request. "They'll get tired and go home."

But the crowd hadn't left. Now one bonfire became three, then four. Drums joined the circle then dancers, then chanting. Passing traffic slowed, stopped and joined the throng.

"Fuckin' Indians," Agent Hodges muttered as he watched the flames and shadowy figures, "Take over the country if we let 'im."

Fox and Bear-Don't-Walk waited in the security

trailer, near the telephone. It had rung three times. A producer from Dateline and Lisa Manygoats. All for David Rollins. The calls irritated Fox. Not because David got them, but because they weren't for him. He could only hope Mara, Christine and Jill had been released. If they hadn't his plan had turned to shit. Fox paced nervously while Bear-Don't-Walk sat with his Stetson low, feet propped up and arms folded. "How the hell can you sleep?"

"I can't when you keep asking me how," the silhouette in the Stetson answered.

The telephone rang. Fox forced himself to reach for it. "Hello."

"Hi, Honey, I'm home," Jill purred in his ear.

"I'm glad," Fox restrained his excitement, as he had coached Jill to do. "Are the kids in bed?"

It was a prearranged question and if answered "Yes" it meant all had gone well and Jill would now await his call.

"Yes, but I think Beth has a cold. I hope Jimmy doesn't get it."

"Uh huh," Fox didn't know what else to say. Jill was skilled at making him feel awkward.

"You want me to wait up for you?"

"I may have to spend the night here."

"But it's been so long since we've slept together."

"I have to go."

"But, honey", Jill pleaded in a low, sultry voice.

"Yes," Fox wanted to be annoyed, but he enjoyed her too much. Was she doing this to tease him, or whoever was listening?

"Ask me what I'm going to wear to bed? Maybe it'll make you want to come home."

"I have to go."

"I'm still all wet from my bath. Could you talk to me while I dry?"

"Pam," Fox said, "I have to ..." His voice failed him as he realized his mistake. He had called Jill by his dead wife's name. His pulse raced. The line was silent. Jill had heard the mistake too. "I'll call you later," he said and hung up.

Bear-Don't-Walk, hidden beneath his Stetson, pretended he was asleep.

Fox sank into a chair to await Mara's call. He hoped it would come. An hour passed. Neither man moved. The distant sound of the drums and the chants were the only sound. Fox found his name slip was more shock than pain. It had been a long time since he had spoken Pam's name. When he did, he expected the pain, but it was mild and slow in coming. It seemed it was all right to think of her. His memories of her were of life not death. Pam was gone, but not far. She was in his heart. He knew he was in hers. He was asleep when the telephone rang. It jolted him awake. He grabbed for it. "Hello."

"Brother," Mara's voice questioned.

"Yes," Fox smiled in the darkness. The name was acceptance, forgiveness and more. It fueled him with deep relief.

"I have the number you need."

"Just a minute," Fox signaled Bear-Don't-Walk. He was quickly to Fox's side with the flashlight. "Okay."

"The one you mentioned is four, seven, nine two."

Fox knew it was the waste disposal plant in Laughlin. He scrawled the numbers on a tablet. "Got it."

"The second is seven, six, oh, four." It was the Lake Havasu facility. Fox added the numbers to the pad. "Okay."

"I hope it's what you need," Mara added.

"I hope it's what *we* need," Fox corrected.

"I do too," Mara agreed.

"Thank you."

The line clicked and a dial tone sang in his ear.

In the FBI mobile command post trailer three blocks away the agent monitoring the call pulled off his headset and looked to Special Agent Clark. "You want me to play back the tape?"

Clark shook his head. "Just numbers, right?"

The agent gestured to a note pad in front of him. "There they are."

"With Fox in there, they know we're listening. It's a code. Run it through the computer. You come up with anything, page me."

"Yes, Sir."

Fox and Bear-Don't-Walk hurried to the executive trailer where the master plans were kept. They found George Manygoats unconscious on the floor. The empty bottle of scotch at his side. The two men stepped over him and began leafing through the large blueprints hanging from a rack on the wall. "Got it," Bear-Don't-Walk announced.

They pulled the blueprint off the rack and spread it out atop a desk sending a lamp, a coffee mug, a pencil can and a calculator crashing to the floor. Bear-Don't-Walk held the light while Fox's finger and eyes searched for measurements. Finally, he found a straight line running from the eastern bank of the Colorado River to the western wall of The White Buffalo's waste disposal plant. Fox read the distance aloud. "Five thousand, nine hundred and forty-two feet."

"That more than a mile," Bear-Don't-Walk added eagerly, "What was Laughlin?"

Fox dug in a pocket for the paper he had made notes on. He found nothing. "Where the hell is it?" He searched a second pocket and found it. Unfolding, he read. "Four thousand, seven hundred and ninety-two. We beat the bastards by eleven hundred feet!"

A knock sounded on the trailer door. Fox and Bear-Don't-Walk stiffened with apprehension. "Yeah?" Bear-Don't-Walk called.

"Hey, Sarge," Merv Scott's voice called from outside. "FBI wants to talk to Fox."

Fox didn't like going to the front gate. He knew in the shadowless light he would be under video surveillance, but not going had its risks too. They were listening to telephone calls. Had they recognized his voice, Mara's? Were they checking to see if he was still there? Had they broken the code? They would. Fox drew in a breath and walked into the light. They were bright glaring balls of light and he resented being in front of them. He forced himself to remain calm. He walked to the gate and waited. Thirty seconds passed. Was this some psychological bullshit? He willed himself to wait another thirty seconds. It was strange knowing both sides. It made him feel smug, but uncomfortable. The lights were a definite pain in the ass. Okay, ten more seconds and they could shine them up their ass.

"John," he heard the familiar voice, but the man was hidden behind the glare. Then Terrence Bell emerged and walked to the gate.

"We're gonna have to quit meeting like this," Fox smiled at his former partner.

Bell smiled and looked at Fox's gloved left hand. "Don't tell me you got a monkey too?"

"Just the glove," Fox answered, flexing his fingers. He did not raise his hand and he wasn't going to talk about it. "You out here on business?"

Bell smiled, "Just happened to see the lights on, thought I'd stop in."

"Anybody else out from the Springs?"

When Bell ignored the question, Fox knew Terrence was wired for sound. "John, they want me to ask you to come out. We don't want to be in a situation where we have to arrest one of our own."

"Do you know what this is all about, Terrence?"

"Indian gaming," Bell answered.

"No, it's about fairness. And what's happening isn't fair. It's not me on the wrong side of the fence, you are."

"Listen, John," Bell pleaded, "don't throw it all away, man. You've worked too hard."

"You think you're here to defend the law," Fox argued. "If I told you what brought you here, you wouldn't believe me. Has nothing to do with justice."

"Jesus, John, you're beginning to sound like an Indian."

"I am an Indian." Fox turned and walked away. Bell stared after him for a moment and then turned into the lights.

25 CIRCLES

"Everything an Indian does is in a circle, and that's because the power of the world works in circles. everything tries to be round.... The sky is round, and I have heard the earth is round and so are all the stars. The wind in its great power, whirls. Birds make nests in circles, for their religion is the same as ours... Even the seasons form a circle, and always come back to where they were...

The life of a man is a circle, as is everything."

Black Elk—Holy man, Oglala Sioux

It was nearly midnight and the bonfires were now little more than glowing piles of embers. The dancing was over. The drums were quiet. The night was full of the throaty hum from the portable diesel generators powering the spotlights illuminating the fence and the facade of The White Buffalo. Darkness and fatigue brought the momentary respite reason could not. Inside the fence the Indians slept while outside the less fortunate cops and FBI agents drank coffee, exchanged war stories and speculated on how long they would be stuck in Parker. An agent from San Francisco suggested Parker be renamed "Lodi."

The shots were sharp with concussion and sound. Bang! Bang! Bang! Hearts stopped as coffee cups were thrown and men on both sides of the fence, clawed at the earth for cover. Jesus! It had happened. Some frightened cop or drunken Indian had fired the shot that would be heard 'round the world. Tension had reached the flash point. Now, all the men, both red and white, who tried to crawl under cars and stacks of lumber and insulation, hoping the deadly bullets wouldn't find them, were brothers because none were ready to die. A long ominous silence followed the volley of shots and a few heads were beginning to show themselves when a fourth shot cut the stillness. BANG!

"Where the fuck is it?" An Arizona Highway Patrolman, with an infrared sniper scope rifle in hand complained as he searched.

"I got 'im...., I got 'im," an excited voice shouted along the perimeter of the fence. Spotlights were being swung. Flashlights were winking on everywhere. The beams danced as the men holding them ran. Guns were cocked "Hold your fire...., hold your fire!" a Sheriff's sergeant cautioned as a wall of armed men raced toward the voice. "Here, here!" the voice called.

A powerful spotlight sweeping along the base of the fence found the voice. Inside the chain link fence, near the far corner at the front stood twenty-two-year-old, casino Security Officer, Jefferson Two-feathers. The young warrior was smiling as he stood, hands high, nine-millimeter browning in one hand, a five-foot rattlesnake in the other. "I got 'im," Two-feathers announced into the glare of the spotlight. "He's dead."

"You dumb fuck, you could have got us all killed!"

"Take his gun. Give 'im a goddamned bow and arrow."

"Shit, now we'll be here two weeks. They've got fresh meat!"

"Fuck you all," Two-feathers slung the big snake at the fence. Most of the cops scattered like rabbits. Others laughed. The police dog clawed at the fence trying to reach the fallen reptile inside.

The insults, curses and accusations through the fence grew as more men arrived on both sides. More than an escalation to violence it was a release of tension. An unspoken celebration of the fact that although blood had been spilled, it was the blood of a snake. The anger gave way to humor, then conversation, as men on one side found familiar faces and friends on the other.

The distraction would be short lived. Sergeants and senior agents were busy redefining lines and duties. Friendship had its place, but duty and loyalty were the real substance of life. The dead rattlesnake would become a story to tell on both sides as well as a new belt for Jefferson Two-feathers.

Warrior versus rattlesnake seemed little more than an irresponsible act by a young Indian but it was more. It was, in fact, a carefully orchestrated diversion. Crouching in the shadows along the dark back wall of the casino were Fox Bear-Don't-Walk and Merv. After the sound of the fourth shot they made a run for the distant chain link fence. Reaching it Bear-Don't-Walk and Merv joined hands. Fox stepped onto their inter-laced fingers and they propelled him up and over the eight-foot fence. Fox landed with a thump in the gravel and rocks on the other side. He scrambled up and disappeared into the darkness. "Touch the wind," Bear-Don't-Walk called after him.

It was dark and moon-less and Fox could see little more than tall brush and the distant horizon as he ran, following the rock-strewn desert floor toward the river. He looked back only once, knowing the glare would rob him of what little night vision he had. He was sweating profusely when the earth leveled and grew soft under his feet. He could feel the cool embrace of air from the surface of the water, "Hello, river," he whispered as if speaking to a friend, and he was. He felt moisture seeping into his shoes. He was wading in mud, reeds and water. Suddenly he sank to his waist. The water felt good. If the dog were following, or if he tracked him later, it would end here. The water was getting deeper, the current swift and cold. Fox pushed into it, swimming further out, drifting down stream with the rapid current.

The chief's story of the bass came to mind as Fox drifted with the current. When the lights at the casino were far behind, Fox swam toward the bank.

Jill, dressed in faded jeans and a short-sleeved blouse, sat in her apartment trying to lose herself in the home shopping network. Tom, a sincere man in his forties was telling of the virtues of a twenty-nine-ninety-five food processor. Jill wondered what it was like to have a home, a kitchen, a life. She had the promise. It had gone unfulfilled. Instead of the kitchen, she got the shaft. She knew she was an attractive woman. She also knew she was over thirty, divorced and a single parent. Beauty was not always an asset. As much as men claimed they sought it, those who found it, often found themselves intimated by it. Jill's beauty wasn't the "let's go home and meet mom" type. It was more "let's get naked." She decided men sought beautiful women for much the same reason they hunted. It was great to bag one, great to show the trophy, great to talk about the hunt, but it wasn't something you could do all the time. Beautiful women, it seemed, didn't have food processors or kitchens or lives. The telephone rang and Jill jumped. She turned off the sound on the TV and picked up the receiver. "Hello."

"Wanna have breakfast in Palm Springs?" It was Fox.

"Do you own a food processor?"

"A what?"

"Would you buy me one?" Tears rimmed Jill's eyes.

"Jill, I just climbed out of the river I'm at the SavMor station near the river bridge."

"I'll be right there."

Fox stepped into the shadows to wait. A few minutes later a set of head lamps approached, slowed and swung into the service station lot near the pay telephone. It was a silver Lincoln.

Fox scrambled in on the passenger's side. He welcomed the warmth of the big car. "Where to?" Jill questioned.

"Palm Springs."

Jill pulled the car in gear and they sped away.

Jill brought a towel. Fox toweled his hair dry and then climbed into the back seat. He dug in a bag Jill had packed, selecting slacks and a pull-over shirt. "You did good."

"Anytime I can contribute to you changing clothes in the back seat, give me a call," she smiled.

Dry, Fox climbed over the seat to settle on the passenger's side. He was comfortable with Jill's driving. She was holding a steady seventy miles an hour. "You look good in a Lincoln."

"Thank you. Are we really going to see the President?"

"I'm gonna try."

"So, like he doesn't know you're coming?"

"Right."

"But he does know you?"

"We've met."

"How are you going to find him?"

"Presidents are pretty hard to hide. We'll find him."

"This isn't something that's going to get you shot, is it?" Jill asked apprehensively.

"Hope not."

They drove on for ninety miles before reaching the interstate. It was a dark smooth ride and the only evidence of the world outside the speeding car was the undulating ribbon of asphalt that raced into their headlamps. Fox was quiet. Jill accepted his trying to show a glib attitude about seeing the President, but she knew how dangerous it was. She had been a cop long enough to know that coming between the Secret Service and the President could be deadly. She was worried about the quiet man at her side. She hoped she wasn't driving him into harm's way. She even dared to hope she had a future with him, but she had learned love couldn't be captured or held. It had to be shared. "So, how are you and Pocahontas getting along?" Jill asked breaking the long silence.

"Mara?" Fox questioned. "Do I detect a tinge of jealousy?"

"Jealous! Why would I be jealous? She's just some gorgeous Indian princess with really big..."

"Jill!" Fox cautioned.

"Brown eyes," Jill quipped.

"Mara's my sister."

"Right, like all Indians are brothers and sisters."

"No, my real blood sister."

"You're serious?" Jill looked at his shadowy profile.

"Yes."

"That's nice," Jill was pleased, very pleased.

At Desert Center, where the highway intersected the interstate Jill pulled onto the shoulder. "Your turn," she said climbing out to stretch and surrender the wheel to Fox. He slid out the passenger's side and walked around the car. The desert night air was warm and rich with the smell of pollen. Jill had her eyes closed, massaging the back of her neck when Fox drew her into his arms and kissed her. She stiffened with surprise, but then yielded to it. He molded himself against her and held her tight. Jill's arms encircled his neck. Breath rushed through nostrils, tongues explored, hands touched and when it ended, they clung to each other breathlessly. "I wanted you to know how I feel," he whispered into her hair. "Earlier I called you by my wife's name. It wasn't because of how I feel about her. It was because of how I feel about you. I know that's a lot to hear, but time isn't always a friend."

Jill kissed Fox gently on the neck. "Thank you." It was a whisper.

"I don't know where all this is going. I don't know how you feel. I only know it was important I tell you."

"John," Jill whispered on his shoulder.

"Yeah?"

"I don't really want a food processor.

They kissed again.

Palm Springs lay sixty miles ahead of them. Interstate Ten was divided, flat and straight. Fox drove at nearly eighty miles an hour. Auto traffic was sparse, but the desert night bristled with the lights of eighteen wheelers. An endless train of trucks flowing both east and west lit the blanket of darkness like a long undulating centipede. Jill was at Fox's side as he drove. She held his arm as if to prevent it all from slipping away. She didn't trust happiness. Excited, eager to know more of one another, they talked. Jill was worried about her mother. The woman had learned Jill worked as a topless dancer in Dallas. Threats and condemnation followed. On the heels of it all her ex-husband sued for custody. Jill suspected her mother engineered it to get the child for herself. Fox listened. That was all Jill wanted. He could hear agony in her voice. The irony, he decided, was they both had lost someone they loved. Fox wondered if it was easier to lose someone to circumstances other than death. He suspected it wasn't.

When Jill grew quiet Fox talked about his awakening with the tribe. He told her of his trip to Washington, meeting Chief Stoner, the President, the excitement of it all. How after the death of his wife, he ran, not knowing where he was going, or why, but only that he had to go. He smiled in the darkness as he spoke of seeing the river for the first time, working in the fields, drinking with Virgil and Sparrow. The tribe was like a big tree, Fox explained. Bear-Don't-Walk had told him the story. A tree with many branches. A tall tree, whose limbs offered safety from the coyotes on the ground and whose leaves provide shade and shelter from the sun and rain. A tree where birds gathered. Birds from everywhere. Some in pairs. Some alone. Some built nests. Others rested. The tree didn't ask why they came. Sometimes the birds flew away, sometimes they stayed, but none of the birds ever forgot the tree. The birds didn't need the tree all the time. But when they needed rest or shelter, a place to land, the tree was always waiting. "It's a great story, isn't it?" Fox questioned.

Jill, her head on Fox's shoulder, didn't answer. She was asleep on her branch.

Fox could see the distant hint of night light along the horizon far ahead. It was the faint glare of Palm Springs and the nearly half million people that called it home. His old tribe, Fox decided. Although he was returning to a community where he had lived, loved, and worked, it did not feel like a homecoming. He didn't feel foreign, but he did feel different. He was a different person. Life had changed. He had changed. The river flowed on. It had cut through the rock. He tried to remember the wounded, empty man fleeing down the other side of the interstate. A bird looking for a tree. He had left alone and in pain. He was returning with hope.

The plan was simple. Fox knew from intelligence briefings in the Bureau, as well as from the media that the President was a morning jogger. More than a sincere effort to ease the impact of fried chicken and French fries, jogging was an easy way to put pictures in prime-time. In the midst of a hard fought, down and dirty Presidential election, the White House, especially on the road, wasn't about to miss an opportunity. The President would jog, between five AM and six, and when he did, Fox would find him. In less than two minutes the President would know the Mojave's, even after spilling their blood on the South lawn, were under attack. It wasn't General Custer's horse soldiers. There were no sabers or long rifles, but the consequence was just as grim. Indians would die. Maybe not from lead rifle balls, but from diabetes, drugs, alcoholism and hopelessness. The President would care.

Fox knew he was facing more than the challenge of finding the President in Palm Springs. He knew he would be facing his past. A past full of icons, memories and pain. A past now drawn in a circle. A past rushing back at him as fast as the occasional moth appearing in his headlamps.

Jill slept with her head on Fox's shoulder as the Lincoln left the mantle of the desert night and emerged into the stark cones of sodium light reaching down from the freeway street lamps. Fox slowed and exited the four-lane highway. The streets were quiet. Tall palms stood like silent sentinels. The streets were familiar but less than comforting. This was a city Fox knew well. Here he was not stranger. He found little peace in it. He felt disconnected. This was no longer home. This was the past. Fox drove past the commercial clutter of Date Palm Drive across the heart of Cathedral City toward downtown Palm Springs. An endless succession of neon light and fast food restaurants swept by. Twenty-four-hour service stations and mini marts illuminated bill-boards and supermarkets beckoned with promises of low prices and the best deal in town. The desert had disappeared. It was covered with asphalt, concrete curbs and sprawling parking lots decorated with hissing sprinklers and flowers in full bloom. Man had conquered more than the Indians. He had conquered the land. Fox felt very far from Parker.

Jill stirred when Fox turned on to the street. The night lighting was softer. Lamp posts illuminated the mailboxes and driveways. Jill said nothing as he pulled to the curb and stopped. Fox switched off the headlamps and engine. They sat quiet in the darkness for a moment before he spoke. "It's the third house on the right."

"It looks nice." Jill said in a near whisper.

"It was," Fox agreed. "Wait here." Fox opened the car door and stepped into the night. Dawn was turning the night shadows pale. The drive had taken nearly five hours.

It felt dreamlike to Fox. The images of his house, his home, cloaked in soft shadows of a new day. The hiss of a neighbor's sprinklers. The scent of the damp evergreen lining the driveway. The thought of walking to the front door, unlocking it and stepping inside to find Pam asleep in bed, waiting, warm and smooth, teased at him. But he knew Pam wasn't there. Fox dug in a pocket for a key.

He unlocked the side door of the garage and flipped on a light. Pam's BMW sat waiting, covered with a mantle of fine dust. Fox touched the car gently as if somehow it was a link to her. The chrome and metal surfaces were cool and reassuring. He patted it and turned to a cabinet over the dryer. There he found a pair of sneakers and a jogging suit.

Jill watched from the car as the light framing the garage door winked out. A moment later Fox appeared out of the shadows. She breathed a sigh of relief as he climbed into the car. "Going jogging?" She questioned, as he handed her the clothes and the shoes.

"Hope so," Fox answered, starting the car.

They stopped at a busy convenience store on South Palm. Jill bought a newspaper, coffee for two and pastries. Fox sipped his coffee as Jill unfolded the newspaper. A picture of the Presidential helicopter landing on a golf course filled the front page. Jill read the copy beneath the picture. "Marine one, shoots for a hole in one as the President arrives at The Westin Mission Hills. Seeking a respite after a five-day campaign swing through the mid-west, the President arrived Monday for two days of what he vowed to be rest and relaxation before the nationally televised debate Wednesday. Tom Cortabitarte, the General Manager of the Westin was on hand to welcome the President."

"Remember that name," Fox said, sampling his pastry.

"The manager's, why?"

"Trust me." Fox started the car.

Palm Springs notorious blue skies and heat were well into the new day when Fox drove up into the palm covered valet entrance to the sprawling Westin resort. There were two Secret Service agents in the polished marble lobby. One, dressed in a golf shirt and shorts, sat in a comfortable deep cushioned chair pretending interest in the Wall Street Journal, while the second, a small brunette, wearing a housekeeping uniform, busied herself trimming a bushy tropical plant. Neither paid particular attention when Fox and Jill entered arm in arm and walked to the long reception desk.

A pleasant looking thirty-year-old in a dark blazer moved to greet them. "Good morning."

Fox pulled his wallet and pushed a credit card onto the countertop. "Reservation for Jack Fox." Jill gave him a puzzled look at the mention of the name, but Fox squeezed her hand and she squelched the reaction.

The desk man punched at the keys on a computer. He watched the screen.

"I asked Tom to book me a golf view king." Fox added.

"Tom?" The desk man questioned with a look.

"Cortabitarte," Fox added. "He is the General Manager, isn't he?"

"Yes, but I don't see anything in the computer."

"Tom and I once went skinny dipping at the Ritz," Fox smiled at Jill. "Just to give them fits. You're gonna like him. He said we'd get together for drinks." He was speaking to Jill, but it was meant for the clerk.

"I'm sorry, Mr. Fox, I don't seem to find anything reserved," the desk man said. "And, unfortunately, we are fully booked."

Fox looked annoyed. "You're kidding me! Check your VIP list. Tom said he'd take care of it!" His tone was ripe with indignation.

"Just a moment please," the tailored suit moved away to confer with a second man further down the counter.

"Stay here," Fox whispered to Jill. He moved down the counter to where the two men stood talking. Pulling a business card from his wallet he gestured with it. "Tell you what, I'll give Tom a call, tell him his oversight just got the Ritz another walkin. What's your name, Sir?

The night manager offered a practiced, disarming G.Q. smile. "That won't be necessary Mr. Fox, I'm sure it's just an oversight. It's been a bit hectic. We apologize for the confusion. Put them in the golf view suite overlooking the eighteenth hole."

"One President can ruin your whole day, right?" Fox questioned.

"We've been asked not to comment," the manager smiled. "You understand?"

"Of course," Fox nodded.

Returning to Jill's side Fox leaned to an ear as the desk clerk worked at the computer. "Make the name on the registration Jack Fox. Use your address in Phoenix." He whispered and walked away.

"If you'll fill this out, Mrs. Fox," the clerk said offering a registration form.

Fox walked to an arrangement of couches and chairs and picked up a copy of the Los Angeles Times. He pretended interest in the newspaper while glancing at the man in the golf shirt and shorts. There was an earphone in his left ear. His eyes went to the woman in the housekeeping uniform, working on plants. She was a petite Caucasian. Not logical in Hispanic filled Palm springs he decided. "Let's get to bed, Jack." Jill said slipping an arm around his. The bellman with her carried their two bags.

As the bellman led Fox and Jill from the lobby the Secret Service agent laid his paper aside, pushed up and walked to the desk. "May I have their names and addresses, please?"

"Yes, Sir."

It was routine with a President asleep in the hotel. Although the President was sandwiched between two rooms full of heavily armed Secret Service agents, new arrivals were still screened. The Secret Service had set up their communications center in room four seventeen. It was a short walk from the main lobby. A video tape of Fox's arrival at the Westin in the rented Lincoln was being played back when the agent from the lobby arrived. "Whatd'ya got?" He questioned the two agents watching the image of Jill climbing out of the car at valet.

"Avis rental from Phoenix," a short haired shapely brunette wearing a shoulder holster answered.

"Fits the registrations," the golf shirt from the lobby offered glancing at the card. "Mr. and Mrs. J. Fox from twenty-one-seventeen Mesquite Canyon, Phoenix, Arizona."

"Run them through the threat and contact file," the brunette said to her older male partner. "Reach back at least twelve months. Use the scramble line."

"Why do I have to do it?" The older agent complained. "I ran the last name."

"Watch my lips and try to concentrate," the brunette said sarcastically. "I graduated from Princeton. I am the senior agent. You are two years from retirement and forty pounds overweight.

"I love it when you talk mean. It makes your nipples hard."

"Fuck you."

26 EXECUTIVE PRIVILEGE

---

*"I have seen that in any great undertaking it is not
enough for a man to depend simply upon himself."*
Lone Man—Teton Sioux

They sat in the darkness of the hotel room in chairs
pulled close to a window overlooking the golf course.
Fox was now dressed in a dark nylon jogging suit and
running shoes. His attention was focused on the golf cart
roadway that ran along the edge of the sprawling green.
Jill's hand was on his knee. She was frightened and
fighting an urge to talk. She needed reassurance, but she
settled for biting a lip.

Fox tensed. A golf cart appeared on the roadway
bordering the green. There were two men in it. Both
wore jogging suits. Secret Service he concluded. The cart
swept by without slowing. "Soon," he whispered. Jill

grasped his knee tighter as if somehow that would stop it all.

Thirty seconds behind the golf cart came two more men in jogging suits. Both had short leashes on alert German Shepherds at their sides. Fox pushed out of his chair.

"John," Jill mouthed in the shadows.

"Quiet," he ordered staring through the glass.

Jill's heart raced. Her eyes were wide with anxiety.

"Here they come," Fox moved for the door. "No matter what... stay in here."

A veteran ABC newsman, and one-time White House reporter, had been traveling with the President for two days, gathering behind the scenes stories for an up-coming television special entitled, "Race for the White House." He was at the President's side as the two men jogged. The President was wearing shorts, a T-shirt and a ball cap given to him by an Air Force fighter squadron. The two jogged at a comfortable warm-up pace. Ten yards ahead and ten yards behind were teams of discreetly armed Secret Service agents.

"Mr. President, John Fox, FBI." Fox said emerging from behind the trunk of a thick palm tree near the edge of the golf cart track.

The President and Donaldson hesitated as Fox approached. His hands were in plain view, fingers deliberately extended.

"Code Alpha!" A tense voice barked over the Secret Service network. Fox had been spotted.

"Mr. President, we met in Washington." The President's eyes found Fox's. Footfalls pounded toward them. "When the Mojave's climbed over the fence," Fox added.

Fox saw the two men and tensed. The President did not. There was nothing he could do. A Secret Service agent knocked the President to the ground covering him. The other agent grabbed Fox in a bar-arm neck choke and slammed him to the asphalt surface of the golf cart drive. A windowless gray van appeared out of nowhere braking to a sliding halt. U.S. Navy was stenciled on its dull surface. A side door slammed open and four men in black jump suits with strapped machine guns jumped out. They gathered and drug the President into the van sandwiching their move with their bodies. The van roared and sped away before the door closed.

Fox's face pressed into the asphalt. He couldn't breathe. "I'm not armed," he grimaced as a knee slammed into his kidney.

"Shut up!" A voice ordered.

"Pat him down," another added.

Four agents rolled Fox onto his stomach. His wrists were pulled behind his back and shackled. A foot pressed on the back of his neck. Pain danced light in his closed eyes. Hands dug in his pockets, pulled at his clothes. "He's got nothing," a voice said. His feet were pulled together as a nylon restraint cinched them cutting into the flesh on his ankles.

More golf carts arrived. "Eagle is secure," a radio announced. "No injuries."

Fox knew who they were talking about.

"Get the package out of here," a voice barked.

A towel was wrapped around Fox's head. He was lifted, shoved into a golf cart and rushed away.

An agent held the back of his neck as the golf cart moved. "Don't move," the man warned.

"Package is being taken to position Delta-echo," the unseen driver of the cart said to a radio.

"Roger, Delta-echo," a filtered voice answered.

The electric motor on the golf art emitted a high-pitched whine as its speed increased. It bumped, turned, sped on. Fox didn't care where it was going. More than disappointed he felt defeated. The plan was foolhardy at its best. Hell, Chief Stoner, David and Paul Manygoats climbing over the fence at the White House made more sense. Their sacrifice bore fruit. His, he was certain, would result in little more than disgrace, a psychiatric exam and probably time in the county jail. It was over. Like the life he once had, like the White Buffalo, it had ended quickly and unexpectedly. He now knew, wracked with pain, chained and blind, how the Indian nations felt when their hope was taken away. Paul Manygoats fate, Fox decided as the golf cart jerked to a halt, may have been better than his. Dying with pride, could be better than living with dishonor. "Come on, asshole," a voice ordered as he was jerked from the cart.

The nylon ankle restraint was cut away. Fox, still hooded with the white hotel towel, hands shackled behind his back, was hustled into a sprawling empty banquet room by eight agents. The chandelier lights were turned on and Fox was shoved into a single chair in the middle of the cavernous room. "Take the towel off."

The towel snapped away. Fox squinted in the light. Five of the men were in jogging attire. The other three wore suits and ties. "Who are you?" A tall lean man with a gray mustache questioned.

Fox studied his accusers. They had once been colleagues. Kindred spirits. Members of the same Federal coalition of law enforcement. Now it was different. He found no fraternalism in the collective cold stare. He looked at each face before he answered. "I am John Fox, a member of the Mojave nation."

"Fuck, here we go with Russell Means all over again," one of the senior agents smirked.

"Who's Russell Means?" A younger agent asked.

"Is John Fox your Christian name or your Indian name?" a mustache pressed.

"Maybe his name is nine fingers," another suggested. "He's missing one."

They laughed.

"My Indian name is Sprite Man," Fox said proudly.

They all laughed. The senior agent quieted them with a hand.

"Well, Sprite Man," the gray mustache challenged, "you may not have noticed, but this isn't the Mojave reservation. This is Riverside County California. Here we make the rules."

"I thought the Constitution did that." Fox suggested defiantly.

"Ah, an educated Indian, huh? Okay, Tonto, let me tell you what the Constitution says about threatening the President of the United States."

The adrenaline the exchange generated was working for Fox. "Threatening the President," Fox scoffed. "I'm a personal friend of his. And when this is over, you're gonna be examining counterfeit one dollar bills in Bum Fuck, Nebraska."

"Yeah, and I'm a personal friend of General Custer's widow."

The agents laughed again.

"Call the Sheriff's Department. Lock Cochise up. Put in the active threat file, even though he won't be around for three to five."

"King-ten this is King base," a radio on an agent announced.

The senior agent reached and took the radio. "King-ten, go."

"King-ten, the Eagle is on his way to Delta-echo. He knows the detainee."

"Fuck," the senior agent growled.

Fox smiled.

"Get the cuffs off him!"

The handcuffs were being removed when the double door at the head of the room opened and four agents escorted the President in. He still wore the ball cap and shorts. His shorter, heavier, bespectacled Chief-of-Staff was at his side. "Mr. President, I really don't think this is wise," he protested as they marched toward the center of the room. The President looked annoyed. "Leon, I told you I know him. Now shut-up."

"Yes, Sir."

The agents surrounding Fox moved away as the President reached them. Fox massaged his wrists. He started to stand up, but the President laid a hand on his shoulder. "Are you all right, John?"

"Yes, Sir."

"Get a chair for the President," the Chief-of-staff barked.

An agent grabbed a chair from the hundreds lining the wall. The President sat down facing Fox. "John, what's this about? Your scared the hell out of a few people. Including me."

"I'm sorry, Mr. President," Fox looked at the circle of faces surrounding them. "Can we talk in private?"

The President turned to his Chief-of-Staff. "Leon. Make it happen."

Leon turned to do as bid. "Everyone out, please."

The agents quickly retreated to the doors surrounding the perimeter of the banquet room. The Chief-of-Staff remained until Fox glanced at him. The President added, "Leon."

The man burned Fox with a look of contempt and moved away.

Fox took in a breath to steady himself. "Sir, I didn't know how to reach you."

The President nodded, "I've heard that can be a problem."

"After we met in Washington, Mr. President, you made your speech about tearing down the fences ... I believed you. The Mojave's believed you."

"I meant what I said," the President defended, "Have they built their casino?"

"They've spent millions building a casino they can't open. A Federal court has ordered them to stop because of a waste disposal built to close to the Colorado river."

"John, I can't get involved in the nuance of all this?

"Sir, the company that built the waste treatment plant on Lake Mead built the plant for the Mojave's. Nine Nevada casinos line the banks of the Colorado north of The White Buffalo. Why haven't they been ordered to be shut down? Their disposal processes are over a decade old. It's a double standard. Mr. President, you said tear down the fences, but someone put them back up. How many broken promises do the Indians have to suffer?"

" I'll have the Attorney General look into this. That's the best I can do."

"Sir, I worked for the government for over ten years. I believed in it. I believe in the Constitution. Never was I prouder than when I heard your speech, but all this doesn't have a damned thing to do with clean water.

"Are people going to sleep safer tonight because an army of Federal agents are surrounding an Indian casino in Parker, Arizona? And what do the Indians want? A chance to work, a decent, schools for their kids. Hell, who do they think they are, Americans? Don't they know who this country belongs to? Why should they expect a fair shake? They never got one before."

The President took off his cap and ran a hand through his hair. He looked hard at Fox. "Damn it, Fox. This is it. You understand me?"

"Yes, Sir," Fox answered.

"Leon!" The President barked. The Chief-of-Staff

moved to them. "Some days being President really sucks," he mumbled.

"Yes, Sir," the Chief-of-Staff announced, reaching them.

"Leon, who petitioned a court for an order against the Mojave's?"

"Is that what this is all about?" The man was annoyed with Fox.

"Answer the question."

"As I recall it was the Coalition for Clean Water."

"Who are they?"

"Well, they're comprised of a number of environmentally sensitive organizations as well as individuals interested in preserving the welfare of ..."

"You're not on CNN, Leon," the President interjected. "Try a direct Goddamned answer."

"Without the benefit of my files...let's see, the Organization for the Waters of the Southwest, The Colorado River Preservation Society, the Committee for Clean Air and Waters."

"Who put it together, Leon?"

"Civic minded businessmen."

"Who, Leon?" It was a sharp order that made the Chief-of-Staff wince.

"Supporters of your re-election, Mr. President. Individuals who have demonstrated their support."

"Contributions?" the President questioned.

"Yes, the television campaign here in the West, as you know, Mr. President, has been expensive."

"Nevada based contributors! Vegas?" Fox suggested.

"I don't think that's any of your business. It's my understanding you're no longer in government."

"And glad of it," Fox quipped.

"Leon," the President said, "It seems some court has found the Mojave's guilty without a trial. That's contrary to both the letter and the spirit of the law. I want the Attorney General to find out what the hell's going on and intervene with a stay. I want the Mojave's water turned on..., and I want it done quickly."

"Mr. President...?" The Chief-of-Staff balked. "This is not a well thought out remedy. I suggest..."

"Leon!" The President warned standing up. "I'm not asking for another suggestion. I'm giving you a directive as the President of the United States, and I want it obeyed. Turn their damned water on!"

"Yes, Mr. President," the Chief-of-Staff turned and marched away.

The President looked to Fox and offered his hand. Fox stood and took it. They shook.

"Thank you, Sir."

"I'm hoping this bunch of Mojave's knows there's an election coming."

"I'll remind them, sir. "

"Goodbye, John."

"Goodbye, Sir."

The President turned, crossed the room. A waiting duo of Secret Service agents opened the double doors and followed after him. The doors swung shut. Fox was alone in the sprawling quiet room. He sank into the chair. "Jesus," he sighed audibly with a look at the ceiling." Thank you."

27 VENGEANCE

> "When a child my mother taught me the legends of
> our people; taught me of the sun and the sky, the
> moon and stars, the clouds and storms. She also
> taught me to kneel and pray for strength, health,
> wisdom and protection. We never prayed against any
> person, but if we had ought against any individual
> we ourselves took vengeance."
>
> **Geronimo—Chiricahua Apache Chief**

The three Indians lay in silence along a hedge that
bordered the driveway of the sprawling Las Vegas estate
of Donald DePalma. Masked in night shadow they had
lain in wait for nearly five hours. Their faces and chests
were painted. These were warriors waiting for their
prey. Bear-Don't-Walk, Sprite-Man and Merv-the-
horse.

Lawn sprinklers soaked them shortly after midnight.

Centipedes and beetles crawled over them and a neighbor walking a poodle came within inches of stepping on Bear-Don't-Walk, but Mother Earth hugged her sons, and the three men with one heart waited.

The headlamps approached shortly after three A.M. The polished limousine slowed as the car swung into the driveway. The automatic garage door hummed and began to open. A soft light winked on inside the garage. The limo with its tinted windows paused to allow the garage door time to complete its track. The quite idle of the engine was the only sound until a series of war cries ripped the night. The three warriors attacked the car as if it were a buffalo.

Merv-the-horse shattered the driver's window with a rock grasped in his fist. The safety glass exploded in a hail of hard pellets. He grabbed the driver by the neck and jerked the frightened man out through the broken window. A knee on the neck and several slams of the head against the concrete driveway quieted the man. Merv-the-horse pulled a nine-millimeter pistol from beneath the man's jacket and tossed it away.

Sprite-Man smashed the window on the passenger's side of the car and Bear-Don't-Walk reached inside and unlocked the door. The interior lights came on revealing Donald DePalma cowering in a corner like a frightened child. "Don't kill me, don't kill me!" He begged with eyes wide, hands extended as if to ward them off. Merv-the-horse reached in on the driver's side and unlocked the door near DePalma. "What is this! What do you want? I'll pay you."

"Shut up!" Bear-Don't-Walk barked. Merv-the-horse opened the back door and grabbed at DePalma. He tried to scream and resist, but it was squelched as Merv-the-horse grabbed him, clamped an arm around his neck and a hand over his mouth. He pushed DePalma's right arm

428

high into the middle of his back. DePalma grimaced in pain. Breath hissed through flared nostrils. Sprite-Man grabbed DePalma's ankles and he was trapped. Leather screeched as the four men crowded the back of the limo. Bear-Don't-Walk grabbed DePalma's free wrist and held it. Leaning close to DePalma's face he growled. "Look at me, you cowardly fuck!"

DePalma opened his eyes and stared into Bear-Don't-Walk's angry, painted face. "I am Bear-Don't-Walk. I am a Mojave warrior," he whispered with restraint. "I have been in your home. Your children and your wife are asleep."

DePalma's eyes opened even wider. "I cut the throat of your dog and we pissed on it. He lays in your kitchen so you will know we speak the truth."

DePalma nodded as if agreeing would lessen the threat. "You are a powerful man," Bear-Don't-Walk granted. "But just a man. You have caused our people pain and trouble. What a man plants he must harvest. If you continue to trouble us, we will return. And we will come until no Mojave remains standing. Do you understand?"

"Merv-the-horse released the hold on DePalma's mouth. "Yes!" DePalma gasped.

"Sprite-Man," Bear-Don't-Walk said without taking his eyes from DePalma's face. "Show him your hand."

Sprite-Man extended his hand in front of DePalma's face and wiggled the stub of his scared and severed little finger. "Your people did this to me."

"I'm sorry, I'm sorry," DePalma pleaded.

"It is easy for a trapped wolf to cry," Bear-Don't-Walk answered. "But it is important the wolf learn the lesson!"

Merv grabbed DePalma's mouth. He went rigid with fear. Bear-Don't-Walk raised DePalma's free hand and a pair of metal wire cutters. DePalma struggled, but it was futile. The wire cutters snapped and DePalma's little finger fell to the carpet. Blood jetted from the stump.

Bear-Don't-Walk leaned close to DePalma's ashen face. "Every time you cause our people trouble, we will return. Spill the blood of a Mojave and you spill your own."

As quickly as the Indians appeared, they were gone. DePalma sat holding his bloody hand grimacing and weeping in the glow of the limousine's interior lights.

EPILOGUE

---

*"Often in the stillness of the night, when all nature is
asleep about me, there comes a gentle raping at the door
of my heart. I open it; and a voice inquires, 'What of
your people? What will their future be?' My answer is:
Mortal man has not the power to draw aside the veil of*
    *unborn time to tell the future of his race. That gift
belongs to the*
    *Divine alone. But it is given to man to closely
    judge the future by the present, and the past."*
Simon Pokagon—Potawatomie

The two men with their wives were from the law offices
of Wisehart and Segal in West Los Angeles. They were
junior partners. One a graduate of UCLA, the other
Berkeley. They were a young, educated and successful
foursome of millennials. They were comfortable driving
a Land Rover, pulling two trailered Yamaha wave

runners. It had been a weekend of fun in the sun at Lake Havasu, chasing Bud light and string bikinis. Now, it was south on Arizona ninety-five, cross the Colorado river at Parker, cut across to Interstate 10 through Desert Center and be back in L.A. in four and a half hours.

The green Land Rover was entering the city limits of Parker when the driver noticed the flashing sign for The White Buffalo Casino. "Check that."

"What is it?" The Berkeley graduate looked.

"The White Buffalo Casino," the UCLA grad answered. "I heard of this place. It belongs to the Indians."

"Grand opening! Let's stop and check it out," one of the wives urged.

The Land Rover slid in among lines of cars, trucks and campers crowding the parking lot. "Place looks busy." Berkeley suggested as they all climbed out to walk toward the casino.

"How much money have you got on you?"

UCLA pulled out his wallet and looked. "About twenty-six dollars."

Berkeley smiled, "Hell, isn't that what the Indians paid for Manhattan?"

ABOUT THE AUTHOR

Novelist & Screenwriter, Dallas Barnes has written nearly two hundred hours of primetime television drama, as well as seven bestselling novels. His writings have won nominations for EMMY'S, in both primetime and daytime, as well as the famed EDGAR ALAN POE AWARD, the IMAGE AWARD and the HUMANITAS PRIZE. Dallas Barnes along with JoAnne have written for over twenty-three of the highest rated, most successful, prime time, dramatic television series, as well as several motion pictures made for television.

As Writers/ Producers of the acclaimed historical docu-drama, "America, You're Too Young to Die," Dallas & JoAnne became the only writers, outside White House staff, to write for, then President, Ronald Reagan.

Along with writing, Dallas Barnes is an executive level hybrid hospitality security professional with a unique blend of management, Law Enforcement and guest services skills. with over a decade of experience in investigations in demanding hospitality and gaming venues linked to a performance in risk management, safety, compliance, and loss prevention.